THE
CHARMED
LIFE OF
ALEX
MOORE

THE
CHARMED
LIFE OF
ALEX
MOORE

MOLLY FLATT

MACMILLAN

First published 2018 by Macmillan
an imprint of Pan Macmillan
20 New Wharf Road, London N1 9RR
Associated companies throughout the world
www.panmacmillan.com

ISBN 978-1-5098-5452-3

1 3 5 7 9 8 6 4 2

A CIP catalogue record for this book is available from the British Library.

Typeset by Palimpsest Book Production Limited, Falkirk, Stirlingshire
Printed and bound by CPI Group (UK) Ltd, Croydon, CR0 4YY

Visit www.panmacmillan.com to read more about all our books
and to buy them. You will also find features, author interviews and
news of any author events, and you can sign up for e-newsletters
so that you're always first to hear about our new releases.

For Yanni –
my beginning, middle and end.

'The world is full of hopeful analogies and
handsome, dubious eggs, called possibilities'
George Eliot, *Middlemarch*

'We all have an old knot in the heart
we wish to loosen and untie'
Michael Ondaatje, *The Cat's Table*

THE
CHARMED
LIFE OF
ALEX
MOORE

As the man flew backwards, he already knew that he was dead. He could feel the blast spreading through his flesh, hot and fast, imploding his organs with something like joy. Seven million lights wheeled around him in a spectacular farewell show and the taste of copper and ozone flooded his mouth. He was still alive when he hit the ground, alive enough to feel the back of his head bounce. Alive enough to watch the last of the lights retreat inside the walls until he was staring into black.

That was wrong. That shouldn't be happening. There would be consequences to that – consequences he should be around to fix. There was so much still left for him to do. So much he had never had time to say. All the seconds he had spent on ridiculous worries, on arguments that didn't matter and people he didn't love, scattered before him like sand, and he longed to sweep up the grains and cram them back into his body's brittle hourglass.

The chill of the stone was seeping through his flesh, the metallic warmth leaching out of the atmosphere. He heard the scuffle of boots, then the rasp of panicked breath as someone knelt beside his face. He had to tell them. He had to give them a chance, even if *he* couldn't, to salvage something from this almighty mess. So with the last of his breath he spoke the words: three words. And as his lungs rattled to a halt and his neurons winked out like the lights that had so swiftly, catastrophically fled, he just about had time to think two final thoughts.

First, he wondered what would happen to the woman.

And then, he hoped, with all his failing heart, that his dear, beloved, pig-headed bloody son wouldn't do anything stupid.

1

Alex took a breath, then froze. For the briefest moment she had no idea how she had come to be standing on this upturned beer crate in this vast and ugly room, staring back at the faces of a hundred hungry strangers.

Tell us, they pleaded with bleary eyes and wetly gaping mouths. *Tell us your secret.*

Before she could stop it, a memory surfaced of her thirteen-year-old self, paralysed centre-stage and stammering like an idiot, in her first and last school play. Seconds later – *oh God, not now, not again* – the memory blurred and shivered. The vertigo drop-kicked her belly. The emptiness opened up inside.

Who the hell was she? Why the hell was she here? She fished around for a mental handhold; felt her thoughts spiral towards the void; was certain, for a moment, that she was about to throw up.

Then: *For Christ's sake, woman.* She swallowed convulsively. *Get a hold of yourself. You know how to handle this. Forget the past. Concentrate on the now.*

She stared down at her flashy heels, an impulsive party-night treat-to-self. She let out her breath in one long blow. *You are strong*, she silently chanted, thinking of the exercises Chloe had taken her through the evening before. *You are powerful. This is your moment. Trust it. Let everything else go.*

The nausea peaked, flickered, dissolved. She cleared her throat. She looked up. She attempted a smile. 'How the fuck,' she croaked, 'did I end up in this fairy tale?'

There was a ripple of laughter, a couple of cheers. Alex took a tentative sip from her beer and felt the void retreat. Over the heads of the crowd she spotted the EUDOMONIA logo that the design guys had smoothed onto the back wall seconds before the first guests arrived. She let the smile widen into a grin. Yes. Pantone Warm Red 172 was perfect, after all.

'I mean, seriously.' She took a proper swig from the bottle and felt the fluency roll back in. 'This can't be right. Six months ago I was stuck in a dead-end job, knackered all the time, barely scraping together the rent. Not to put too fine a point on it, really quite miserable. Then . . .' She paused and felt the weight of their stares pressing against her. She was glad, now, that she'd taken that reckless hour to get her high-lights refreshed. She held the silence for a few more seconds. 'Well, frankly, it feels like a miracle.'

A collective sigh.

'I mean, people don't just change overnight.'

A rumble of *Huhs*. A few weary nods.

'And yet . . .' A wry shrug. 'Hell, perhaps it's karma. Lady Luck. Divine intervention. Allahu Akbar! Of course, we've still got a long way to go. This is just the beginning. But to

4

have come so far so quickly . . .' She gestured from the huddle of wheeled desks on one side of the room to the glass-walled meeting pod on the other. 'Well, it's obviously what I'm meant to be doing. At bloody last!'

A tide of whoops. A froth of applause.

'Although,' Alex went on, as the whistles died down, 'it's really Lenni who should be up here, not me.' She smiled down at him where he stood beside the beer crate, his pink scalp visible through his white-blond hair. 'Seriously,' she said, well aware that Lenni would much rather be celebrating alone with a spreadsheet and a storm of Finnish techno crashing through his headphones, 'Eudo would still be a pipe dream if this guy hadn't agreed to meet me for coffee in Farringdon, one Wednesday six months ago.' She held out her hand, freshly manicured in the closest the Filipino girl had been able to find to Warm Red 172. 'Let's hear it for Lenni.'

A roar. Lenni ducked his head and waved them away.

Alex widened the gesture to embrace the room. 'And it goes without saying that we owe a big debt of gratitude to all of *you*, for taking a risk on us so early on. The remarkable fact that we're able to gather here in our first proper office – sorry, *co-working space* – is down to our incredible angels Ahmed and Dale. It's not exactly Google Campus, but it's a damn sight better than the table in my flat. Especially seeing as we're going to be recruiting like mad over the next few months. Talking of which, if any of you knows of a COO-in-waiting with a trust fund, give them my number, now.'

A third crest of cheers and laughter petered out into expectant silence.

Alex ground a £600 lime-suede toe into the splintered wood. 'I suppose,' she said softly, 'what I really want to say is this: don't underestimate yourselves. Because, I promise you, even if you've been a total loser for your entire adult life, if you can just let go of your own bullshit – anything is possible. Literally anything.' Eyes up. 'Okay, heavy stuff over. Go and get pissed.'

This time, the roar was deafening. Alex jumped down from the crate.

'Alright?' she murmured to Lenni as they pushed their way through the slapping hands and jabbering voices.

'Very good.'

'Bit corny?'

'They're drunk. Corny is good.'

The air con was fighting a losing battle against the combination of month-long heatwave and a hundred under-deodorized, post-work people. Alex discreetly tried to billow a breeze under her vest as she fended off incomers with apologetic smiles and headed straight for Ahmed and Dale. The investors were caught in a thicket of neon-jeaned twenty-somethings, being buffeted by pitches. Turning herself into a windbreak, she pressed fresh cold Shoreditch Blondes into their palms.

'Christ!' She blew into her new fringe. 'That was embarrassing.'

'Oh, you know what you're doing,' Ahmed said, appraising

her from haircut to heels. 'I picked up a copy of *Flair* at Victoria yesterday. That interview was spot-on.'

'Great!' Alex touched his wrist. 'I'm so glad you like it. Oh, it's a bit fluffy, obviously, but we've already seen a huge spike in web traffic and a shedload of new sign-ups.'

'It's like I said, Alex.' Ahmed swilled a mouthful of beer. 'You're Eudomonia's biggest asset. Personal profile pieces like this are just what we need, and you're obviously a natural. I think it's time to aim higher than a Tube rag. I'll make a few calls.'

'Too fucking right.' Dale slapped her on the back, leaving a damp palm-print on the silk. 'Most of my founders are barely out of nappies and they can only speak in sodding ones and zeros. You're special, doll.' He raised his bottle. 'To you. To us. To Eudo.'

They three-way-clinked, spotlit in a dozen envious stares. 'To Eudo.'

Ten internally monitored minutes later, Alex handed the angels off to Lenni and sought out the hacks. By some communal freeloading instinct, they had congregated near the big rubber buckets of drinks and ice, the lifestyle editors eyeing the tech bloggers like beasts at a watering hole. Imagining herself as an alpha lioness, Alex stalked into their midst and fielded their predictable questions with a few piquant soundbites. Next, she sashayed over to the desks to smooth the nerves of a bundle of twitchy new-hires. She couldn't remember all of their names, and she wasn't entirely clear who was on her payroll and who was a plus one, so she stuck to general joshing and piss-takery. Then, replenished with another beer from a beautiful girl with a scarlet-tinted Afro, possibly one of the interns, she headed down to the far end of the room. It was time for some bonding with the other start-up that shared the sixth floor. Their product – brightly packaged organic protein balls – hung in clusters from six-foot plastic trees stationed around the walls.

She was just passing the sofas that divided their spaces when someone grabbed her arm. She turned, a charming rebuff on her lips, and found that it was Harry.

'Very slick,' he said. 'You really should have told me you were so miserable, six months ago.'

'*Harry.*' Alex caught sight of her own face, sparkling with exhilaration in the mirrored wall of the kitchen module behind him. 'Very funny,' she murmured, punching his shoulder. It took some effort to drag her gaze away.

Harry smoothed the sleeve of his jacket. He was looking incredibly handsome, in exactly the right amount of chestnut stubble and a new silver tie. 'Your parents are here,' he said, moving aside to reveal Alex's mother, looking tiny amongst the oversized scarlet cushions, unwrapping a protein ball.

'Mum!' Alex perched on the arm of the sofa and leaned down to give her mother a hug. The cloud of Joy that engulfed her threatened to unleash a thousand memories and she experienced a wave of dizziness. She quickly pulled back. 'Mum,' she mumbled, focusing on the grain of the pleather beneath her palms. 'I'm so glad you're here.'

'We wouldn't have missed it for the world, darling.' Her mother patted Alex's hand, took a small bite from the ball, chewed vigorously, then refolded the packaging over the remainder and hid it in her lap. 'I like your new hair. Very smart. I always said you should go short. And what a shindig! But are you sure they won't mind all this catering? Your angels? I mean, what in the name of heaven is birch water? This must have cost an arm and a leg.'

The dizziness passed. 'It's all sponsored, Mum,' she sighed, straightening up. 'Where's Dad?'

Her mother shifted, squeaking. 'He went to hide in the toilets, but that was quite a . . . Ah, there he is.'

Alex turned to see her father ambling over from the direction of the buckets with a brimming plastic cup in either hand. At the sight, so reminiscent of dozens of parties from her childhood, where she'd watched her father topping up the drinks of red-faced authors and agents from her sleepy nest on the kitchen sofa, the bottom inexplicably dropped out of her stomach. Bile surged into her mouth. She stumbled back into the people behind her. *For fuck's sake. Why is this happening? NOT NOW.*

'Hey there, Kansas, steady.' He was there to catch her rebound, cups skittering across the floor, his deep transatlantic drawl cutting through the buzzing in her ears. He steadied her shoulders and held her at arm's length, studying her face, but she pressed forward and folded into his chest. With her cheek squashed into the worn corduroy of his shirt, and the smell of soap and vodka filling her nose, the vertigo rushed back so violently that Alex thought she might actually faint. But then her father levered her gently upright and the memories receded. The laughter and the hip-hop flooded back in. It was okay. She was here. She was now. She was new Alex, extraordinary Alex, Founder-CEO.

'Stupid heels,' she muttered. She cleared her throat. She shook out her hair. 'Sorry, Dad. You lost your drinks.'

'Don't be silly,' he said. He rummaged in his pocket. 'Here. I got something for you.' He uncurled his knuckles to reveal a novelty USB stick topped with a canary-coloured block of Lego. 'Somewhere to store your plans for world domination, I thought. Help pave that Yellow Brick Road you're galloping down. I gather that paper is passé.'

'I love it.' Alex slipped the USB into the pocket of her jeans and studied her father in turn. He had made an effort, in his best city jeans with his beard neatly trimmed, but his skin looked grey and there were purple hammocks under his eyes. The vertigo flickered. *Here and now*, Alex told herself firmly. She stepped back. 'I'm so glad you let me drag you out of your cave,' she said brightly. 'I know how much you hate the Big Smoke. It feels like twenty years since I last saw you guys.'

'Seven months.' Her mother struggled up from the sofa, shooing away Harry's arm. 'You haven't been to Fring since' – she waved from the games station to the miso vending machine – 'all this.'

Alex felt her cheeks get hot. 'I know. I'm sorry. I've just been so—'

'It's a good thing,' her father interrupted. He squeezed her mother's shoulder. 'We're proud. You're flying high now, Kansas. It's the way it should be.'

'Although perhaps,' Harry said, appearing on her other

side and placing a hand on the small of her back, 'you should go easy on the beer.'

'I'm fine,' Alex said, sidestepping and defiantly taking another swig. 'Just tired, that's all. It's been such a manic week.' She glanced over her shoulder. Good. The massage girls were doing the rounds. Gemma was laying out the goody bags near the door.

'We should go,' her father said. He scooped up their coats from the sofa. 'This is your night. We're raising the average age in here by at least three decades.'

'No! Please. It's so early!'

'It's gone midnight, Al,' Harry said, then muttered, 'your mum's feet are playing up.'

'But you've haven't met *anyone* yet. You haven't tried the—'

'Don't fuss, darling,' her mother said, wriggling into her cardigan. 'We'll see you tomorrow. And you know what I always say. Last to arrive, first to leave. That way . . .'

'You're always welcome,' Alex recited. 'I know.' As her father gave her another hug, she felt like she wanted to say something more. But the music was too loud, and over her mother's shoulder she could see the intern flirting with Dale.

'I'll walk you back to the Premier Inn, Liz,' Harry said. 'I've got an early start.' He brushed his lips across Alex's cheek and murmured, 'I need to see you.'

'Oh, baby, I told you. It's been crazy here. I've barely even been home.'

'We need to talk. Will you come over for dinner tomorrow?'

'Ah, I'd love nothing better, but tomorrow night I have this women in tech event and—'

'Alex.'

'Honestly, I'm really sorry, but this big corporate sponsor is going to be there and—'

'*Alex.*' Harry turned so that his back shielded them from her parents. 'I talked to one of your employees tonight,' he said, his voice suddenly clipped. 'Toby, was it? Tom? Malnourished teenager with dreadlocks.'

'Oh. Tim. He's one of our community managers.'

'Tim, then. Well, Tim, who seemed to think I was a waiter, kindly filled me in on your "deal" while you gave your little speech. He said that you'd narrowly missed a life of domestic slavery, before you'd seen the entrepreneurial light. I believe the exact phrase was "dead-eyed desk monkey about to become a baby machine".'

Alex sighed. 'Harry, please. Tim is . . . well, Tim is Tim.'

'But you as good as implied you thought the same, Alex. Up there, in front of everyone. You were pretty clear on how relieved you were to have escaped this life of terrible mediocrity. *Our* life, for the past five years. Our future, I rather thought.'

'Oh, baby, come on. You know that I was talking about me – about my own issues – not about us. And look, I know I've been neglecting you, but Lenni says we just need to—'

'Oh yes,' Harry interrupted, his blue eyes narrowing. '*Lenni.* You've obviously got very close to Lenni.'

'Oh, *Harry.* Please.' Alex rose up on her toes and planted

12

a kiss on his lips. 'Okay. You win. I'll skive the event and we'll do dinner. I do miss you too, you know.'

Alex watched Harry usher her parents towards the lifts. Her mother, marching beside him in her low heels, kept up a steady rill of conversation. Her father, trailing behind them, turned and winked. Alex clicked her heels together and blew him a kiss. Harry didn't look back, she noticed. She knew she had been neglecting him. But right now wasn't about Harry's jealousy or insecurity, or whatever it was. Right now was about what was going right, and she was damn well going to enjoy it.

East Road was uncomfortably hot, even at 2 a.m. The faint breeze did nothing but waft a sour cocktail of tar and night-bus fumes across Alex's face, but she didn't care. She was full to the brim, electric with connection. The manhole cover ringwormed with gum, the gutter frotted with ash, the perox-ide wig nesting beneath the stunted sapling: they all served to make her night even more magical, because they were proof that it was real.

She hooked her bag over her shoulder, clenched the sleeve of her laptop under the same arm and swiped her phone to life with her thumb, unveiling a glitter of alerts. Flicking across the screen, only dimly aware of the blisters on the balls of her feet, she slid into autopilot. Right into Chart Street, the lights of the council-flat balconies sputter-ing in the corner of her eye. Round the silent black rectangle of Aske Gardens basketball court. Left onto Pitfield Street. North, towards the canal.

Of the many new habits that Alex had developed over the past few months, the ability to cull digital bumf was one of the best. After years spent wading through the bogs of social media, wasting whole hours rubbernecking disingenuously curated lives, she was now a ruthless ninja at sifting the genuinely useful from the seductively inane. Within minutes she had bulk-accepted fifty-seven LinkedIn invitations, bulk-deleted fourteen Facebook friend requests and archived sixty-one non-urgent emails. Harry aside, she could already feel the success of the evening gushing through her digital tributaries: sparking new alliances, reinforcing the old, leaving a wake of excitement that she knew would continue to froth over the next few days. When her eye caught on some charity-spam for a Sudanese flood – or possibly a Vietnamese drought – her electric sense of connection was so strong she not only *texted to donate* twenty quid, but filled out the Gift Aid form.

Shouts and the shiver of chain-link rang out from Shoreditch Park. A quick scan confirmed nothing more menacing than bored teenagers throwing cans at the tennis-court fence. Alex turned back to her phone. There was one voicemail from an unknown landline – a landline, ye gods! – and another from Mae.

She pressed to play the landline message, but the moment the Celtic accent came down the line, she realized it was the woman from that academic institute – SOAS, was it? CGAS? – who had been bothering her about some research project all day. She saved it for later, glanced up at the shuttered shops and scaffolding of Whitmore Road, then skipped

forward to the message from Mae. Her friend was apologiz-
ing – barely audible over the sound of Bo's screams – that the
babysitter had let her down. Poor Mae. But it had probably
been for the best. Tech launches weren't really her scene.

Alex crossed the bridge onto De Beauvoir Road. She was
just logging into the back-end of Eudo, to get a head start on
tomorrow's behind-the-scenes party blog, when the man
slammed into her.

She flew a good couple of feet before she hit the pavement.
As she rolled onto her back, he planted his knees in her stomach, pinning her down. One of his hands splayed over her
mouth and his thumb pressed into her eyelid, making the
darkness warp and spark. The other wrapped around her neck,
the pads of his fingers rough-skinned behind her ears.

He smelled of body odour and fast food, and he was
breathing in laboured gasps. A single drop of sweat splashed
from his skin onto her lips as she lay beneath him, lungs
burning, heart rabbit-drumming in her chest. He shifted his
weight and she managed to reach for her right foot, jack-
knifed up beneath her left buttock – just as he reared back
to reveal an old-fashioned farmer's shotgun.

In one desperate motion, Alex stabbed five inches of
hand-stitched stiletto heel into her attacker's solar plexus.
Finally catching her breath, she screamed. He reeled back
with a strangled grunt while she rolled over the kerb and out
into the road. Scrabbling against the tarmac, she got onto
her hands and knees and screamed again.

'Oi! OI!'

There were shouts and footsteps, and now another man

appeared, a different one. Oh God. A gang. The new man was moving towards her now, ready to take his turn.

'NO,' Alex cough-shouted. 'GET . . . AWAY . . .'

'Awight, lady, awight.' The new man took a step backwards into the orange puddle of the street light, pushing back his hoodie, holding up his palms. He was a boy, really: pasty, stubbled, slightly overweight. His face glistened with sweat. 'Wasn't me, lady. Wasn't me. Mi boy just run after him. You awight?'

Alex remained on her knees, staring at him mutely for a second. Then she slumped down onto her heels with a sob. Tried to get up. Sank back down. Unbuckled her remaining shoe, with shaking fingers. Eventually got to her feet.

'You awight?' The boy was keeping his distance.

'Fuck,' Alex said. '*Fuck!*'

'You get a look at him?'

'He had a *gun*. A massive, fucking' – her voice wobbled – '*shotgun*, like Mr fucking McGregor.'

The boy, looking worried, squinted beyond Alex into the dark. 'Din know he was packing. We only saw his back. Came running when we heard you shout.'

He indicated over his shoulder to a paved courtyard in front of a council block. Beyond this, Alex knew, was a bollard-lined strip of grass where the De Beauvoir kids liked to hang out. Walking on the canal path below, she had more than once clocked the skulking hoodies with their lurching Staffies and expensive phones.

The boy's expression brightened. 'S'awight. Here he is.'

Alex turned to see a lean boy in a white vest jogging

towards them. He gathered up her bag, laptop, phone and shoe as he approached and held them out to her at arm's length.

'Couldn't get him,' he said. His cornrows were bleeding sweat and his hands, when she brushed them to take back her stuff, were slippery. 'Weren't big, but he were fucking fast. You awight, lady?'

'Yes,' Alex replied, clasping the laptop to her chest like a shield. Instantly sober, she could feel the chill of shock on its way, the delayed seeping-in of the pain. 'Thank you. Thank you so much.'

'He had a gat,' the white boy said to the black boy.

'*Fuck.*' The black boy dragged up his vest to reveal a skinny, hairless chest. He wiped the vest over his forehead. 'Good thing he were fast, then.' He nodded at Alex. 'Should call the feds.'

'Yes. Yes, I will.'

'Din even get yer lappy, did he? Wanker.'

She called the police, shivering, and spoke to a woman who said a car was on its way. The boys waited with her until headlights flashed over the speed bump at the end of the road, before jogging off, the podgy one giving her an awkward gun-salute wave.

The police took a statement. They were sympathetic but circumspect about the chances of an arrest.

'You'd be surprised, the number of guns circulating around here,' said the policeman, a tired-looking guy in a Sikh turban. 'Rare to see one, five years ago. I blame *The Wire.*'

'You're sure you don't need to go to hospital?' asked his partner, a girl who looked about fifteen.

'No, really, I'm fine. I'd rather get home.'

'Is there anyone who can come and stay with you?'

'I'll call my fiancé. My flat's just over there.'

Thankfully her bag had been zipped, so her wallet and keys were still inside. They walked her to her door, and the girl handed her a leaflet with the details of a trauma helpline.

'Nice,' she said, holding up the evidence bag containing Alex's right shoe.

'Thanks.' Alex gave her a weak smile. 'It was a magical evening. Until this.'

'Get inside. Have some tea, plenty of sugar. Call your fiancé. We'll be in touch.'

Standing in the lift, Alex felt her throat begin to thicken and her sinuses sting. A dozen memories of other lonely, tearful moments spent in the lift over the years crowded in. The vertigo rushed up again, her stomach lurched and she felt the bright patina of the evening shiver and slide. Beneath it, she sensed the void, lurking. Felt how easy it would be to let it crack open, let herself tumble in.

Alex took a deep breath, cleared her throat and swiped at her eyes. She reminded herself of all the good things that had happened that evening, of all the lovely things people had said. She forced herself to recall how she had felt up on that crate, after the initial wobble had passed: powerful, admired, fully alive. Extraordinary. Bulletproof. She had wondered whether she should tell someone about her little

18

episodes, as she had come to call them. Perhaps Mae. Or Chloe. Wasn't she paying Chloe to coach her through exactly this sort of psychological self-sabotage? But she'd read all about founder burnout. She knew they'd simply tell her to slack off. And she certainly wasn't about to do that, just as her fledgling new career reached its first real tipping point. She simply had to stay focused on the present. She wasn't the kind of woman who did tears, or irrational fears.

Not any more.

Inside the flat she double-locked the door, dumped her stuff on the floor and pulled up Harry's number on her mobile. Then she paused, her thumb hovering over the screen. Harry would get a cab straight over, he would love the chance to fuss, and that was the last thing she wanted: victimhood, cosseting. It would seem like proof that evenings this good weren't allowed. That months – that *lives* – this good weren't allowed. That, more to the point, as a woman alone, she wasn't strong enough to handle the flipside. It would be tantamount to letting that crackhead win.

Throwing her phone onto the pile, Alex veered into the bathroom and inspected the damage as she peeled off her jeans and vest. There was a long scrape on her right arm, a cut on her knee, bits of gravel and glass embedded in her palms. She'd probably have a lot of bruises in the morning – well, later in the morning. But other than surface scratches she was, as she had told her unlikely saviours, unhurt. She got into the shower and stood under lukewarm water for almost half an hour until the shaking stopped. She rubbed her hair dry, applied cream and plasters, and pulled on Harry's Durham

Uni T-shirt. In the kitchen-lounge-diner she made herself a cup of builder's with three sugars. Then she went through to her bedroom and twisted the blinds shut.

Six months ago this would have crippled her. She would have stayed at home for days, let Harry wrap her in cotton wool, made some stupid phone call to Ahmed and Dale. Crumbled. Fucked it up. But not now. She was a very different Alex from the one she had been six months ago.

Alex climbed gingerly onto her bed. She reached into her beside cabinet and fished out a couple of paracetamol, feeling her limbs already starting to stiffen and her head ache.

What sort of shit retro mugger used a shotgun, anyway?

2

Walking the Kingsland stretch of Regent's Canal at commuter o'clock was like playing a late-nineties computer game. Emerging from a tunnel with her neck cricked sideways, Alex had to hop over a jumble of empty cans, swerve as a grizzled man loomed up at her from a bench, then veer back into the weeds as the ping-ping-ping of a bike bell rang out.

She had spent most of her youth gaming on the old Gateway in her parents' attic, while her father laboured over paper and ink in his study across the corridor, trying to coax his next novel to life. She wasn't entirely sure, now, why she'd spent so many hours glued to the pixellated screen in that chilly, cobwebbed room. She'd hated fight scenes, so her career as a gamer had mainly involved wandering around sparsely populated fantasy scapes, tumbling aimlessly over the walls of ruined temples and breaststroking jerkily through underwater caves. Looking back from her current perspective, her teenage self seemed like a prehistoric ancestor, her actions inexplicable and her motivations mysterious. Just thinking about her, in fact, was starting to bring on the dizziness that heralded an episode.

Alex quickly shut down the memory. What did it matter if her past self had been pathetically directionless? Today she had so many micro-goals to hit she could barely afford the time it took to cover half a mile of towpath. But when it had come to leaving the flat, she couldn't quite face taking her usual route to work. Despite her resolution to forget the . . . the *random and meaningless incident*.

Alex knew that the best way to outscore last night's mugger was to ignore him. She would launch her own modest war on terror by diving straight back into work. She'd armed herself with a long-sleeved black tee to hide the scrapes, and a pair of box-fresh white trainers to cushion her sore soles. And it soon became obvious, as she switched between tabs and apps on her phone, that the party had been a hit. The bloggers and super-members they'd invited had uploaded reams of content. There was already a thick grassroots layer of buzz.

She had been a little worried, as her mother had hinted, that the whole thing might have seemed presumptuous or profligate for such a young brand. But Gemma had nailed the tone: wholesome, unpretentious, playful. Eudo was all about mixing the high with the low, the healthy with the indulgent. Their hero message was that you could pursue personal development whilst also giving back, and the early comments suggested they'd hit just the right note. One of the Pinterest gurus had even created a graphic based around Eudo's tagline – a collage of sepia photos from the evening set behind a hand-drawn exhortation to *Be Your Best Self* in various shades of red. Squashing herself against an overflowing bin to let a man in Lycra huff past, Alex fired off an email to Gemma asking her to bike the girl some branded meditation beads. As she pressed Send, a small hit of oxytocin sent a soothing ripple through her body. It was like Chloe said: when you finally opened yourself fully to life, your energy resonated through the universe.

Nevertheless, Alex had to clutch onto the railings as she climbed the steps up from the canal onto New North Road. There was bruising deep in her muscles, and the overdose of cortisol the night before meant she had woken feeling tired and queasy. It hadn't been helped by her dreams, in which she had fallen, feeling as if her chest were about to burst, through chasm after chasm of light-spangled dark. Chloe would probably say the dreams had an important meaning. But then Chloe thought everything had an important meaning. Sometimes, Alex reflected, it was best to forget about meaning and get on with your foot-long to-do list.

Her phone vibrated as she ducked into a cafe just past the bridge.

'Hello?'

She mouthed an order for a triple espresso at the barista and, realizing that she hadn't eaten since yesterday lunchtime, scanned the counter for the lowest-calorie food. Harry had said, more than once, that he preferred her 'with softer edges'. But then Ahmed had been spot-on when he'd told her that the Eudomos needed her to be what they hoped to become. And what the Eudomos hoped to become was at least seven pounds below her natural weight.

'Hi Alex, it's Jacob?'

'Sorry, who?'

'The intern?'

'Oh, right. Hi.' Alex studied the label on a pouch of Superfood Breakfast Bites.

'Are you coming into the office this morning?'

'I'll be there in five.'

'Okay, great; it's just that there's a guy from the BBC who says he's here for an interview?'

Alex put down the packet. She frowned into the phone. 'The BBC? Are you sure?'

'Well, there's nothing in your shared calendar, but I don't know if you have a separate one or forgot to put it in or something? He seems pretty insistent, though?'

'*Shit!*' Alex waved away the coffee. This had to be one of those contacts Ahmed had promised to tap up. She'd seen a text arrive from him while she was walking, but had assumed it was a well-done on the party. 'What have you done with him?'

'Well, he's just sort of standing here?'

'Is Lenni in?'

'Not yet? Should I—'

'Put him in the meeting pod. Offer him coffee. And pastries – buy some pastries.' She paused, struck by a terrible thought. 'Does he have a camera? Like a TV camera?'

'I don't think so?'

'Okay. Good. Tell him I'm on my way.'

Sprinting the rest of the way down East Road was a bad idea. It made every inch of her that wasn't yet hurting hurt. It also meant she then had to spend another five minutes in

24

the loo, trying to fix her sweaty mess of a face. Thank God she'd washed her hair; the sharp new bob (technically, a bronde lob with blunt bangs, according to the hairdresser, who had assured her it made her look like Uma Thurman crossed with a sexy schoolgirl) covered the bruises below her jaw. A quick touch-up of make-up helped to conceal the black eye, but there was nothing she could do about the general puffiness and fatigue. Deciding that distraction was her only hope, Alex slicked on some red lipstick and strode out across the sixth floor.

At least the cleaners had done a good job; the place looked spotless. She swapped banter with the protein-ball people as she walked towards the Eudo meeting pod, her eyes fixed on the dark shape visible behind the frosted glass. Outside it, a mixed-race boy in knee-length denim shorts, presumably Jacob, was attempting to open the door. A tray of baked goods wobbled precariously on his non-existent hip.

'Hang on, hang on,' Alex murmured, rushing up. 'What's his name?'

Jacob stared at her. 'Name?' The tray tipped and a cinnamon bun hit the floor in a nuclear puff of icing sugar.

'Jesus, forget it!'

Alex slid open the door, Jacob blundered in and the man from the BBC turned to face her.

'Oh,' Alex said.

He was young, very young. She had expected some middle-aged dome-head in a suit, but the man-boy before her looked barely older than Jacob. He had a bony face, badly cut ink-black hair and a broad-shouldered, whippet-hipped body. He

25

also looked like he had been styled for an AllSaints ad campaign: grey flannel shirt buttoned up to the neck, tight grey trousers tucked into mid-calf lace-up boots and a battered grey canvas holdall at his feet. He was, undeniably, what Mae would call ugly-hot.

Alex found herself, to her irritation, blushing. It was silly of her to be wrong-footed; no doubt this was exactly the kind of child who now populated the renovated corridors of Broadcasting House. In any case, as his gaze roamed from her crimson lips to her trainers, it became clear that she, too, was far from what he had been expecting. She plugged in her most businesslike smile and extended her hand.

'Hi. I'm Alex. I'm afraid we're a little chaotic at the moment. I hope you haven't been waiting long.' The man-boy didn't move. Undeterred, Alex reached across and clasped one of his hands with her best authoritative-young-Founder-CEO grip. With something that could only be described as a growl, the man-boy jumped back, jerking his fingers out of hers.

'You're Dorothy Moore?' he croaked.

Alex blinked. 'No,' she said. 'Well, yes. Strictly, it's my legal first name, but I haven't gone by Dorothy for years. How did you . . . ? Oh yes, of course. The *Flair* piece.' She rolled her eyes in a from-one-broadsheet-reader-to-another way. 'Honestly, you'd have thought they'd broken WikiLeaks, they were so pleased to have uncloseted that little skeleton. Just imagine, Dorothy Moore! So old-fashioned! So pre-web! That's exactly why, as soon as I was old enough to know

26

better, I insisted that everyone I knew called me by my middle name, on pain of death.'

'Death?' He looked ever so slightly in pain himself. His brow was furrowed, his skin had a distinct blueish tint and his voice was hoarse, under the accent – Welsh, maybe Scots. That would keep the regions happy, Alex thought. She gave a self-deprecating laugh.

'I was a dramatic eleven-year-old.' She pulled out a couple of chairs. 'Please. Have a seat.'

The man-boy took a step back, still eyeballing her shame-lessly. After a few more seconds, fearing that her aching knees might buckle, Alex sat. 'Can I get you a drink?' She gestured to Jacob's tray. 'A pastry?' He didn't even give them a glance. *Paleo*, Alex thought, observing the tautness of his thighs through the rough fabric of his trousers. *Just the type.* Another few awkward seconds passed. 'So.' She reached for a coffee. 'How do you know Ahmed?'

The man-boy looked at her hand wrapped around the Be Your Best Self mug. He looked at her chest. He looked at the interactive whiteboard, then at the frosted wall, then back at her face. Quietly he said, 'Do you know who I am?'

Wow. Alex let her eyebrows inch towards her fringe. She almost admired his balls. 'I'm so sorry,' she said. 'My assistant didn't quite catch your name.'

The man-boy raised his hand to his throat and grasped something tucked into his shirt. He licked his lips. His eyes were flint-grey and glittering. 'Dorothy Moore,' he said. 'Do you know where I'm from?'

Alex added a touch of razor to the smile. 'Please,' she said,

'Alex. And yes. We're very grateful you found time to talk to us. Although I must admit, we don't really care about that sort of thing around here. Beeb, bloggers, we like to treat everyone the same.' She spread her hands. 'Look—' Nothing. 'Sorry, your name?'

After another long minute of staring he said, slowly, as if he was testing her, 'I am John Hanley. From the BBC.'

The name sounded vaguely familiar. Good on him. Although if he was already a name, he'd probably be offended if she asked whether he was digital or print. She'd have to wing it. 'So, John' – she just about resisted the urge to add 'from the BBC' – 'why don't you tell me more about the angle of your piece? Then I can make sure I give you exactly what your readers are looking for.'

'*Readers?*' He took another step back, fumbling at the thing round his neck. Noticing the indigo flash of an elaborate Celtic tattoo coiling out of his sleeve, Alex repressed a faint urge to laugh.

'Okay, then, sorry – clients, consumers, whatever it is you call them nowadays. What I mean is, we both have targets here. So let's figure out how we can make this a win-win, shall we?'

Nothing. Calculating how many hours she had left before she could take another Nurofen, Alex took a gulp of flat white. Was the silent glaring some kind of journo technique, designed to draw out deep, dark truths? If so, he was out of luck. Beeb or no Beeb, Dorothy Alexandra Moore was no longer easily intimidated. If some young gun was going to insist on subjecting her to his trademark master-and-commander schtick, she was going to counter it with candyfloss charm.

'Did you want to focus on the holacratic business model?' she asked brightly. 'The proprietary tech? Our culture anti-manifesto? Or are you more interested in the creation-myth stuff? My own story, I mean?'

'Your story!' John Hanley literally choked on the word, lapsing into a coughing fit. When he had managed to catch his breath, he croaked, '*Yes*. Why don't we discuss *your story?*'

And there it was, Alex thought. The chip the size of a cliff that had been perching on John Hanley's not-inconsiderable delts from the start. Mr Superior Snake-Hipped Hipster Hack Hanley, who probably considered himself some sort of shit-hot business reporter, had obviously been ordered to pen a fuzzy-wuzzy hottish-youngish-woman-in-overnight-success human-interest puff-piece. A piece his editor knew would drive thousands more clicks than a hard-hitting Tech City exposé.

Oh, but Alex would enjoy this.

She rebooted the smile and patted the chair beside her. After a moment, John Hanley stepped forward and sat, every inch of his carb-free body protesting, on the edge.

'Well, John,' Alex began, sliding seamlessly on-script, 'to understand what happened, you'll need a bit of context. Six months ago I was working as a marketing manager at a security software firm – you can probably find out where, but I'd rather you didn't name them in the piece, if that's okay? Anyway, I'd stumbled into the job after uni and stayed for almost a decade and, frankly, I'd turned into a zombie.'

'A *zombie?*'

Alex snorted. 'Okay, so I know it sounds dramatic, but when I bring up my memories of those years, that's exactly what I feel. Hollow. I was going through the motions without really living and, frankly, I don't think it's all that rare. Anyway, one day in February—'

'Tuesday the seventeenth of February? You're talking about the seventeenth?'

At least he'd done his research. 'Yes, that's right. On the morning of the seventeenth, my boss, Mark, offered me a promotion. A big promotion. More responsibility, a greater workload, even a stake in the company. It was a surprise, and not necessarily a good one. So I asked him to let me sleep on it.'

She hesitated, considering telling him about her session with Chloe that night, the emotional breakthrough they'd made. It would be worth it, just to see his reaction to the words 'holistic self-transformation coach'. But after a moment she took pity. Hanley was looking more and more ropy, his hollow cheeks sheened with sweat. The room seemed pleasantly cool to her, but then at this point she was probably metabolizing her own fat stores. Picking a flake off one of the croissants, she took her mobile out of her pocket and IM'd Gemma, asking her to crank up the air con. Then she looked back up into the young man's flinty stare.

'As it turned out, I only managed to sleep on it for a couple of hours. Come midnight, I found myself wide awake, my heart racing, my whole body prickling. It was as if some sort of inner floodgate had burst.'

'*Inner floodgate?*' Hanley fumbled again at his throat, and she finally caught sight of what he was grasping at: a hideous gap-year-style man-necklace, a carved pebble strung on a leather thong. Oh Lord. She noticed, too, that his fingers were shaking. Could he be an alcoholic? Were journalists that big a cliché?

'Can I offer you some water?'

More silent staring. It's a mixer, darling, Alex only-just didn't say.

'Okay, well,' she ploughed on, 'I'm not a psychologist, but it seems pretty obvious to me that the idea of staying trapped in the same old meaningless grind for another ten years somehow brought all my frustrations to a head. Now, there's this interesting leadership development model. I don't know if you know it, John. It says that for meaningful change to happen, you need a high volume of D multiplied by V multiplied by F. That's dissatisfaction with your current situation, multiplied by your vision of the future, multiplied by your concrete first steps. And all of *that* must add up to a force greater than R, which symbolizes your resistance to change. I can only assume that my D, my dissatisfaction with my life, had become such a tidal wave that it finally overwhelmed my R and set my V and F free. You see?'

John Hanley closed his eyes briefly. 'Are you trying to tell me this is an equation you have developed? To alter your consciousness?'

'No, no.' Alex laughed. 'I can't take the credit. Gleicher's Formula was created by organizational theorists decades ago. Look, are you sure you don't want a drink?'

Hanley swiped at his forehead. The hand was shaking badly now, and there was a drop of sweat rolling down his hawkish nose. '*Please*. Just tell me. Tell me what you did.'

Christ, he must desperate to get out of the office and into the nearest dive bar. 'Well, John,' she said gently, 'I spent the next few hours working out my vision of Eudo, down to the tiniest detail. Then I emailed Lenni – that's Lenni with an i, Kauppinen, K-A-U-P-P-I-N-E-N, he's Finnish – who used to be a housemate of a friend of mine. I'd seen from Facebook that Lenni had done well for himself over the years, sold his first start-up at uni, then founded an award-winning design agency. He was quite a big deal in Silicon Roundabout. So I asked if he could meet me in my lunch break. Now, well-being isn't exactly Lenni's natural interest area. I mean the closest he's ever got to self-development is ordering a pair of personalized Nike iDs.'

She paused for the laugh.

'*Okay* . . . so anyway, despite that, he saw the potential of Eudo right away. I'd thought through everything that sleepless night: competitors, target audience, USP. I knew I'd need to give Lenni a killer elevator pitch, so I told him that I saw Eudomonia – that's ancient Greek for well-being, by the way, John, but then I'm sure you knew that already – I told him that I saw Eudo as a well-being hub. A transmedia community for content and conversation about being your best self. We would pull in the best UGC alongside expert features on everything from quantum physics to hair masks. We would create a boutique stable of like-minded partners. Set up a suite of forums. Do some disruptive on/offline

32

influencer outreach. And then Lenni started talking about merch opportunities and immersive events, and by the time I remembered to look at the clock, half the afternoon had flown by. When I got back to the office, I was so sure that we had something real, I resigned on the spot.'

'So you . . .' Hanley was looking anguished. 'You're saying that you've invented a new technology?'

Sarcastic little cock. 'Okay, look, I'd be the first to admit that what we've done isn't exactly cutting-edge. But it's a combination of the world's most inspiring emergent people-focused tools, and I strongly believe that Eudomonia is far greater than its parts. Lenni and I, and the Eudo team, see ourselves as the curators, not the creators, in this space. The true creators are our Eudomos – that's what the most passionate members of our community call themselves. The key, John, is to make them feel part of a movement greater than any individual. Eudomonia isn't just a website, you see. It's a *fellowship*. And finally I feel like I'm helping others. That I'm doing something worthwhile.'

It was only then, turning back from where she'd been gesturing at the shapes of her team beyond the glass, that Alex realized that Hanley's eyes were squeezed shut. He appeared to be taking deep breaths, the tendons in his neck protruding, his nostrils pinched. There were dark, wet patches spreading out across his broad chest from his armpits, and the knuckles around the pebble at his throat were white.

She looked down at her phone. Should she text Ahmed? She was reluctant to admit that the opportunity he had set up with such alacrity was not going well. Scrolling through her contacts, she recalled that Mae's older sister had once done some freelancing for the BBC.

Su, she tapped. *Need ur help. I'm in an interview w a BBC journo John Hanley. He's in a bit of a state. U ever hear anything about him? He have issues?*

'You know what you're doing, don't you?' Hanley had opened his eyes and was speaking from between gritted teeth. 'You know exactly why I'm here, and you're playing with me, aren't you, you're pluuuhhhh—' He lurched forward over the table, gulped from the spare coffee, then exploded in another coughing fit. Alex took the opportunity to jump up from her chair and wrench open the door to the pod.

'WATER!' she yelled.

Fifteen heads shot up from their screens. Lenni, damn him, was still nowhere to be seen. Jacob sprinted to the kitchen module and returned with a bottle of Fiji and two Pantone Warm Red 172 beakers, which he thrust into her hands.

The door whumphed shut behind him as Alex poured John Hanley some water. His hands shook as he took the cup. When he drank, the plastic banged against his teeth. He set the beaker down and swiped at his mouth with his sleeve. 'Why?' he hissed. 'If you won't tell me how, at least tell me *why.*'

Alex's phone lit up: *Ally! Hows things!! M says ur a total celeb now :) Yeah I met JH. Seemed an OK bloke. No issues*

34

*that I know of but not current with all the goss. Didn't know
he had changed dept tho?! Sx*

'Look, I've tried to explain,' Alex murmured, frowning at
the screen in her lap. She opened the browser on her phone
and typed *John Hanley BBC* into the search bar. 'Maybe
you've always been an achiever, John. Maybe you can't
empathize with what it feels like to fail.'

'You think *I* don't know about failure?'

About 480,000 results, the front page declared. At the top
was a Wikipedia entry, followed by a LinkedIn page, a Twitter profile, a BBC bio, a list of news articles. 'Then maybe
you don't know what it feels like to be desperate, John. Like,
I don't know, somewhere deep inside you just want to blow
everything apart.' She clicked on the bio.

'Are you mocking me? You . . . you . . . *Whatever you are?*'

She looked up into his eyes then, and what she saw
stopped her breath. It wasn't only his expression – a white-
hot roil of pain and anger and a whole searing mess of other
things she couldn't name. It was the way his gaze bored into
her, like he was seeing her more deeply and clearly than
anyone had bothered to in a long time. Most of all it was the
way that she could see, reflected back at her, exactly what
those flinty drill bits had mined. She could see him see what
was inside her. She could see him see what *wasn't*.

Could he really see it? That dangerous little crack
between the Alex she used to be and the Alex she was now?
The secret hollow at the heart of her wonderful transformation? Had this total stranger somehow spotted the void?

Whatever you are.

Then he shut his eyes again, and the spell broke. Alex looked blankly back down at her phone until the image on the screen suddenly slid into focus. Fuck. Oh, fuck. Certainly John Hanley worked for the BBC, and he did indeed appear to be one of the corporation's fastest-rising stars. But he also happened to be a big bald black man, currently reporting from Brussels on a recently uncovered jihadist cell.

'Would you excuse me for just a second?'

Calmly, Alex stood up and left the pod. She shut the door behind her and stood surveying the room for a moment. Then she walked over to Tim, who was hunched over a laptop beside the window.

'Yo, boss. Whassup?'

'That guy in the meeting room?'

'Man from the Beeb?'

'Yeah, well, it turns out he isn't. From the Beeb, I mean. I was so frazzled this morning I didn't even think to ask for ID. And, well, you know those bullshit merchants bringing the IP suit against us? I think he's one of them. Also, I'm pretty sure he's drunk. Or on drugs, or something. Can you get him out of here? Now?'

'Yeah. No problem.' Tim got up and wove between his colleagues' erratically placed desks. Alex, who had never quite believed the rumour that Tim taught Mixed Martial Arts in his spare time, watched his narrow form disappear into the meeting pod, then reappear as a dark shape inside the door. After a few seconds the second dark shape, seated at the table, stood up. The two dark shapes remained like that for a moment, then the Tim-shape moved forward with

36

one arm outstretched. There was a muffled yell, and the two dark blurs became one big dark blur that started barrelling around inside the pod.

Fourteen heads shot up from their screens. From inside the pod, a strangled shout just about conveyed the words 'LOCKIE, MATE'.

Lockie, their six-foot-four Czech data analyst, got up from his desk, lumbered over and went in.

Shortly after that, the meeting-pod door banged open, and Tim and Lockie emerged with Not John Hanley secured in a two-man headlock. As soon as he caught sight of Alex, Not John Hanley started shouting, flecks of spit flying from the corner of his mouth. 'WHY DID YOU DO IT? WHY?'

'It wasn't personal,' Alex said sternly. 'I saw an opportunity and I worked incredibly hard, along with all these people right here. And I'm sorry if it didn't work out for you guys, my friend, I really am. But this isn't a zero-sum game.'

'Jacob, mate,' Tim said, dragging his prize towards the lift. 'Get this douche's bag?'

Jacob scurried into the room and retrieved the holdall. He took one brave step forward, then put the bag down on the floor and shoved it to Tim across the polished concrete.

'DOROTHY MOORE!' Not John Hanley yelled, his man-necklace swinging wildly back and forth. Tim grabbed the strap of the bag with one hand, while Lockie used his elbow to call the lift. 'DOROTHY MOORE!' Not John Hanley yelled again. The doors pinged open. Tim and Lockie hauled themselves, the bag and their prisoner inside.

A final bellow rang out. 'DOROTHY MOORE! TELL ME! WHY DID YOU KILL HIM?'

The doors slid shut.

For several minutes, in total silence, everyone in the room – Eudomonia people and protein-ball people – watched the blue digits on the panel above the lift turn from six to five to four to three to two to one to G. They were just starting to move when it changed back from G to one to two to three to four to five to six.

The doors slid open. Tim and Lockie walked out.

There was a sudden surge of movement and noise. The protein-ball people became very busy. Tim meandered over to where Alex was still standing, beneath one of the plastic trees. 'Dude was stronger than he looked,' he said. 'Still, the dank stuff can do that to you. Or so I've heard.' Lockie lumbered past them without a word. 'Talking all that bullshit,' Tim clicked his tongue. 'Hallucinating like a motherfucker, no doubt. Hey, boss. You okay?'

Alex forced her lips into a rictus of a smile.

'Of course,' she said. 'Never better.'

3

As the Uber inched away from Old Street roundabout, Alex closed her eyes and let her head fall back against the cool leather headrest. The car was an extravagance. She'd be early for lunch with her parents. But after the drama of the past eight hours she'd decided to skip the brainstorm for their mindfulness pop-up and give herself some much-needed headspace.

Now that the shock and indignation had faded, she almost felt bad for Not John Hanley. She had hardly been able to believe it, a month ago, when she'd received the snail mail from some two-bit Surrey law firm accusing Eudo of intellectual-property theft. Sure, Opa! also had a Greek-derived name, and it too had tried to corner the digital market in holistic health. But its motto – *Find Your Awesome* – was as far away from *Be Your Best Self* as Jeff Bezos was from Buddha. Not to mention that the whole outfit had folded while Eudo was still in seed-round. However, Alex knew all too well how tempting it was to pin the blame for your own mediocrity on those around you. How depressing it could be to watch your peers soar while you shuffled along the ground.

Of course, the accusation of actual murder had been a surprise. She hoped that Not John Hanley had been referring to Opa! as a business, personified. She could understand that impulse. It was all too easy to think of Eudo as her child. The more worrying alternative was that Opa!'s failure had driven someone in their team to suicide. She'd already checked on her phone and confirmed that the founder – a pompous Dutch-Russian she had once met at a networking event – was still tweeting away. But it was certainly possible that some fragile designer or bipolar developer might have been tipped over the edge by Opa!'s untimely wipeout.

It was a terrible thought. Alex was pretty certain that, even in her worst pre-Eudo moments, she had never seriously considered killing herself. Although she couldn't be entirely sure. She found it impossible, now, to remember – really remember – how it had felt to be such a failure, from the inside. As her stomach twinged and the familiar nausea rose up her gullet, she quickly steered her thoughts back to the now. Lockie had friends in the force; she'd asked him to find out whatever he could. If there were some secret tragedy behind the slander, she'd try and find a way to help the family. Without admitting any corporate responsibility, obviously. An anonymous donation, perhaps.

In the meantime, rather sadly, it had become obvious that Not John Hanley's outburst would only add to her cachet. Word, Google Alerts told her, had already got round. From the evidence of the gossip on the digital street, the intensity of the guy's ire had only illuminated the sparkle of her own rising star. The poor sod had proved that she was literally one to watch. What's more, Alex thought grimly, remembering the intensity of his gaze, misogyny certainly had a part to play. If the past six months had taught her anything, it was that people still – in the twenty-first century, for Christ's sake! – couldn't handle the idea that a woman could succeed. Openly admitting that she believed in her vision, daring to hustle, allowing herself to be exposed in the public spotlight . . . Despite their surface enlightenment, most men *and* women still seemed to believe deep down that these were not feminine qualities.

Whatever you are.

Stop it. Stop dwelling. Move on.

Alex cracked open the car's complimentary mini-Evian and downed a couple more painkillers. She straightened her spine. She murmured the power affirmation she'd crafted with Chloe: *I steer my fate, I embody my dreams.* Of course she *had* wondered, for a few stunned minutes back at her desk, whether this morning's nutter and last night's mugger might have been one and the same. But that was the sort of narcissistic paranoia that old Alex would have pedalled – *I've put myself out there, so they're out to get me: retreat, retreat!* No, she would not let them force her into becoming fearful or cynical. In fact she would go one better. She would sprint to the other end of the scale. Put her heart right out on the line.

The driver, who was 0 per cent The Knowledge and 100 per cent outdated satnav, was busy executing a seven-point turn in a dead end off the Strand. Perfect. A rare window of writing time. Settling back against the seat, Alex pulled out her phone and began to draft the bones of a post for her Founder's Blog, entitled *Speaking Out: 10 Hard-Hitting Truths on Gender in Tech.*

She was still typing when the car finally deposited her onto a roasting, heaving Charing Cross Road. Weaving through the tourists and the ticket touts, Alex switched apps to send her mother a text letting her know she'd arrived. Seconds later the reply came through: *The early bird catches the worm! Except the work i still looking at soap doshes in Heal's. Find yur father in Foyyle's see tou there. Mum x*

She found him easily, obscuring a large chunk of Fiction on the first floor. He was scanning the 'M's, big shoulders rounded, hands stuffed into the pockets of his city jacket. One frayed shoe was stabbing the floorboards in an unconvincing show of nonchalance. As Alex approached from behind, she saw him remove his right hand from his pocket and run his thumb along the row of spines, all the way from Brian Moore's *Lies of Silence* to Richard C. Morais's *The Hundred-Foot Journey*. He paused, reversed the process, then slowly dropped his arm.

As quietly as she could, Alex crept back down the stairs to the tables just inside the door. She finished the blog on her phone, then forced herself to lock the screen and zip it into her bag. Realizing that she hadn't been inside an actual bricks-and-mortar bookshop for at least a year, she selected a random hardback from one of the tables and started flicking through the pages. As far as she could tell, it was yet another high-concept psychological thriller. Albeit one making a bid for award status, by dressing up the convoluted plot in weari-somely literary prose.

'I thought you only downloaded those things nowadays.'

She closed the book and smiled into the screaming face of the woman on the cover, then suddenly noticed the *Novus Young Novelists to Watch* sticker plastered in the left-hand corner. Shit! Smile sliding off her face, she replaced the book and, trying to block the Novus display with her back, turned. 'Dad!'

'Hello, Kansas.' He held out his arms and she burrowed into the bearlike warmth of his chest. 'That's a terrible book, by the way,' he added as she emerged before an episode could take hold.

Alex glanced back down at the screaming woman, then grinned back up at her father. 'Derivative movie bait?'

'You got it, Kansas, you got it. Then again, those folks at Novus never had any taste. They'll put any old rubbish on that damn list. I should know.' His beard creased in a smile and he winked, but she could tell that he was putting on a show.

'Shall we go and find Mum?'

'Excellent idea.'

They were almost out of the door when a freckled, red-haired girl in a red-and-black name badge stepped into their path.

'I'm terribly sorry,' she said, 'but are you by any chance Tom R. Moore?'

He did this shrinking action whenever this happened,

deflating his chest and ducking his head, as if he was trying to deny his name with every inch of his flesh.

'Yes,' Alex's father said.

'Oh my God.' The girl looked around her, as if she was surprised not to see a clamouring horde gathering at her back. 'Well, I'm sorry, because normally we're not supposed to bother people, but I couldn't pass up the opportunity. *The Switch* is literally my mum's favourite book. She made me read it when I was, like, fifteen. She rereads it every year.'

'Well, thank you for telling me,' he murmured. He flashed the beard-crease and shoved his hands back into his pockets.

'This is so great. Could I get you to sign a copy? I'll just see if we—'

'Oh, well, I was—'

'Please? Please,' the girl pleaded, looking around again. 'God, my manager will kill me, but it'll only take me a sec. Let me go and check the database.'

Alex snuggled into her father's arm as they waited beside a rotating stand of grown-up colouring books. 'That was nice,' she said.

'I'm fine, sweetheart.' Her father twisted so that he could look down into her face.

'Of course you're fine, I just know you . . . hate that kind of fuss.'

'Seriously,' he said, extricating her from his arm. 'Alex.' He put a hand on her shoulder. 'You do know that, don't you? That I'm fine with this. With all this. By now.'

Alex looked deep into his pouchy eyes. 'Seriously, Dad, I

44

do. I don't underestimate you, unlike those short-sighted publishing dicks or those lazy journos looking for an easy headline. Look, I know the press gave you a hard time for a while, and I'm sure it's still tough at moments like this' – she gave him a playful prod in the stomach – 'being reminded that there are still so many rabid fans out there waiting on you. But Dom obviously still believes that Book Two is worth waiting for. And I know that underneath it all, you've got a core of steel.' She put her hand on top of his. 'We're the same, Dad, you and I. I never realized how true that was, until everything kicked off with Eudo. Now I've found my work, my real work, I *get* it, I really do. You and I might take our time, but we get there in the end. Other people's expectations don't matter, not deep down. We have our vocation. We're much stronger than everyone thinks.'

She paused. Her father was looking at her with an odd expression. She was about to ask what was wrong when she realized how strange it must be for him, not having seen her since the whole Eudo rollercoaster began, to witness how much she really had changed. His meek little Kansas, who had clung to him like a life raft for so long, had finally, at the age of thirty-one, blossomed into a woman. There must be a hint of sadness in that for him, mixed with the relief. Alex was just trying to find the words to let him know how much she still needed him, when the girl returned.

'I'm so sorry,' she panted. 'It looks like we don't currently have it in stock. Or anything else by you right now.' She smiled apologetically, her freckled skin blooming pink. 'I'm sure you understand what it's like, Mr Moore. Shelf space.

Overheads. So I wondered if you'd mind . . .' She held out a
Novus Young Novelists to Watch flyer. 'My mum would love
it if you could sign this. Thirty years on from your lot, right?
And they only do it once every ten years? Amazing to think
Mum was my age back then, when you guys were the first
ones ever. Oh, hang on.' She jogged over to the display table
and grabbed one of the screaming-woman hardbacks from
the top of the pile. 'You can lean on this.'

Alex's father took the book and the leaflet. From his inner
jacket pocket he withdrew one of the black Fineliners that
lived about his person like elongated tics.

'You didn't come along last week?' the girl asked, as he
scrawled his name without looking down. 'To the announce-
ment drinks? They invited all the alumni from the previous
two lists. I kept looking for you, but I couldn't see you there.'

'No.' Tom gave another tight beard-crease. He handed the
book and the leaflet back, then glanced at Alex.

'Sorry, of course, I won't keep you any longer.' The girl
stepped back, clutching her prize to her chest. 'Thanks so
much, Mr Moore. My mum is gonna *die*.'

Alex called her mother, who was still in Heal's. They
agreed to meet her there and began the short walk north to
Tottenham Court Road. Her father still seemed subdued, so
Alex took the opportunity to show how much she needed
him by confiding the problems they were having at Eudo:
streamlining the CRM system, defining the freemium
model, recruiting a half-competent COO. It did feel weird
not to mention either the mugger or the Opa! guy – she and
her father had no secrets from each other – but she didn't

46

want him to worry. She was only too aware how much of her new life her parents would find inexplicable. How could they be expected to understand, from the suburban tranquillity of Fring, that crazy shit like that just happened in the cut-and-thrust of the London start-up scene? It would be hard enough for them to believe that such attacks weren't personal. Even harder, from the evidence of the frown still lingering on her father's face, to believe that their conflict-averse daughter had finally grown the balls to more than hold her own. Still, it stung, that little lie of omission. Alex found herself longing to reach for her father's hand, as if he was *her* child.

They found her mother in the bedroom department, lecturing a terrified-looking boy on duvet togs. 'If they don't know their products,' she grumbled as they left the assistant to contemplate his inadequacies, 'they can't exactly complain if they're replaced by robots. Hello, darling. You look thin. And tired. What time did you get to bed?'

The only space left in the cafe was a row of high chairs at the marble bar, surrounded by people hammering away on laptops. Alex's mother ordered bacon rolls for all three of them, then launched into a thorough update on life in Fring. The lowlight of this was an ongoing feud between herself and the co-chair of the Local History Committee. The highlight was the news that Alex's father had been asked to trial a regular book-review column in a Sunday broadsheet.

'Dad!' Alex gripped his arm. 'You didn't tell me.'

He glanced at her from under his brows. 'It's just a trial, Kansas. On a sinking ship.'

'Oh, don't be so modest. It's amazing. And Dom must be pleased.'

Her father grunted. 'Dom is.'

Then their food arrived and her father ordered two beers and her mother said, 'So what's going on with Harry?'

'What do you mean, going on?' Alex, sighing, replaced her roll on its plate.

'Well, I heard you having a bit of a squabble last night, and he was as sweet as ever to us, of course, but it's quite obvious he's unhappy. You still haven't set a date?'

'Liz!' Alex's father murmured.

'Well, I'm sorry, darling, but everyone keeps asking.' Her mother leaned across and took her hand. 'Darling. I don't mind in the least whether you've changed your mind, but I can't help but wonder what's going on. You said it would definitely be this summer and, well, *tempus fugit*, and we haven't heard a peep.'

Alex sighed again. In all honesty, she'd barely given the wedding a moment's thought. Harry had tried to broach the topic a few times since New Year, but she'd been so busy that she'd fobbed him off, without really wondering why. She traced her fingernail round the rim of her plate. 'I've been so busy, Mum . . .'

'Of course you have,' her mother said, squeezing her hand. 'And I want you to know, darling, that we *are* very proud. It's incredible, everything you've achieved since we last saw you. I can't say I understand what Eudo *is*, exactly—'

'*Mum*.'

'No, darling, I don't, but it doesn't matter. It's quite obvious

48

that all those people at the party think it's going to be a great success, and they're the ones who should know.'

There was a pause.

'What?' Alex said.

'I just wonder,' her mother said, 'if you're going about it all a little . . . wholeheartedly.'

Alex groaned. 'Mum. That's the point. Don't you see that the exact reason I was so directionless, all those years, was that I never did anything with my whole heart? I mean, sure, nothing was awful, and getting engaged to Harry was lovely, but nothing was great, either. Nothing was *extraordinary*.'

What was extraordinary was how she had been for so long; how she had allowed herself to be. The days spent sitting in interminable meetings discussing meaningless targets. The evenings wasted on the sofa, watching trashy teen dramas with crusty-edged ready-meals. The hours lost flicking through magazines and dreaming about the amazing life that had to be just round the corner, but which never actually arrived.

Starting to feel queasy, she switched her focus to her new day-to-day. She relived how it had felt to see Eudo's beta-release go live. She mentally traced the exponential curve of their sign-up figures. She reminded herself of the members who said that visiting the site was the highlight of their morning. She recalled the deals she had calmly brokered in roomfuls of men. And yes, damn it, she thought about the parties, the new wardrobe, the sight of her retouched face on the front cover of *Flair*. Slowly, Alex felt a warm swell of conviction spread through her chest. The change she'd undergone recently – no, the change *she'd made happen* –

might be hard for her parents to understand. But she knew it was authentic, because it was, quite simply, working. It was making that amazing life, the one she'd daydreamed about so ineffectually for so many years, finally come true.

'Committing my whole heart to Eudo is exactly what broke the cycle, Mum,' she said. 'It's like my life coach, Chloe, says: you can only become the person you're truly capable of being if you unleash all your secret power.'

'Darling.' Liz raised her eyebrows. 'Life coach? And she sounds a lot like Margaret O'C from the Baptist Church.'

Alex gave her mother a calm smile. 'I know it can be hard to understand,' she said. 'Chloe warned me that an empowered attitude can be very threatening. English people, in particular, hate it when someone approaches their vocation in a *wholehearted* way. But Dad gets it, don't you, Dad?' Alex shot her father a look of appeal, but her father was still staring at her with that unreadable frown.

Her mother's eyebrows had all but disappeared into her hairline. 'All I'm trying to say, darling,' she said, 'is that you seem to have changed so very much in such a short time. It reminds me of that summer you were eleven, when you moved to St J's. All of a sudden my happy little girl seemed to turn into this miserable shadow overnight. It seemed so dramatic. So abrupt. Oh, of course, back then a lot of it would have been hormones, the pressure of a new school, but I can't help but be reminded of it now. I'm worried about you, that's all.'

'But back then I turned from happy to miserable, Mum, and this is exactly the opposite.' Alex spread her palms. 'I remained that miserable shadow for so many years, and now, well, now I'm . . .'

A ripple of sickness. A quiver of vertigo. She leaned over the side of her chair and reached into her bag, pretending to check her phone while she breathed the episode down. As her vision cleared, she saw a ghost army of missed calls and message symbols lurking behind the lock screen. Amongst them were four new voicemails from that anomalous landline she didn't recognize. She really should . . .

'Yes?' her mother prompted gently. 'Who exactly are you now, darling?'

Alex sat up. 'Well, I'm back to being that happy little girl,' she said. 'Only I'm not little any more, am I? I've finally grown up. I'm independent. I'm strong.'

'And Harry?'

'Harry's Harry. Harry's lovely. Harry and I are fine. I'm just too busy to focus on sugared almonds right now, and he's finding it a bit tough to adjust to my new obligations, that's all.' She paused. 'It seems he's not the only one.'

'Darling—'

'It's okay, Mum.' It was Alex's turn to reach for her mother's hand. 'I understand. You're only trying to protect me. But you have to trust me, really, I don't need protecting any more. Now why don't you tell me how things are going at the Abbey?'

Her mother gave her a knowing look and a laden sigh, but took her cue. As she embarked on a dissection of the political maelstrom that was the Fring Abbey summer fete, Alex glanced over at her father and winked. But her father was still watching her with that strange expression, and the smile he summoned up was as tight and shallow as the one he'd given the bookshop girl.

4

'Al! I haven't heard from you in *ages*. How – Bo! Sorry, hang on. BO!'

Leaning over the sink in the deserted Eudo loos, Alex added a third layer of mascara in an attempt to widen her tired eyes. On the counter beneath her, her mobile speaker-phone disgorged the sound of Bo's tinny voice negotiating for 'yog raisnis' over the *Peppa Pig* theme tune. It had been a relentless afternoon. First, she and Lenni had interviewed five potential COOs. Not one of them had been right. Then she'd had to jump in and help Gemma defuse a flame war about breastfeeding, on the Eudo messageboards. And throughout it all she'd been distracted by the conversation with her parents, unable to shake the feeling that she was under attack at a time when they should have been most proud. At least, thank God, Lockie's police contacts hadn't been able to dig up anything sinister about the Opa! guys.

'Sorry.' Mae came back on the line. 'How *are* you? I'm so sorry I couldn't make the party. Was it like one of those Apple launches? Are you going to start wearing nothing but black turtlenecks?'

Alex snorted. 'It was fine. No, actually, it was great. Except

Harry got all jealous, and some nutter tried to lift my hand-bag on the way home. And this morning some other nutter lied his way into my office and basically accused me of destroying his life. And then my parents decided to have some sort of crisis about me finally finding my mojo.'

'No! Al! What? What do you mean? Are you okay?'

Alex sighed and swiped two determined lines of blusher across her cheekbones. 'Honestly,' she said, 'it's all petty non-sense. I don't even want to talk about it. I'm totally fine. Except—'

'BO! I *told* you.' There was a volley of sobs. 'Hang on.' Alex heard a cupboard door bang, the crackle of a packet, abrupt silence. 'Sorry.' Mae reappeared. 'Just rewarding bad behaviour. He was supposed to be in bed half an hour ago, but he's had way too much attention today. And way too much cake. What were you saying?'

'I wanted to ask your advice about something.' Since the night of Southampton Uni Freshers' Ball, when a tiny, bolshy Singaporean-Mancunian had told Alex in no uncer-tain terms that she was never to wear yellow again, Mae had been the one friend Alex could trust to give her an honest perspective on her life. Not to mention that Mae was the only real friend that her semi-reclusive student self, who scurried home from university on the train every weekend, had managed to make. As the memories of their friendship bubbled up – Mae dragging Alex along to parties, Alex proof-reading Mae's essays, the pair of them getting fits of giggles in the solemn art-house cinema – the dizziness that threat-ened an episode rose in their wake. Alex shook it off impatiently and focused on the task in hand. 'Or, rather, I want your advice about someone,' she corrected. 'About Harry.'

'Ah,' Mae said.

Alex paused, lipstick hovering in the air. '*Ah?*'

'What? No. I don't – well, I just mean I've been wondering if you'd changed your . . . I mean, if something's changed between you guys.' Mae paused. 'I mean, obviously I've got all your round-robin emails and group WhatsApps, but we haven't actually talked since February.' The slightest edge crept into Mae's voice. 'You haven't returned any of my calls.'

'I . . .' Alex was about to defend herself, but then she realized she really didn't want to bullshit Mae. 'I know,' she said quietly. 'I know I've been crap. I've been a bit . . . a bit burnt-out. I don't know, Mae, somehow it makes it harder, being with people who knew me. Who knew me before. When I'm trying to focus on all the amazing opportunities coming up now.' She paused, swallowed. 'To be honest, Mae, thinking about the past? Remembering what a loser I was? I get these . . . It makes me feel physically ill. Not that you're my past,' she added hurriedly, 'God, no, you're still my best, my only—'

'Al,' Mae interrupted laconically. 'I get it. Don't sweat it. You're a famous badass businesswoman now. Although, for the record, you really weren't that much of a loser before.'

'I really am sorry. Once this first phase calms down and I have time to get a bit more sleep, venture further than Zone One—'

'Al,' Mae insisted. 'I understand. This is your time, and

you should make the most of it. It's my fault for living out in the sticks. Now what did you want to ask about Harry?'

In the background Bo started singing along tunelessly to a plinky-plonky song. Alex planted her hands either side of the sink, took a deep breath and looked in the mirror. 'Harry's wonderful, isn't he?' she asked her reflection, its brownish eyes made glamorous by glittering shadow, its brownish hair highlighted to almost-gold. 'About as good a guy as any woman could hope for? Thoughtful, successful, upstanding, kind?'

'Um,' Mae said slowly, 'aren't you the one who should be telling me?'

'I know, I know,' Alex sighed. 'And I *know* he's all those things, Mae. He's always treated me like a princess. Our relationship is great. We never argue, except when he goes on one of his jealousy crusades, and that's only because he loves me so much. I can think of a hundred women who would be desperate to marry Harry.'

'Okaaaay. So?'

Plink-plonk, plink-plonk.

'So . . . I just . . .' Alex paused. 'Can you remember how I reacted, when he proposed?'

'How you *reacted*?'

'Because I remember calling you, telling you he'd popped the question, but I can't quite remember how I *felt* about it, weird as it sounds. I mean, was I excited? Did I sound – did I sound certain? Did I seem *happy*?'

Plink-plonk, plink-plonk. As Alex tried to focus on the memory of that New Year's morning, picturing Harry on his knee in her parents' frosty garden, his handsome face smiling

56

up at her, his grandmother's sapphire glinting from the open box, she felt the details start to slip and blur like wet watercolours and the vertigo start to slosh against her mind.

'. . . don't exactly like to talk about your feelings,' Mae was saying. 'Or you didn't, back then. You've always been such a closed book, Al. Not like now. It was like you used to silently analyse every little action for all its potential consequences, like you were watching out for hidden traps. And then there's the commitment issue. I mean, we both know you always had trouble committing to things – wholeheartedly, that is—'

The word landed like a bullet, shattering the encroaching episode. 'Exactly!' Alex cried, slapping the countertop. The void snapped shut and oxygen swept back through her veins. 'God, Mae. That's exactly what this is about.' She shook her head incredulously, watching her hair catch the light. 'Poor old Mum. I was starting to get so defensive, but as usual she was basically right. I've been in danger of running away like I used to, buying into the bullshit, limiting my power. That must be what my procrastinating with the wedding has been about. A trace of scared old Alex clinging on.' She paused. She smiled deeply into her reflected eyes. She murmured, 'It's okay now, Alex. New Alex. I'm here. She's gone.'

From the phone: 'Al? Are you okay?'

'You know what,' Alex said, hurriedly slicking on two curves of lipstick, 'I'm better than okay. I'm bloody brilliant. And I love you very much. And I'm sorry for being so rubbish recently, but I'm late for something very important, and I really have to go.'

'Al—'

'I'll call and explain tomorrow. I promise I'll try and call tomorrow. Okay?'

Mae hesitated, as if she had been about to say something else, but then she said, 'Fine.'

Alex hit the red circle on her phone and scooped up her bag.

Harry had tried to get Alex to come to his flat. She was relieved, now, that she had held her ground and insisted they go out, on the basis that she'd had a terrible day and needed a treat. Gemma had pulled some last-minute strings, and when she rushed up the worn stone steps of L'Antiga Capella – the big new venture from a Catalan chef who'd made his name throwing word-of-mouth supper clubs – she saw that the setting could not have been more perfect. A stern Spanish hostess escorted her up the steps of the deconsecrated chapel and across the nave. Harry was at a table near the back, stabbing at his BlackBerry from behind two untouched shot glasses of red goo.

'I'm so sorry I'm late.' Alex allowed herself to be tucked under the stone slab. 'You'll forgive me everything, when you hear about my day.' Unbidden, an image of Not John Hanley's Gormenghast face and ballet-dancer thighs superimposed itself on the snowy tablecloth. Alex forced it away and focused on Harry's Hollywood jaw, his Air Force-blue eyes, the classical proportions of his Virgin Active physique. 'God, I'm starving. Do you mind?' She downed both amuses-bouches.

' – pacho,' the waiter said. He paused. 'May I explain the menu?'

While he droned, Alex gazed at Harry, bathing his lovely features in attention – until a flash of bling from the dim cavern beyond his shoulder caught her eye. 'Shit!' she hissed. 'Helena Pereira! Three o'clock! Shit, Harry! She would be the perfect, literally the perfect, brand ambassador for Eudo. Do you think it would be totally inappropriate for me to—'

'Yes,' Harry said. 'I think it would.'

Alex collected herself. She unfolded her napkin. She let the silence settle. 'You're right,' she said. 'I find it so hard to switch off. But I know I need to, Harry, I do. I need to get some balance back. And on that subject, there's something I want to say.' She took a deep breath and gave him a shy smile from under her lashes. 'What I want to say to you is . . . let's do it.'

Harry frowned, glass of tap halfway to his lips. 'Do what?'

Alex let the smile spread into a grin. 'The wedding, you idiot! Let's bloody well get hitched.' She leaned over the table and wrapped her arms round his neck for a kiss. He was slow to respond, obviously dazed. She felt a pang of guilt. How long she had kept him waiting. How nearly he must have given up hope. 'You've been so patient,' she said, settling back into her chair. 'I know Eudo has kind of taken over everything recently, but I've been doing a lot of thinking today, and I'm ready now. I really am.'

'Alex—'

'No, wait.' Alex held up her hand. 'Lenni, Ahmed, Dale,

everyone at work would say I'm mad to be thinking about a wedding right now. But I don't care. I don't want to hold myself back on any front any more, professional *or* personal. And I know your parents might not like it, but honestly, I'd rather not get bogged down by some big fat St Albans do. Let's just take ourselves off to Shoreditch Town Hall one weekend and tie that knot as tight as we can.' She stretched out her hand and cupped it over his. 'Baby, I'm not afraid any more. I know we can make this a success.'

The waiter brought the food. Alex stuffed a forkful of something beige and grainy into her mouth. Harry adjusted the position of his knife.

'Have you phoned Mae?' he asked.

Alex blinked. 'Have I what?'

He looked up, the Air Force blues direct on hers. 'Did you call Mae today?'

Alex squinted at him. '*Mae?* Well, yes, I did, as a matter of fact, half an hour ago. That's why I was late. I needed to ask her opinion on – on Lenni. But what on earth has that got to do with . . . Harry, did you hear what I just said?'

Harry lowered his gaze and fiddled with his napkin, looking shifty. 'Okay. In that case, I apologize. I admit, I thought you'd forgotten about Bo.'

'*Bo?*' Alex paused, thoroughly confused. 'Forgotten what about Bo?'

Harry stopped fiddling. His eyes narrowed. 'So you *did* forget?'

'Forget *what*? What are you trying to—'

'It's Bo's second birthday today, Alex,' Harry said. 'Bo, your godson. Did you even mention it? Or were you too busy talking about Lenni?'

'I don't . . . what has this—'

'Let alone a card? A present?'

Alex set down her fork. 'Harry? What's going on?'

Harry sighed. 'I didn't want to come here. To come out. I wanted to talk properly at home.' He hesitated. 'I had no idea you were planning to bring up the wedding yourself.'

Alex felt the mush start to curdle in her chest. 'I don't understand. I thought you'd be over the moon. Why are you so upset about one tiny slip concerning Bo?'

'It's not Bo. Well, it's not only Bo. It's symptomatic.'

Alex forced herself to swallow. '*Symptomatic?*'

Harry sighed again. 'You've changed, Alex. Look, I'm sorry, I know it's been an important period for you, these past six months, and you've achieved an awful lot. But, frankly, I feel like you've become a very different woman from the one I first met.'

Alex closed her eyes. Silently she repeated Chloe's affirmations three times. Then she opened her eyes again and gave Harry the same calm smile she'd bestowed on her mother. 'Darling,' she said. 'It's alright. I know this must be challenging for you. I know that the power dynamic in our relationship has shifted pretty fast. But you have to understand: I'm still the same Alex underneath it all. Just with the rubbish bits taken out.'

'But that's exactly it,' Harry said. 'I'm beginning to suspect that what you consider to be your "rubbish bits" weren't rubbish to me at all.'

'Come on.' Alex gave an incredulous laugh. 'You can't seriously mean that you liked the fact that I was so miserable? So directionless? So . . . so *weak*? Even thinking about it now makes me—'

'But you see, what you call weak,' Harry interrupted, unsmiling, 'I experienced as moderate and thoughtful and sensitive. The woman I fell in love with didn't forget her godson's birthday. She didn't fail to ask what was going on in other people's lives because she simply assumed they couldn't be as interesting as hers. She didn't air her private thoughts in public, she didn't want to spend all her time with a rabble of autistic men. And she certainly didn't think that having her name splashed all over a Tube weekly was the ultimate achievement in life.' He paused, flushed. The waiter approached their table, smiled, opened his mouth, then veered away without breaking pace.

Quietly Alex said, 'Listen to yourself, Harry. Are you seriously saying that you loved me when I was small and fearful, but you can't handle me now I'm spreading my wings? Are you really that *Victorian*?'

Harry was wearing the face she hated most, what she called his Puritan face. In one expression, it summoned the St Albans Bell Ringing Society, his black Marks & Spencer work shoes, his dislike for olives and the fact that his favourite book was *Tuesdays with Morrie*.

Alex shovelled up another forkful of mush, even though she had entirely lost her appetite. 'Be honest,' she said, after a long silence. 'Is this a God thing?'

The Puritan face reached its Platonic ideal.

'Because I've never let it get in the way of our relationship, Harry,' she continued, chomping vigorously. 'I've made a lot of effort to respect your beliefs. But if this is some kind of deep-rooted, Old Testament Madonna-whore crisis, I—' She gulped down a great soggy bolus. 'I mean, Jesus, you don't really buy that stuff anyway, do you? You don't go to church. You don't hate gay people. You don't even pray.'

'This is precisely what I mean,' Harry said coldly, looking with distaste at the bits of grain she had sprayed in his water glass. 'I think you're the one who needs to listen. I don't recognize the woman saying those words.'

Alex took a deep breath and searched Harry's eyes for the man she loved, for the man who always talked to the most awkward-looking person in a room and who used to make her packed lunches with notes hidden inside. She reminded herself of his addiction to old Astaire and Rogers movies. She thought about the way he adored Bo.

'Okay,' she said, leaning forward. 'You want the truth? Half the time I don't even recognize *myself*. This transition isn't exactly easy for me, either, you know. It's like this great force has exploded inside my brain, inside my body, and I'm having to sprint to keep up. I'm knackered, Harry. Sometimes I feel like I'm on the edge of this . . . this *void*, and that if I stop sprinting for just a second I'll fall right in. But I also feel free for the first time ever, and I have no alternative but to keep going, now I've got out of my rut. I'm sure things will settle down soon, but honestly' – she shook her head – 'honestly, I can't believe you can't see how much better I am now.'

Harry sighed and rubbed his forehead. 'I did know that you weren't entirely happy,' he said stiffly. 'I suppose I felt guilty that I couldn't seem to help you more, these past years. That I couldn't make you happy myself. And recently, well, of course I'm in awe of all you've achieved.' He paused. 'But it seems so radical, the way you've transformed yourself so thoroughly to make it all happen. It rings a little hollow, to tell the truth. And I don't want to speak for anyone else, but I know there are others in your life who feel the same way.' He shook his head. 'It's not that I don't want you to succeed, Alex, but I don't understand why you have to abandon so many things that make you *you*, in order to do so.'

Alex didn't want to ask, but she had to know. 'Including us?'

'I think,' Harry said slowly, 'that you're on a particular journey at the moment, and I'm obviously getting in the way. I hope – I very much hope – you'll find more of an equilibrium soon, but I'm not sure that a shotgun wedding is the right thing just now.'

'Don't buy into the bullshit, Harry,' Alex said quietly. 'I refuse to believe that it's impossible for a woman to have both a brilliant career and a brilliant marriage.'

Harry refolded his napkin beside his untouched food. 'I'm sorry if this wasn't the conversation you were expecting, but I really think you should spend some time thinking about what I've said. About what you want, and about who you want to be.' He stood up and shrugged on his jacket. 'I'll sort the bill on my way out.'

After he left, Alex sat alone for another half an hour, letting the tinkle of glass and the murmur of small talk wash over her jumbled thoughts. She came to when Helena Pereira led her entourage across the flagstones in a backwash of whispers, looking like a time traveller from some perfected future race. Alex was just constructing an argument about Pereira being the consummate case study of having it all – the iconic modelling career, the jewellery business, the adoring husband, the trilingual twins – when the sound of a commotion broke out from the chapel's vestibule.

The rumble of raised voices quickly escalated into a single shout, immediately followed by a female scream. Then a cacophony of yells and the scuffle of struggling feet followed. Three men in aprons came thundering through the restaurant from the open kitchen at the back. Several diners stood up while others froze, gripping the backs of their chairs. After a moment's silence, the room erupted into babble. Someone dropped the word 'bomb.' A few men got out from behind their tables and made bold yet dithery movements towards the source of the noise.

The maître d' emerged.

'Please,' he called, 'ladies and gentleman. Our apologies for the disturbance. There is nothing to worry about. We had an unfortunate incident with a lone individual who has now been delivered into the charge of the police.' He bestowed a comradely smile on the hovering men. 'Do resume your seats. I hope that you enjoy your evening.'

Why, Alex thought wearily as she stood up and hoisted her bag onto her shoulder, was the world full of so much spite and fear? Chloe was right: people saw life through such blinkered eyes. Alex had noticed that the more she pushed her own boundaries, the more those around her seemed to do the opposite, entrenching themselves more deeply into their narrow beliefs. Navigating your way through all their twisted versions of reality really was exhausting sometimes.

Feeling a little wobbly, Alex got the Tube to her flat. She was tempted to nip back to the office and steal a march on the next day's work. But she knew that would have been a classic old-Alex avoidance technique. Instead she made herself a cafetière of Blue Mountain, rubbed some arnica into her bruises, sat on the sofa and did what Harry asked. She set out to think.

But as soon as she tried to review his accusations, her thoughts began to fracture and slide. Despite the expensive food she had forced down, she felt hollow. Instead of embarking on the rigorous burst of self-examination she had intended, she found her mind drifting off into a cold, windy no-man's-land. As she sipped her coffee, it skittered between the mugging, Not John Hanley and a mess of fuzzy memories that took her dangerously close to the void.

Abruptly, Alex snagged her thoughts back onto the safe ground of the present. Perhaps, to a certain degree, Harry was right. Perhaps, just perhaps, it was time for her to stop ignoring her episodes. They were clearly a signal that, whatever Chloe said about boundless power, she needed to back off a bit with work. But then how else was she supposed to keep up the momentum when, as Ahmed liked to remind her on a regular basis, she *was* Eudo? It was the sort of entrepreneurial pressure that Harry would never understand, with his steady analyst's job in a global shipping firm. Ever since he had left Durham, his days had been navigated by a constellation of reliable data, anchored by process, churned along by a thousand habits. Whereas she was having to free-style every moment, imagine her own horizon into existence, fight for every stroke.

They had always been different, she and Harry. That's what had made them so great together, in the past. But suddenly the differences seemed . . . different. Clashing, not complementary. Was she admitting, then, that Harry was right? After five rock-solid years, could their relationship really have crumbled in a mere six months?

Again, for some reason, she thought of Not John Hanley, sweating and shuddering in her office like an injured wolf in a glass tank. She thought of his stare, hungry and merciless. *Whatever you are.*

But then an image that had been slowly but firmly taking root in Alex's mind since she spoke to Mae reasserted itself. A vision of her life in five years' time. It featured Harry opening a bottle of rosé in the high-ceilinged kitchen of a Highgate townhouse, while three small and unruly children chased a rescue Saluki around the patio. And it didn't make her feel sick at all.

'No,' she said, punching a cushion. 'No, Harry boy. *That's* what I am. That's what *we* are. And I won't let it go.'

She jumped up and paced her kitchen-lounge-diner's ninety square feet while a distant soundtrack of electro-bhangra and backfiring mopeds floated in on the stifling breeze. It wasn't Harry's fault. Social Stockholm Syndrome, Chloe called it: the reluctance of people to open the door of the cage that society had shut them in. At least Alex had the advantage of half-American blood. Harry was as English as Earl Grey. Was it any wonder that, seeing the shrinking violet he had treasured for a decade suddenly shoot into a tall poppy, his instinct was to whip out the scythe?

It had been unfair of her, Alex admitted, to expect him to trust in her transformation. It was obvious to her now that all those who had known her before Eudo were struggling to come to terms with her transition. God – as she had told Harry, sometimes she barely trusted it herself. But this was no time for self-pity, old-Alex-style. She had put so much effort into her game plan for Eudo that she'd neglected to do the same for both her health and her relationships, and it was her responsibility to put that right.

Alex returned to the sofa. She picked up her iPad, opened her project management app and created a new workstream called FAMILY. Under Mission Statement, she typed: *To build a satisfying, stimulating and mutually supportive family life.*

It would do.

She organized the project into three colour-coded substreams – Harry, Children, Property. Then, in the spirit of Chloe's principle to throw it all out there, because you never knew what might bounce back, she added Parents, Friends, Pets, Holidays, Transport, Relaxation and Fun. Then she tapped on the Harry tab and contemplated possible tasks.

Prove to Harry that I am still the woman he loves, she typed.

Accurate, but too vague.

She deleted the sentence, swallowed more coffee and closed her eyes, trying to recall the specifics of each accusation Harry had made. After a few minutes she opened her eyes and resumed typing, and moments later she had five robust tasks:

1. Put aside more time for self-reflection and meditative calm.
2. Demonstrate that I am not obsessed with Eudomonia.
3. Provide evidence of generosity / sensitivity / spirituality / thoughtfulness.
4. Give Harry the space he needs to realize that his life is incomplete without me.
5. Courier Bo 2nd birthday gift.

Alex opened her browser and found a garden yurt suitable for twelve months and up, in a toy shop near Twickenham. Five minutes later she had spoken to the shop owner, secured the yurt and paid extra to guarantee same-day delivery. Delighted that she had already completed her first concrete action – her fingertip prodded the Bo-task tick-box so hard that it left a brief digital halo behind – Alex poured some more joe and contemplated the remaining four.

She was just wondering whether taking up Pilates might provide evidence of renewed spirituality when an order confirmation from the Twickenham toy shop popped up. She

opened her mailbox, wondering whether she should forward
it straight to Harry. On balance, she decided not, but then
the subject of the message beneath caught her eye:

Attn Miss D.A. Moore: Invitation to Collaborate on International Research Project

Feeling particularly benevolent after her gift-buying coup,
Alex decided to break her digital-bumf rules this once and
double-clicked:

Dear Miss Moore
[the email began, with rare formality]
    I am not sure if you have received my previous emails
or telephone calls, but I hope that you will excuse my per-
sistence in attempting to contact you on a matter of some
urgency.
    Here at the Global Centre for Autobiographical Studies,
or GCAS (European Chapter) we are working on a unique
research project in which we are very eager for you to
participate. We are chronicling powerful stories of personal
transformation from across Europe. Our hope is that they
will become a spur for international understanding, collaboration and enlightenment for all those struggling to live
lives that give back to the global community.

There were a lot of good words here, Alex thought. Very
good words. She felt the beginning of a buzz that had nothing to do with caffeine.

The Charmed Life of Alex Moore

Having recently read an article on the website of 'Flair'

[and that's what you get from half a million monthly uniques, Harry darling, Alex thought],

we believe that your own Story would make a central and timely contribution. Considering the many national, racial and religious conflicts dominating the news at present, we aim to complete and collate our interviews as rapidly as possible. We would therefore like to invite you to visit us at your earliest convenience, for as long as you can spare, with all travel and accommodation costs paid.

The European Chapter of GCAS is based on Iskeull, a privately owned island in the Orkney archipelago and a living embodiment of untouched native ecology. This is a rare opportunity to visit a microstate set in one of the most unspoilt landscapes on earth.

Archipelago. It practically reeked of nobility. Ancient wisdom. Dragons. Not to mention air; air and light and quiet.

It sounded like somewhere she could slow down, if only for a couple of days.

Somewhere she could breathe.

All profits from the research paper will be ploughed back into GCAS's ongoing work, which is focused on the preservation of indigenous ecosystems and the promotion of the free flow of human thought across the world.

Please do get in touch as soon as you receive this message. We look forward to arranging your journey.

Yours sincerely, Sorcha MacBrian, S.R., Director, GCAS (European Chapter)

Alex googled Orkney.

5

The doors beeped closed seconds after Alex jumped into the carriage, breathing hard. She couldn't believe she'd come so close to missing her train, after paying so much for a last-minute ticket. Who would have thought so many people wanted to go to Scotland at 8 a.m. on a Friday? But she had been determined not to fail at her very first goal – clean, lean, planet-friendly nourishment – hence the M&S carrier bag banging against her shins. Two boxes of organic fruit salad, three packs of free-range chicken breast strips, a bar of Fairtrade 90 per cent dark chocolate and a six-pack of Highland Spring. She was off to an excellent start.

She wobbled her way to her allocated seat and hoisted her rucksack – which she had started to think of, for the purposes of this trip, as her valise – up onto the rack. Brand new underwear, spare jeans, a couple of vests, a Breton-striped pullover and some emergency cashmere. It was the ideal capsule wardrobe for a few back-to-nature days by the sea.

The woman in the aisle seat, who had already spread a sheaf of printouts across the table, sighed and stood up to let Alex squeeze past. Thanking her with a patient smile, Alex settled into the worn upholstery. It wasn't long, after all, since she herself had been dull-complexioned and borderline-podgy, spending her mornings doing soulless paperwork. The train was already speeding through the outskirts of London, offering up a cinemagraph of sagging washing lines and broken trampolines. Harry, Alex thought with a swell of magnanimity, had been right. She'd barely given a thought to the world outside Eudo since it all kicked off. As if on cue, the suit sitting opposite folded his *Times* on the table and hunkered down for a nap, knocking her ankles with his feet in a brief territorial dance.

'Excuse me?' Alex said. He reopened one eye. 'Do you mind if I . . . ?' The suit swept a permissive hand towards the paper, before tucking his hand back under his armpit.

Tingling with the thrill of the contact – they must be out of London, to transgress the privacy of public transport with such insouciance! – Alex picked up the broadsheet and shook it out. But as she flicked through the pages she found herself struggling to concentrate for more than a paragraph. Abandoning it, she turned on her phone, despite her vow to leave it off until York, just to check the time.

Seven minutes? Seven? Only . . . 253 to go.

But then as Chloe would say, Alex reminded herself sternly, the journey was the destination. When Alex had proposed her itinerary to the Director of GCAS (European Chapter) last night, the Director of GCAS (European Chapter) had tried to persuade her to take the quicker option of a flight. But Alex knew that a slow, contemplative *Anna*

Karenina-style odyssey by rail and sea would sound far better to Harry than a business-like hop from Heathrow.

Harry. She had promised herself not to contact him until she was back, to *give him the space he needs to realize that his life is incomplete without me.* But it would be a shame for him not to realize the effort she was making on his – no her, no *their* – behalf. She thumbed open their message thread.

H. I'm off to Orkney for the wkend to collaborate on research project for international enlightenment. Going to think about what you said. A. She hesitated, then added *x.*

She waited for a few minutes, but there was no reply. To the irritation of the woman beside her, who was now brutalizing her printouts with great swathes of highlighter, Alex reached up for her bag to retrieve her iPad. She opened the e-book she had downloaded for her journey the night before: *The Collected Poems of George Mackay Brown.* He was, apparently, the definitive bard of Orkney. Wishing that her father could see her, she tapped on a random hyperlink in the Contents and started to read:

> *Further than Hoy*
> *the mermaids whisper*
> *through ivory shells*
> *a-babble with vowels*
>
> *Further than history*
> *the legends thicken*
> *the buried broken*
> *vases and columns*

Further than fame
are fleas and visions,
the

But then it was probably unreasonable to expect her to jump straight into poetry when she hadn't read so much as an airport thriller in months. Alex logged into the Virgin East Coast wi-fi, intending to select something a little more palatable. Surely there would be tons of trashy Tolkien-lite set in 'one of the most unspoilt landscapes on earth'? But although her menu bar claimed to have five full bars of connection, it soon became obvious that her menu bar was full of shit.

She checked her phone. Nothing from Harry.

Not to be discouraged, she opened the webpages she had cached in case of just such an emergency and began to pore over the research that she'd barely had time to skim the night before.

There wasn't much. The GCAS website was a grey holding page with a clunkily symbolic logo – a figure-of-eight inside a circle – at the top. There was a sentence about the institute's aim to 'promote the free flow of human thought across the world', then a list of its seven 'Chapters'. Each of these linked out to a native-language microsite. When she navigated to the European one, Alex found that it was barely more helpful. It simply repeated the logo, added a border of blue runic symbols, and repurposed the copy from Sorcha MacBrian's email – explaining that the Chapter was located on an island that was 'a living embodiment of untouched native ecology'. At the bottom was a stern reminder, in bold caps, that:

ISKEULL IS A PRIVATELY OWNED AND FUNDED MICRO-
STATE, INDEPENDENT OF THE BRITISH GOVERNMENT
AND UNSERVICED BY PUBLIC TRANSPORT. VISITORS BY
APPOINTMENT ONLY. CONTACT INFO@GCASEU.ORG

Alex skimmed through the microsites for the other Chapters, with the help of her browser's auto-translate. The decorative borders were an international art-history tour of ancient-looking motifs. The names of the islands differed, obviously (Pasca Nui, Menikuk, Belyando, Gave, Yíngzhōu, Buyanin). As did the governments from which they declared independence (Chile, Canada, Australia, Comoros, Japan, Russia). Each Chapter also had its own email address – which appointment-only visitors were ordered, in no uncertain bold caps, to contact. Otherwise, each one replicated exactly the same minimalist template and eco-friendly blurb.

Other search results for GCAS had been dominated by various engineering, accounting and automative firms that happened to share the same acronym. She'd only managed to find one mention of the European Chapter in social media, buried deep in the postgrad section of a student chat room. A member called **anniem411** had started a thread called 'Help! Opportunities in GCAS Orkney – advice?!!', asking, 'any of you know about "GCAS" in Orkney nr Scotland? Phd w/ specialism in critical theory, narrative & psychology looking for research job, having trouble finding application info for this place??' A lone reply from someone called **smilenthwrld** said, 'seem to be local offshoot of some kind of international NGO. prob cherrypick from other courses/places. looks residential only tho, sure u want to be middle of nowhere?'

As for Iskeull, a Wikipedia entry confirmed that it was the northernmost island in Orkney and the second largest, at 170 square miles. It added that it was three miles away from its nearest neighbour, North Ronaldsay, and had an estimated population of 8,000. There then followed three stark and distinctly familiar sentences:

> Iskeull is a privately owned and funded microstate, independent of the British government and unserviced by public transport. It is home to the European Chapter of the Global Centre for Autobiographical Studies (GCAS) and provides a protected environment for the preservation of ancient native ecology. Members of the public are permitted to visit the island by private appointment only.

The only other mentions she had been able to find were cut-and-paste jobs on travel sites, reproducing the same few lines of text.

The other islands that made up Orkney, however, were another matter. Alex scrolled through page after saved page of Historic Scotland PDFs and websites of 'world-renowned' distilleries and fisheries. She jumped from ugly local domains compiling legends and dialects, to unwieldy art-festival microsites. She skimmed articles on Bronze Age archaeology, articles on Viking DNA, articles on World War wrecks. And then there were the photo galleries, featuring thousands of shots from professional photographers and tourists alike. It was standard northern-idyll stuff: rainbows arching over glistening heather, dramatic rocky crags, weird Neolithic grassy humps and freezing-looking beaches. Alex imagined the selfie she would send to Harry, featuring her pink-cheeked, clear-eyed, internationally-enlightened self standing on the edge of a cliff beside a bunch of earnest academics. Wild sunset, check. Rune-covered monolith, check. Soaring eagle, check-check-check. No bloody filter required.

She checked her messages. Nothing. But then he was probably in a meeting. The sort of meetings in which highlighter-woman spent her days. The sort of meetings in which Alex had once frittered away her life, before she broke free. Poor Harry.

She returned to her iPad and opened the file containing Director MacBrian's instructions. She was to catch the ferry from the mainland, arriving late that evening into Kirkwall. This was the capital of Orkney, located on its largest island – which was called, confusingly, Mainland. Alex would then be picked up by one of MacBrian's colleagues and taken to a nearby B&B. The next morning, weather permitting, they would fly to Iskeull by private plane. Alex would stay over on the GCAS (European Chapter) campus, and then they would fly her back to Kirkwall for her return journey, weather permitting, on Sunday night.

When they'd spoken on the phone, MacBrian had seemed gratifyingly eager to get Alex onto the island, if somewhat lacking in the niceties of social intercourse. She had repeated the offer in her email that Alex should stay as long as she could. Alex had repeated in turn that, with Eudo at a crucial point in its growth cycle, even a weekend was pushing it. Two days would provide plenty of time to fill her lungs with fresh coastal air and her soul with a fresh contribution to the global community. By Monday, she'd once again be the woman that her mother approved of, her father adored and Harry wanted to marry. Just without the crap job, the emotional constipation and the hopeless hair.

She wondered, frankly, if they had forgotten quite how hopeless she had been. Against her better instincts, she opened her photo library and scrolled back past six months' worth of design mock-ups, whiteboard captures and publicity headshots to the first pre-Eudo photograph. Back then, Alex had hated having her photo taken, which was obvious in the image she now made full screen. The scene was New Year's Eve in her parents' kitchen. Harry must have been behind the camera. Her mother was in the middle of the frame, her red-cardiganed back bending to take a dish out of the oven. Her father was on one side, wine bottle in hand. Alex was on the other, already heading out of shot with a saucepan lid and a novelty dishcloth.

Alex studied the Alex in the photo with appalled fascination, feeling the familiar sickness start to rise but unable to pull back, like a child probing a wobbly tooth with its tongue. Startled by the flash, her eyes were the reflective red discs of imminent roadkill, her mouth half-open in a grimace of surprise. Her mousy hair, *sans* highlights and lob, straggled around her shoulders, limp with cooking steam and crowned with a lopsided paper hat. She was wearing an unflattering navy jumper that she had owned since sixth form, and which she'd recently dumped in a clothes bank.

Twelve or so hours later, Harry would propose to that creature. God, she had been lucky. What had he seen in her? Why hadn't she booked the venue there and then? What on earth had been going on behind those scared scarlet eyes?

And then the sickness intensified, and the vertigo rolled in, and beneath them she felt the void crack open its shadowy maw and wait for her to slide, slide, slide . . .

NO. Alex snapped shut the cover of her iPad, took a deep breath and refocused on the window, which was now unspooling twiggy brown parcels of scorched countryside. Enough. Last night, in her bracing state of self-scrutiny, she'd promised herself that she would stop pretending the episodes weren't a problem. It was time to tackle this psychosomatic crap head-on.

She unpocketed her phone again – still no message from Harry – waited until it found a couple of blobs of signal and speed-dialled Chloe. To her relief, Chloe answered after a couple of rings.

'Alex!' The soft voice wafted into her ear. 'Namaste!'

'Chloe,' Alex said, eager to get to the point before she lost her blobs. 'Is this a good time for a quick chat?'

'You're paying for 24/7 remote support, Alex,' Chloe replied, with a fluting laugh. 'My time is yours. But I'd like to stop you for a moment before we continue. I can hear quite a lot of tension in your voice. May I ask you to sit and breathe? Reconnect? Where are your shoulders right now, Alex? Where are the soles of your feet?'

Alex closed her eyes. She located her shoulders. She located the soles of her feet. 'The thing is, Chloe,' she said, opening her eyes again, 'I'm a bit short on time.'

'As Jim Rohn said, Alex, either you run the day, or the day runs—'

'Indeed,' Alex interrupted, hearing the connection crackle. 'And that's very true. But I need your help with something specific. Can I run it past you?'

A zephyr of a sigh. 'Of course, Alex. But don't forget, all I can do is guide you to unlock the potential you already possess to empower yourself.'

'Absolutely. Great. Okay. So, I know we've talked a lot about the challenges that going through a personal transition can bring, but there's one thing I haven't mentioned. The fact is, Chloe, my memories appear to be making me sick.'

There was a long pause. Alex was just checking the signal when Chloe said, softly, 'Wow, Alex. That's a very powerful image.'

Alex checked that the suit in the seat opposite was still asleep and that highlighter-woman was still absorbed in her printouts. 'That's the problem,' she said in a low voice. 'It's not an image. It's a physical reality. Whenever I remember anything that happened before I . . . became my true self, it makes me feel ill. Not just nauseous, but really weird, unbalanced, dizzy, like I'm skating on ice. And if I try to hold on to the memory for too long, I feel the ice crack and I . . . I

82

don't know. I start to fall into a . . . I start to fall.' She paused. Silence. 'It's been going on ever since the night I started to change,' she admitted. 'The night after our first session, back in February. For a while I put it down to overwork, but recently it's been getting harder to avoid. Whenever I spend time with my family, old friends, even with Harry – anyone who reminds me of my old life, really – the worse it gets. It's starting to become a real issue.' Silence. The signal was fine. 'Chloe? Is this normal? What should I do?'

At this, there came another sigh, feather-light. 'You know what to do, Alex.'

'That's the problem, Chloe. I kind of don't.'

'When the caterpillar becomes a butterfly,' Chloe said, 'do you think he feels no pain?'

'So this *is* normal?'

'What we're witnessing, Alex, is your *old* normal battling with your *new* normal. Have you heard of cognitive dissonance?'

'Isn't that like – when you say you love animals, but you eat meat and squash flies?'

There was another pause. Alex was about to check the signal again when Chloe proclaimed: 'In psychology, cognitive dissonance is the mental stress or discomfort experienced by an individual who holds two or more contradictory beliefs, ideas or values at the same time. Or they might perform an action that is contradictory to one or more beliefs, ideas or values. It also occurs when the individual is confronted by new information that conflicts with existing beliefs, ideas or values.'

'Oh,' Alex said. 'Right. I—'

'Leon Festinger's theory of cognitive dissonance focuses on how humans strive for internal consistency. An individual who experiences inconsistency – dissonance – tends to become psychologically uncomfortable. They will become motivated to reduce this dissonance, as well as actively avoid situations and information that are likely to increase it.'

'Wow,' Alex said, after a moment. 'Okay.'

'In short, Alex,' Chloe said, 'your brain is struggling to assimilate your new belief system. *Feel* the conflict. Feel the conflict, then let it go. I suspect that you're not so much afraid of giving up your outgrown self, as scared that she'll come back. But all you need to do is trust, Alex. Persevere. Be strong. Keep gathering evidence that refutes your old, limiting beliefs. After a while your brain will realign. You'll be able to look back on your memories with the fondness of a wise mother for an ignorant child. You'll become more powerful than ever before.'

'Wow.' Alex blew out a breath. 'That's . . . extraordinary.'

'No, Alex,' Chloe said. 'The world is extraordinary. It's so much bigger and stranger than most people want to believe. And you've become a true part of it now, Alex. *You're* extraordinary. I'd like you to say it to me.'

'What?'

'I'd like you to say that you're extraordinary. Out loud.'

'Oh.' Alex glanced around. 'This isn't really the—'

'As Brené Brown said, Alex, shame erodes our courage.'

'Okay, okay.' Alex lowered her voice to a whisper. 'I'm extraordinary.'

'Alex.'

'I'm extraordinary,' Alex said.

'Alex . . .'

'I'M EXTRAORDINARY!' Alex bellowed, making the suit jerk awake with a snort and highlighter-woman send a great arc of green skidding across her page.

Three and a half hours later the train pulled into Edinburgh. Alex, given a wide berth by everyone in her carriage, stepped stiffly onto the platform. Across the bustle of the concourse she spotted the awning of a Caffè Nero and broke into a jog. Having secured a chair beside a power point, a triple flat white and all the signal a civilized human being could desire, she spent forty-five glorious minutes fielding emails and delegating tasks to the office.

And, finally, a message popped up.

Sounds interesting. Hope it's rewarding. H

No *x*. No *x*? Really? Okay, Harry. If that's how you want to play it.

Thx. Think it will be. Sounds like a great bunch of blokes. Hoping to forge some lasting relationships. Prob won't be in contact. Signal likely to be bad. A

One minute passed. Another minute passed. Then:

What sort of blokes?

Alex counted out a minute.

Brainy but outdoorsy. Top academics, gifted students, passionate young conservationists. Think they'll really help me reconnect with my true self.

Thirty seconds.

Okay. But watch yourself. I'm positive they have their own agenda.

Oh no. They just sound super-excited to meet me & explore my journey. Have to throw myself into this wholeheartedly if I'm going to make the most of it, after all. You were right. I've been too wrapped up in myself. It's time I took an interest in others for a while.

Ten seconds.

Don't go out of contact entirely, though. Not safe.

Alex smiled. *I'll do my best.*

Speak soon? x

Of course. xx

Spirits back in full sail, Alex closed the thread and allowed herself a quick dip into the frothing rapids of Twitter. She had just tweeted a pithy comment about haggis and Harry Potter when a re-tweet from a foodie blogger caught her eye:

> Wasn't me I promise!! RT @LifeandStyle Helena
> Pereira stalker detained outside L'Antiga Capella
> yesterday: http://bit.ly/1qgyKsj

Alex clicked on the link:

STALKER DETAINED IN SKIRMISH
AT A-LIST EATERY

A man has been detained on suspicion of stalking the model and jeweller Helena Pereira after a fight broke out outside Marylebone restaurant L'Antiga Capella yesterday evening.

Pereira was dining inside when doormen became suspicious of a young man acting strangely, as he waited for over an hour near the restaurant's steps. The model has been dogged by similar troubles with 'superfans' in the past.

Gabriel Noguerra, the doorman, was injured after the man ignored repeated requests to leave. 'This guy looked like he was high,' Noguerra told The Guardian. 'He was sweating, shaking, mumbling some s**t about libraries, freaking out every time a car came past. When I put my hand on his arm he reacted like a wild animal. He started yelling that he needed more. I guess he meant drugs. It took four of our guys to pull him away.'

Both the police and Ms Pereira's press office declined to comment on the incident. But this is not the first time the critically acclaimed restaurant, which opened in January of this year, has faced controversy . . .

Alex returned to the photo gallery beneath the headline. The first image was a glossy press shot of a naked Helena Pereira crouching beside a panther, draped in strategically positioned ropes of her own jewellery. The second showed the top of Pereira's bowed golden head, glimpsed behind the outstretched arms of two burly assistants. They were hurrying her down a set of broad stone steps towards a black car. Studying the white-shirted figure framed in the arch behind them, Alex recognized the open-mouthed face of L'Antiga Capella's maître d'. The third and final image was smaller and blurrier, and it showed two policemen bundling a man into the back of a van. The stalker's features had been swallowed by the dim interior and his body was little more than a grainy hump. But Alex could just about make out the detail of one distinctive calf-length lace-up boot, bracing against the ledge as they pushed him in.

She looked up from the screen, feeling as if her ears had popped. She scanned the people in the café around her warily. No hot-ugly man-boys. No grungy boots.

Catching sight of the clock, Alex suddenly realized that she only had three minutes before her connection left. Thrusting her iPad and phone into her bag, she sprinted towards platform seventeen. For the second time that day, she jumped through train doors moments before they shut. She slumped into a seat as the train jolted away from the station, her heart thumping, and told herself to get a grip.

London was full of people wearing the same shoes. London was full of weird and violent men. The moment she started linking everything that she saw back to herself was the moment Harry would be right, and she really would have disappeared up her own backside. She was extraordinary, she reminded herself. No tears and no irrational fears.

Not any more.

She pressed in her earbuds and cued up the music she had downloaded last night: Peter Maxwell Davies' first symphony, apparently composed on the Orkney island of Hoy. The Scottish Rail train was small and rickety, the landscape now properly coastal, with scrubby banks giving way to vistas of glittering, white-tipped grey. As glockenspiel tinkled and woodwind squawked beneath a surge of violins, Alex watched surf explode over coal-black rocks and gulls pick their way across pipe-and-rope strewn pebble beaches under a flat, hot sky. She whispered the names of the stations as they stopped, then shuddered on – Inverkeithing, Kirkcaldy, Leuchars. By the time the train squealed to a halt, her carriage was empty and her mind was still.

Seven and a half hours after she'd left London, Alex fed her ticket into the barrier and stepped out into a shopping centre. She spent a bleary hour wandering round the outlets buying vitamins, antibac gel and a bright yellow fisherman-style anorak. Then she used Google Maps to navigate across the small patch of concrete that separated the mall from the ferry terminal.

By the time she'd squeezed through the ticket-check bottle-neck, all the seats were taken. Who cared? Now that she was seaborne, her hard-won Zen was starting to segue back into excitement. Alex decided to celebrate her voyage with a drink. She pushed her way to the bar and ordered a double gin and tonic, which cost more than it would have in Soho, then made her way onto the deck.

Spray and rain pricked at her face and, as she watched the navy waves churn, she felt cool and fresh for the first time in weeks. The moon was already up, a pale nail-paring in a vast paler sky. She stared romantically at the water, sipped from her drink and once again indulged in the Highgate day-dream. She imagined the gleaming glass-fronted kitchen, the tousle-haired toddlers, the garden-facing study where she could work on Eudo – home-mixed martini in hand – once they had gone to bed. Her memories might be broken, but at least her vision of the future was as crisp as a salad from the local farmers' market, and dewy with emotional verve. Alex knew that if other people could see it, most of them would tell her she was unrealistic, that real life didn't work like that. She didn't care. After all, six months ago she would have said it was unrealistic for her to imagine that she would be here and unafraid. She'd never have guessed she'd be at the helm of her own business and on a trip through unknown waters. But here and unafraid she undeniably was.

'To being extraordinary,' Alex toasted under her breath. 'To brain realignment. To a brilliant career *and* a brilliant marriage.' She stayed outside until the plastic cup was empty and the air grew chilly. Then she headed back in for a cheeky top-up.

She had only started drinking the day after her miraculous transition began, the day she'd gone to meet Lenni for lunch and quit her job at Minos. That evening, suddenly finding herself unable to remember why she'd insisted on remaining teetotal her entire adult life, she'd asked Harry to mix her a celebratory G&T. Unfortunately, this meant it still only took one to get her really quite drunk.

Now she had four.

The rest of the voyage was a blur of strip-lit corridors, impossibly tiny toilets and groups of people curled up in refugee camps built from sweatshirts, sweets and magazines. She vaguely remembered a man in a paper pork-pie hat depositing a steaming wedge of red-brown stuff onto a plate.

Then she was alone, curled in a reclining chair in a dim, mutter-filled room – rocking up and down, down and up, up and down.

Alex pressed her hot cheek to the reinforced glass and fell through the dark.

MacBrian's colleague was waiting for her at the dock, standing beside the front bumper of a hire car. He clocked her as soon as she walked through the sliding doors, one of the last to leave, then watched her approach, without moving or offering to take her bag.

'Miss Moore?' He was as broad and square as a wrestler, his heavily lined face inscrutable from beneath a thatch of short, dark hair. He was dressed in all black and his accent, like that of the Director's on the phone, was indefinably Celtic. He possessed more than a touch of *Gladiator*-era Russell Crowe.

'Hi,' Alex whispered.

There was a silence. The man was still watching her as if he was waiting for her to spring a surprise chokeslam. After several long minutes Alex whispered, 'Sorry. Where are my manners. You're—?'

'I'm Iain MacHoras.' He finally tore his eyes away from her, performed a three-sixty scan of the emptying car park, then looked down at her bag.

Alex handed it to him. 'Thanks.' He hefted it, then without a word tugged open the zip and began to rifle through the belongings inside. 'I, er, I—' Alex stammered, but before she could formulate an appropriate expression of outrage, he had handed it back.

'Get in,' he said.

Too exhausted to quibble, Alex climbed into the passenger seat while he got in beside her and slammed the door. He started the engine, stalled, put it in gear, revved ferociously, stalled, revved, moved off. The radio was playing rousing fiddle folk, and the window let in a draught of air as cold and sweet as a Glacier Mint. The headlights, jerking as he repeatedly braked and accelerated, panned across the ferry, lumbering away from the harbour like a yellow-eyed sea beast.

'Excuse me,' Alex said faintly.

Iain MacHoras braked sharply and turned to look at her with implacable grey eyes.

'I think I might—' Alex gulped. 'I think—' She gulped again, then vomited a fountain of bile, gin and microwave lasagne into the footwell.

6

'Stoornway puddin'?'

The proprietor of Hrossey B&B waved a pile of steaming black offal under Alex's nose. Alex smiled weakly and shook her head, holding her breath.

'Do you have any coffee? Proper coffee, I mean?'

'Coorse.' The woman disappeared back into the kitchen with her dish, bellowing 'Rob! Git yin Nescaffy!'

Alex turned back to the text message from Harry.

Have you arrived? x

On main island, she tapped. *Off to institute shortly. Stayed overnight here with bloke called Iain. Bit of a silent muscly tough-guy type. Already had a good poke thru my stuff – think looking for city spores that might harm native ecology or sthing. Dorothy's not in Hackney any more! This is going to be fun! x*

Be careful. I'm still here for you, A. Stay in touch. x

She placed her phone face down beside her empty plate, already feeling better. Overenthusiastic celebrating, unexpected spore-hunting and cheeky Harry-baiting aside, wasn't this already genuinely fun? Waking up in a chintzy little room, opening the window to the sea air, sitting amongst fellow wayfarers sharing a wholesome repast? Chloe was right – when you practised noticing the positive, the positive bloomed everywhere. Alex sat back and smiled, with real warmth this time, at the two old boys tucking into fry-ups at the next table. Hrossey B&B's breakfast room evidently did double duty as a popular local hangout. Nearly all of the tables were full of sturdy-looking Orcadians chomping their way through greasy hummocks of food.

'Is that a local speciality?' she said, leaning towards the nearest old man and pointing at his huge lumpy scone. He looked up at her, glanced over at his friend, made a tiny movement with his shoulders, and went on eating.

'Are you from Mainland?' she asked.

The man grunted.

'It must be so wonderful to live here. The air! It's so pure. And the food must be so nutritious. Do they have rules about what you can spread on the fields?'

The man gave her another brief appraisal, then returned to his food. 'Thoo'll need mair maet lass, thoor turnin' tae a rookle o' bones,' he said.

'Mmm!' Alex said enthusiastically. 'And were you born in Mainland?'

The man sighed and put down his fork. 'Yoor a ferry-louper?'

'I'm a – oh, yes, exactly. Just off the ferry, ha-ha.'

'A peedie break i'Kirkwall, is it?'

'Ah, no, sadly I'm only passing through,' Alex scraped her chair closer. 'I'm actually off to Iskeull later this morning, to do some work at GCAS. European Chapter. Well, I hope I am.' She peered over his shoulder, relieved to spot the hire car on the gravel outside the window. 'I got stupidly drunk on the ferry, you see, and—'

Alex realized that both her friend and his companion had stopped eating and were staring at her. Damn. Misstep. Hadn't she read that most of them were Calvinists?

'Yi din wan' t' waste time wi Iskeull folk,' the companion said slowly. 'Thir's nowt tae see o'er there.'

Ah. Of course. She should have known. She had read about the Orcadians' fierce sense of independence, as well as their aversion to self-importance. Or, as one travel blogger had put it, with the bitter ring of reported speech, their dislike of 'fancy airs'. She could only imagine the sort of hostility that the private ownership and grandiose global vision of GCAS might stir up.

'But surely you support their environmental work?' Alex suggested gently. 'Don't they help preserve the native landscape? Keep the ancient ecology alive?'

The man gave a laugh of such dark astringency that she wondered, for an uncharitable moment, whether he was one of those rural people who moaned about the destruction of the old ways while secretly wishing Tesco's would offer him half a million to bulldoze his patch of Neolithic burial site.

'Aye, thee could say yin,' he said. Then he stopped laughing and leaned across the table, the brown skin of his forehead ploughed into two deep furrows. Alex leaned closer in turn, getting the impression that her new friend was about to impart some urgently important folkloric truth.

'Miss Moore?'

Iain was watching them from the doorway, the hire-car keychain dangling from his fist. Alex's confidant flung up his head in something like panic, curled in on himself like a snail and returned with great concentration to his plate.

'Oh, hello, Iain, yes!' Alex's voice rang loud in the small space. The other customers had become suddenly and silently intent on their kippers.

'The plane is ready,' Iain said.

'Oh, great. Brilliant.' Alex grabbed her valise from the floor. 'See? I'm all set. And I promise: no comestibles! No mad cow! No spores!'

Iain didn't react.

She jumped to her feet, then stood still for a moment, regretting it. 'It was lovely to meet you,' she told her neighbours. They ignored her, still staring down at their food. But she got the feeling, as she followed Iain out of the door, that they were watching her back.

In the car, Alex made an apologetic comment about city slickers and sea legs, which Iain ignored. He maintained his silence on the ten-minute drive to Kirkwall airport and, secretly relieved, Alex wound down the window. She let the breeze clear her head as they lurched past wide, glassy lakes and long, low hills that were the almost too-green green of a spirulina shake. In the car park, Iain tucked the keys under the front wheel, then set off without a word across the tarmac.

'I love that.' Alex rushed to catch up in with him. 'That level of trust. I suppose everyone knows everyone out here, right? Although it seems like you might be caught up in a bit of local politics? With GCAS? I mean, you certainly look and sound like you grew up in these parts yourself, but those two characters in the B&B—'

'We keep to ourselves,' Iain said.

'Right. I'm sure. But there must be quite a few people like me coming in and out? Collaborators, and so on?'

'Fewer than you'd think.'

'And what's your position here, Iain?' She had to jog for a few strides to keep pace. 'I mean, what's your specialism?'

He turned to look at her then. 'Security,' he said.

Alex laughed. She'd read about the dry sense of humour. 'Well, I promise not to cause any trouble. I'm a pacifist.'

If she hadn't already primed herself to make concessions for northern dourness, she might have interpreted his expression as positively hostile.

Iain came to a halt on a patch of runway in front of a very small blue-and-white plane that looked like something a 1940s schoolboy might glue together from a kit. He opened the door of the plane and let down a set of flimsy fold-down steps.

'Get in,' he said.

Alex looked across the tarmac to the series of hangar-like buildings that she had assumed to be the terminal. 'Don't we have to check in or something?'

'We have a special arrangement.'

'Oh! Okay. Wow. How glamorous.' Alex climbed the steps and buckled herself into one of eight tiny seats. 'Where's the pilot?'

Iain stooped to the front of the plane. He crammed himself into the pilot's seat and reached for a headset.

'You're the pilot?' Alex called. 'How—' She was saved from having to complete her sentence by the roar of the engines. Frankly, she thought, how terrifying, considering your performance with a Ford Fiesta. But then she stopped thinking and concentrated on keeping the plane in the air with sheer willpower.

If the weather on their flight had passed the 'permitted' test, Alex couldn't imagine what it would have taken to ground them. It wasn't too bad at first, once she grew used to every tiny buffet of wind flip-flopping her guts. As the wing dropped to give her a panorama of the islands, she felt a burst of genuine happiness that had nothing to do with Eudo or getting her life back in balance, or anything other than vast quantities of light and air. She started formulating a metaphor for her first 'Postcard from' Eudo blog, involving emerald velvet patchwork and swathes of cerulean silk.

And then the sky turned black.

At one point, as their scrap of airborne foil shuddered and dropped and banked and baulked through a churning maelstrom of doom-laden grey, Alex started to yell. Yelling seemed necessary, although she was unclear exactly what she was begging Iain to do. Stop? Pull in? Turn around? Eventually she closed her eyes and hummed as loudly as she could, a vigorous military march that she later realized was the *Dam Busters* theme. Then a phrase she'd heard from a speaker at an entrepreneurship unconference – '*you have to jump off the cliff and assemble your aeroplane on the way down'* – started, rather unhelpfully, circulating in her head. Next she had a premonitory vision of her mother, weeping in black Boden, at her funeral. By the time they landed, she felt as exhausted as if she had swum to the sodding place. It hurt to straighten out her fingers, which had curled into bloodless claws around the armrest.

Expressionless, Iain stooped his way to the door, wrenched it open and unfolded the steps. Wet wind swooped into the cabin. Determined to salvage the shreds of her pride, Alex took her time wriggling into her new yellow anorak, squeezed past Iain's solid bulk and climbed, shakily, out.

Iskeull airfield consisted of a strip of scrub that ran from a low stone hut to the edge of a perpendicular cliff. On the grass below the steps was a solitary figure in a waxed cape, silhouetted against the rolling grey muscle of the sea.

Alex wobbled down the steps, took a moment to make sure she wasn't going to fall over, then stepped forward and offered her hand. 'Director MacBrian? Great to meet you.'

A plain, sallow face excavated with black moles shone out from beneath the hood. Iain walked past, bent his face close to MacBrian's ear and muttered. When he had finished, MacBrian gave a single nod, then finally gripped Alex's hand, a little too hard.

'Miss Moore,' she said. 'Welcome to Iskeull.' Her accent was strong, and her English a little slow and over-precise, as if she didn't use it much.

'Please, call me Alex. And I must say, I'm relieved to have made it. That was quite a trip!'

'We're glad you could join us. We've been most impatient

to meet you. Most' – eyes the colour of the sea swept Alex from head to toe – 'most intrigued.' MacBrian said something unintelligible to Iain, who nodded and headed back towards the plane. 'It's only a short walk to the main facility.' She gestured beyond Alex's left shoulder to an ugly stone building perched on the cliff to the north of the airfield. Beyond it could be seen the outskirts of what looked like an old town, half-concealed by the drizzle. 'Please, follow me.'

Alex tramped beside her across the turf, grappling with the hood of her anorak as the mud squelched over the tops of her trainers. The rain had an ominously persistent feel. 'I'm a little unprepared for the weather, I'm afraid,' she laughed. 'We're having a heatwave in London, you see.'

'Indeed,' MacBrian said, after a pause. 'Here we are experiencing quite unseasonal storms.'

'Climate change, right? At least we have people like you looking out for the planet.'

MacBrian flashed her a sideways look.

'I'm serious,' Alex said. 'It's so impressive. I can't wait to see what you're up to, conservation-wise. I'm convinced most of my recycling goes straight into landfill.'

'I'm afraid,' MacBrian said, 'that the reserve on the peninsula at the north of the island is out of bounds to all but staff. I must ask you in the strongest terms to respect our boundaries, Miss Moore. Some of the species we protect on the peninsula are extremely rare, and even the best-intentioned intrusion might upset the ecology. However, our agricultural governor may be able to arrange for you to have a look at some of our working farms here.' She indicated over her shoulder and Alex swivelled to look at the land beyond the airfield.

Oh. She stopped, and drew in a sudden, rain-laced breath.

Before her spread perhaps fifty unbroken, treeless miles, illuminated with oyster-coloured shafts of light. There were pennants of shivering golden-green barley; valleys bathed in purple-grey mist; ridges crowned with jagged standing stones. Hundreds of weathered settlements covered the slopes, from single houses with sheep-studded paddocks to big barns clustered around ant-busy yards. In the middle of them she saw the gaping mouth of a quarry and, beside the glassy inlay of a loch, the giant wheel of a mill. Yet unlike the monocrops and apocalyptic pig farms of her childhood, Iskeull had clearly nailed the art of keeping agriculture in harmony with its environment. Even through the driving rain she could see the riot of wildflowers stippling the grass in a nearby field and the birds of prey circling the distant, yellow-dusted coastal heath. Beyond the heath she could just about make out a thin rind of white sand and, beyond that, the faint, scalloped hem where the sky met the sea.

'Shit,' Alex murmured. The panorama was spine-tingling, bordering on surreal. Blindly she fished her phone out of her pocket, and it was only when she swiped to unlock the camera that she realized the screen was a sunburst of lines.

'Shit!' Fuck – that damn plane. 'Ah well, not to worry,' she said brightly, rooting around in her bag for her iPad. But when she pulled out the tablet she found that not only had its screen also fractured, but the casing at the back had warped, as if its circuitry had melted. 'This is ridiculous!' She turned to MacBrian, waving her useless devices. MacBrian recommenced her march up the slope.

'Ah well,' Alex panted as she tried to keep pace. 'As my mother says, don't trust anything that doesn't have a smell. And I'm sure you'll have a few bits of old hardware up at the campus that I can borrow?'

'I may have failed to mention,' MacBrian said. 'We have no electricity.'

Alex tried to decipher what she meant. 'Oh. Okay. So just broadband?'

'No. No telecommunications, no wires, no satellites. I'm afraid that Iskeull isn't on the grid at all. It's necessary, for the conservation. Other than Iain's plane, the only transport we have on the island is by horse. We have some powerful energetic leylines here and, as you can see, they have a tendency to interact rather badly with man-made technology.'

By this time even MacBrian seemed to be getting an inkling of the impact her words were having. She stopped walking and peered round her hood.

'But . . . I . . . you have email!' Alex declared triumphantly. 'And a phone!'

'We maintain a small property on North Ronaldsay equipped for such purposes. You are welcome to fly over and use it, weather permitting, of course.'

Alex cast around, panicked, as if a sacred circle of radio masts might suddenly spring up atop of the hills. 'But you didn't . . . I can't—'

'Sorry for the inconvenience,' said MacBrian, who didn't sound sorry at all. 'Here we are.'

Numbly Alex followed MacBrian into the ugly building, passing a metal sign engraved with GCAS's name and logo. There was also a warning that **ALL VISITORS MUST REPORT TO RECEPTION. 24-HOUR SURVEIL-LANCE IN OPERATION**. The lobby, which contained nothing but an unmanned reception desk, was dim and musty-smelling. It also appeared, Alex noticed with sinking disbelief, to be lined with oil lamps. Iain, who must have rejoined them without Alex noticing, walked round to take their coats. Stripped of her cape, MacBrian was squat and muscular, with a greying pixie crop. She wore leggings tucked into sturdy ankle boots and a navy tunic cinched by a leather belt, with a large silver figure-of-eight brooch pinned above her left breast. If it wasn't for the moles, she would have been a ringer for Alex's old Brown Owl.

'But how do you work?' Alex persisted. 'How do you research? How do you write?'

'Books,' MacBrian said. 'Pen and paper.' Something flickered behind her shark's eyes. 'We have an excellent on-site library.'

'You must have some kind of generator?'

'We'll make sure you have everything you need. Now we'd like to start the interviews as soon as possible. But first I'll show you to your room, give you some time to prepare. This way, please.'

As MacBrian led the way through a side door and into a deserted, whitewashed corridor, Alex tried to talk herself down. Her father, an intransigent technophobe, would be delighted to hear that she had been forced into a two-day digital detox. She could just imagine the gentle jibes he'd give her when she told him how panicked she had initially felt. And he would be right; the lack of electricity would force her to rest, to connect with herself rather than others, to re-immerse herself in the natural world. Eudo would hardly collapse without her hand at the helm over a single weekend. Right? She could rely on Lenni, and this would in fact be the ideal opportunity to stress-test their new team. And then there was Harry. Wouldn't her inability to send Harry a single email, photo or text give him exactly *the space he needed to realize that his life was incomplete without her*?

Feeling better, she turned to MacBrian, somehow sensing that they'd got off on the wrong foot. 'So how long have you been at GCAS, Director?' she asked. 'I'm always delighted to meet a fellow woman in leadership.'

'A long time,' MacBrian said. 'A lifetime, you might say.'

Alex gave a low chuckle. 'I know how that feels. So you worked your way up the ranks?'

'Indeed,' MacBrian said. 'I was only appointed Director here on Iskeull earlier this year.' She stopped at a door.

'But that's fabulous,' Alex gushed. 'Congratulations!' She leaned closer. 'Finally dislodge some old duffer who'd been incumbent for decades?' she whispered, playfully elbowing MacBrian's thick waist.

Before she knew it, Iain had grabbed her from behind, his fingers locked in a vice around her upper arm.

'Excuse me!' Alex spluttered. 'What do you think you're—'

MacBrian said something sharp and indecipherable. Iain dropped his hand and stepped back without a word.

'What the hell?'

'My – our – apologies,' MacBrian said. 'Captain MacHoras was simply being over-protective. Everyone is a little . . . tense right now. Director MacCalum was an extremely popular man, and his death was an untimely tragedy.'

'Oh God.' Alex turned from glaring at Iain and put her hand to her mouth. 'He died? Jesus. I'm so sorry.'

'We're all very sorry, Miss Moore,' MacBrian said. She was studying Alex's face. 'It has caused incalculable pain. And made my position very difficult. Very difficult indeed.' She turned the knob. 'I'll be back in an hour. You should have everything you need.'

As soon as MacBrian had shut the door behind her, Alex slumped down on the bed and took stock. The iron-framed bedstead was one of only two pieces of furniture in the high-ceilinged room. The other was a nightstand, on which stood a ewer and jug, a folded towel and a misshapen bar of hand-made soap. The walls were streaked with damp, and a single window of thick, warped glass looked out onto rain-lashed cobbled streets. On the plain bedspread beside Alex was a chipped tray bearing a glass of milk, a dark heel of bread and a round of white cheese.

A draft whistled in from the window frame and Alex wished, suddenly, that she was in her flat. She longed to be curled up on the sofa with Harry, watching YouTube videos, familiar and safe and warm. The silence of Iskeull, the rawness and scale of its nature, the chilly reception she had received from Iain and MacBrian, even the rain – they all conspired to make her feel more like old miserable-shadow Alex than she had in a long time.

But then she thought again of how proud her father would be of her, and of what Chloe would say, and she made a concerted effort to push the self-pity away. The room, she told herself firmly, was a masterpiece of homespun elegance that would cost 500 quid a night in Gloucestershire. And sure, Iain might be on the troglodyte end of the male spectrum, and MacBrian might be somewhat lacking in social graces, but then that was academics for you. The poor closeted brainiacs were obviously in the midst of dealing with a tragedy, not to mention a considerable organizational shake-up. Unlike old Alex, new Alex knew better than to take their behaviour personally. New Alex relished opportunities to push her boundaries. New Alex had the courage and humility to *walk a mile in their shoes*, as her mother liked to say, even if those shoes were orthopaedic-looking ankle boots. She peeled off her soaked shorts, changed into fresh jeans and ripped off a small piece of bread.

By the time the knock came, Alex had polished off all the food and was in the midst of a power-nap. Blearily, she opened the door, to find MacBrian standing in the doorway beside a tall, thin woman holding a leather bag.

'This is Bride MacDiarmid, our resident doctor,' MacBrian announced. 'She'd like to conduct a physical examination.'

'Oh. An . . . oh?' Alex looked at the doctor's bag. 'I wasn't really expecting—'

'We ask all of our contributors to provide us with a full

medical history and undergo a few rudimentary checks, so that we can incorporate physiological and genetic factors into the research.' MacBrian paused. 'So far everyone has consented, but of course, if you don't feel comfortable . . .'

'No, no.' Alex smiled and opened the door wider. 'Of course. That's fine. I'm surprised, that's all. Impressed, actually. It's so rare to find an academic project with such a holistic approach.'

'Very good.' MacBrian moved aside to let MacSomething Else pass through. 'I'll wait outside.'

At first Alex tried to coax some small talk out of the monosyllabic doctor, but as the checks became increasingly unrudimentary, she lapsed into silence. When the doctor snapped on a pair of gloves, Alex gave herself a bracing reminder that she was dealing with the penetrating methodologies of science here, not the broad strokes of PR. She even felt a faint frisson of pleasure at being treated like some kind of entrepreneurial athlete. By the time she had straightened her clothes, she had already turned the scene into a comic vignette to retell in London over a stiff cocktail.

The doctor spent several minutes making notes, then embarked on a series of precise questions about Alex's family tree. Thankfully, Alex was able to answer to a decent level of detail. Her American grandmother, Dorothy, had traced the Moores all the way back to the *Mayflower*. And although the thoroughly English Wrights thought researching their bloodline was conceited, she had recently dug everything she could out of her mother's side for a project Eudo had run in partnership with FitBand. On the mental rap sheet she was able to claim a healthy smattering of depression, an anorexic cousin and an obsessive-compulsive great-grandfather. As the doctor pressed her with a faintly disappointed air, Alex confided about several Moores whom she'd always suspected to be functioning alcoholics. Physically, her inheritance was robust, even vigorous. There was another cousin in remission from breast cancer and a diabetic aunt, but most of her relatives had died old. Her parents, as her mother loved to relate, had been the bare-minimum burden on the NHS.

Alex received the impression that the doctor had been hoping for something a little juicier. She hoped they weren't trying to prove some damaged-genius hypothesis. *Talent is a habit, not an inheritance* was one of Eudo's core brand values, after all.

'It's so quiet,' she said when it was over and MacBrian was leading her further along the corridor. 'My university was borderline chaos. Where are all the students?'

'It's a national holiday,' MacBrian replied tightly, her eyes fixed ahead, her stride brisk. 'They'll all be taking a break in the farmland or spending time in the town.'

'Ah yes. I got a glimpse of the town through my window. It looks so quaint. I'd love a tour.'

'Perhaps later. Once we've made some progress with the interviews. The rest of the faculty are extremely eager to meet you. However, I managed to reserve this afternoon for you, me and our Head of Scholarship to talk – before the others insist on their pound of flesh.'

'I'm sorry again,' Alex said, after a pause. 'I'm afraid I

rather put my foot in it with my comment, earlier. Were you very close? To your predecessor, I mean?'

'Not personally. We had somewhat divergent views on how to run things here.'

'But he was a good Director, you said?' Alex probed.

'He was an extraordinary . . . extraordinarily good at what he did.'

'And popular, you said?'

'Very much so.' There was a distinct tightening of Mac-Brian's jaw.

Ah, Alex thought. 'Do you mind me asking,' she said gently, 'how he died?'

'Perhaps,' MacBrian said, stopping outside an identical-looking door, 'we could focus on asking some questions of our own first?'

The room they entered was the same size and shape as Alex's bedroom, except that here the furniture was a flimsy-looking antique table and three mismatched chairs. The chill was softened by a small open fire that gave off the heady whiff of peat. Seated at one of the chairs, behind a sprawl of loose papers, was a lanky middle-aged man.

'Miss Moore!' he cried, scrambling up from his chair.

'This,' MacBrian said, 'is our Head of Scholarship, Taran MacGill.'

Taran MacGill had a long face, a big nose and straggly iron-grey hair. He was wearing crumpled brown trousers and a stained oatmeal jumper with the same logo-brooch as MacBrian's pinned onto his chest. He was staring at Alex as if she were a particularly rare and beautiful species of snow leopard.

'Alex,' Alex said. 'Please call me Alex.'

He gave a crooked smile. 'Alex, then. And please call me Taran, Alex. How very . . . fascinating to meet you.'

As Taran shook her hand, damply and for far too long, Alex began to harbour some serious suspicions about the impartiality of the selection criteria used to recruit GCAS staff. Despite Iain's muscle-bound stature, MacBrian's statement crop, the doctor's thinness and Taran's general dishevelment, their monochrome colouring and stark features pointed strongly towards a common ancestry.

'Before we begin, Miss Moore,' MacBrian was saying, 'Professor MacGill and I would like to express in advance our gratitude for your willingness to collaborate in our investigations with full openness and honesty.'

'Absolutely.' Alex extricated her hand from Taran's. 'I'm very grateful for the invitation. You seem to have a wonderful set-up out here. Who . . .' She paused, fishing for a diplomatic way to frame the question. 'Now, how does the Chapter here work exactly? Is it a – a family enterprise?'

'We're all—' Taran began.

'It is a rather unusual arrangement,' MacBrian interrupted. 'GCAS is an umbrella organization that operates across seven islands located around the world. Each of those islands is owned and run by its original indigenous tribe. We are all united in a shared endeavour to protect our unique native ecologies and promote the free flow of human thought between our continents. Here, on Iskeull, we go straight back to the Picts.'

'But that's incredible,' Alex said. 'Like the street artists near our office. They've been squatting in this historic warehouse for months, refusing to move, because the council have sold it off and some Russian magnate's trying to turn it into a boutique hotel.'

There was a brief silence.

'I'd imagine it's difficult, though?' she ploughed on. 'Oh, you must have an awesome sense of community, but don't you feel a little isolated? Especially with the whole anti-tech leylines thing? How do you get your news?'

'Ah, but you see we have access—' Taran began.

'We have access,' MacBrian said, 'to a different kind of news. Collective storytelling, you might say.'

'You mean spoken word?' Alex shook her head and blew out a puff of air. 'God, you know, with all due respect to your comms team, I can't believe you guys don't get more exposure. Interdisciplinary, international, sustainable, authentic . . . I mean, there are some real similarities with what you're doing here and what I'm trying to do with Eudo. If more people in London knew about this, oh my God – well, let me just say, they would go *insane*.'

'I'd love to—' Taran began.

'They'd destroy it,' MacBrian snapped.

There was another tense silence.

'No, no, you're right,' Alex said, after a moment. 'It's so sad, but you're so right. You'd have tour companies and bloggers and billions of spores rampaging over your ecology in no time.'

'Yes, well.' MacBrian pulled out the chair beside Taran. 'We're on a very tight schedule. Do you think we could start?'

'Of course.' Alex smiled graciously and sat.

MacBrian took the chair on Alex's other side, then opened a notebook, moved a red bookmark to the back and clicked up the nib of a biro. 'Are you ready?'

Taran had a gratifyingly intense expression of anticipation on his face. Alex arranged her features into the very picture of collaborative transparency.

'Shoot.'

7

'We need your story,' MacBrian began. 'Your personal account of exactly what happened on the night of February the seventeenth. The article in *Flair* was helpful to a degree, but we need to know your every emotion, sensation, thought.'

Here we go again, Alex thought. She settled back in her chair.

'Well, to understand what happened on the seventeenth, you'll need a bit of context. At the time I was working as a marketing manager at a security software firm – you can probably find out where, but I'd rather you didn't name them in the research paper, if that's okay? But I'd sort of stumbled into the job after uni and, honestly, it made me feel dead inside.'

'Dead?' MacBrian, who was already scribbling furiously, looked up.

'Totally. Oh, there was nothing wrong with it in particular, but there was nothing right, either, and I knew it wasn't where I had expected to end up by the time I was thirty. In terms of personal life, I had a wonderful fiancé – that's Harry Fyfield, feel free to include him in all this, he's been absolutely central to my journey. But I was so ground down, I couldn't even summon the energy to organize our wedding.' She shook her head. 'I really was quite a different woman from the one you see now.'

'Different? In what way?'

'Well, that's the question, isn't it? What was holding me back? I was always coming up with these grand projects that were going to unlock my true talent – art classes, creative-writing courses, coding lessons, marathons – but somehow I could never make a go of anything I tried. After a burst of enthusiasm, it would always sort of . . . fizzle out.'

'Your true talent.' MacBrian's eyes narrowed. 'And what do you think that might be?'

'Well, obviously now I realize it's all about helping others – building communities, inspiring people to be their best selves – but for a long time I had no idea what I really wanted to do. Oh, I was confident when I was a child, very precocious, I had all sorts of big dreams. But the rot began when I was around eleven years old.'

'The *rot*?' MacBrian exchanged a look with Taran. 'What do you mean by rot?'

Alex chuckled. 'My poor mother could tell you all about that. I won a scholarship to a fancy school, and suddenly there was all this pressure to perform. I had gone from being a big fish in a small pond to just the opposite, and I guess that's when I started to doubt my abilities. I started to build up this narrative inside myself that everything I did was doomed to fail. I began to invent excuses not to go out with my friends, contracted mysterious illnesses that meant I had to stay at home. And I spent more time alone mucking around on the computer, made less effort with schoolwork. Thereon in, I can only assume it became a self-fulfilling prophecy.'

Alex sat back and reached into her pocket. There were the seeds of a promising podcast here; she liked that bit about the 'narrative inside'. It wasn't until she had patted a full circuit of her hips that she remembered her phone was lying broken in her room.

MacBrian was writing again. 'And there was a second shift – a reversal of that *narrative inside*, if you will – on the seventeenth?'

'Exactly, Director – exactly. I couldn't have put it better myself. You see, on the morning of the seventeenth, my boss, Mark, offered me a promotion. I suppose that the prospect of plodding on with my miserable non-life for another decade made me finally come to my senses.' Alex gazed contemplatively into the fire. 'By that point I must have had almost twenty years of untapped potential inside me, ready to erupt.'

MacBrian looked up. 'Erupt?'

'I can't take full credit, of course. I owe a lot to Chloe.'

'Chloe?' MacBrian leaned forward, pen poised. 'Who is Chloe?'

'Chloe Apostolou. My holistic self-transformation mentor. Now' – Alex leaned forward and stabbed a finger at Mac-Brian's notebook – 'the woman from *Flair* cut all mention of this, but it could be a really fruitful avenue to explore in your research. Personally, I have no doubt that Chloe's method was instrumental in what happened that night.'

'Her method?'

Alex stifled a sigh. She reminded herself that if she lived on a remote island, instead of the middle of the city, her horizons would be much less open, too. 'Look,' she said, 'I know that the Western scientific establishment can be sceptical about alternative approaches, but Chloe has so much integrity. She's approach-agnostic. She combines whichever tools she thinks will be best for each individual client, everything from Shiatsu to Jivamukti to NLP.'

MacBrian seemed to be struggling to know what to write.

'Anyway,' Alex said, 'the point is, that evening I had my first session with Chloe. I'd never seen a therapist before. I hated any sort of self-examination back then. However, my friend Mae had bought me a voucher for Christmas, and Harry plays squash on Tuesdays, so I forced myself to give it a go.' She sighed. 'It didn't start well. I resisted opening up.'

'Opening up?'

'Mentally. Emotionally. But Chloe was so great. She put on some binaural beats, took me through a Kabat-Zinn body scan, made me do some Pranayama breathing, and eventually I . . . well, I suppose I simply released. I started crying and I couldn't stop. I sat there for the whole hour with tears streaming down my face.'

Another glance at Taran. 'Why? What were the tears about?'

Alex sighed again. 'I have no idea. The old doomed-to-failure narrative, I suppose. I still didn't have the language I needed, at that point, to put my issues into words. But it was obviously the first step in blasting through some major blockages.'

'Blasting?'

'Personally, I'm certain that my brain must have processed my old emotions during REM, or perhaps consolidated Chloe's positivity during a period of deep wave. As Chloe pointed out, I was thirty at the time, right at the end of my Saturn Return. It's a natural time for transition. All I needed was the right nudge.'

MacBrian was frowning. 'You have contact details for this Chloe? We need to talk to her as soon as possible.'

'Of course!' Alex groped at her hip. 'Oh. Well, I'll send them over as soon as my phone's back in service. Chloe would *love* it out here.' She paused. MacBrian was still writing. Taran was still watching her with his hungry stare.

'Is this helpful?' Alex asked him. 'I'm not sure exactly what you guys are looking for.'

'Nor are we,' Taran said, with his crooked smile. 'But this is all very interesting.'

'Good. I'd love to see some of your previous research.'

'I'd love to—'

'And after that,' MacBrian cut in, 'you went straight home?'

Alex gave Taran a sympathetic glance. 'That's right,' she said. 'Harry goes back to his place after squash, so it was a night alone.'

'What did you do?'

'The usual.' Alex grimaced. 'Back then, anyway. Box set and bed.'

'Any drugs? Stimulants?'

Alex laughed. 'No. God, no. I didn't even drink in those

117

days. Just a ready meal and a chamomile tea. I went to bed early and dropped off right away.'

'But you woke shortly after?'

'That's right. It was amazing. The moment I woke, I felt like an entirely different person. So powerful, so clear, so calm. There was no way I was going back to sleep. So I grabbed my iPad and started brainstorming. By the time my alarm went off, I had a full business plan. Oh, I'd dabbled with ideas for start-ups before, but this time I knew it would work. Something major had shifted inside.'

MacBrian underlined a word several times. At least, Alex thought it was a word, until she craned over and saw the rows of meticulous symbols that crowded MacBrian's page. 'Wow!' She whistled. 'Is that, like, ancient Iskeullian?' She paused. 'You are publishing the research in English, right?'

MacBrian abruptly closed the cover. Somewhere in the distance, a bell boomed, twice. It sounded more like Big Ben than a class alarm.

Alex reached for her absent phone. 'It can't be only two o'clock.'

'It isn't,' Taran said. 'The bells mark shifts on the . . . um, on the reserve. It's four o'clock. Would you like a break?'

MacBrian gave him a look. 'We should really carry on,' she said.

'Oh no, sure.' Alex shrugged. 'This is fun. By all means, crack on.'

MacBrian reopened her notebook just wide enough to let in the tip of her pen. 'That morning. What was it that made you wake?'

'Nothing.' Alex took a sip of water. 'Nothing at all.'

'No dreams?'

'Oh, yes, those were pretty psychedelic. A sense that I was falling, a feeling of panic, millions of lights flashing around me then winking out. My fault for choosing paella. Late-night carbs are never a good call.'

MacBrian looked at Taran. 'And was there something specific that made you wake up? A thought? A sound?'

Alex combed her fringe with her fingers. 'No, no, I just . . . I just woke up.'

'Physical sensations? Changes in temperature? Feelings of release?'

Alex shifted in her chair. 'You know, I think maybe I wouldn't mind that break after all.'

'Any pain?'

Alex stared at her hands.

'You're telling us that nothing happened other than dreams, Miss Moore?' MacBrian pressed. 'Nothing at all?'

Alex continued to study her flaking red manicure, feeling her face grow hot under their double gaze. Finally, she let out a groan and held up her palms in mock-surrender. 'Okay, okay. You got me.'

MacBrian looked at Taran. She said, slowly, 'What do you mean?'

Alex gave a rueful grin. 'Oh God, Lenni will kill me. But I suppose if I have a veto over what gets publicly shared . . . ?' She thought of Harry, and was suddenly overcome by a heady sense of self-sacrifice. 'You know what? Screw it. God knows how this is relevant, but you guys are scientists. I can't feed you the same spin we give the press. The truth is that Eudo was born in a spray of puke.'

Alex paused as the dizziness rushed in.

'There's no nicer way to put it, I'm afraid. The fact is, I woke up because I threw up. All over my duvet.' She swallowed. She hadn't allowed herself to remember, really remember, this part of the story ever since Lenni had declared it out of bounds. 'It was just awful,' she murmured. 'I mean, that paella was past it's sell-by date, I should've . . .' Her stomach lurched. The vertigo arrived. The room began to pixellate. 'There was this terrible pain, deep inside my chest, and I honestly thought I was going to—' Her guts spasmed once, twice, the void cracked open, and then suddenly she was falling. She was falling and falling and falling and the void was rushing up to meet her as she tumbled towards the bottomless nothingness and she knew she must not in any circumstances let herself slide slide slide . . .

Alex closed her eyes, breathing hard. Through the ringing in her ears she heard MacBrian and Taran exchange a few sharp, urgent sentences of gibberish. She focused on her breath. In, out, in, out. *Here and now, here and now.* Iskeull. MacBrian. Taran. White walls. Hard chair. Scarred wooden tabletop. Gradually, gradually, as she felt her way back into the room, the tightness in her chest loosened and the sickness began to recede.

'Alex.' She opened her eyes. Taran was crouching beside her chair, studying her with a kind of scientific fascination. MacBrian was standing beside the open door, whispering with Iain, who had reappeared from nowhere.

'God,' she croaked. Her head was banging. 'How embarrassing.' She sat up carefully.

'Captain MacHoras has sent for Dr MacDiarmid,' MacBrian said, watching Alex from the doorway as if afraid she might explode.

'No.' Alex shook her head, then regretted it. 'Please. I'm fine. It happens, when . . . when I get overtired.'

MacBrian and Iain conferred briefly again and he left, shutting the door behind him. MacBrian returned slowly to her chair.

'Really,' Alex said, summoning a wan smile. 'I'd rather we all pretended that didn't happen, okay?' She forced herself to straighten up. 'Look, we're just getting to the good bit of the story. When the energy and the ideas and the confidence began to flow.'

She smiled harder at MacBrian and Taran, who were still watching her with a sort of enraptured horror.

'Look, I know it's gross. It doesn't make for the greatest story. That's why Lenni and I decided to keep it out of my public script. We don't exactly want to advocate bulimia as an effective strategy for entrepreneurship. But Chloe – and I know this might sound a bit woo-woo, to you guys – Chloe doesn't think it was the paella. Chloe thinks that my mind-body was expressing its metamorphosis by physically ejecting the past. Out with the old, in with the new. And I think that's kind of beautiful, don't you?'

There was a brief silence, during which Alex kept trying to project a breezy positivity. But underneath her game face she had to admit that she really didn't feel well after all. That had been the worst episode yet. Her chest still felt hollow, her limbs were pricking with pins and needles, and the headache was threatening to evolve into a migraine.

Brain realignment, she reminded herself. Caterpillar. Butterfly.

'Are you sure you don't want to—' Taran began.

'There's just one more thing I'd like to cover before we break,' MacBrian said. 'If you're capable?'

'Of course.' Alex rallied herself. 'Fire away.'

'This idea that you came up with.' MacBrian scanned her notes. 'This business. *Eudomonia.*' She pronounced it carefully, elaborately, like it was a spell. 'Could you explain exactly how it works?'

Alex let out a breath and smiled properly, this time. 'Now that,' she said, 'I could do in my sleep.'

But MacBrian was obviously about as far away from Eudo's target audience as it was possible to be, and she seemed to have trouble grasping even its simplest aspects. She spent a long time grilling Alex on the technology behind the platform, apparently under the impression that Eudo operated via some sort of digitally supercharged witchcraft. She also seemed to have extraordinarily high expectations of the impact Eudo might have on members' lives. Alex had an arsenal of stats proving that Eudo was a facilitator of genuine transformation, rather than a well-designed collection of woolly truisms and expensive yogawear. But now she found herself in the unusual position of downplaying its influence.

'Look, I do believe we've built something truly powerful,' she concluded after at least another hour of questions. She was feeling ever more ill and wishing that she had taken Taran's earlier opening to escape the smoky room. 'But I admit that I don't feel comfortable making *too* many claims about its lasting effects, especially to scientists like you. Eudo's still in its very early days, Director. The only person I can be one hundred per cent sure it has changed, and changed forever, is me.'

She sat back, utterly wrung out. MacBrian was still writing. Taran cleared his throat. 'Sorcha,' he said. 'It's getting late.'

MacBrian looked up, frowned, then shut the notebook. 'Yes. Of course.' She turned to Alex. 'I'm afraid we have rather a lot to deal with at the moment, so we won't be able to join you for dinner. I will arrange to have some food brought to your room.'

'Of course,' Alex smiled. 'I just hope I've given you something useful.'

MacBrian stood up. 'So do I, Miss Moore. So do I.'

Whether the culprit was a mind over-stimulated by the interview, the bowl of fish stew she'd wolfed down or the Nordic white night disrupting her body clock, Alex found herself stubbornly awake as the night wore on. Switching sides on the lumpy mattress, she reached for her phone for the hundredth time, then tossed the useless slab of plastic down onto her bag. She lay back under the heavy coverlet, staring at the damp on the ceiling and listening to the rain patter down outside.

The afternoon's interview had left her feeling distinctly on edge. It seemed obvious that she'd somehow let the professors down. Perhaps they had expected a more intellectual, less intuitive framework for her success. It seemed Lenni had been right all along about keeping quiet about the throwing up part, too. It had obviously rattled them. Still, there was another full day to go, which should be plenty of time for MacBrian to get what she wanted, despite all her pushiness. And Alex had a soft spot for the geeky Taran, who seemed to find her fascinating – to the point, she was beginning to suspect, of a crush. They probably didn't get many young women taking up positions in GCAS Europe, let alone young women with haircuts that made them look like Uma Thurman crossed with a sexy schoolgirl.

Sighing, Alex flopped over again and started to compose work emails in her head. She was halfway through a mental press release about the GCAS project when the distant bell boomed out again, three times. As the resonant chimes faded away, she heard her mother's voice, exasperated and affectionate. *You think too much, you and your father. Honestly, sometimes it's like living with two brains in a jar. If you're feeling strange, just get some air in your lungs, Alex. Get up and get out.*

Her mother was right. It would do her no good to lie here thinking until morning. Alex pushed the blankets aside and slid her feet down onto the cold floor. She dressed by moonlight, then crossed to the door and lifted the latch.

The oil lamps in the corridor had been lowered to the merest glow. The only sounds were a mouse-like scurrying, a nest-like rustle, and the odd coo or hoot from a bird. When she reached the lobby, Alex noticed with a shock that Iain was sitting behind the reception desk, although slumped in his chair and obviously asleep. She crept across the flagstones and tried the main door, only to find it locked. Unwilling to wake him, she started back in the direction of her room. But then the thought of lying in that hard bed without distractions for seven more hours made her swing round again.

She tiptoed across the lobby to the opposite corridor. Groping her way along the flagstones, she was relieved to find that this wing seemed identical to the one she had just left. There was a single long corridor with the same row of doors, and the same atmosphere of abandonment. She inched open one of the doors and saw an empty shell of a room, its walls patched with peeling plaster and its corners furzed with mould. MacBrian's urgency started to make sense. Obviously the Iskeullians badly needed to prove their worth to whoever allocated funding from GCAS's money pot. A high-profile, zeitgeisty research paper was probably their best shot. Perhaps, Alex mused, she could offer to build them a digital strategy, on top of the interviews. It wouldn't be hard; a microsite, a teaser campaign, a sexy infographic about the DNA of success.

Above and beyond, Harry, she thought. *Above and beyond.*

She continued to the end of the corridor and passed through an arch into a cold, damp anteroom. There was what looked like another outer door here, a thick old slab of wood. It was secured with a padlock, but the hoop was flaky with rust. Telling herself it was about to fall off anyway, Alex found it only took a tiny bit of jimmying to pull it apart. Then, feeling like some shlocky Hitchcock heroine, she pressed her shoulder against the door and stepped out into the night.

8

She was standing at the end of the building's east wing, with her back to the airfield and the farmland beyond. Before her, the town that she'd glimpsed from her window unrolled like an oily black fleece. Delighted by the prospect of exploring without a pre-planned route or pressing end-goal for the first time in weeks, Alex wandered slowly into the streets. The cobblestones were slippery under the soles of her trainers, and as her hair began to clump and drip, she wondered where Iain had stowed her anorak. But in the wake of the squall the droplets were light, and now that she was out in the soft salty air she didn't want to go back. In any case, getting wet felt good. Appropriately *Wuthering Heights*.

The sun had finally dropped beneath the horizon but the darkness remained translucent as she wove her way further in. Here and there, the flickering flame of a gas lamp danced in a puddle that was caught in a patch of broken cobbles or the foot-worn hammock of a step. She passed low stone houses with elaborately carved lintels and roofs scaled with rectangular slates. She peered into the dark maws of shop fronts and workshops, catching the glint of a jewelled necklace, a shrine-like pyramid of tinned pineapple chunks, a loom beside a heap of folded cloth.

Now and then she heard a shout or a laugh. Once she saw a bowed couple hurry round a corner; shortly afterwards she heard the tail-end of an argument traded in a harsh Gaelic-sounding dialect as a distant door opened, then banged shut. After a while, as she circled through street after street, Alex realized that the town was arranged in one loose, interconnecting spiral, with residential houses on the outer loop and commercial buildings closer in. Just as she was wondering whether she ought to turn back, she found herself emerging onto a circular sweep of sand-compacted earth.

She could only presume this was the town centre, the snail in the centre of the spiral shell. Obviously used as some sort of arena, it was bounded by rings of stone seats, with a few open-fronted stalls between them and a low stage set off to one side. In the middle of the sandy ring was a huge column of rock, mounted on a plinth. Alex had dismissed it as an abstract sculpture until, rounding the perimeter, she looked back and saw the face, picked out by the moonlight.

She cut across the arena to get a better look. So far, only the head and shoulders had been hewn out of the rock, but they were masterfully done, eerily lifelike. As she brushed the rough surface where the feet would be, Alex was struck with the absolute certainty that she had seen this man before. He was beautiful, with his hawkish brow, high cheekbones and full lips. His muscled shoulders were as round as basketballs, his thick hair was raked back from his face and his blank stone eyes were fixed longingly north – over the roofs to whatever was on the other side of the town. It was him, she knew it. It was the dead Director. And, with that thought, the vertigo surged forth and the void ripped open and swallowed her whole.

The falling. The blackness. The million glittering lights. The terrible sense of loss.

She came to curled on the wet sand, her skin slick with sweat and rain. She was exhausted, she told herself as she clambered shakily to her feet. She was disoriented, she was sleep-deprived. He must have reminded her of someone else, someone from her loser-Alex past. But however hard she tried, none of the excuses would stick.

Shivering, keeping her back to the statue, she returned to the street.

After she had wound her way through the town for another half-hour, the buildings began to thin out. Between them, the horizon had turned a pale, wavering gold. Alex wondered just how many hours she had been walking, and whether anyone back at the main building had noticed she wasn't there. It was only when she emerged round a final cobbled curve and out onto a broad avenue that she saw that what she had taken to be the dawn was fire.

She had reached the top of Iskeull. A few feet from where she was standing the avenue crumbled into cliff, and the cliff crashed back into the sea. But a hundred feet or so across the waves, connected to the mainland via a broad stone causeway, was a whole other mini-island. It was fronted by an unbroken line of stone buildings, with a huge glass-domed rotunda set in the centre like a jewel. Every window cut into the facade appeared to be ablaze, and behind the buildings a second wave of light blanched the grainy early-morning sky, as if a thousand bonfires had been set alight on the land beyond.

After the intimate darkness of the town, Alex was as shocked as if nocturnal Haggerston – street lamps, head-lights, smouldering joint-ends and all – had followed her from London and transplanted itself wholesale onto a lump of Atlantic rock. So here at last was the islanders' famed reserve. She had to admit that she was impressed. Their academic processes might be archaic, but these nepotistic Celts were obviously tirelessly committed to the conservation of their land.

She wondered what such vigilant night-time duties might involve. Burning heather – was that a thing? Studying bats? Harvesting . . . wild orchids? Dew? Feeling a surge of obstin-acy sweep aside her lingering wooziness from the episode, Alex strode towards the bell tower that gave access to the causeway. Yes, the Director had asked her not to trespass, but she wasn't about to go nicking eggs from nests or dropping gum. They probably had her pegged as a hopeless city slicker anyway, so if anyone caught her, she'd simply say she was lost. And for some reason she knew she had to see what the statue was looking at with such blank-eyed desire.

Unfortunately she hadn't accounted for the presence of four big black-clad men, clustered at the open mouth of the bell tower in some sort of strategic huddle. With a jolt of surprise, she recognized one of them as Iain. It seemed that he hadn't been joking about his job in security, and he was evidently leader of the pack. Alex could see the other eco-bouncers attending to his muttered speech with the same stagey active-listening expressions she recognized from many a feudal boardroom. Fortunately, they were all too busy being earnest and attentive to notice one small, sodden woman slink round the far side.

As she crept through the passageway, Alex passed the open doorway of what looked like an empty guardroom. Inside were a row of galoshes and a line of hooded waxed capes hanging from pegs. Before her conscience could object, she had ducked in and grabbed one of the capes, dragged the heavy folds over her shoulders and pulled up the hood. She'd put it back, for goodness' sake, but now that the exhilaration of the walk was fading, she was starting to get cold. In any case, she figured that remaining anonymous for the duration of her so-very-short-and-harmless peek at the reserve was a good thing. It would prevent Iain from wasting unnecessary energy and resource on trying to throw her out.

Crossing the causeway was pleasantly scary. Alex allowed herself one thrilling glance at the waves embroidering the rocks a hundred feet beneath her feet, before fixing her eyes on the peninsula ahead. Already she could make out figures scurrying along the road in front of the line of buildings, milling in and out of the rotunda's double doors. There were horses, too, hairy yellow prehistoric-looking things, trotting up and down. It was a veritable hive of activity, and she was sure it would not be hard for one stranger to blend in.

Alex followed the path off the causeway and strode straight towards the rotunda as if she had several very urgent and important things to do. Keeping her hood up, she climbed the steps, then came to an abrupt halt just inside the double doors.

It was some sort of vast reference room. The walls were lined from floor to dome with thousands of leather-bound folios. In the middle of the room was a second, circular tower of shelves – some kind of chamber, judging by the door set into the middle of it, which was encrusted with a spiralling mosaic made from fossils and minerals in various shades of grey and blue. In the doughnut of space between the outer and inner shelves were dozens of glass cabinets, containing colourful hand-inked tables, maps and diagrams. Between the cabinets sat circular stone desks, each one bathed in the soft yellow glow of an oil lamp. The moonlight, refracted through the rain-spattered dome, spangled a pattern over the flagstoned floor. At the far side of the room, a huge arch stood open to the night, letting in wafts of cool air.

At least a couple of hundred people were moving around the space, their voices and footsteps mingling with the drumming of the droplets overhead. The atmosphere was one of quiet efficiency. Some moved in and out of shadowy doorways set into the shelves. Some browsed the cabinets. Some studied at the desks. Others crawled up and down ladders to retrieve or replace folios. Most activity was centred around the arch at the back, where people passed in and out of the night in a steady stream. Beyond them, Alex could see the orange-yellow twinkle of hundreds of lights dancing across the reserve outside.

She stepped into the human traffic and headed straight

for the arch, trying to look purposeful while sneaking glimpses of the islanders from under her hood. They covered a wide range of ages, and there was a gratifyingly even gender split – but they were all, to a man or girl, pale-skinned, dark-haired and grey-eyed, with their own version of the same heavy bone structure the professors shared. Catching snatches of their conversation, she recognized the same harsh and impenetrable Gaelish dialect that she had over-heard back in the town. Iskeullian, presumably.

As she wound her way round the central chamber, the door flew open and the sounds of a ruckus echoed out. Two men in black emerged, dragging another man in grey – who was yelling incomprehensibly – backwards through the door frame. As the others in the room froze, rubbernecking the trio with a gamut of expressions from disgust to delight, Alex took advantage of the distraction and increased her pace. She could just about make out a series of tall black shapes looming outside, in the semi-darkness between the fires. She was already halfway through the arch when someone pushed past her, knocking her roughly against the stone wall. With-out thinking, she shoved back, looking up at them with a glare.

The shock hit her like a punch in the stomach. The person who had knocked into her was the angry man who had caused the ruckus. And the angry man was Not John Hanley.

He glanced back over his shoulder but, still caught up in his own drama, he took a moment to recognize her. Then his face contracted in confusion and slowly warped into a mime of disbelief, anger, and a trace element of something that looked strangely like fear.

Ordinarily, faced with such a look, Alex would have turned and legged it. On receiving such a look from a man she knew to be a drug-addled psychopath with a misguided personal grudge, legging it was the only sane response. Unfortunately, now she was out in the full glow of the firelight, Alex was also granted her first proper look at Iskeull's nature reserve. And it wasn't, after all, a haven for bats. Nor was it a plantation of wild orchids. It was a network of towers. Vast, ancient stone towers. Hundreds of them, spread across the peninsula in a hexagonal grid, lit by spluttering flares.

Her muscles stopped working.

Not John Hanley grabbed her arm. He pulled her back through the arch and across the rotunda, then through one of the doorways on the right-hand side of the wall. He had dragged her quite a way along a narrow, dim corridor before her brain, still trying to process what she had seen, caught up with her stumbling feet. He must have seen her prepare to yell, because he suddenly pulled open a door behind them and bundled her through. Alex yelled anyway, but her voice was immediately swallowed by thick stone walls. The room was small and high and lined, from floor to ceiling, with ranks of carved cubbyholes. In turn, each cubbyhole was crammed with what appeared to be hundreds of multicoloured index cards.

She skidded to the back of the room while Not John Hanley stood with his back against the door, eyeballing her wildly.

'What the *fuck* is going on?' Alex spat.

He continued to stare at her in silence. She would never have made the mental leap between the grungy London smackhead and the genteel Iskeull hippies – yet now it all seemed blindingly obvious. Not just the *Game of Thrones* clothes and the accent, but the jutting cheekbones, the flinty eyes, the black, toilet-brush hair.

'Oh God,' she said. 'Is this an Opa! outpost? Some sort of souped-up research facility? Have you lured me out here with this elaborate cover to take some sort of twisted revenge? Because I meant what I said back in London. I'm very sorry if you guys didn't make it, but I don't see how you can possibly blame—'

'Are you an alien?' Not John Hanley burst out.

It was so ridiculous that Alex's anger fizzled to a stop. '*What?*'

He raked a hand through his hair. 'Artificial intelligence? Some kind of experiment?'

'What the fuck are you *on?*'

But as Not John Hanley paced, she could see that, however angry he was, whatever he had been taking in London was no longer in his bloodstream. His skin was clear. His colour was high. His hands, which she was monitoring closely for potential threat, had no hint of a shake. It made him look even younger – not to mention stronger. She watched the muscles flex under his shirt as he tugged at his hair and tried not to think about how much harm they could cause.

'Taran thinks you're harmless,' he said, scanning her from head to toe in that excoriating way she remembered so well.

'With your questions and your smiles and your . . . your *charm*. But I know you're stringing them along. It's a front, isn't it? A blind. I think you know exactly how strong you are. I think you know exactly what you're doing.' He shook his head, let out a groan. 'Is that why you were sneaking onto the peninsula? Did you want to see the damage you've done?'

'Look,' Alex said slowly, trying to sound as calm as she could. He was just a boy, she told herself. A messed-up boy. 'Whoever you are, whatever you think I've done, I can assure you, you're making a big mistake. Now, please, I'd like you to move away from the door. Let's walk out of here and talk it through like rational adults. Okay?'

'Talk this through?' He came right up to her and leaned forward until he was inches from her face. She could feel the heat radiating off him, see the top of another tattoo peeking out from between the undone buttons at the neck of his shirt. 'You kill my father and you want to *talk this through?*'

'Your *father?*' Alex blinked. 'What in Christ's name are you—?'

'Ah!' He gave a horrible laugh, his breath hot on her cheek. 'So this is religious? Some kind of God complex? You've found some clever way to manipulate your Story and now you're on a mission to—'

'I'm not on a mission to anything!' Alex swallowed. 'Please. Listen. I promise, on my life, I have literally no idea what you're talking about.'

'You're lying!' He backed off and started to pace again. 'Dorothy Moore, London. That's what he said. Three words.

Three names. And you're the only one it could be. The others were dead ends; they searched for months. You're the only one who tried to hide your identity. It *has* to be you.'

Pressing herself back against the cubbyholes, Alex felt a small, sharp object dig into her right bum-cheek.

'You told me *yourself* you did it.' He scrubbed his fist back and forth across his scalp. 'The night of the seventeenth. You *boasted* about how you had "released your inner floodgate". How you had "unleashed a new power in your Story".'

Without taking her eyes off him, Alex slowly slid her right hand into her back pocket and closed her fingers around her father's novelty memory stick.

'Why?' Not John Hanley groaned. 'Why would anyone do this?'

'Listen,' Alex said soothingly. She pushed herself away from the wall, drew out the USB and rotated it inside her fist. 'I'm sure this is all an honest misunderstanding. As I said, if we could just go back into the library and talk—'

It was the wrong thing to say.

'So you *do* know about the Library!' Not John Hanley barked, striding back up to her. He thrust his arms over her shoulders and into the cubbyholes, caging her in. 'I knew it! I told them! I – *GNUH!*'

The cage released as he grabbed at the soft flesh at the base of his throat, into which Alex had stabbed half an inch of metal flash drive. Leaping sideways, she bolted for the door and managed to wrench it open just as she felt the tips of Not John Hanley's fingers brush against her back. She crashed out into the corridor, slammed the door shut with

137

her shoulder, then sprinted towards the rotunda. Plunging through the doorway, she skidded across the flagstones, ducked under someone's arm, banged into someone else's hip and hurtled out of the nearest arch.

Those towers. There weren't just hundreds of them, but hundreds upon hundreds, each one at least sixty feet tall. Each one was uplit by a flaming torch, each one accessorized with a tethered horse. Alex's thoughts leapt and blurred as she ran. What the Jesus fuck had she been sucked into? A secret nuclear armoury? A breeding colony of killer sodding bees?

The paths that snaked between the towers were dark. Alex veered onto the nearest, sprinting as fast as she could, her trainers sliding on the waterlogged ground. She heard a shout behind her and somehow doubled her pace, careering around and between the soaring walls, her breath ragged and her chest burning with a stitch.

Another shout. The pound of footsteps: near, too near. She cast around desperately for somewhere to hide. And it was then, threading through the panic, that she felt it. It was a pull, a sort of inner tug – irresistible, cell-deep – calling to her from inside the nearest tower. It was coming, she realized, from a crescent-shaped black gap where the earth didn't-quite-meet the base of the wall. *You know me*, it said. *You know what I am. Come here, Dorothy. Come home.*

Two yells rang out, one answering the other. Nearby. Alex swerved over to the tower and, flinging herself onto the sandy mud in front of the gap, found herself staring into a chute of polished stone. She looked back, suddenly scared, but then the pull lassoed her heart again and whispered its siren song. *You know what I am, Dorothy. Come home.*

Closing her eyes, Alex plunged head-first into the opening. Thrusting her feet against the earth, she slithered down into the darkness with startling speed. After only a few seconds her momentum slowed, as the smooth slope levelled out. When she pushed forward, she felt the chute begin to rise up again and sensed a faint, warm breeze on her hands. She wriggled forward and felt the breeze strengthen, the promise of an exit inches away. She stretched up, and her fingers found and then closed around a rounded stone lip. Heart pounding against the wall of the chute, she hauled herself up and over the edge. Elbows. Belly. One knee. Both.

Collapsing, exhausted, onto the earthen floor of the tower, she found herself washed in a glorious swell of calm. Everything was fine. Everything was possible. Everything and everyone was here. Breathing in wave after wave of warm, sweet ease, Alex opened her eyes. Inches from her nose, there was a soft grey boot. She stared at it for a moment, then rolled sideways onto her back. Above the grey boot was a length of grey-trousered leg. Above the leg was the half-naked torso of a woman. A heavily tattooed woman, who appeared to be pulling a rainbow out of a galaxy of stars.

9

There were by now at least a dozen people assembled around the table at the other end of the room. Despite the indecipherable dialect and the drum of the rain on the glass dome above, it was clear they were having a furious argument.

'Hadron Colliders?' Alex called from the high-backed wicker chair that Iain had unceremoniously deposited her in. They ignored her. 'Big agra? A next-gen GM nursery? Oil?' But what she had seen had looked more like circuitry, perhaps even some sort of crazy new biochemical VR. Alex paused. 'Oh, shit,' she said slowly. 'I know exactly what's going on. You're not Opa! at all, are you? You're *Google*.'

There was yet another knock. The door opened and the harassed face of the secretary appeared in the gap. The secretary said something apologetic to MacBrian, and MacBrian, who had two red patches high on her white cheeks, wearily sculled her hand. The secretary withdrew, and yet another monochrome-faced, silver-brooched islander strode into the room. By now, Alex knew the score. The newcomer cast around; saw her; subjected her to a long, wary and increasingly incredulous stare. Then he turned and made some impassioned comment to the group, causing a further eruption to break out.

'Hey!' Alex called. *'Hey!'*

She wasn't entirely clear on the sequence of events that had just occurred. She'd lain on the floor of the tower, staring up for a few shocked seconds at the woman who was manipulating that spectacular airborne mass of coloured sparks. Then a second woman had run at her from behind and pinned her down. Moments later Iain had appeared through the chute and dragged Alex back under and out. A gang of black-clad men was waiting for them outside, watching her emerge as if she were the victim of a particularly horrific car crash. The strange peace she had felt inside the tower had evaporated instantly. Steely fingers digging into flesh that Not John Hanley had bruised only minutes earlier, Iain had then all but carried her back the way she had come. Back between the towers, back under the arches, back into the rotunda – their glowering posse following their every step. As they crossed the flagstones to the chamber at the centre of the room, all the employees, or students, or whatever they were, had stopped whatever it was they were doing and gawped at Alex as if a wild animal had just been led into their midst.

Iain had left their escort outside the fossil-encrusted door and marched her through. They'd passed into an antechamber, where the startled secretary was rising to her feet, then through a second door and finally into the room at the core of the dome. This turned out to contain ranks of empty bookshelves, faded squares of plaster where paintings must once have hung, stacks of unpacked boxes, teetering piles of paper – and MacBrian. The Director had been alone, poring over a ledger on a vast circular stone table. Her expression, when she looked up, had said car crash, wild animal, and more. Still clamped between Iain's hands, Alex had started to shiver – a cartoon-like, core-trembling, teeth-clattering shake. She hated that she'd shivered. She hated more than anything that Iain had felt it. Now, she tried to cover the wobble that kept creeping into her words with brisk counter-attack.

'Hey!' she bellowed again. Everyone turned. 'You'd better tell me what is going on here, right now,' she demanded, looking MacBrian squarely in the eye. 'You people are harbouring a violent criminal.'

MacBrian snapped something to the group behind her and strode across the room to Alex's chair. 'I have been trying to protect you, Miss Moore,' she said, her face thunderous. 'Unfortunately, when you trespassed into—'

'*Trespassed?*' Alex choked. 'I went for a bloody *walk*. It's not my fault that you've got some sort of top-secret steampunk project going on. And I like your idea of protection! Employing some insane addict to stalk me through London? Luring me out to your fucked-up family island, so that he could abduct me when I nipped out for a breath of fresh air? What I don't understand is why you didn't just let him cut me to pieces back down in Wildfell Hall.'

'A – what?' MacBrian looked over at Iain in, Alex thought, a piss-poor show of confusion. 'I have no idea what you are talking about.'

142

'Oh, come *on*.' Alex spread her palms. 'You really expect me to believe that you didn't send Not John – I mean who- ever that fucked-up kid really is – to ask me the exact same questions you asked me yesterday? What was that: some sort of twisted audition? Did his crack habit ever so slightly hamper his data-gathering abilities?'

The group, which Alex could only assume to be the rest of the leadership board, exploded into a fresh bout of bickering. MacBrian, ignoring them, exchanged a rapid back-and-forth with Iain. She turned back to Alex. 'Let me get this straight,' she said. 'You're saying that someone from Iskeull visited you in London?'

'Right, as if you didn't already know.'

'Miss Moore. We know nothing about this. Are you sure?'

'Of course I'm bloody sure! It didn't click at first, which, okay, was pretty stupid. But once I saw him back there amongst his bloody brethren, I realized.' She paused. 'Who *else* do you think I was running away from?'

'You were running *away*?'

Alex threw up her hands. 'What the hell do you *think* I was doing? No, I did not spot your Neolithic Tardis planta- tion and decide to go play Doctor Who. That guy was about to kill me, or at least inflict some pretty grievous bodily harm. And all because I wouldn't tell him why I killed his father, because, um, I HAVE NOT KILLED ANYONE AT ALL.'

Silence, punctuated by the hiss and patter of rain. In a tight voice MacBrian asked Taran a question. Taran replied, holding his hands up now too, in a gesture of helplessness. Everyone looked at Iain, who shook his head, then Iain and

Taran started arguing, with a lot of head-shaking and hand gestures, until Iain turned abruptly and left the room.

'Hey!' Alex called again. 'Hello? Can someone talk to me in English?'

'This is—' MacBrian swung round. She looked pained. 'I . . . We had no idea.'

Taran walked over to stand beside MacBrian. 'Alex,' he said. 'Can you describe the man who came to see you?'

Alex sniffed. 'Well, he's one of you, basically. Pale, dark hair, grey eyes. Skinny but muscly. About twenty, maybe. And he has a tattoo – a tattoo just like the one I saw on that woman doing whatever the fuck she was doing in that tower. Anyway, he'll be pretty easy to spot. He's got a Lego USB stick rammed into his neck.' She paused. 'Did you seriously not send him to get me?'

'No,' MacBrian said. She looked around her colleagues. 'I expressly forbade anyone from making contact Outside.'

'Outside what?'

A white-haired man talked over MacBrian in Iskeullian, loud and angry.

'No,' MacBrian replied wearily in English, shaking her head. 'It's too late. She's seen the Library. And the way the situation has been progressing, or rather not progressing, we probably would have had to tell her soon anyway.'

'So I've seen your bloody library, so what?' Alex flung up her hands. 'My Kindle comes with more free downloads than all the books you have in there. Even if you're hoarding the Da Vinci Code or something, I promise you I don't care.'

'This,' MacBrian said, turning back, 'isn't the Library. This is just the index room for the archives, which are stored in the buildings to either side. It's those towers you saw outside that—'

Several professors bellowed something that even Alex could tell meant *NOOOO*.

MacBrian briefly closed her eyes – presumably sending a prayer to some Pictish god – then opened them and turned back to Taran. 'Taran?'

Taran spread his palms, twitched his shoulders. 'I – well, really, this is your decision, Sorcha . . .'

The door banged open and Iain re-entered the room. Beside him, being dragged by the upper arm, was Not John Hanley. There was a small clot of crusted black blood at the base of his throat. His eyes wheeled around the room and found Alex, and Alex was gripped by an aftershock at what could have – had almost – happened. She gripped the arms of her chair. As the others broke into dark mutters, Taran walked over, placed his hand on Not John Hanley's arm and spoke quietly to him in Iskeullian. Not John Hanley ignored him.

'Miss Moore,' MacBrian said. 'Is this the person who came to see you in London?'

Alex nodded, holding eye contact with him, forcing her voice to stay firm. 'That's the fuckbag.'

'Can you explain to me exactly the circumstances of your meeting?'

The others fell quiet again as Alex described Not John Hanley's visit to her office. Then, in vicious detail, she gave them a run-down of his latest assault. Throughout her speech the young man's face remained hard, his stare unwavering.

'But that's not all,' Alex added, once she'd arrived at her escape into the . . . the *thing*. 'I was attacked twice before, in London. I was mugged on the street near my home, the night before this guy lied his way into Eudo. And a few hours after that, another man was arrested outside a restaurant where I was having dinner. A violent nutter wearing those exact same boots.'

Everyone looked at Not John Hanley's boots.

Alex wrapped her arms around her chest. 'I didn't want to believe it at the time. I hoped I was being paranoid. But, you know, when he came to the office he had this bag with him, this holdall, and I reckon he must have had the shotgun inside the whole time. And . . . God, yes, the paper said the man outside the restaurant was shouting something about wanting more, as in more drugs or whatever, but of course he must have meant *Moore*. Me, Moore. All in all, it seems that this guy has tried to attack me no fewer than *four times* over the past four days.'

'No,' Not John Hanley said in English, shaking his head. 'No, no—' He fired an urgent stream of Iskeullian at Taran.

'Don't tell me he's trying to deny it?' Alex said incredulously. 'Who *is* this kid, anyway?'

'It's . . . complicated,' MacBrian said.

'No shit.'

'He's – his name is Finn MacEgan. He's not in his right mind. He should never have made it off the island. I assure you, he will be contained. Iain, take him away.'

But when Iain tried to turn his prisoner towards the door, Not John – Finn MacEgan – resisted, twisting in his grip to glare at MacBrian. 'You're behind this, aren't you?' he hissed. 'You always resented my father. You hardly waited for his ashes to cool before you took his place.' The others' heads whipped between him and MacBrian with a mixture of alarm and delight. Finn MacEgan turned his glare on them. 'You all know it,' he spat. 'You know she's a snake. You only elected her because you were desperate.' He turned back to MacBrian. 'They'll never love you like they loved him, *Director*, however many henchmen you surround . . . *UH!*'

He grunted as Iain wrenched him round. The bigger man pulled him across the room, but at the last moment he managed to brace himself in the doorway. He turned to Taran, to whom he said something low and fast and pleading, then twisted to look back at Alex.

'You,' he said. His eyes darted over her again, as they had the first time they'd met in the office, although this time they were more confused than hostile. 'You, whoever you are – if you're not . . . if you really don't . . . Please, just *don't trust her.*'

At that, Iain pressed his thumb into the crust of blood on Not John Hanley's throat. As Finn MacEgan yelped, Iain was finally able to pull him over the threshold and out of the room, kicking the door shut in his wake.

The room burst into uproar. MacBrian stood staring at the door, the spots on her cheeks burning like coals. Taran began to talk at her, rapidly.

'Hey. HEY!' Alex slammed her hand down on the arm of

the chair. It bounced off the wicker with a faint creak. 'Talk to me! I have a right to know. Who the fuck are you people? Why the hell does that guy want me dead?' The action-movie words sounded ridiculous, even as they came out.

MacBrian turned her back on the shouting islanders and, looking only at Alex, raised her hand. One by one, the others reluctantly lapsed into silence. 'I believe her,' MacBrian said shortly. 'But whether you agree with me or not, we don't have any more time for games. The simple fact is that our finest have tried and they have failed. We need her help.'

After a moment, the white-haired man started to speak again, half-heartedly.

'No, Sim,' MacBrian cut across him. 'The Covenant is meaningless if there's no Library left to protect. If Dorothy – Alex – knows what she's doing, then our secret is already out. If she doesn't, we need her to understand what's at stake, and find a way to stop doing it.' She turned to Iain. 'Tell your men on North Ronaldsay to send word to the other Chapters. We're going to have to take her into one of the Stacks.'

Close up, in the drizzly early-morning light, the towers looked less sinister but more strange. Each one appeared to have been made from a single piece of rock, without the need for bricks or mortar, creating the disconcerting illusion that they had grown straight from the ground. Their rough, lichen-stippled walls tapered towards conical roofs, and they covered the cliff in concentric circles, forming a honeycomb pattern against the sandy paths. The overall effect was of a colony of colossal beehives.

Taran, walking beside Alex, pushed back his hood. 'How do you feel?' he said.

Alex stared back at him as Iain and his bevy of black-clad heavies led the way along one of the paths. 'I'm thinking—' she began numbly, then stopped. 'There is no research project, is there?' she said. 'I'm such an idiot. I knew it was too good to be true. Is there even such a thing as GCAS?'

'Oh yes,' he said. 'GCAS exists. Just not in the form you think. Our cover has changed several times over the centuries, but the GCAS front has served the Library very well for the past few decades.'

'And you're telling me that this,' Alex gestured limply at the soaring walls around them, 'is some sort of library?'

'*The* Library,' Taran corrected. 'Your Library. Mine. Ours. Everyone's. Or at least one of the seven sites across the world where it shows itself above ground. You'll see, Alex. But while we have a chance to talk, I'd like to ask you how you've been fee—'

'Here we are,' MacBrian interrupted, indicating a figure doing a deep side-bend beside one of the towers up ahead. As they approached, Alex saw that it was a woman of about her own age, lean and muscular, with her dark hair pulled back in a fishtail plait. She was wearing a grey outfit identical to Finn MacEgan's, and she appeared to be going through some kind of callisthenic warm-up routine.

'This is the Stack I've managed to temporarily requisition for our use,' MacBrian said. 'And this is Curstag MacRob, one of our most gifted full-time Readers. She'll be showing you how it works.'

'I know how to read,' Alex said weakly.

'How to *Read*,' MacBrian corrected, coming to a halt in front of the woman. The heavies arranged themselves in a loose semicircle behind them while Iain stalked on, scanning the paths.

Dad? Alex thought helplessly. *Mum? Harry? What the hell have I got myself into? A religious cult, driven mad by inbreeding? A Scientology-style indoctrination camp?* Alex gazed around her, wondering if she could, at a push, run. But she was already weak with delayed shock and exhaustion, and Iain's heavies looked very heavy indeed. And there was something else. Something she didn't really want to admit to. Something she couldn't rationalize or explain.

Despite the seriously crazy turn that her rural adventure had just taken, despite the bruises on her arms, despite the nonsensical bullshit the pretend professors were all suddenly spouting, the only thing Alex knew for sure was that she wanted more. She had to have another taste of whatever it was she had felt inside that tower a few hours before. She knew she should be trying to figure out the real agenda these crackpots were peddling, making a plan for how to get safely out of this mess. But the craving for another shot of that delicious calm was stronger than her impulse to escape.

The MacRob woman dropped onto her belly and disappeared head-first into the gap at the base of the tower. 'You next, Miss Moore,' MacBrian said.

Alex got down on her hands and knees and stared into the half-moon of darkness before her face. She glanced back over her shoulder. MacBrian, Taran and four heavies stared back. She thought for a moment that she might cry. But then it reached out for her, the pull – twining itself around the roots of her hair, reaching into the marrow of her bones.

She became hyper-aware of the chill of the sandy earth, the rhythm of the drizzle pattering on her back, the roar of the wind. The pull wrapped itself around her heart like a memory, an ancient memory; a memory made of nostalgia and hope and the promise of finally being back where she belonged. Before she had made a conscious decision, Alex found herself plunging into the chute head first.

It took only a few seconds to slither under and up, with the walls angled to give her weight momentum, and the stone polished smooth under her chest and ribs and thighs. Before she knew it, she felt two hands grab hers, then her arms jerked in their sockets and she flew over the lip of the chute and out the other side. Curstag MacRob met Alex's startled gaze for the briefest of moments, then turned and walked away while Alex scrambled to her feet.

Back in MacBrian's office, she had tried to label what she had seen. A planetarium, a control panel, a circuit board. This time, as she stood and stared, her veins once again flooding with that strong, sweet calm, Alex simply accepted it as beautiful.

The whole of the inside of the tower was made of some kind of glass. Thick, gnarled, ancient-looking glass. Its surface was covered with thousands of spherical indentations, as if someone had attacked it with an ice-cream scoop. And behind the glass ran a river of blackness. Rich, muscular blackness, stewed out of the darkest shades of all the colours in the universe. Blackness that looked unfathomably deep, despite being trapped inside a wall that Alex knew to be no more than ten feet wide. Blackness that never stopped moving, and that carried within its distant currents what looked like a million tiny pearls.

All across the tower, the pearls were somehow pushing their way out of the blackness and into the walls. Approaching from the depths, they somehow passed through the surface of the glass, then grew in size until they fitted snugly inside the spherical nooks. They nestled there, thousands of spheres the size of oranges, their translucent skins pulsing with silvery light. Waiting. Alex could feel them waiting. Then, as if disappointed, they slid back beneath the surface, returning to the blackness. Within seconds, another set of pearls had thrust their way through. And so the cycle went on: spheres emerging and retreating in a ceaseless, seemingly random pattern, as if they were dancing to the rhythm of some secret choreography.

Alex let out a breath that she felt she had been holding for thirty years.

'Welcome to the Library. Iskeullian Chapter. Stack I-10, to be precise.'

She looked round to see Taran untangling himself out of the chute. She had no idea how to reply, but it seemed that her expression said it all, because he suddenly smiled, a flash of white in the soft light. A moment later, MacBrian thrust herself efficiently up after him.

'You feel the radiation very strongly, the first time,' she said, straightening her tunic. 'It won't be good for you to stay inside for long. Follow me, and don't touch anything until I say.'

She led the way over to the wall. The air was several degrees warmer than it was outside and had an indefinable taste of copper, salt and overheating hard drive. Up close, Alex could see through the oversized pearls' lustrous skin to the source of their glow. Each one of them contained countless tiny, dazzling silver-white sparks.

'These . . . these things, these pearl things, they're . . .' Alex shook her head. She wanted to say they were impossible, but the impossible thing was that she *recognized* them, as instinctively as she recognized the sight of a human face. She wanted to panic and protest. But then came the calm, the soothing, cradling calm, blanketing all disbelief and fear.

'The spheres are called Stories,' said MacBrian. 'So named because they generate and store our life stories, Miss Moore. Don't be afraid. We all have one. They're perfectly natural. Curstag will show you how they work.'

She nodded at Curstag MacRob, who was waiting in the centre of the tower. MacRob nodded back, then shrugged off her cape and dragged her shirt unceremoniously over her head. Beneath it was a sort of grey linen sports bra, a rippling four-pack and the same full-body tattoo Alex had glimpsed, briefly, on the woman in the other tower. It began at her wrists, with matching infinity symbols that sprouted thick, elaborately knotted indigo ropes. The ropes twisted up MacRob's arms and over her shoulders, crossed between her shoulder blades, curled around her ribs, then docked into a third infinity symbol beneath her diaphragm. It looked like a harness for a sport that Alex was not eager to play. Oblivious or indifferent to their stares, MacRob bent her knees, the figure-of-eight beneath her ribs bulging and shrinking as she breathed deep into her abdomen. She raised her arms and wriggled her fingers like a pianist about to tackle a concerto. Then she positioned her hands above her head and became very still.

Nothing happened for several long seconds. Then, without warning, the skin of one of the 'Stories' that was docked near the ceiling ruptured. A swarm of silver sparks burst from the breach into the air. Flashing, darting, rolling, the sparks spread into a glittering canopy across the tower. Alex didn't realize that she'd raised her arms in a shield, until she felt a hand on her elbow, pulling it down.

'They can't hurt you,' MacBrian said. 'They're Memories.'

'*Memories?*' Alex reluctantly lowered her arms as the sparks clustered and shimmered and swooped through the air, too fast to track.

MacBrian nodded. 'With a capital "M". These are the originals, created in the moment of experience. They're the physical records your brain draws upon when you remember. The hard copies, if you will. Some Memories are heavy and rich from having been activated many times. Some lie dormant for years. Some fade instantly, while others gradually lose significance and crumble away. However, the power of Memories does not lie in their individual natures, but in the relationships between them. Now if you watch . . .'

'You must be out of your . . .' But Alex's half-hearted protest faded away as hundreds of 'Memories' began to break away from the glittering canopy above their heads. Flocking to the centre of the tower, they clustered into a figure-of-eight loop directly above MacRob. The loop began to whir round, twisting faster and faster until it gave off a mingled yellow-green glow. For the next few seconds the loop's colour steadily intensified, from pistachio to lime to a burning chartreuse. Then, without warning, the whole thing exploded in a silver spray, scattering its Memories back out across the tower. Moments later, a fresh set of Memories had swarmed out of the canopy and formed another loop above MacRob. When this loop began to spin – more slowly than the last one – it glowed a pale red-brown. It circuited lazily for several seconds, its colour deepening to a rich mahogany rust before it, too, burst apart. And so it went on. Now a wisp of watery blue; now a helix of grey tinged with rose. Then back to the rusty rope again – as if someone had set off a manic firework display in the dark tower.

'Now those loops,' MacBrian said, barely glancing at the spectacle above, 'are Storylines. Patterns made up of Memories. When they join together in particular combinations, our Memories create narratives about who we are. And those narratives, in turn, influence how we behave. When we're young, we test out and discard dozens of Storylines. But as we get older, certain Storylines stick. These grow stronger and stronger, pulling in more and more new Memories. In this way, over time, our Storylines reduce in number and stabilize. In other words, our narratives about who we are become more predictable, more rigid, and our behaviour follows suit. Now, this isn't necessarily bad. Some entrenched

Storylines continue to be sources of great energy for their owners, for good or otherwise. But others, especially ones underpinned by very old Memories, can become over-dense and sluggish. They start to slow their Stories down, like plaque clogging the arteries. And that's where we Readers come in.'

She gestured towards MacRob, who was studying the lightshow above, her fingers still poised in the air.

'I don't—' Alex began weakly, fighting the calm, trying to resurrect some rationality. But then MacRob closed her eyes and lifted her hands higher and Alex saw the red-brown loop quiver. Drop an inch. Quiver again. Then it plummeted all the way down through the roiling silver air to cuff MacRob's wrists. MacRob snatched her fingers into fists. The loop shivered for a second, as if trying to break apart. Then it settled, and held.

'Miss Moore?' MacBrian said. 'Stand behind Curstag, please.'

Her body responded to MacBrian's order before her brain had a chance to intervene. The calm washed over her, the Storyline called to her and wonder outweighed doubt. Prickling from her scalp to her toes, Alex approached MacRob.

'It might sting a little at first,' MacBrian's voice said, as if from a hundred miles away.

MacRob's face was perfectly composed, but the muscles in her shoulders were straining and her skin glistened with sweat. As Alex came up behind her, MacRob unfurled her left fist and dipped her forefinger down so that its tip touched the rusty current of light.

'Put your hands on her back and close your eyes.'

Again, Alex hesitated, trying to question what she was doing, to summon her shattered thoughts, to evaluate. But as the calm flooded her lungs, her mind dissolved into pure sense. She felt the crackle of the current, the heat on her scalp, that visceral smell. And the pull, again. The pull. It knew her. She knew it, too. Alex let out her breath and planted both her palms on MacRob's slippery shoulder blades.

'GAH!' She jumped back, shaking her fingers. 'What the fuck was that?' She looked at MacRob, who hadn't moved an inch.

'Curstag has Read thousands of Storylines,' MacBrian said. 'Hundreds of thousands. All you need to do is relax, Miss Moore. Don't try to understand. Just let her do the work.'

'Are you sure you want to go on?' Taran asked, stepping forward. 'If you don't feel quite ready . . .'

But Alex was already closing back in, reaching out.

It wasn't pleasure. It wasn't pain. It wasn't sight or smell or sound or touch or taste, but all and none of them at once. It was beyond language, a multisensory data storm of images and emotions and thoughts and ideas. And there was no interface to help her navigate.

His clumsy hands, on the night of his wedding, turning his caresses into battering rams.

His mother calling him stupid boy, with real and terrible rage.

Sitting on the floor of the pantry in the darkness, spooning honey out of a jar.

157

The eyes of his daughter, which were his wife's eyes, shouting at him useless man.

His lover's dark nipples, and the feel of them: electric shame.

Decades raced past in minutes, as Alex was drenched in wave after wave of someone else's ossified past. Someone else's life, resurrected in blasts of nerve-flare and muscle-tweak and hormone. Things he had done, things he had said, things his wife and mother and lover had done and said to him. Dreams, paintings, the feeling of his bare feet on soil. The scent of perfume, a particular piece of music, abstract moments of private reverie. It wasn't remembering, fuzzy, faded and half-felt. It was vivid, urgent, immediate sensory experience – except it belonged to someone else. Some Memories passed through her light and quick. Others snagged and sank, clotted with significance. As the Memories accumulated, the Storyline moved more slowly, and Alex began to feel heavy and slow, too. Just as she was wondering how much more she could take, she felt the Storyline pause, then tremble, as if it had snagged. Pause. Tremble. Pause. Tremble again.

Beneath Alex's hands, MacRob's back expanded in a long exhale. Her shoulder blades dropped an inch. Another breath, another softening. Again. And again.

And then the one Memory that had been resisting MacRob's touch gave way and Alex tasted it, a hard little kernel lacquered by sixty years of fear. It was the sight of his grandfather's face, on the night his grandmother died. The image faded into a moment of perfect stillness. Then, out of the stillness, something blossomed. A meaning, like a single drop of essential oil on her tongue. An *I . . . a . . . an I . . . a love . . . love . . . loss . . . my . . .*

Someone was gripping her arm, pulling her away. There was a brief and horrific rush of desolation. Then the calm filled the tear and, all at once, it was done.

'Miss Moore?'

Taran was on one side, peering into her face. MacBrian was on the other, appraising her with a frown. In front of her, Curstag MacRob was rubbing her balled-up shirt over her face. The tower was dim. The cloud of sparks was gone. Alex looked up at the wall. The Story from which the Memories had released had closed over again, its skin flawless and glowing, its precious cargo trapped safely inside. As she watched, it began to slip back through its hollow, returning to the blackness behind the wall. Within a few seconds it had vanished. Except, except . . . yes, there – another silvery orb was already pushing its way out of the blackness, passing through the glass and docking into the same hollow. Another Story waiting to be Read. Another human being's entire inner world.

Alex felt a moment of pure, free-falling vertigo.

Taran moved a hand towards her, then away.

Alex opened her mouth, then closed it.

'What was the overall meaning of the Storyline?' MacBrian asked MacRob.

MacRob pulled her shirt back over her head. *'Love will make me lonely,'* she said.

The phrase shivered through Alex like a premonition, or a memory, or something between the two.

'There was resistance to being Read,' MacRob said. 'The Storyline was very old. The root Memory that it grew from was strong.'

'Likelihood that the owner will be able to stop the Storyline from re-forming?'

MacRob shrugged. 'Ten per cent?'

'That's a ten per cent chance that the Story's owner goes on to permanently disperse that particular Storyline – and the unhelpful narrative it creates within him about who he is,' MacBrian said to Alex. 'Being Read kick-starts the process, but it will be up to . . .'

'Dardan Ismaili,' MacRob said, picking up her cape. 'Male. Sixty-five. Kosovan.'

' . . . Mr Ismaili whether he takes that opportunity to dismantle the Storyline for good. Unfortunately, once they get established, Storylines are stubborn. Very stubborn indeed.'

Alex stared up at the Stories. There were so many of them, docked into the glass around and above her. So many lives – glowing, waiting, asking. She felt a hand on her arm.

'The first time is always disconcerting, even for an islander.' It was Taran, too close, his face bright pink. 'For an Outsider . . . well. The last time *that* happened was on Menikuk in 1895. It was part of an experiment by their scholarship department to secretly enlist Outside psychologists. Their very first candidate went quite insane, and unfortunately they were forced to abort the project. Although,' he added quickly, 'there's no reason for that to happen. Physiologically, I mean. Other than shock.'

Alex gazed at the thousands of oversized pearls bulging

160

out of the wall. She looked beyond them to the other distant Stories twinkling in the river of blackness, awaiting their turn. Dizziness battled with calm as the traces of a sixty-five-year-old Kosovan man's life sparked and dissolved inside her. She closed her eyes and saw red-tinted darkness perforated with thousands of pinpricks of shadow-light.

'I must say,' MacBrian's voice said, 'you're behaving very sensibly, Miss Moore. I admit that I was prepared for the worst. Now, if you're feeling strong enough, we'd like to proceed to I-537 forthwith. There's a chance that a spot of Reading-by-proxy might have helped your own Story to dislodge.'

Alex opened her eyes. 'My—'

'There's a problem with your own Story,' MacBrian said. 'That's why you're really here.' She exchanged a glance with Taran. 'Well, that and what happened to Director Mac-Calum.'

10

Whatthefuckwhatthefuckwhatthefuckwhatthefuckwhatthe-
fuckwhatthe

Out of the tower and back in the rain, all trace of calm gone, Alex couldn't decide whether to laugh or scream. Or throw up. Or all three. Her head was throbbing, her legs were shaking, and her chest felt like it had been scraped out with a spoon.

'It'll pass, Miss Moore,' MacBrian said.

The radiation sickness or the fucking existential crisis? Alex would have bellowed, if she wasn't too busy freaking out to speak. The worst part was that, beneath the rat-scrabble panic of her mind, every instinct was insisting that what she had just experienced was entirely real. More real, in fact, than anything she had experienced for a long time. You want to know about cognitive dissonance, Chloe? she thought savagely. Try stumbling across the biggest fucking secret on the planet, and see what *that* does for your psychological fucking discomfort.

'I-537 is some distance away,' MacBrian said. 'We're going to have to ride.'

Alex, who had been staring at her trainers as if they might

162

suddenly transform into ruby slippers, lifted her head. Each of the heavies who had escorted them to the tower from MacBrian's office was now mounted on a sodden yellow horse, and Iain was holding three others by their reins. Alex made eye contact with the nearest, which flicked its loo-brush tail and stamped one of its dinner-plate feet.

'No way,' she said.

'I know you must be feeling rather shaken up,' MacBrian said, 'but there are seven hundred Stacks here and we need to limit the disruption to our work. You have to understand: you being here is quite as disconcerting for us as it is for you.'

'Shaken up,' Alex echoed incredulously. '*Shaken up?*' Then, as she cast around for something – anything – that would reassure her this was all a fucking dream, she spotted her audience. There were islanders everywhere: beside, or in between, or emerging from, the towers. Some were on horse-back, some on foot. A small army of men and women, all of them in soft grey shirts, grey leggings and calf-length boots. As Alex watched, they began to cluster into pairs and groups, whispering. And not once did a single one of them take his or her eyes off her.

One of the heavies muttered something.

'Miss Moore,' Iain said, cupping his hands beside the stirrup of one of the monsters. 'Get on the horse.'

Alex got on the horse.

As their group cantered around tower after tower, forging deeper into the maze, Alex had to use all her concentration to stay in the saddle. Nevertheless, she couldn't help but glimpse white faces turning to watch her pass, or flashing up at her as they emerged from the chutes.

'What *are* you people?' she asked Iain, when they finally came to a halt beside a tower. Two guards were stationed outside. Iain lifted her out of her saddle as if she weighed nothing at all. Her feet hit the ground, her knees buckled and, to her shame, she found herself having to grab onto his meaty arms to stop herself from falling.

'What are *we*?' he said quietly. 'What are *you*—?'

'We're not anything,' Taran interrupted, shambling up beside her, having evidently overheard. Iain led their horses over to the guards without looking back. 'People from the Library islands can Read. People from anywhere else on earth cannot. That's the only difference.'

'So what did Iain mean, just now? When he asked me what I am? Not John . . . I mean, Finn MacEgan said something similar when he came to my office.' *Whatever you are.*

'Ah, well,' Taran said. 'You're special.'

'But I'm not,' Alex pleaded, searching his grey eyes. 'Honestly. I'm simply a thirty-one-year-old nobody who came up with the idea for a website. We haven't even monetized yet. Please, you have to understand, you've got the wrong . . . whatever you're looking for.'

'On no.' Taran smiled. 'You're her, alright. You're extraordinary, Alex. More extraordinary than you know.'

There was a crunch and a squelch. Alex turned to see the soles of Curstag MacRob's boots disappearing into the chute at the bottom of the tower.

'In you go,' MacBrian said, marching up beside them. She looked round, frowning, at the towers nearby.

'But I'm—'

'Quickly, if you please, Miss Moore. We're causing enough disturbance as it is.'

Alex looked at Taran, who smiled. She looked at Iain and the guards, who didn't. And there was no choice but to keep moving, to keep playing, to get on her hands and feet in the dirt and plunge into the dark.

The moment she entered the chute, Alex knew something was wrong – a wrong that was way beyond all the other incalculable wrongness that had suddenly wrapped itself around the world. Unlike the other towers, this one was sending no welcoming pull to encourage her in. On the contrary, as she slid along the stone she felt an instinctive pang of dread, an immediate urge to turn back. When MacRob yanked her over the lip, the only thing she could see was the greasy yellow halo of a lamp, placed on the ground a few feet away beside the wall. But that, she suddenly realized, was exactly the problem. In Stack I-537 there were no glowing spheres docked in the wall, no distant others roiling behind them. There was no velvety calm to soothe her hammering heart. The air was dark and dry and cold, and the only smell was that of her own fear.

MacRob walked over to the lamp and began to remove her cape and shirt, casting billowing, distorted shadows across the rock. There was a rustle from inside the chute and Alex turned to see MacBrian climb out, carrying a second lamp. Moments later Taran emerged too.

'What's going on?' Alex asked, her voice a child's squeak.

In reply, MacBrian simply nodded at MacRob. MacRob clipped the lamp onto her belt, then scooped a handful of white powder from a pouch on her belt and clapped it between her palms. She slotted her left boot into one of the spherical hollows in the wall that should have held a sphere. She reached her hand into another hollow above her head, then boosted herself up, grabbing and thrusting her way up the inside of the tower with silent, startling speed. Perhaps thirty feet up, just before the wall domed into the roof, she stopped. She found her balance in a set of indentations, then unhooked the lamp and raised it above her head.

The flames illuminated a single Story bulging out of the wall. Even allowing for the distance and the colour of the lamp, Alex could see that it looked odd: dim and cloudy, as if it had been frosted, with a sickly yellowish tinge.

She didn't need to ask. It was like the sight of her own face in a mirror, or the smell of her own skin. She just knew.

Shitshitshit. It was hers.

No. Not exactly. It wasn't hers. It was *her*.

She tried to breathe. She swallowed. She whispered: 'What's wrong with it?'

'We were rather hoping,' MacBrian said grimly, 'that *you* would be able to tell *us*.'

'Is MacRob going to Read it? Going to Read . . . me?'

'That's the problem. She can't. None of us can.'

Alex dragged her gaze away from the Story and back to MacBrian, who was studying her, unblinking, her face all angles in the flicker of the lamp. Behind her, Taran was a looming shadow. Alex swallowed again. 'Why not?'

'We're not entirely sure. As you can see, the skin has thickened, so we can't see what is going on inside. We've never seen anything like it. All of our best Readers have tried to open it, and every one of them has failed. Professor MacGill's scholars have searched centuries' worth of records, but they have found no precedent so far.'

Alex dug her nails into her upper arms. She could hear her own breathing, fast and ragged. She looked back at the Story.

Get out, she told it.

Not a flicker. Not a twinge.

Get out, she thought. *Whatever you're doing, stop it. GET OUT.*

She looked back. MacBrian was still staring at her. 'I can't—' she stuttered.

'Breathe, Miss Moore.'

'But how am I supposed to control it?' Her chest was tight. 'What am I supposed to do? I don't . . . I can't . . .'

A weight on the back of her scalp, pressing her head down. Alex closed her eyes and grabbed her thighs, hauling in shallow gasps. She heard MacBrian shout something, and lifted her head just in time to see MacRob scuttle back down the wall in a riot of rocking light. She stared at the patch of darkness where she knew her Story to be.

'Please,' she said. 'Tell me what the hell is happening. Tell me why I'm here.'

MacRob thumped down softly beside them, exhaling little

puffs of steam in the chill atmosphere. At a word from MacBrian, she gathered up her cape, jogged over to the chute and slipped silently away. MacBrian waited until the light from her lamp had dissolved in the dark, then turned back to Alex.

'Egan MacCalum wouldn't stop Reading,' she began. 'All our Directors scale down their shifts or stop Reading altogether, once they take office. All except Egan. He was one of the most accomplished Readers that Iskeull has ever known. A prodigy really. He made it a condition of his appointment that he be allowed to continue to work his usual shifts.'

'He couldn't live without it,' Taran said.

MacBrian's jaw twitched. 'Taran and Egan,' she said, 'were very close.'

The whites of Taran's eyes shone in the gloom. 'He was my best friend,' he said. 'My only friend.' He gave a humourless hiccup of a laugh. 'Oh, Egan was the first to admit that he wasn't a natural politician. He'd been pressured into standing for the Directorship because he was handsome, charismatic, a true athlete. He certainly knew the Library better than anyone. But he hated the administration, the paperwork, the endless squabbles between the island Council and the international Board. He told me it was only when he was Reading that he felt free.'

Alex thought of the statue's blank eyes, gazing out across the town to the peninsula.

'A pity,' MacBrian said stiffly, 'for his own sake, and ours. I didn't hide the fact that I disapproved of him continuing to

Read, when he had neither the time nor the energy. Others on the Council felt the same. We were all relieved when, in March last year, he finally bowed to the pressure and announced that he was stopping for good.' She paused. 'Unfortunately, as it turned out, he was lying. A fact we discovered on the seventeenth of February. Taran? I think you should take it from here.'

Taran withdrew a flask from his pocket and took several noisy gulps. 'Just after third bell on the seventeenth,' he said, 'that's ten o'clock, a young Reader called Dughlas came to my study, where I was finishing some paperwork. Now Dughlas was a sensitive boy, an orphan, impressionable, eager to please. He absolutely idolized Egan. Anyway, Dughlas admitted that Egan had been working his shifts for months. Apparently' – he glanced at MacBrian – 'Egan had told Dughlas to keep the rota unchanged, and to fabricate Reading records for each shift.'

'Reading records?' Alex said faintly.

'Ah, yes. We have details of every Reading that has occurred, give or take the odd slip-up, since the system was introduced – in the International Library Administration Treaty of the 1580s. It's all there, noted in the records, stored in the archives, cross-referenced in the index. The data the Chapters have collected over the past few centuries has transformed our knowledge of the Library and helped improve our work.' The whites of his eyes were shining again, but this time with fervour, not grief. 'Some of us believe that the world's strongest Storylines will combine, over time, to create some great text of wisdom. Others, like Sorcha here, believe that such theories are sentimental nonsense. Nonetheless, we do undoubtedly observe high-level collective Story behaviours that can—'

'Taran,' MacBrian said, 'this is not the time for science fiction. Could we stick to the matter in hand?'

Taran sighed. 'Well, as Dughlas told me the whole sorry tale, it was obvious that he had been thrilled to be taken into Egan's confidence. To be made his accomplice, if you will. At first. But as the months wore on, he began to feel increasingly guilty, and anxious about what would happen to him if anyone found out. What's more, he complained that Egan had become increasingly distracted and short-tempered as the year went on.'

'An observation,' MacBrian, added darkly, 'not restricted to Dughlas MacFionn.'

'I must admit that Egan did not seem . . .' Taran paused, twisting the cap on his flask back and forth. He blinked several times. 'I knew him better than anyone. We had trained together. Even when we were boys he far outstripped my abilities. But then I was always more interested in ideas than in the act of Reading itself. And when I was appointed Head of Scholarship, and Egan became Director, well . . . He might not always have understood the importance of the work we do in the archives, but I was still the one he confided in. The one he came to, when he needed to let off steam. But even with me, over those last few months, Egan was . . .' – twist, twist, twist – 'not entirely himself. I've wondered whether I should have paid more attention, probed harder, but then we always had so much work to discuss. And I had distractions of my own.' He looked down at the flask as if he had only just noticed it, and shoved it back in his pocket. 'My sister is not well.'

There was a short pause. 'The night of the seventeenth,' MacBrian said.

'Yes.' Taran inhaled sharply. 'Well, that night, apparently, Egan had been particularly strange. Called Dughlas in here, accused him of conspiring with Sorcha to depose him—'

'Which is of course nonsense,' MacBrian added. 'I had no idea what they were up to.'

'Threatened to get Dughlas banned from the Library if he ever betrayed his confidence, shouted at him to leave. It seems that Dughlas's conscience and, yes, perhaps his wounded pride, finally intervened. So he came to me.' He paused. 'I will always regret that I didn't immediately tell someone else, or go to the Stack myself straight away. But Egan . . . I knew better than anyone how badly he craved Reading. How much he needed it. I didn't want to be the one to take that away. So I thanked Dughlas and told him I would talk to Egan, then went back to my paperwork.' He shook his head. 'I couldn't concentrate. I knew something wasn't right. So I held out for two hours and then I left the archives and made my way out here.' He looked up into the dark. 'When I poked my head up out of the chute into the Stack – this Stack – everything looked normal. Your Story was open, and Egan was standing in the centre of the floor, right there, Reading its heaviest Storyline. Certainly I could see that he was struggling. His body was shaking, and it was clear that the Storyline was very old and powerful. The Memories were resisting – they did not want to give up the pattern they had formed for so many years. Nevertheless, the Storyline was moving, albeit slowly, circuiting his wrists. He was getting through it, Memory by Memory, steadily coaxing it apart. But then he reached the root Memory at the heart of the Storyline, right in the middle of the figure-of-eight. He stood there, touching that Memory, for a long time. His knees looked ready to buckle. Then he took a deep breath, and I thought it was about to yield. But then, before I could understand what was happening, the whole world turned silver-white.

'I can only have been unconscious for a few seconds. When I opened my eyes, I was back in the chute, wedged in like a cork in a bottle, face-down. I was in great pain, but it must have saved me, being flung back beneath the earth like that. I slowly managed to pull myself back up the chute and into the Stack. And the first thing I saw was your Story. It was right up there in the wall, like it is now. Your Memories had flown back inside it, just as they normally do at the end of a Reading. And your Story's skin had closed. But it wasn't undocking. It seemed to be stuck. And all the other Stories docked into the wall around it were sliding away. They weren't simply returning to the blackness behind the wall. They were riding its currents all the way down to the sea of Library energy that lies deep beneath the earth. They didn't want to be anywhere near this Stack. It was like they knew they might be in danger. Like they knew that something they didn't recognize had happened here.' He paused again, his expression inscrutable in the lamplight. 'I've never seen anything like it,' he said quietly. 'Never imagined it was possible.

And then I looked down. And I saw him. I saw Egan.' He gestured at the ground beneath them. 'He was lying right there, on his back.'

Alex looked down, as if she might suddenly see the statue's beautiful face shattered under her soles.

'I hauled myself across to him as quickly as I could,' Taran said. 'He was still breathing. I said his name, and after a moment he opened his eyes. He managed to say three words – Dorothy, Moore, London. But a minute or two later, he died.'

Alex couldn't look at him. She couldn't look at either of them, or at the floor where the man everyone loved had died. She certainly couldn't look at the wall where the thing – her thing, her wrong, hideous thing – lurked. She pulled her cape around her tightly, as if she might be able to hold together with a piece of cloth the world that she knew. She stared at her feet until the silence stretched so thin she could hardly breathe.

'Look,' she said, 'I'm sorry that my . . . my Story thing is somehow mixed up in this. And I'm *really* sorry about what happened to your friend. But this all sounds like a horrible accident.'

'No.' MacBrian sighed. 'Certainly, it seems that Egan was going through some kind of personal crisis. The pressures of the Directorship are intense, and he had been dealing with them for fifteen years. He was no longer a young man. Perhaps, just perhaps, his skills were beginning to fade. He may well have been getting frustrated that Reading was becoming harder for him than it once was. But' – she paused—'but,

Miss Moore, Egan could not have caused this damage, either to you or to himself. He could no more *do* anything to your Story than you could control him using psychic powers. That's simply not the way the Library works. The very skill of Reading requires us to suspend our own Stories. To become a neutral physical conduit, so that someone else's Story can take a few minutes of time and space outside the Library to reorganize. We cannot change so much as a single Memory in someone else's Story. If we tried to Read in any other way, the Story we were working with would simply close.'

'So what are you trying to tell me?'

'Egan died from a surge of energy to the chest. All our doctors agree. A great blast, which essentially disintegrated his heart.' MacBrian paused. 'Now, everything we know about the Library tells us that this is impossible. Stories draw on the energy of the Library to make Memories and form Storylines. Nothing more. Nothing less. They cannot direct that energy in any way. They certainly cannot use it to kill. Except that is exactly what seems to have happened, with yours. It seems that your Story somehow took advantage of Egan's weakened state and . . . well.'

There was another silence. Alex felt utterly disembodied, as if she was gliding through some weightless new atmosphere.

'Anyway.' MacBrian cleared her throat. 'As soon as Taran alerted us to the tragedy and reported Egan's parting words, Iain sent a team over to our base on North Ronaldsay to research who the owner of this renegade Story might be. It was not hard to find out – thanks to all the information available online nowadays – that there are twenty-three Dorothy Moores currently alive and living in London. Identifying which of them was the Dorothy Moore we were after, however, was far more difficult.

'Of course we had no idea whether this person knew what she had done, or whether she intended to do it. The Chapters are scrupulous in maintaining the secrecy of the Library – you can only imagine what would happen if it became a pawn of the world's religious leaders and governments. Yet many on the Board feared that there had been a breach, somehow, and that the killing of the European Director was the opening salvo in a larger attack. And so we decided to invite as many Dorothy Moores as possible to Iskeull, interviewing them under the guise of GCAS. We even tried sending some of Iain's men out into the field to investigate. However, as you have seen for yourself with Finn MacEgan, that is an ineffective approach. The same genetic quirk that gives Library nations the ability to Read keeps them tied to their islands, you see. All Iskeullians are born with a unique Storyline that connects them to Iskeull. The same goes for the Menikuki Readers and the island of Menikuk, the Gavians and Gave, the Yíngzhōuese and Yíngzhōu, and so forth. If anyone here spends more than a few days away from Iskeull, a terrible form of homesickness rapidly cripples both their body and mind. So, frankly, I was starting to believe we faced an impossible task. Until a new lead surfaced this Monday.'

Alex thought of the questions Not John Hanley – Finn

MacEgan – had asked in her office four days before. She said, numbly, 'The interview in *Flair*.'

'Precisely. The team found an article that revealed your true name. A name you had kept concealed throughout your adult life.'

'But I didn't *conceal* it!' Alex looked from MacBrian to Taran, pulling the cape around her even more tightly. 'Look, are you seriously suggesting that ever since I told my family to call me Alex – when I was eleven years old – I've been hatching a grand plan to become some kind of . . . evil psychological murderer?'

'It wasn't just your name,' MacBrian continued steadily. 'It was your account, in the same interview, of how dramatically your life had changed that night. It had all the hallmarks of a successful Reading, an *extraordinarily* successful Reading. The coincidence was too great. I convened a meeting of our Council and consulted the Board, and we formulated a plan to bring you here.'

Alex could feel her Story lurking there above her in the dark. *GET OUT*, she told it. *GET OUT. GET OUT.* She took a step back into the shadows, shaking her head. 'Look, I'm sorry.' Her face was hot, her heart banging in her throat. 'I wish I could help. But I have a business to run, I have responsibilities. I have *deadlines*.' She glanced up at the wall one last time, then back at MacBrian and Taran. 'I'm not going to deny this has been . . . I mean, *fucking hell*. I don't know how I'm going to – how I'll be able to . . . But that's the point, isn't it? You're the ones born to all this. The ones with the centuries of scholarship, the ninja skills. So if something has gone wrong here, I think it's clear that it's *your* responsibility to sort it out.'

Before they could reply, she turned and strode back towards the chute, breathing hard. She heard the clank of lamps as MacBrian and Taran made to follow, but she was on her belly and sliding under and up before they could reach the opening. She clambered out and started walking back along the path towards the rotunda's distant dome. Not running, but walking, with fake-calm determination. It must have confused the heavies, because no-one grabbed her.

For exactly twelve seconds. She counted.

But when Alex turned to yell at whatever testosterone-pumped lackey had taken hold of her wrist, she saw that it was MacBrian. The Director had an expression of such open desperation on her face that it stopped the shout in Alex's mouth. Iain was already running over, but MacBrian turned and barked a command. He jogged, frowning, to a stop. In the distance, Taran's dishevelled head popped out from under the tower.

MacBrian turned back to Alex. 'Please,' she said. 'Please listen to me. I believe you. I do. I believe that you did not do this consciously, or with malice. And I will make sure every-one here understands that, too. But do you feel this?' She dropped Alex's wrist and lifted her own palms to the rain. 'These storms are flooding our fields. They're rotting our crops, endangering the lives of our fishermen. Whether or not you intended it, this is happening because of you. The Library is part of the fabric of this island, part of our stone and our water and our earth. The health of the Library determines the health of the island. And every day your Story is stuck in that Stack, it gets worse.'

Alex shook her head. 'Shut up,' she said.

'Even if you don't care about us,' MacBrian pressed on, her voice husky with urgency, 'you must care about your family. Your friends. Whatever happened with your Story has triggered a total shutdown in I-537. Not a single other Story has surfaced within that Stack for the past six months. As long as your Story is still docked in that wall, they're simply refusing to come up. That's a million people who have had no chance to be Read, any one of whom might be your mother, your father, your fiancé.'

Alex shook her head. 'I don't want to hear it.'

'Dorothy—'

'Don't call me that.'

'The problem is bigger than you can imagine. The Library runs deep, deep beneath the earth. Every Stack is connected, in every Chapter across the world. With I-537 out of action, the entire Library has started to slow. All over the globe, people are stagnating, entrenching, falling back on old Storylines rather than having the courage to change and grow.'

'So what are you saying?' Alex opened her eyes and gave a high, quavering laugh. 'You're saying that I'm . . . what – just sort of really slowly fucking up the entire human race?'

'Then there's you,' MacBrian added quietly. 'You saw the state of your Story in there. And we saw how you reacted when you tried to recall the night Egan died. Who knows what damage is going on behind that clouded skin? For all we know, whatever has happened inside your Story is slowly destroying you, too.'

At that point, because she could think of nothing better to do, Alex sat down. The mud seeped up around her, soft and cool. MacBrian had fallen silent, although she could hear Iain muttering gruffly somewhere. The rain pattered onto her hood and dripped off the brim, gradually filling the cradle of her lap. Her trainers were sodden, her socks soggy. Her feet were very cold. She tried to think of her father. She tried to think of her mother; of Harry, of Mae, of Bo. She tried to think of Finn MacEgan, and the anguished look on his face when he had asked her why she killed his dad. She tried, briefly, to think of everyone in the whole bloody world.

But right at that moment all she could think of was strong, powerful, extraordinary new Alex and her harmless little episodes.

11

'Professor MacGill?'

Behind Iain's shoulder, a plump young man was bouncing up and down, waving. He caught Alex's eye and gave her a beaming smile. Hustled back through the rotunda, she'd kept her head down at first. Then she hadn't been able to resist glancing up and had seen them ogling her from their desks, peering down from ladders, craning around cabinets like birders in a hide. Some of them looked unmistakably hostile, but others, particularly the younger ones, were whispering and gesticulating excitedly.

'Some of us were wondering, Professor,' the plump young man called, 'whether we might be permitted a few minutes with Dorothy Moore?'

Iain took a step forward.

The plump young man danced back. 'As President of the European branch of the Story-surging Society,' he shouted, darting sideways, 'I think it's only fair that some of our members get a chance to—'

But Iain was on him, twisting the collar of his tunic, strangling the rest of his sentence. Taran rushed over, exclaiming. After a moment's hesitation, Iain loosened his grip. Grasping

Iain's wrist with both hands, the young man wriggled round to glare at MacBrian.

'Story-surging is a legitimate theory,' he gasped. 'It's the only theory that fits. You can't silence us just because you disagree with us. Is that what happened to Dughlas, Director? Did that poor boy say something that you and your personal guard dog here disagreed with? Did he worship your predecessor a little too strongly? This isn't a dicta-torsh—'

Iain twisted again.

'That's enough,' MacBrian snapped, the red spots burning on her cheeks. She gestured sharply at Iain. 'Enough. All of you. Get back to work. Taran, I'd thank you to control your department. We don't have time for histrionics.' She hustled Alex through the fossil-encrusted door and past her secretary, to whom she barked a terse command. Inside her study, she went over and stood with her hands on the big table for several seconds, with her back to Alex. Then she turned and pulled out one of the wicker chairs. 'Please,' she said. 'Sit down.'

Cautiously Alex sat, shedding flakes of drying mud. The rain was loud on the dome overhead. She had no idea what time it was. She had reached a stage of shock and exhaustion that was almost pleasant in its numbness.

'What did he mean: what happened to Dughlas?' she asked. 'Wasn't he the one who fabricated Egan MacCalum's Reading records? Did you punish him, then?'

'No,' MacBrian said. 'I did not. And I'd thank you to keep the information about the Reading records to yourself. No-one knows about Dughlas's involvement in Egan's death, outside of the Council and Egan's immediate family. The time straight after the – accident – was a period of deep instability, and Egan had already been cast in the role of tragic hero. The Council made it clear to me that smearing Egan's name would only make things worse. In any case, Dughlas was just a boy. *Is*. A poor deluded boy. But unfortunately, last week Dughlas disappeared.' She sat down, pulled her notebook towards her and began flipping through the pages. 'We have no idea what's happened to him, although my detractors will find any excuse to place outrageous accusations at my feet. Personally, I fear the worst. Dughlas obviously blamed himself for what happened. And I very much hope he hasn't done something rash. But, frankly, his disappearance is a complication we could do without.'

Alex took a moment to digest this, and failed. 'And what did he mean, about Story . . . Story . . .'

'Story-surging,' Taran said, shutting the door behind him. He came to sit on the other side of Alex, looking more rumpled than ever. 'I apologize, Sorcha. Ailbeart didn't mean any harm. None of them do. They're excited, that's all. And he's right, of course. It's increasingly clear that Story-surging is the only viable explanation for all this, however unorthodox it may be.'

The numbness was fading. A nest of snakes stirred in Alex's belly. 'What,' she asked, 'is Story-surging?'

Taran looked at MacBrian. MacBrian sighed, then nodded. Taran shuffled his chair closer to Alex. 'The concept of Story-surging has been mocked by traditionalists for centuries,' he said, 'as have many of our most creative ideas. Ideas such as Memory-sharing, Story-hopping, even *Editing*.' He paused, eyes shining, as if expecting Alex to dredge, from her choking miasma of incredulity, some new and special kind of amazement. 'These ideas have mostly survived in the form of fiction, because it is appallingly hard to secure funding from the Council for proper research.'

'*Because*, Taran,' MacBrian said wearily, 'there has never been any actual evidence to suggest that those ideas are anything other than a fantasy.' She hesitated. 'Until . . .'

Taran smiled broadly. 'Exactly, Sorcha. Until now.' He drew a circle on the table and stabbed at the middle of it with one bony forefinger. 'The more open-minded among us, Alex, have always believed that the Library is slowly evolving. That, at a certain point in the future, Stories are bound to start displaying different behaviours, that they might even develop new powers. And that's exactly what I think is happening with your Story. I believe that your Story is the very first to surge.'

'*Surge?*'

'Until now, Stories have only been able to use the energy of the Library as fuel, to create Memories and Storylines. But according to the theory of Story-surging, Stories will at some point also learn to push that energy *outwards*, beyond their own skins and into the physical world. And that's exactly what your Story appears to have done. It blasted Egan with Library energy. It *surged*.' His finger shot out of the circle and across the table towards Alex, making her jump. 'We've been in close contact with our international counterparts on the other islands, and we haven't found evidence that any other Stories have surged. Yet. But if Story-surging did become widespread, the Library could become the greatest generator on earth. Perhaps even the universe. The development of Story-surging would effectively allow us to harvest some of our vast collective mental energy. To use it as a *tool*. Even a weapon, you might say, although' – he gave a conspiratorial smile – 'the hope has always been that it could be harnessed positively. And not just to keep light bulbs shining, or cars on the road. You yourself have felt how potent this stuff is, from the tiny amount of radiation that leaks into the Stacks. You recall that sense of endless possibility? That calm? Imagine the potential uses. If Stories start to surge Library energy out into the world, and we can find a way to collect and administer it, Library energy could be used in all sorts of ways. To create a fruitful atmosphere for political negotiations. To treat mental illnesses. Perhaps even as a widespread pharmacological supplement, to increase the empathy and creativity of our entire species. Moreover, certain scholars recently suggested that Story-surging might evolve in parallel to digital technology. That it represents the response of human consciousness to artificial intelligence. And the timing of your . . . display appears to prove them right.'

Alex stared at him. The snakes twitched.

'In other words,' MacBrian said, 'your Story may have somehow learned to project its energy beyond the boundaries of the Library and into the outside world. You might be the first person ever born with a Story that can surge.'

Alex closed her eyes and pressed her fingers into her lids,

lighting up a halogen map of veins. 'Let me get this straight,' she said. 'First you tell me I'm a killer. Now you're telling me that I'm some sort of psychological mutant?'

'No, Alex, no,' Taran insisted. 'You're not a mutant. Not at all. You're a *pioneer*.'

Alex opened her eyes. The snakes began to thrash. 'But what does that *mean*? What does this *all* mean? For me?'

'If the Story-surging theory *is* correct,' MacBrian said, glancing at Taran, 'it is, in some ways, good news. It gives us an idea of how you might be able to dislodge your Story from the wall of the Stack. If you can do that, the other Stories should return, all those poor people will be Read and Iskeull's climate will stabilize. What's more, you might even learn to direct and harvest your Story's energy in new and productive ways, as Taran suggests.'

'Oh. Right. And how exactly am I supposed to do all that?'

'Well. If – and only *if* – the theory is correct, we know what triggered your Story to surge. Your Story only unleashed its fatal blast of energy when Egan tried to Read one particular Memory – the Memory at the heart of your oldest and strongest Storyline. It follows that, to gain control over this new talent your Story has acquired, you have to get hold of that root memory. That's where the trigger for this new surging power lies.'

Alex put her head in her hands. Tried to breathe deeply. Tried to think. 'Get hold of – which means what, exactly?'

'It means that you must identify the narrative that dominated your life, up until February. The one that changed so abruptly the night Egan died. And then you must understand the key event or experience that caused that narrative to form, and why.'

Alex looked up incredulously. 'You mean . . . you're saying that I have to save the world with a *self-help exercise?*'

'Not at all.' MacBrian was shaking her head. 'It won't be enough just to name that Storyline. You'll have to *feel* your way into the very heart of it – not only with your brain, but with your Story. This is not something that can be done with a book or some deep breathing. It will require true self-knowledge. Deep emotional insight. Thankfully, we have something that should help.' MacBrian withdrew a red index card from between the pages of her notebook and slid it across the desk. 'This is your Reading record.'

Alex stared down at the indecipherable runes inked onto the feint-ruled card. She remembered mistaking it for a book-mark in their interview the day before. The interview that had happened a million, billion light years ago.

'You're lucky,' MacBrian said. 'Some Stories present them-selves to be Read regularly, but many never surface at all. Your record tells us that you've had one previous Reading, back in 2005, from one Greum MacTormod. Unfortunately, the record gives us no details about which Storyline he tack-led, because it was only partially Read.'

'And what does *that* mean?'

'It means you're a feinter.'

'A *what?*' Alex looked up from the runes.

'Your Storyline broke apart before MacTormod could complete a full circuit and penetrate its root Memory. Ordin-arily, that would mean that, despite being dissatisfied enough with your life to surface your Story for Reading, you lacked the conviction to follow through. However, if Taran's Story-surging theory *is* correct, you may in fact have been trying to protect MacTormod. By feinting, you might have been trying to prevent him from reaching the deadly mutation at the heart of that troublesome Storyline.' MacBrian sighed. 'I spoke to MacTormod back in February, when we first retrieved the records for all possible Dorothy Moores. Unsurprisingly, he doesn't remember one specific feinting Storyline from ten years ago. But the record does still leave us with one crucial piece of information. The date.' She leaned over and tapped a stubby finger on the card. 'The question is, Miss Moore, what happened to make you reassess your life on Saturday the sixteenth of July 2005?'

'Seriously?' Alex said.

'Seriously,' MacBrian said.

Alex looked at Taran, who nodded, flashing her a nervous smile.

Alex looked back down at the impenetrable marks on the card. She could barely remember what she had been doing last Monday, let alone one day in July ten years ago. And the harder she tried to remember, the sicker she started to feel.

She sat back. 'No. I'm sorry. This is all too much. I can't—'

HOW AM I SUPPOSED TO FISH ONE ANCIENT FUCKING MEMORY OUT OF MY BRAIN WHEN EVERYTHING I THOUGHT I KNEW ABOUT THE WORLD HAS BEEN TURNED INSIDE OUT?

'Take your time,' MacBrian said. 'Think again.'

Alex swallowed. She looked back at the runes.

'Classic reasons for a Story to surface,' MacBrian said, 'include getting a job, failing to get a job, the beginning of a new relationship, the breakdown of a relationship, reloca-tion—'

'Wait.' Alex suddenly stiffened, goose pimples shivering across her skin. 'Shit,' she breathed. 'Shitshitshit! Dom. Dom's thing in New York.'

'Dom?' MacBrian prompted, turning her notebook to a new page.

'Dominic Bernam. My dad's literary agent. My godfather.' Alex frowned, trying to fan the flicker of recollection. 'Shit. Yes. That was the day Mum threw a surprise lunch for my dad, because it was the anniversary of this list of hot young writers he'd been put on twenty years before. Dom took the opportunity to announce that he'd found me a job. Dad's big novel was published the year after I was born, you see. Dom had seen me grow up. He was always trying to look out for me. His agency was starting a new office in New York, and he had somehow managed to arrange me a bottom-rung position – if I was willing to go.'

She stopped. The thought of Dom, of her father, of her mother – even of her mother's noisy, nosy friends drinking Pimm's on the patio – made her want to sob. And now the vertigo was starting to take hold, making MacBrian's and Taran's faces blur and slide, as the details of that long-past afternoon clarified.

'So you decided to move to New York?' MacBrian asked, writing hard.

'Oh . . . no. No, I . . . I turned him down. I'd just accepted a job in an IT firm in the town where I grew up, the same place I'd always temped in the holidays, and I . . . Well, it's difficult to imagine now, but back then, I didn't like to stray far from home. It's difficult . . . to remember' – she took a deep breath – 'exactly why I wouldn't have jumped at . . .'

MacBrian was nodding, oblivious, head bent over the page. 'It has all the hallmarks of a Reading trigger. And which Storyline, which narrative about yourself, would this job offer have threatened so very much?'

Alex swallowed. *Here and now. Here and now.* 'Like I told you before, perhaps it was . . . perhaps a sense that I'm never good enough? Fear of change? A belief that anything new I tried would . . .' But it was too much. The void cracked open, freezing nothingness whistled through her chest, and the world tilted and slid. She gripped onto the edge of the table, trying to anchor herself to the cool stone. 'I can't . . .' she murmured, 'I can't . . . I get these – these episodes . . .'

'Like the one you experienced yesterday, when you tried to recall the moment of Egan's death?' said MacBrian's voice, from a long way away.

Red card. Round table. Wicker chair. Glass dome. Iskeull. The Library. My Story. Holy fucking fuck.

It took a long time to come back, this time. When she eventually opened her eyes, MacBrian was watching Taran sketch out some kind of messy diagram.

'Alex,' Taran said, looking up. 'How do you feel? How does it feel when that happens?

'Here.' MacBrian reached for a decanter in the middle of

the table, poured an inch of amber liquid into a tumbler and passed it across. Alex mutely accepted the glass. She sipped, then dissolved into a coughing fit as the burning taste of bacon and fag-ends slammed into the back of her throat. 'I'm . . .' she choked, trying to find the words to describe how utterly not alright, on all levels, she was.

Taran nodded. 'It's . . . fascinating, quite fascinating to observe. Can you tell us exactly when these episodes occur?'

Alex turned the tumbler in her hands, watching the whisky slosh.

Hadn't she known? Honestly, hadn't she known all along just how deeply wrong the episodes were, whatever Chloe said about cognitive dissonance?

'Whenever I try to remember,' she murmured. 'They happen whenever I try to recall anything that happened before that night, I mean before the Director was . . . I mean, before the seventeenth. I can pull up the basics – images, sights and sounds – but if I try to remember how I actually felt . . .' She took another sip of the whisky, felt it start to sedate the snakes.

'You see?' Taran said to MacBrian, slapping his diagram. 'You can't deny it any longer, Sorcha. This really is the beginning of a new era for the Library. For humanity. Everything fits.'

Alex looked up. 'You think this is part of it, isn't it? It's all part of that . . . Story-surging thing.' She lifted the glass to her lips, then downed the remaining whisky in a single gulp and gasped, 'Am I going to die?'

MacBrian sat back in her chair with a heavy sigh. 'Quite

honestly, we don't know. Taran believes that these episodes are a self-protective mechanism that your Story has activated. He thinks it might be restricting your access to your own Memories, in order to stop you identifying the one that has mutated, and thereby gaining control over its ability to surge.' She sighed again. 'Precisely what impact it's having on the rest of you, however, we can't say.'

Five, Alex thought, glancing up through the glass dome at the coal-coloured clouds overhead. It couldn't be much more than five hours until her ferry left from Kirkwall. 'Please,' she whispered, 'please. I've tried to help you. I've told you all I know. Just let me go home.'

'Trust me, I wish we could. But you have to unstick your Story, Miss Moore. For your sake, as well as ours.' MacBrian reached for the decanter beside her elbow, hesitated, then poured herself a measure and knocked it back in one efficient shot. 'Fortunately, we do have three clues as to the nature of this crucial Storyline. The first two come from your Reading history. We know that the job opportunity your godfather offered you in 2005, and the promotion you were offered by your employer this February, both challenged this Storyline enough to make your Story surface. And there are obvious themes linking these two incidents, as you say – themes around fear of commitment, reluctance to change, lack of belief in your abilities, and so forth. Those help us understand what it's about.' She flipped back through the pages of her notebook. 'But we also have a third clue – a hint about *when* the root Memory that originated this particular narrative might have formed.'

Alex looked longingly at the decanter. 'We do?'

'You mentioned in our interview yesterday that a major change in your self-belief occurred around the age of eleven, when you changed schools and also changed your name. You said, and I quote, "I started to build up this narrative that everything I did was doomed to fail."' MacBrian looked up from her notes. 'That's a powerful description of the genesis of a new Storyline. And, by your own admission, it's exactly the narrative that exploded when Egan Read you on the night of the seventeenth.'

Oh God. What was it her mother had said at lunch? *It reminds me of that summer you were eleven, when you moved to St J's. All of a sudden my happy little girl seemed to turn into this miserable shadow overnight.*

'Okay.' Alex said slowly. 'So this thing was hiding inside my fear of failure? And you think it had been there since I was *eleven years old?'*

'Yes, fear of failure, or something similar. Unfortunately, without full access to the relevant Memories, it will be impossible for you either to identify the exact nature of this Storyline, or connect with its root Memory in any meaning-ful way.' She closed the notebook. 'I think the time has come for us to consider our back-up plan.'

'Sorcha,' Taran began. 'Sorcha, she can't—'

'No, I'm sorry, Taran. Nobody's going to like it, but con-sidering we've already gone this far, I can't see what we have to lose.'

'But she's tired, she's already weak, I'm not sure—'

'I get it,' Alex interrupted bleakly. 'I'm not stupid. If a

Story's essentially my consciousness, then it dies when I die, right? So if I can't get it out of the wall of that tower, you will have to kill me.'

'*Kill you?*' MacBrian stared at her. 'What on earth gave you that idea?'

'Come on.' There was a high, thin ringing in her ears. 'One small mutant sacrificed, one fucking massive planetary problem solved.'

'Miss Moore,' MacBrian said.

Alex fought the urge to laugh.

'Miss Moore.'

Molars grinding, Alex met MacBrian's level gaze.

'We do not kill people, Miss Moore. The International Library Covenant of 1122 states that every Story is of equal and inestimable value. It is our job to protect them. That's one reason we go to such lengths to ensure the Outside world remains ignorant about the Library. You have to understand that we are the servants, not the dictators, of mankind.'

Another airless silence.

'So if you're not going to get out the shotgun,' Alex finally croaked, 'what exactly is the back-up plan?'

The rain finally dribbled to a stop. Alex pushed back her hood and paused at the top of the cliff path to see a double rainbow blossoming in the bruised sky. Freed from its battering, the air filled with the scent of herbs and seaweed and salt, and seconds later a gull-like bird with white-tipped wings dive-bombed her hair.

Taran stopped his descent and glanced back. Behind her,

she heard Iain's tread fall silent. Beyond that, she could hear the distant clink and rustle as their horses grazed heather beside Taran's house, a dilapidated-looking hulk of stone on the promontory above.

For a moment she could almost pretend she was alone, with the early-evening breeze swelling her lungs and the babble of nature filling her ears. Hundreds of miles away, in the garden in Fring, her mother's dahlias would be bobbing their blowsy heads. The sweet chestnut would be ripening its conkers over her father's bench. The wood pigeons would be cooing their throaty lullaby. All unaware that the child that had grown up beneath their impassive gaze was a . . . a what? A mutant? A killer? The villain, as it turned out, in the sort of mindfuck fantasy that would merit its author a place on the Novus Young Novelists to Watch list?

Oh, Daddy, Alex thought, as the breeze shivered the hairs on the back of her neck: real neck, real hairs, real breeze. *Not even your brilliant brain or your big arms can save me from this.*

Had Egan MacCalum known, as soon as her Storyline had locked around his wrists, that he was going to die? She kept seeing him, lying on the cold floor of the Stack while the pulsing lights around him went out. Had he stared up at the Story that had killed him, wedged in the wall like a tumour, while his heart struggled to process its fatal blast? Had he heard Taran drag himself across the stone, and summoned the last shreds of his strength? Had he been determined to hold out until his friend could reach him, hoarding the name of the woman who had killed him inside his mouth like a coin?

According to these people, she was a unicorn. A mermaid. An impossible creature that existed only in books. Although they were the ones who should be a myth. But then she had felt for herself the ancient truth of the Library. She had seen that thing stuck in the wall. She had unquestioningly known it to be hers. And she couldn't deny that, six months ago, something unnatural had happened inside her. Hadn't she always known, deep down – despite Chloe's spiel about turning points and latent potential, despite all her own patter about talent and karma – that change simply didn't work like that?

Alex pictured her Story, lonely and damaged in the dark. She pressed one hand over her heart and another across her forehead, and tried to feel her way in from outside.

LET GO, she thought. PLEASE. LET GO.

But her heartbeat was just her heartbeat, and the words were just words, after all.

You're a couple of cows, her mother said, *you and your father. Always chewing your own cud. Get out into the world, darling. Muddy boots, clear mind.*

Alex lowered her hands. The rainbow, which had started to blur, came back into focus. Fixing her eyes on it, she set off again down the path and, after a moment, Taran moved off ahead. Both Iain and MacBrian had tried to insist that a walk was too risky, considering the general anti-Alex sentiment on the island. But then Taran had suggested the isolated cove below his house, on the other side of the causeway, and Alex had refused to back down. Now, however, she wondered whether she secretly wanted to be spotted, abducted, lynched. Wasn't it only what she deserved?

The path was rough, twisting steeply between banks of willow scrub and lime grass. For a while Alex had to focus all her attention on navigating the pits and humps. Then they rounded a sharp turn and the cove appeared: a deep white horseshoe stamped into the foot of the cliff, ridged like bark and riddled with worm casts. It was as deserted as Taran had promised, bracketed by jagged spines of rock, the water riddled with oily patches suggestive of deceptive cross-currents below.

When she stepped down onto the beach, however, she found that the atmosphere was surprisingly calm. To the north a high russet escarpment, layered with sediment and guano like a giant red velvet cake, blocked the worst of the wind. The cliff behind, tangled with pink and yellow flowers, created a fragrant cradle for the air. Alex shrugged off her cape and, without asking either man for permission, began to run.

Her trainers were sodden within seconds, but she continued right down the length of the beach and back again, pumping her arms, savouring the crunch and the spray. Only when her brain was as numb as her toes and her side was burning with stitch did she slow, panting, and come to a halt in the threadbare lace where the breakers met the shore.

Above her head, puffins growled in their nests. In front of her, waves flung diamonds into the sky. Off to one side, on a jut of black rock, a shining jumble of seals jostled and argued. It seemed unbelievable that a few minutes' flight to the south would take her back to Kirkwall, with its tourists and cars. That an hour north would deposit her in Scandi-lands, full of gaming start-ups and next-gen smartphones. Gradually her exhilaration faded and her breath steadied, and the sound of the surf was again drowned out by the desperate patter of her mind. As the gunmetal sun dropped into the gunmetal sea, Alex felt, inch by inch, the cold, hard forever of Egan MacCalum's death lodge itself inside her bones.

'How do you feel?' Taran asked from behind her.

HOW THE FUCK DO YOU THINK I FUCKING FEEL?

'I still don't get what I'm supposed to do, tomorrow,' she said. 'How I'm supposed to get inside my Story – *physically*.'

Taran came round to face her and started, excitedly, to say something about micro- and macro-manifestations, but when he finally logged her expression, he stuttered to a stop. 'Honestly?' he said. 'We can't explain it. We never have been able to, not fully. But that's the beauty of the Library, Alex. There are so many mysteries, as you yourself are proof. We're only just starting to scratch the surface after all this time.'

'So you're asking me to go into something – or is it a somewhere – you can't explain?'

Taran gave several hiccupy laugh-gasps. 'Forgive me, but you haven't been able to explain the workings of conscious-ness for the past thirty-one years, and I doubt that bothered you for one minute. What matters . . .' He trailed off. Alex turned to follow his gaze.

A distant figure, hunched against the wind, was peeling away from the escarpment and striking out along the shore: a small black comma, curled against the ashen page of the sea. There was a crunch and Alex turned to see Iain, coming up on her other side. As the shape drew nearer, Alex realized it was a woman. She looked lost in thought, her eyes fixed on the ground and her bowed head haloed by a dark corona of hair.

Taran swore under his breath. He said something to Iain and jogged gracelessly off.

'Stay here,' Iain murmured, moving round to Alex's side.

As Taran got close, the woman's head shot up and she came to an abrupt halt. She half-raised one hand, although when she noticed Alex and Iain, she slowly let it drop. Taran approached her with his arms spread, as if he was trying to herd a wary dog. As soon as he reached the woman, he took hold of both of her shoulders and tried to turn her back towards the escarpment. She shook him off, pointing at Alex and Iain. Taran shook his head and tried to turn her again. She began to shout, her voice drifting across the bay.

'Who is that?' Alex asked.

'Just stay where you are,' Iain said.

Taran grabbed the woman, and for a moment Alex couldn't work out whether he was trying to hug her or wrestle her to the ground. Then he stood back and she saw that he was now holding a palm-sized rectangular object. The woman stamped one foot like an angry child and pushed at Taran's chest. He held his palms up, still clutching the object, apparently trying to appease her. But then she ducked under his arm and started to run towards them.

Iain wrenched Alex behind him and pulled a nasty-looking leather truncheon from the back of his waistband.

'Iain!' Taran pounded up, pink-faced and tousle-haired. He seized the arm of the woman, who had already stopped several feet in front of them and was staring at Alex. Taran said something low and fast to Iain. Iain, not taking his eyes off the woman, growled back.

The woman looked exactly like Taran; or rather a beautiful female version of Taran. Set against that storm-coloured cloud of hair, the long face, strong nose and wide mouth were compelling rather than ungainly. What was lanky in him had become statuesque in her. But she also looked haggard beyond her years and, now she was close, Alex caught the unmistakable whiff of alcohol, steaming from her skin and her clothes.

The woman licked her lips and said something slow and hoarse. Taran turned away from Iain, keeping hold of the woman's arm. They exchanged a subdued back-and-forth. Alex realized that the object in Taran's hand was a leather-bound flask.

'Um,' Alex said, 'what the hell is going on?

'You're the one, then,' the woman said in English, turning back round. Her words were ever so slightly slurred. 'You're Dorothy Moore.'

'Al – oh, never mind,' Alex said. 'Yes. Whatever. I'm the evil Dorothy Moore.'

'Evil?' The woman's big grey eyes tried to focus. 'They

said you didn't mean it, in the gathering down in town, at lunchtime. They said you didn't know. They said you were giving your full cooperation.' She smirked at Taran. 'Or so I heard. I wasn't allowed to go.'

'Where's Cait?' Taran asked, his hand still on her arm.

'She had to leave. Beitris came and told her that Finn had been taken to the guardhouse.' She looked back at Alex. 'They say he tried to kill you.' She shook off Taran's hand. She leaned forward. 'What is it like?' she whispered, her breath sweet and stale. 'In London? What's it like, living Outside?'

'Freya.' Taran retook her arm.

She ignored him. 'Did you come here on an aeroplane?' She seemed to be trying to drink in Alex's face. 'How many aeroplanes have you been on? Have you been to America? Have you seen the desert? Tokyo?'

'Freya!' Taran hissed, then added a pleading tumble of Iskeullian.

'Is there someone you love in London, Dorothy Moore? Is there a man waiting for you, ready to show you the world?'

Iain said something and stepped forward. Taran replied, shaking his head, and managed to yank his twin around. Eventually she gave a shout, threw off his arm and began to tramp away across the beach towards the path. Every few paces, she turned back to look.

'I'm sorry,' Taran said, once her hunched back had disappeared round the turn up the cliff. He was bright pink. 'I had no idea she would be here.'

'She's your sister.'

'Yes.'

'Your twin.'

Suddenly seeming to realize that he was still holding the flask, Taran slipped it into the pocket of his cape. 'Yes. She shouldn't have been out here alone. Freya is . . . not well.'

Alex studied the professor's flushed face. As he gave her a reflexive smile that didn't reach his eyes, she realized how easily he could be one of the data wonks she met in London on a daily basis. He had that same combination of unnerving intensity and evangelical obsessiveness, leavened with the endearing vulnerability of the lifelong underdog-nerd. 'Can I be honest?' she asked. 'She seems to be the first sane person I've met. I mean, if I was born here, I think I'd probably spend most of my time blind drunk. How the hell do the rest of you cope?'

Taran shrugged. He waved towards the sea. 'Everyone gets to visit Kirkwall every three months, for a couple of days. We get monthly shipments of Outside books and magazines, English translations from all over the world. We import medicine, of course. We bulk-buy stationery. We correspond with our international counterparts. We try to remain as self-sufficient as possible, for security's sake, but we're not entirely cut off.' He looked down, kicked a pebble. 'Some struggle. Most find it's better not to think too much about Outside at all. Others, like Egan, go the opposite way: hoard Outside stuff, write about the people they've Read. Egan used to order things for Freya. He thought he was helping her, but really it only made her worse. If *I* can be honest, Alex' – he looked back up, his eyes silver-bright – 'Outsiders are the ones I feel sorry for. What's the point in being able to travel the world if you never get a glimpse inside the control centre of the human mind?'

Everything, Alex thought, desperately. The taste of a place when you first get off a plane. The embrace of an unfamiliar climate. The freedom of walking through streets surrounded by thousands of people you don't know. The stink of New York. The heat of the desert. The noise of Tokyo. But it seemed, suddenly, too cruel to say out loud. And it was taking her dangerously close to tears.

Behind them, Iain growled something.

Taran sighed. 'Yes. It's getting late. They'll want you back for training. We should go.'

Over the sea, the light was fading to purple-grey. Exhausted and cold as she was, Alex suddenly dreaded having to leave the horizon and head back inside.

'Alex?'

No tears. If you start, you'll never stop.

'Alex?'

NO TEARS. 'Fine. Let's go.'

She couldn't trust herself to speak as they started back along the shore, Taran gabbling about Story-surging again, Iain trailing a few silent paces behind. Through the dozens of questions churning in her head, the one that finally popped out was: 'What's going to happen to Finn MacEgan?'

Taran stopped talking. 'He's been charged with breaking the Covenant. They'll allocate him an advocate, put him on trial before the Iskeullian Council and then refer him for sentencing to the international Board.'

'What happens if they find him guilty?'

'Most likely he'll be assigned to some sort of manual labour, moved into supervised housing. All Outside trips revoked.' He paused. 'I hope you don't mind me saying this,' he added slowly, 'but I will do everything in my power to get Finn released. Being banned from the Library will be more than enough punishment. Reading is Finn's whole life. He's wanted to become a full-timer ever since he was a tiny boy. What he did was foolish, but he was grieving. Lashing out at you was an impulsive mistake.'

'I am sorry, you know,' Alex said after a while. 'About what happened to his dad. More than you can know.'

Taran looked out to sea. 'It's not your fault.'

'But this thing's part of me, isn't it? Part of who I am? Shouldn't I have been able to stop it, somehow? Like I did the first time with that Greum guy back in 2005 when he tried to Read my Story?'

'I believe,' Taran said, 'there's a greater force than any individual at work here. I think it would have found its way out, one way or another, even if it had been delayed for a few more months or years. You're part of something enormous, Alex. You're the instrument of mother nature. Of *evolution*. You're the vanguard of a change that began with one terrible, terrible tragedy, but that could in the long term have unimaginable benefits for us all.' He sighed. 'I like to think that Egan would have taken solace in that. I like to think that, even in the moment of his death, he might have realized that it wasn't a waste, but a brilliant sacrifice.'

Alex followed his gaze out to the horizon. 'Did MacBrian

mean what she said? About letting me go home? As long as I go down there tomorrow? Even if I can't . . . get it under control?'

'You don't believe her?'

'Finn told me not to trust her.'

'Finn was upset. And Sorcha . . . well, Sorcha . . .' He grimaced, glancing over his shoulder towards Iain. 'Let's hope she knows what she's doing.'

'Oh, great.'

'I'm sorry. We're sailing in uncharted waters, with you.'

At the top of the cliff the wind hit her, flinging hair into her eyes. Taran went to untether his horse while Iain helped Alex clamber on. As they rode away, she looked back over her shoulder at Taran's house, at the smeared windows with their rotten-looking shutters and lichen-bearded sills. Then the horse jolted from a trot to a canter and she had to focus on not falling off. But before she turned around, she was sure she had seen a glimpse of a white face in one of the windows, staring back at her from beneath a halo of storm-cloud hair.

12

Darkness rolled over Alex's head, heavy as a wave. She released her grip on the last swaying rung and thumped onto the ground. There wasn't the faintest bleed of light, despite the fact that Taran and MacBrian were standing with lamps on the edge of the hole less than ten feet above. She tried to shout up to them, but although her lungs did all the right things, the darkness swallowed the sound.

Breathing down a swell of panic, she turned back to the tunnel. Her eyes battled to focus, convinced the darkness might suddenly solidify into a biting thing. The ground beneath her trainers was steeply sloped and as springy as a forest floor. When she stretched out her arms, her fingers brushed against fibrous walls that felt like they were made from aeons of compacted fossil and root.

Just keep going. That's what MacBrian had said. Alex's senses were screaming at her to reach for the rope ladder dangling above her head. They were begging her to climb straight back up into the cramped normal-darkness of the tomb that lay above. This was the tomb they'd ridden to straight after breakfast, cantering along the boggy paths between the Stacks through the relentless morning rain. The tomb that was hidden beneath a low grassy mound, right in the centre of the maze. The tomb that concealed the mouth of this tunnel, which led – they said – into the depths of the Library. At the end of the tunnel – they said – she would somehow be able to enter her own Story, gain access to all her Memories, and be able to Read her screwed-up Storyline. They'd said a lot of things to her over the past twenty-four hours. She was no longer sure which of them she believed, or even understood. Except for *just keep going*. She understood that one. It was one of her mother's favourite pieces of advice. And it seemed pretty much her only option, in the circumstances.

So instead of trying to scramble back up to the waiting islanders, she took one tentative step forward. Then another. Then another, with one hand still brushing the wall of the tunnel and the other stretched out. This was the bargain, she told herself, as she stumbled down, trying not to imagine suddenly touching something warm and wet and soft. If she did this, they'd promised to let her go home. Which meant that every step she took was a step closer to freedom. To sanity. To a world where accessing your consciousness was something you did in an evening class. All she had to do was walk.

At first she tried to count her strides, but she was on such primal high-alert that the slightest sound – a gurgle from her guts or the scrape of a stone underfoot – sent her straight back to nought. This blackness wasn't simply an absence of light. It was alive. She could feel it breathing with her, probing and pressing her, as if she was being digested in the belly of a giant snake. And as she walked and walked and walked,

Alex slowly felt herself becoming the one thing she'd been trying to avoid since the moment she was born: alone.

This wasn't the pleasant solitude she felt pounding the Hackney streets, when she sometimes imagined a camera was recording her movements to a jaunty rom-com soundtrack. Nor was it the aching emptiness she had felt the morning after her first and last one-night stand in her narrow university bed. This loneliness was older and deeper, primordial and brawny. It threatened to unleash all the monsters that a life-time of dinners and books and soft furnishings had tried to fend off.

Alex thought about her father. She thought about her mother. She thought about Harry, Mae, Lenni, Dom. She rifled through the headshots of the Eudo team, shuffled through her pack of work contacts, brain-checked old family acquaintances and called up the faces of reliable bit-players in her life. She recalled the barista in the cafe over the bridge, the homeless guy outside the off-licence near her flat. She even tried to summon the thousand miniature smiles of her digital not-quite-friends. But the figures came out flat and dead, like shadows jerking out of a zoetrope. The bul-wark of people she had built up around her, back on the surface of the earth, had failed. No-one was coming to save her; no-one could. This was her tunnel. This was her dark.

Alex walked. And walked. And then walked some more. More than once, pausing to swipe the cold sweat on her forehead with her sleeve, she found herself experiencing a wave of full-body paralysis. It took all her willpower to resist the temptation to sit down and never get up. Calves and thighs cramping, outstretched arms aching, she lost all sense of distance and time. As she grew tired she began to stumble: skidding against a patch of loose rocks, catching her foot in a hoop of root. Her palms became grainy with scree, her elbows raw, the water flask in the back pocket of her jeans ominously light.

It smelled dank and earthy and ever so slightly of that metallic musk that she remembered from Dardan Ismaili's Story the day before. If Chloe were here now, Alex knew she would say that the definition of insanity was doing the same thing over and over and expecting a different result. But then Alex's concept of insanity had grown rather baggy over the past thirty-six hours, and putting one foot in front of the other seemed the only sensible thing left to do.

Of course it *was* still possible that all this was happening in her head – super-realistic sense data and primordial instincts aside. Perhaps she had crashed, in Iain's ridiculous plane. Perhaps she was strapped to a bed in Kirkwall hospital, tripping on heavy-duty painkillers. Her mother and father might be standing above her right now, clinging to each other and weeping while they watched her eyelids flicker, willing her to wake. Perhaps, just perhaps, if she tried hard enough . . . If she relaxed every muscle and breathed really deep, she would be able to simply open her—

'Fuck!' Alex felt rather than heard the shout inside her head as the blackness slammed into her face. She staggered back in a fizz of pain, grabbing at her nose with one hand while she flailed with the other to ward off attack. It took a few seconds of stumbling about, banging into the walls, before she realized.

She'd found the door.

They'd been telling the truth, then. The tunnel wasn't just a very long grave. And the door to her Story – if it was indeed her Story – was exactly as MacBrian had described. It was firm but not rock-hard, slightly rough and faintly warm. Sweeping her hands over the surface, Alex felt the dip and curve of carved letters and used her fingertips to trace the words.

Dorothy Alexandra Moore.

They were right about that, too, then. Although neither MacBrian nor Taran had been quite able to describe how, exactly, this one tunnel could take whoever travelled down it to their very own Story, every time. Mouth dry, heart leaping, Alex pressed both palms against the door and pushed. It shifted, then jammed. She put her shoulder against it and shoved with all her might. It remained firmly stuck.

She'd asked them about this, as well.

'If my Story is sealed from Readers,' she had said, opening one eye from where she stood in the middle of MacBrian's office, 'what makes you think I can get in?'

'Because you're still coherent,' MacBrian had replied, watching MacRob hoick Alex's arms back up above her head with a frown. Alex had always been rubbish at sports, and it was looking increasingly likely that she would prove no better at Reading than at netball. Even holding the basic Reading posture for more than a few seconds seemed beyond her. 'If you were shut out of your own Story, you'd have lost all language, all sense of self. You'd have gone insane.'

'It seems likely,' Alex had said, irritably shaking off MacRob, 'that I have.'

'For Library's sake,' MacBrian, who was visibly losing her headmistress cool by the minute, had snapped, 'we don't know what's going to happen when you try to Read yourself, Miss Moore, but you'll simply have to try. For your sake, as much as ours. *Try.*'

But trying, it seemed, wasn't going to be enough. Even though she had proved to the Library that she was 100 per cent committed to Reading her own Story, by dutifully slogging all the way down into its subterranean guts. Reading someone else's, up above ground in the Stacks, was starting to look easy in comparison – give or take a special gene or two, and decades of training. She braced her shoulders against the door, dug in her heels and strained with all her might until her back almost gave way. Panting, she rested her hands on her knees and gazed back up the tunnel.

Was that really it, then? Game over? Return to Go, a dozen miles uphill in the dark? Do not collect the Shield of Self-Knowledge or the Sword of Truth? Traipse back up and beg the Games mistress to give you another Life?

Alex turned and rested her damp forehead against the door.

A heartbeat later the door swung inwards and she was floundering forward into thin air, scrabbling at nothing. An updraught of warm wind scoured her face and her pupils contracted with the sudden transition from dark to light. Her right foot found solid ground, but the left continued to grope, sickeningly, for purchase, until her vision began to clear and she found herself staring down at a narrow walk-way suspended above a fathomless abyss. Panicking, she tilted sideways even further. And for a moment it was as if it had already happened: the slip and the fall and the endless weightless tumble through the buffeting air. But then she managed to grab onto the doorframe, plant her left foot next to the right one and steady herself.

Alex clung to the slippery doorframe, her eyes fixed on her feet, her heart hammering. The walkway was narrow and the currents blowing up from the chasm were strong. She could still climb back through. She could still change her mind. But as the telltale taste of salty copper crept into Alex's mouth she felt the calm wash through her, a hundred times stronger than it had been in Dardan Ismaili's Stack. She tried to blink away the last of the dazzle, until she realized the darkness itself was shimmering. She looked up.

'Room' wasn't really the word. There was no floor, no roof, no walls. The only architecture, if you could call it that, was the walkway she was standing on, which terminated in a small circular platform fifty feet from the door – although quite how she was supposed to move along it, without any-thing as sensible as a handrail, she wasn't sure. The walkway was made from a cream-coloured matt substance that looked suspiciously like bone, and its surface was being lapped from above by washes of rainbow light. Alex looked higher.

Fuck fuck fuck fuck fuck.

There had to be hundreds of thousands of Memories

scintillating in the blackness high above the platform. In constant succession – so quickly that she could barely distinguish one from the next – silvery sparks from all over the chamber were swarming into loops, orbiting in bursts of colour, then shattering back out. It was so beautiful it made every hair on her body stand up in salute. So powerful it made her want to fall on her knees and stammer out a prayer. And, beneath the awe, she felt once more that eerie sense of déjà vu, as if she'd been in this immeasurably vast, deeply intimate place countless times before.

She raised her arms to either side, improvising a tightrope-walker's pole. Then, taking a deep breath, she stepped out across the walkway. The calm blew against the backs of her legs, roiling up over her shoulders and buoying her towards the platform. And now, pupils dilating, she realized that Memories were forming right before her eyes: pinpricks of silver, blinking out of the air. They were, presumably, what she was seeing and feeling and thinking right now. Memories, she thought dizzily, about Memories. The new Memories were darting up to join the Storylines forming and re-forming overhead. But as soon as any of the newborn sparks touched a Storyline, the loop would give a discordant flash and burst apart. She was evidently struggling to fit this experience into what she thought about the world. About herself.

She took another step along the walkway. She was barely conscious, now, of the chasm below, and the calm carried her forward until she reached the centre of the platform. Dropping her head back, she gazed up at the Storylines far above. A twist of mint-green was rotating so fast its Memories had dissolved into one smooth blur. Moments later it exploded in a glittering spray, giving way to a silky lasso of blue and grey; then a short ochre cable; then a loose loop of pinky-red. But she could already see there was something not quite right about these Storylines – at least compared to those that had emerged from Ismaili's Story the day before. Whereas his had shone with a clear, almost unbearable radiance, hers gave off only the faintest cloudy bloom. It was as if they were coated with a layer of glaucous mould. And then, as Memory after Memory was sucked inexorably into a new Storyline, she knew, without a doubt, that she had found what she was looking for.

It was twice as fat as the others and as big as a python, so dense that it was entirely opaque. Stuttering round sluggishly in a muddle of yellowish-brownish-greenish shades, it emitted an even dimmer, sicklier glow than all the rest. It hung above the platform for several minutes, much longer than any other Storyline. Then, when it finally broke apart, the Memories sheared away heavily, in uneven plasmic clumps.

'Remember,' MacBrian had said, 'you don't have much time. You won't just be exposed to radiation in there, you'll be immersed. The sooner you get through this, the sooner you can go home.'

Home. Remember home. Time to press play. Level one: Practice run.

Alex tried to gather her whirling senses. She shuffled her feet until they were hip-width apart. She went through the routine MacRob had shown her: unlock knees, drop weight, relax shoulders, lift arms. She pulled calm deep into her lungs fifty times, and fifty times let it out in a long exhale. By the time she had finished, she felt as still as stone, as heavy as earth, as light as air. Her mind sank and spread into a cool, glassy pool. She floated in it for a moment, breathing in stillness until every cell was washed clean. Then she looked up at the Storyline that had formed above her – a pale-orange braid. She closed her eyes. She dropped its image into the mind-pool. She raised her wrists.

The Storyline locked on almost instantly, barely an inch from her skin, blood-warm and crackling. Instinctively, Alex jerked back. Her eyes sprang open, and she found herself staring at a silver mist of Memories, already swarming back up into the darkness above.

'Reading your own Storylines is a perfectly natural process,' MacBrian had said. 'You don't need the genes and the skill that are required to Read someone else's – just a little attention. The important thing is not to react. Don't think too much. Don't judge and don't reach. Just let go.'

Don't think too much. Just let go.

Alex got back into position and closed her eyes. It took her longer this time to establish the rhythm of her breathing, to still the last stubborn skitters of her mind. But the calm did its work, and after a while she was able to sink back into the mental pool. By this time the sheared-off Memories had re-formed into the hideous python. She wasn't about to touch that until she'd got the hang of the others, so she had to wait until it had once again slowly sloughed apart. As soon

214

as the next Storyline gathered – a long mauve lasso – she shut her eyes and offered up her wrists.

This time, when it cuffed her, she tried to focus on nothing but the sensations: the tingle, the energy, the warmth. Carefully, she bunched her hands into fists. The current held. She felt a rush of victory, then immediately felt the energy flicker and ebb.

No, wait . . . No. Don't panic. Don't think.

She latched back onto the familiar cycle of her breath.

Don't think. Don't reach. Just let go.

Her pride dissolved. The wind picked up, eddying around her ears, lifting her fringe. Slowly, Alex uncurled her right hand and twitched her forefinger towards the current. She felt an electric nip on the fleshy pad and then – *Ohhh*.

She was twenty-three, having lunch with her mother in John Lewis on Oxford Street. Alex was staring at a Caesar salad while her mother ranted about a family friend, who had recently caught her husband cheating for the second time. 'The thing is, darling,' her mother was saying, 'love is as much about what you *don't* as what you do. It's about the impulses you resist far more than the grand gestures you make. Your father might not buy me flowers; in fact he often neglects to say a single word from breakfast until dinnertime. But I know he would never purposefully do anything to hurt me, and that's everything, Alex. Everything.'

Back on the platform, Alex's stomach lurched. There was something wrong. The details drawn out of her Memory were as vivid as the crispest HD – she could see the brown

215

edges on the iceberg leaves, taste the salty cream of the dressing, feel the hard seat of the chair. But it all somehow felt empty. Fake.

Even if she hadn't experienced the rich, fatty savour of Ismaili's Memories, she would have known, with some visceral instinct, that hers were deeply flawed. Reading them was like encountering something both hers and not-hers, like scratching at her own dead leg. Alex felt a spasm of revulsion. But now that the Storyline had locked on, it had its own momentum and, before she could pull away, the next Memory was there.

She was in the maternity ward of West Middlesex University Hospital, staring down at Mae. Her friend was propped up in bed, pale from blood loss, cradling a mole-rat swaddled in a pale-blue beanie and a bear-print onesie. Mae was pulling off the beanie to show off Bo's thick black cap of hair. Alex was reaching out a finger to touch the baby's scurfy cheek.

Again, every Memory was as smooth and shallow as plastic. Again, Alex tried to wrench her wrists apart, but the hold of the trance was too strong. She simply had to stand there and take it, as the Storyline jerked on in a unchronological tumble: watching *Lady Chatterley's Lover* at a teenage sleepover; walking down the aisle as a bridesmaid at her cousin's wedding; hearing Harry propose on New Year's Day; listening repeatedly to a Bryan Adams song in her bedroom; kissing Joe Vickers at Fring youth club. And although the Memories were as vivid and detailed as real, in-the-moment experience – she could see the exact blue of her childhood sleeping bag, feel the itchy fabric of the bridesmaid's dress, smell the bergamot musk of Joe Vickers's CK One – not a single one of them inspired a single tweak of emotion, good or bad.

Yet still the Storyline lurched forward, Memory by Memory. She was watching her guinea pig die; masturbating to online porn in the attic; finding herself sitting beside a gorgeous man in a bus stop, the day she first moved to London. Alex had no idea how many Memories had passed through her when, without warning, she suddenly felt the current snag. Here it was: the root Memory that had first formed the Storyline. As MacBrian had instructed, Alex tried to stay centred and focus on her breath. After a few moments she felt it bulge, then give.

She found herself aged seven, sitting alone with her paternal grandmother in the living room of her grandparents' New Jersey house. She was blinking at the acrid cigarette smoke and listening to Gramma explain how the only man she had ever really loved had married someone else.

For all its sensory detail, the root Memory was as emotionally bland as the rest: a dull plastic bead in place of Ismaili's richly lacquered jewel. Nevertheless, as the image faded and the Storyline stalled, Alex felt a swell of hope. This was the moment when the Storyline's meaning was supposed to emerge. But what came out, with a retching heave, was not a profound personal truth, but a sickening, sliding afterbirth of almost-meanings and half-words.

Quite simply, her Storyline didn't make any sense.

Trance broken, Alex let her hands fall down by her sides. When she opened her eyes, the shattered loop was already beginning to re-form, far above her head. She felt weariness wash through her, lapping up around the edges of the calm. She realized that she was panting, her jumper soaked with sweat. Distantly, she became aware of a faint throb in her shoulders, her arms, her abs, her knees.

What the fuck? What the actual fuck. This wasn't supposed to happen. According to Taran, the problem lay in her recall, not in the Memories themselves. Memories were supposed to be perfect, inviolable storage units of consciousness. The whole premise of the back-up plan was based on the fact that Reading her Memories, from inside her Story, should have allowed her to bypass whatever was blocking her recall. But from what Alex had just experienced, it was clear that her Memories weren't being blocked.

They were damaged. Rotten, from within.

The issue wasn't that Alex's mental search engine was faulty. The very files she was trying to retrieve were corrupted.

Fingers shaking, she pulled out the flask. As she took a long drink, she noticed that there was a thin blue leather thong knotted around her wrist.

'There is a danger,' MacBrian had said on the edge of the shaft, briskly tying the knot, 'a real danger that you won't come out. Reading your own Story is highly addictive, and the energy inside the Library masks the physical toll it takes. Let this bracelet be a reminder to you. You have to stay focused. You do one trial run. Then you Read that mutated Storyline. You find its root Memory, the one that surged at Egan. Then you get out.'

But MacBrian hadn't discussed what to do if the Memories

themselves were screwed. Although she *had* been right about the addictiveness. Despite the nauseating wrongness of what she had just experienced, Alex could feel a deep, muscular craving for another Read already tugging away inside. Horror fought with hunger, and it took less than ten seconds for the hunger to win.

There was a purple figure-of-eight circling vigorously overhead. Alex settled back into the posture and breathed in calm until her mind grew still. She felt her whole body sigh as it found its level. Then she shut her eyes, let the image cohere and hungrily raised her wrists.

Nothing happened. She opened one eye. The Storyline was still there, orbiting fifty feet above, but it showed no sign of coming to her call. She closed her eye again. She mentally traced its amethyst curve and reached higher, demanding it lock on. Nothing.

She felt a stab of impatience. The tension in the air slackened. She opened both eyes, only to see that the Storyline had disappeared, replaced by the silky grey-blue lasso she had seen before. She gave a little groan, feeling the craving tweak at her guts, and realized that she was wanting rather than waiting. Trying to pull the Storyline in, rather than letting it dictate the pace.

Don't reach, MacBrian said. *Just let go.*

Alex redistributed her weight, shrugged her shoulders up to her ears and dropped them back down. She studied the Storyline. She closed her eyes. She raised her wrists.

She breathed into the words. *Let go. Let go. Let go.*

It locked on. As she closed her fists, she felt a pang of

mingled anticipation and dread. The current wavered. She exhaled and let the moment of emotion fade. The current held. Slowly, she uncurled her right fist and dipped her forefinger down.

She was walking across the airfield with MacBrian, feeling the rain prick her scalp and sensing her hair start to frizz; she was fidgeting in the wings before going on stage at a conference two years before, tying and retying her ponytail; she was fourteen, hacking at a tangle with a pair of scissors; she was walking out of the salon in March, feeling the lightness of her new haircut; she was staring at a Pre-Raphaelite painting on a school trip; she was scrolling past an online image of unruly seventies pubes; she was pausing on a black-and-white movie still of Jean Seberg.

Empty, all empty. Memory after Memory was slippery, glassy, bleached. Even the last, tough root Memory at the heart of the Storyline – a sleepover with a girl she had known at primary school, with beautiful auburn curls – prompted no emotion at all. And when, eventually, the moment of suspension came, the meaning that slithered out was another dismembered, nonsensical mess.

Alex found herself back on the platform. Her toes and fingers were cramping, her legs wobbling dangerously. But it was only a few seconds before the calm rolled back in. Before she could question what she was doing, she had looked up for the next Storyline and closed her eyes.

The more she Read, the stranger she felt – both sick and excited, as if she had binged on too much greasy junk food. Every Memory was slick and hollow; every Storyline ended with an abortive jumble of nonsense and a horrible come-down. And yet Alex still felt a twisted compulsion to keep Reading. She held up her wrists again and again, like a child poking its tongue into a toothless gum.

She was about to launch into her fifteenth – fiftieth? – Storyline when her legs gave way. Her left hip hit the plat-form, hard, and her head banged down against bone. She lay on her side for a few shocked moments, then dragged herself up to sitting. With detached surprise, Alex observed that her body was shuddering, her skin drenched, her throat parched. When she reached for the flask, her hands shook so badly that it took her several tries to pull it out of her pocket. And it was only when she tilted her wrist to drink that she noticed the strip of blue leather tied around her wrist.

The what?

Alex stumbled to her feet. The calm was already obliterat-ing the pain, and the craving for the next Read had started up more sharply than ever before. Yet MacBrian's low-tech safety mechanism had broken the spell.

God knew how long she'd been down here. And however badly she wanted to stay in the warm, radiant dark of her Story, Reading every Storyline, she knew it wouldn't be long before she was too weak to climb back out.

She couldn't avoid it any longer. She had to progress to Level Two: Bad Storyline time.

It took Alex far too long to get into the zone. Time after time, she managed to breathe herself down. But as soon as that murky snake re-formed in the glittering air, a spike of fear would rupture her composure and she'd have to start all over again. Eventually, by the tenth or fifteenth time the bad Storyline reappeared, she found she was too tired even to be afraid. And at that moment – the very moment when she'd lost all hope – the calm simply scooped her up and buoyed her back into that clear pool.

Alex shut her eyes and raised her arms.

13

'Yes?'

Alex stared at her newly purchased replacement phone, which was flashing manically as a backlog of messages downloaded from the cloud, and found herself suddenly incapable of saying a word.

'Hello?'

Alex gazed around the cafe. There were so many people, slamming and shoving and slapping things around. The tinny blare of muzak collided with dozens of ringtones. The air stank of coffee, cinnamon, body spray. She ran a finger under the filthy blue strap around her wrist. Surely, if anyone would believe her, it would be him.

'*Hello?*'

Her father would be standing at the hall table in his slippers with a mug of black coffee, the landline handset wedged beneath his chin. Her lifelong safety net. Her staunchest ally. Her rock. But that was the problem. He loved her too much. If he found out what she really was . . . Alex swallowed the lump.

'Dad,' she said as brightly as she could. 'It's me.'

'Well, well. Hello there, Kansas. How's life in the fast lane?'

'I've – I've been away.'

'Your mother told me. Some college in Scotland?'

'Orkney.'

'Ah. Hobnobbing with the Vikings.'

Alex looked at the fingers curled around her cardboard cup of cooling cappuccino. The same fingers that had traced the walls of the tunnel. The same fingers that had Read – whatever it was she had Read. 'To be honest, Dad,' she whispered, 'it was all a bit odd.'

'That's academics for you.'

Alex put down the coffee and fiddled with a napkin on which she'd written *Dad/Mum. Dom. Chloe. Mae. Harry*, with the waitress's pen. 'Do you guys have plans over the next couple of days?'

'Why? Could Ms Founder-CEO be thinking of visiting Fring?'

'Yes, yes, I need to – talk to you both. There are some things I need to . . . that I'm trying to remember for this research project.'

'That sounds mysterious. Well, if your mother has made plans, I'll cancel them.'

She blinked. She swallowed. She drew on the napkin, beside the list, a wobbly figure-of-eight. 'Dad?'

'Mmm?'

'What would you say drives me, as a person? Like, which one narrative would you say has most shaped my life?'

A pause. 'What kind of a question is that?'

'Just humour me. What would you say?'

A long pause. 'Kansas . . .'

224

'Fear of failure? Commitment phobia? If I was a novel, what would the blurb say?'

'Alex. What are you asking me?'

'Or say I was a film. How would the voiceover start? "Alex Moore had spent her entire life believing . . ." What?'

'Sweetheart—'

'Dad, do you think I'm a bad person?'

Another long pause. 'I don't think there are good people and bad people, Alex,' her father said slowly. 'I think there are just things we do. And I also think that all of us make mistakes.'

'But some mistakes change everything.' Her voice had grown dangerously high.

'Alex—'

'No, forget it. I'm being stupid. Sorry, Dad. We'll talk when I see you. I'm tired.'

'*Alex*—'

'No. Please. Ignore me. Tell Mum I'll let her know when I've booked the train. I—' she squeezed her eyes shut. 'I love you.'

Swiping at her eyes, she googled the offices of Bernam Keene Literary Agents and asked to be put through to Dom. He was delighted to hear from her and would put himself at her disposal all evening; the Crystal Pistol Crime Novel of the Year Awards could, apparently, go hang. Chloe didn't pick up, so Alex sent a text asking if they could meet. Mae's mobile was engaged. Finally she called Harry, who picked up at the first ring.

'Alex! At last! Are you okay? I thought you were due back yesterday. What the hell happened out there?'

'I . . .'

'Alex?'

'I'm sorry. It's . . . complicated. I got ill. I had to reschedule. I've just come off a flight.'

'Are you okay?'

Alex stared bleakly at her coffee. 'I'm fine.'

'I must have left twenty, thirty messages. Texts, calls, emails.'

'Yes. I saw.'

'You warned me that the signal might be bad, but there's no way they didn't have wi-fi.'

'I'm sorry. They—'

'I know I suggested that you get some space, but I didn't expect you to disappear entirely.'

'I'm sorry. Really.'

A pause. 'I didn't mean we were over, Alex. I just wanted you to take stock, do some thinking. I didn't want you to . . . I apologize if I gave you the impression—'

'Please, Harry, it's fine. It was me. My fault. I simply – couldn't call.'

Another pause. 'Alex. Tell me truthfully. Did you meet someone out there?'

'What?' Alex thought of Finn MacEgan close up against her in the archive room; his breath on her cheek, that sinewy arm locking her in place, the anguish radiating from his hot flesh. She wondered whether he was still locked up, or whether Taran had already persuaded them to let him out.

226

She wondered if he still hated her as much as he had. 'Oh no,' she said miserably. 'Quite the opposite.'

'Really? Because it sounded like—'

'Harry.' She thought with exasperation back to herself, on the train three days ago, merrily laying the bait. So arrogant. So naive. 'You've got nothing—' Her voice broke, and she had to take a moment before she could speak again. 'You've got nothing to worry about.'

'I'm glad,' Harry said eventually. 'I'm more than glad. I was seriously worried, Alex. When I didn't hear from you, and you didn't come back, all these ideas came to mind, all these awful images and—' He stopped. 'Look, I *do* owe you an apology. In fact, I've been doing a lot of thinking myself. There are some important things I want to say. Will you come over this evening?'

'I'm sorry. I'm seeing Dom tonight. But I need to speak to you, too. Ask you some questions for this thing I'm working on. Tomorrow?'

'I want to see you tonight. I want to see you now. But if tomorrow is best for you, tomorrow it is.' Another pause. 'I can't wait to see you. It's felt like a very long time.'

Alex gulped. She tried to speak. Eventually she managed to whisper: 'I know.'

She sat in a daze on the Heathrow Express, picking up voicemails while she watched the industrial parks whizz past. One of them was from Hackney police. She called the number they left and was transferred to Commander Holland of Special Operations, who explained that the tests on Alex's shoe – her impromptu weapon – had, unfortunately, returned 'corrupted DNA'. In fact, the lab technicians were very keen for Alex to come into the office and answer some more questions about her assailant. Alex explained that she was in the middle of a family emergency and promptly hung up.

On Paddington concourse she kept bumping into people, tripping over bags, letting chuggers thrust leaflets into her hands. As she passed through the barrier into the Underground, she saw a pale, dark-haired man all in black run towards her, and froze. But he was too old, he was Asian; he was swerving around her and smacking his Oyster onto the sensor next to hers. As she stood staring after him, the barrier snapped closed against her stomach, exploding into angry beeps. The TfL man, coming over to let her through, muttered, 'Wake up, love.'

The Tube was crammed and stifling. Alex found a handhold near the doors and stood swaying, staring at the tunnel, her reflection superimposed with blue-and-white sparks. Her legs were weak, her breath shallow. She wondered if she was about to faint.

'Good afternoon, darling.'

A large Jamaican woman was hanging onto the loop beside her, fanning them both with a magazine. Alex smiled politely and looked back at the door. Seconds later the front cover of the magazine appeared, hovering under her nose: a photograph of a child reading a book on a beach, and a headline: 'Discover the Word of God – It Is Alive!'

'Have you read the story of our Lord?'

'No. I mean, yes, I have, but no, I'm not interested, thanks.'

'Oh, but it can save you. It can save your soul, line by line.'

Alex turned. The woman was watching her with deep, hooded eyes.

Quietly Alex said, 'I have no idea what you're talking about.'

The woman bent closer. 'Don't you understand, darling? I've been sent to you. I'm here to help.'

Alex glanced at the vacant faces around her. 'You mean,' she whispered, leaning in, 'you're from *the Library*?'

The woman straightened up and sighed, re-rolling the magazine. 'Next stop, darling. Get out at King's Cross and follow the signs.'

At the co-working space, they'd changed the key fobs. Lenni came down and fetched Alex from the lobby.

'Thought it was a sensible precaution, after the scene with the Opa! guy,' he said as they entered the lift. 'So. What the hell happened out there?'

'It's . . . complicated.'

'You said the signal might be bad, but we didn't expect you to go completely off-grid.'

'I know. Nor did I.'

'Okay, whatever. I hope it was worth it. Gemma's drafted a press release, though she found it hard to work out exactly what this research project's about. Their website's prehistoric.

But good for a vlog at least, I hope? You got some nice photos? Ponies, sweaters, bogs?'

'My phone broke.'

Lenni sighed. 'Well, I've cleared all my meetings this afternoon, and if you work through the evening we might just triage the worst.'

'Oh. I have to go and see someone tonight.'

Lenni gave her a look. 'Alex. I understand that you needed a break, but now I need you to focus. You'll barely have enough time to prep for tomorrow as it is, and there are some serious issues I need to bring you up to speed with. You're a leader now.'

'Please, Lenni. I'm not – I'm just—'

Lenni pursed his thin lips. 'You know Harry called me when you were away?'

'Harry? Why would Harry call you?'

'He wanted to know if I'd heard from you, apparently. And he wasn't exactly friendly about it, either.' Lenni shrugged. 'Look, I get it. It can be a tough juggling act. But you're playing with the big boys now, Alex. You can't afford to be held back by people who don't understand.'

The doors slid open and Alex followed Lenni out across the sixth floor. Eudo people began to scramble up from their desks, clasping iPads, but Lenni batted them away. 'No way,' he called. 'You'll get your turn later. This afternoon she's mine.'

He ushered Alex into the meeting pod, where both of their laptops were already on the table, plugged in and booted up. A rail-thin Indian girl with pink-and-white ombré hair pushed her way backwards through the door with two bottles of brackish green liquid and two lumps of foil. Alex thought of Finn MacEgan, sweating and shaking in the exact same spot, racked with anger and pain.

'Where's Jacob?' she asked faintly, remembering how he had kicked Finn's heavy holdall across the floor.

'Who?' Lenni was already typing with one hand, tearing into one of the foil parcels with the other. 'Oh, that kid. He got poached by the wearable guys on three. Now, we have to run through some prospective COO CVs in a minute, but first I need to show you some comments we've been getting on the site.' He turned his screen to face her. 'The community team—'

A new email alert popped up on Alex's screen, tagged with a red exclamation mark. The subject header was *Research Project: Follow-Up*, and the sender was <u>sorcha.macbrian@ gcaseu.org</u>.

'Sorry,' she said. 'I just need to—'

'Oh no.' Lenni reached across and closed the lid. 'No, you don't.'

'I just—'

'Alex!' Lenni grabbed at the laptop. There was a brief tug-of-war before Alex let go. Lenni sat with his hands flat on the lid for a moment, then lifted them and gave her a thin smile. 'Okay. Thank you. Now, take a breath and let's get to work. Here. Have a burrito.' He thrust a foil slug into her hands. 'So.' He turned back to his screen. 'Unexpected as your digital detox was, it turned out to have an interesting silver lining. Obviously, while you were away, Gemma had to press pause on the personal PR. So we took the opportunity to make an assessment of our progress, advocacy-wise. Pull in some feedback.'

Alex bared her teeth in a semblance of a smile.

'Now, we always knew that our positioning would take some tweaking. We've been playing it by instinct, and we've done pretty well, but it's essential that we keep evolving as our network matures. And as it turned out, when we looked through the data, some interesting themes emerged. You see this?'

Alex dragged her gaze back from the window. Lenni was pointing at the red-and-grey matrix of Eudo's online discussion boards. He'd pulled up a thread called *Inspiring everywoman or cash cow?* 'Go on,' he said. 'Scroll down.'

> **LucyLoo**: Did anyone see that piece in *Flair* about Alex Moore? Um, is it just me or is she a *bit of a bitch*??!! OK so the mods will prob trash this as soon as I post but I can't help it: she TOTALLY comes across as cold & self-involved . . . (maybe I'm in a bad mood . . . !)
>
> **EuKnowIt**: **~LucyLoo** No! OMG totally! I am like the biggest fangirl but I have to admit that AM is starting to p me off. She only ever talks about how great she is an how easy it is to just get off ur ass an 'find your power'. Makes me feel like she secretley thinks like the rest of us are idiots, like shes superior
>
> **LucyLoo**: **~EuKnowIt**: Um, exactly, idiots she can *make money out of*

CarrotttCake: *~LucyLoo ~EuKnowIt* One word: smug.

YogaBunny51: Eudo has a good mission but honestly I dont think she is some one I can relate to. I think she is stop being a normal person

CarrotttCake ~YogaBunny51: One word: Goop.

LoveLife000: Great hair, tho ;)

'There's plenty more where this came from,' Lenni said, clicking between tabs. 'And the comments we get whenever we publish under your name . . .' He shrugged. 'Let's just say there's a hell of a moderation queue.'

Alex stared at him. 'You think they're right, don't you?' she whispered. 'You think I'm a fake.' She felt something land on her thigh and looked down to see her fist clenched around a twist of pulped foil, a glob of salsa on her jeans.

Lenni sighed. 'This isn't about me, Alex. It's about our members. And I'm afraid the engagement figures correlate. We're still hitting our targets overall, but there are big red flags when it comes to your content. We ran an on-site poll, and we also had an agency do a small offline survey. The keywords that people associate with Alex Moore are successful, powerful, focused . . . and cold. This is a big issue. Cold is not going to shift merchandise. Cold is not going to promote premium memberships.' He saw her expression and sighed again. 'This is business, Alex. You can't take it personally.'

Guacamole dripped onto the salsa. 'How can I not take it personally? You're talking about me.'

'I'm talking about the public perception of you.'

'And do you think I'm cold?'

'All I'm saying is that I think it would help, for the next phase of our development, if we found some ways to make you appear a little more . . . human.'

'*Appear?*'

'You know what I mean.' He shook his head. 'I warned you, Alex, when we first talked, that if we were going to build the brand around your personal story, you were going to have to develop a thick skin. I thought you understood. You seemed . . .' He shrugged. 'Honestly, I thought you were bulletproof. But if you're going to shy at the first hurdle . . .'

Alex blinked up from the gore in her lap. 'What do you want from me, Lenni?' she asked wearily.

Lenni smiled. 'Now that's the attitude I'm looking for. So Gemma and I have been discussing this, and we absolutely think we can turn it to our advantage.' He maximized a document on the screen. 'Have a look at this.'

Alex tried to concentrate. But by the time Lenni finally closed his laptop at five, she realized she had barely taken in a word he'd said over the past two hours. 'Okay.' Lenni stood up and stretched, then gave her a little pat on the back. 'Good work. I've got to show face at Seedcamp now, but I think we have the beginnings of a game plan. And tomorrow will be the perfect opportunity to test it out. See you at the studio, five sharp?'

'The studio?'

Lenni paused, his laptop sleeve half-zipped. 'Yes, Alex, the studio.'

'Okay, sorry, yes. Of course. The studio. See you there.' She would find a way to wriggle out of whatever she was supposed to be doing tomorrow. There was no way she could afford to waste another afternoon. The thought of having to appear normal – through some interminable photoshoot or product collaboration kick-off, or whatever it was – sent a lance of panic stabbing through her chest.

Lenni walked to the doorway, then turned back. 'You sure you're alright?'

Alex gave what she hoped was a reassuring smile. 'Of course.'

'Well, eat something. You look terrible.' Another thin smile. 'Must be all that country air.'

Alex watched his blurred form through the frosted glass, walking to the lift. The doors opened and closed. She sat for a moment listening to the whirr of servers, the clank of the coffee machine, the laden silence of twenty people plugged into earphones. Then she turned back to her laptop, opened the lid and clicked on the email:

Dear Miss Moore,

Greetings from Iskeull. I know you were extremely drained by the time you left us, so do let me know that you have arrived back safe and well.

We are very eager to receive news of the research you committed to undertake in London. The weather here remains very unseasonal, and continues to challenge both the equilibrium of our habitat and the morale of our staff. The sooner we can push towards completion and reallocate our resources, the better it will be for us all.

I am sure I do not need to remind you of the need for <u>absolute discretion</u> when it comes to our project. The work we do here must be protected from outside agendas at all costs. I look forward to hearing from you at the first possible instance.

Yours sincerely,

Director Sorcha MacBrian (on behalf of the International Board of GCAS).

Alex hit Reply:

Well, I'm back, and I suppose I should feel grateful for that, although I wouldn't exactly say that I'm well.

Was she still raw from her overdose of Library energy? Or was the thing inside her Story getting stronger, leaching her strength from within? Either way, she felt permanently on the verge of an episode, and it was taking all her energy to appear half-normal. An effort that, from the evidence of Lenni's comment, wasn't working particularly well.

But the problem isn't just physical. The thing is, I'm not really an Outsider any more, am I? I'm back Outside, but I'm also the only one Outside who knows THE BIG SECRET, and that feels, well, pretty damn horrible. But don't worry, I'm not going to say anything. I literally couldn't explain what the fuck I saw over there, even if I wanted to. Also, everyone would simply think I'm mad. Which, at this rate, I very soon might be.

Alex sat back and pressed her fingers against her eyes, but that only seemed to bring into sharper focus the scene she was trying to avoid summoning up. How was it that the one Memory she wanted to forget was the most vivid of all? Within seconds she could feel the warm air rushing up from beneath her feet and taste the copper in her mouth. Before she could pull back, she found herself reliving, for the hundredth time since she had struggled out of the tomb, her bad Storyline.

It had been worse than any of the others, much worse; not just rotten, but violently fetid. All the relevant Memories from 17 February had been there – Mark's offer of promotion, the session with Chloe, waking up vomiting in bed. But although each one had diffused through her in exquisite detail, they hadn't offered the slightest hint of how she had actually felt. It had been the same with the Memory of Dom's job offer from 2005. She had been able to smell the side of poached salmon on her parents' kitchen table, see the exact look of bewilderment on Dom's face when she turned him down. But she hadn't experienced one iota of emotion.

And again with the Memories from the awful summer of 1995. She had experienced the hours that eleven-year-old Alex had spent reading alone in her bedroom, the mysterious bug that had taken hold of her when she was supposed to go on holiday with her best friend, the arguments with her mother. She relived the early days at St Joseph's, spent wandering the corridors alone between classes; the evenings spent hammering aimlessly away at the computer in the attic. But exactly what those crucial Memories, so carefully preserved, had meant to her remained a mystery.

What was worse, the whole 'fear of failure' theory hadn't seemed to hold up. Her bad Storyline proved to be full of Memories that seemed to suggest the opposite, from the afternoon when she had set up an artisan cupcake stall in Broadway Market and sold out in a matter of hours, to the time she had smashed her first 5K. What's more, she had found nothing about Egan MacCalum. Nothing that looked like a decision to attack him with a fatal burst of energy. There were no repressed thoughts or scenes that suggested she had somehow, somewhere, been aware of her secret 'Story-surging' talent. The talent that had allowed her to blast consciousness out of her Story and into the defenceless flesh of another human being. The talent she never asked for. The talent she wasn't even sure she believed she had.

But then, after the Storyline had completed its hideous cycle, she had approached its root Memory. And oh, boy, had she finally been forced to acknowledge that Taran was right. She had known, with every shivering, prickling atom she owned, that something powerful was waiting for her in that Memory. Something powerful, and dangerous. The trigger was real, and the catch was off. But then the void had opened up faster and wider than ever before and swallowed her whole.

When she woke, cheek burning against the platform, it had taken all her remaining strength to stumble her way along the walkway and out of the door. She had no idea how long she'd lain curled in the tunnel. All she knew was that, once she had managed to stand up again, the climb back up to the tomb had seemed to take years. When she'd finally felt the bottom of the rope ladder brush her hair, she hadn't even had the energy left to cry.

Back in Eudo's meeting pod, Alex swung round just in time to retch strings of drool down the side of the chair. Her stomach spasmed and her skin shrank, as if it was trying to slough away from her flesh. Wave after wave of adrenaline coursed through her body. RUN, her nerves screamed, RUN RUN RUN. Except there was nowhere to run, because the monster she needed to escape was inside.

Alex sat up and wiped her mouth with the back of her shaking hand. Slowly, slowly, the hormones and white blood cells – whatever the fuck had tried to rush to her rescue – slunk uselessly away. Suddenly freezing, she unzipped her bag and pulled on her jumper, which was torn and filthy and stank of sweat and soil. She warmed her hands on the bottom of her laptop, then placed them back over the keyboard.

Honestly, Director? I'm not sure that I can trust you, because I'm pretty damn sure you don't trust me. I told you the truth about what happened down there, I swear. I wish it had been different, I wish I had been strong enough to get my hands – my brain? my heart? – on that root Memory. But I wasn't. I couldn't handle it. I passed out. I – ha – failed.

Alex blinked up at the huge silver pipes that criss-crossed the ceiling. No tears, she told herself. Nonononononono-nono. She turned back to the screen.

239

Look, I know I messed up. And I'm not going to go back on my word. I promised you that I would do everything in my power to get at that Storyline from the outside, once I was back home – and I will. Frankly, we both know I don't have any choice. Oh, sure, every person I see, I wonder whether their life is already worse because of me. But there's also the selfish reason, i.e. I do not want to die, which from the way I'm feeling right now seems a distinct possibility. Although now I think about it, that's probably your preferred outcome anyway, International Covenant or no.

But you know what?

What? What did she know?

Alex stared at the cursor. The cursor blinked back. She had been moving towards a point, building to a righteous climax, but suddenly she had no idea what to say. She knew too much, she knew nothing. And every second that passed, on seven islands across the world, seven billion Stories lost a little more of their light. She realized what she wanted to type, then. She wanted to type, in bold, underlined, 72-point scarlet letters: IT'S NOT FAIR.

But then, as her mother was so fond of saying, *Fairs are for clowns, darling.*

Alex rose stiffly from her chair and left the meeting pod. Went to the loo, drank a pint of water, nibbled the edge of a protein ball. Sat cross-legged on the floor, closed her eyes, took fifty deep breaths and tried to summon that bastard Storyline from inside. Gave up after ten minutes and stood beside the darkening window for a while, looking through the reflection of her face at the evening lights of the city.

Then she returned to her laptop, highlighted all the text and pressed backspace.

Director MacBrian, I am proceeding with my research with the utmost discretion and all possible speed. Yours, Alex Moore.

14

'Alex Moore. You are a terrible person.'

'I . . .'

'I'm joking!' Mae laughed. 'I just meant you never called.'

Oh God. She had to tell her. She couldn't hide from Mae.

'Al?'

Weaving between the early-evening revellers on Dean Street, Alex tried to imagine what Mae would say. But Mae was firmly on the non-fiction-and-documentary end of the imagination scale. She would insist on getting health services involved, in seeking out 'practical help' that would be anything but. And knowing, even if she didn't believe it, might put her in danger – whatever Taran had said. Alex wouldn't put anything past Iain's 'scrupulous security', especially with MacBrian calling the shots. Perhaps literally. She glanced around her, but there were too many black-haired people, too many pale complexions, too many watchful pairs of eyes.

'Alex? I was joking. Are you there? Are you okay?'

More pretending, then. Ignore the ache in your head and the shake in your hands and the terrible weight in your heart. As Chloe would say, act like the person you want to be. Act

242

like someone for whom consciousness is nothing but a fuzzy psychological concept. *Breathe deep. Smile.*

'Sorry, sorry, yes. My signal cut out.'

'Good. I thought you'd hung up on me for a moment there.' A pause. 'Well, I've just got my impossible son to bed and poured myself an enormous glass of wine. How are you?'

Alex imagined Bo in his cot, fat cheek squashed against the mattress, and Mae, curled on her toy-strewn sofa, downing Merlot. *No. Stop. Breathe deep. Smile.* 'I'm fine,' she said. 'I had to go away, to collaborate on a research project. Last-minute thing.'

'Yes, Harry told me. Guernsey, was it?'

'Harry? Why were you talking to Harry?'

'Oh, he – he wanted to know if I'd heard from you. To be honest, I think he was on one of his, um, jealousy crusades. He said you weren't answering any of his calls.' A pause. 'So . . .'

'So what?'

'So did you?'

'Did I what?' She clipped shoulders with a woman talking on a mobile.

'Hook up with someone out there?'

Alex ground to a halt. The plea in Finn MacEgan's voice when he'd told her not to trust MacBrian. The desperation on his face as Iain had wrestled him back through the door. Had he really wanted to hurt her, or simply to scare her into telling him why she had done what she had done? Wouldn't she shoot someone without a second thought, if she found out they had hurt her dad?

A young couple split around her. Alex started moving again. 'Of course not. My phone broke, that's all. To tell you the truth, most of them were pretty hostile.'

'Ah, well. Dickheads. Their loss.' Another pause. 'You haven't seen him yet, then?'

'Who?

'Harry.'

'No. I'm seeing him tomorrow for dinner. Why?'

'Oh, nothing. No reason. I'm just – I'm glad to hear from you.' Another pause. 'I was a bit worried about you, after our last conversation, Al. You seemed . . . not quite yourself.'

'I wasn't,' Alex said quietly. 'I mean, I'm not. Or, rather, I am, but I'm really not sure I know who that is. Was. Any more.'

Without warning, her face began to crumple. She swiped at her eyes with her sleeve, accidentally elbowing a man in a leather jumpsuit. The man whirled round with a moue of outrage. SORRY, Alex mouthed. SORRY, SORRY, SORRY.

'Oh, Al. This has been such a crazy time for you. It's natural that it would take you a while to catch up with all the change. I'm relieved, really. It was getting a bit weird for a moment there. That whole old-Alex-new-Alex shtick.'

'That's what I wanted to ask you about.' Alex did a side-shuffle dance with an Indian guy carrying a box of oranges. 'Hang on.' She slipped into a doorway and lowered her voice. 'Mae. If you had to summarize my character – I mean my character before all the Eudo stuff kicked off – what would you say?'

Mae laughed. 'What a question! Um, okay, how about Alex Moore: queen of navy jumpers? Embarrassing Bryan Adams fan? Arch-enemy of coriander?'

'No, seriously. What would you say was my overriding self-belief? Before everything – before I – changed?'

'Oh. Is this a Chloe thing? Some kind of exercise?'

'Would you say I suffered from a fear of failure?'

On the other end of the phone, Mae paused.

'I did wonder that, once or twice,' Mae said carefully. 'You're so damn smart, Al, you could have made a success of any of your big ideas, if you'd really decided to give them a go. They always started off so well. That cupcake thing. The film blog. The marathons. But every time, just as something looked promising, you'd suddenly freak out. You'd stop making an effort, decide it wasn't . . . *you*. It was like you were holding yourself back for some reason. Like you just couldn't . . . let go.'

'Let go? Let *what* go?'

'I don't know, Al. Whatever you were holding onto so tightly inside.'

'Like a fear of failure?'

A sigh. 'Maybe. But, you know, that doesn't totally add up. Look at uni. You could've easily got a first – you know you could. But it was, like, whenever you started getting As, you'd slack off, miss lectures, spend your afternoons mooching around in the common room. It was kind of annoying, actually. I had to work my ass off to get a two-two, and yours was like some kind of self-inflicted booby prize.' Another pause. 'Now I sound like I'm getting at you. I don't mean to. We're

245

all afraid of failure, aren't we? You were still amazing back then, Al. You were just a normal human being, hang-ups and all.'

'Meaning what? That I'm not normal now?'

'Well, no, to be honest, you're not. Look at all you've achieved since February. You're a bloody Superwoman.'

You're extraordinary, Alex, Taran had said – although inside her head his earnest voice had turned into a mocking singsong. *More extraordinary than you know.*

Alex gripped the phone. 'Do you remember that job Dom offered me, our first summer after uni? The agency gig in New York?'

'Uh, yeah. Of course.' A pause. 'Is that what this is about? You think you squandered the opportunity? But surely that doesn't matter now. You've got Eudo. You're virtually famous. And Harry . . . well, I know for sure that Harry loves you. Aren't you getting the life you always wanted?'

Alex stared out at the people streaming past. That manic-looking woman marching past, both arms laden with shopping bags: was a Storyline about *the right wardrobe will make me happy* dominating her life, because her Story couldn't surface in Alex's Stack? That man standing on the corner of Old Compton Street, shouting puce-faced down the phone: was he getting stuck in the rut of his habitual anger, as the Library inexorably slowed down?

'. . . come and see you?' Mae was saying. 'It's a nursery day tomorrow. I could get Mum to do the pick-up, jump on a train.'

'No.' If she was face-to-face with Mae, there was no way

she would be able to keep up the charade. 'No, honestly. I'm fine.'

'Please. I'm worried. I don't know what's happened to you this week, but—' Three police cars whooped past. When the sirens died down, Mae was saying '. . . practical help.'

'No, really, I don't need it. Honestly. Look, I have to go. Give Bo a kiss from me. Tell him—'

But she had no idea what to tell Bo, and when an ambulance followed the police cars, she took the opportunity to kill the call.

The bored blonde behind the desk couldn't find Alex on the guest register, until Alex thought to ask for Dorothy. Dom had always refused to accept her new name. Every time she'd tried to insist, over the past nineteen years, he'd simply smiled and said, 'But Dorothy Parker, dear.'

She spotted him as soon as she reached the top of the stairs, ensconced on a velvet sofa, jabbing with his forefinger at a smartphone.

'Well, well, well!' Dom hauled himself up as Alex wove between a table of people in heavy-rimmed glasses conferring around a laptop, and a trio of armchairs exhibiting three surreally good-looking men. As she leaned in for a kiss, Dom grabbed her by the shoulders. His smile switched to a frown. 'Dorothy. Are you ill?'

'Just tired,' she said, summoning a smile. 'Hello, Dom.'

'Well, no wonder you're tired, now that you appear to have become some sort of media mogul.' He gestured for her to sit on the sofa opposite. 'I assume you've come to tell me that you want to write a bestseller? One of those awful American-ized business books, with case studies about coffee shops and exercises to fill in?' He waved at a passing waiter. 'What'll it be? Sparkling or still?'

'Actually, I think I need a proper drink.'

Dom's pale eyebrows swept up his forehead. 'Goodness. All change, indeed. I bet your father's pleased.' He lifted a tumbler from the low table between the sofas. 'Whisky?'

Alex swallowed. 'No. I'll . . . maybe just one G&T?'

It must have been at least eight years since she'd last seen Dom. The fat that had aged him then seemed to have preserved him now, like a giant potted shrimp topped with a slick of grey-blond hair. As she snuck glances at him, moments from her childhood burst inside her brain like the liquid-centred sweets he used to bring her in paper bags. She remembered Dom carrying her around literary festivals on his massive shoulders, stopping to greet someone every second stride; Dom sitting beside her in a corner at a book-signing, showing her how to make origami cranes; Dom and her father having one of their arguments about grammar over the dinner table – until her father started to throw full stops at him, otherwise known as peas.

But the juice they gave out was flavourless, and her recol-lections of Dom's more sporadic visits throughout her teenage years evoked no more emotion than a stranger's holiday snapshots. As the dizziness rose, she sat abruptly on the sofa. She was afraid, for a horrible moment, she might throw up.

Dom was watching her. 'It is very lovely to see you,' he

said, irony shunting abruptly into earnestness. 'What little of you there is left. How are you really, my dear?'

Alex, still breathing her way out of the episode, met his gaze for less than a second. 'I'm fine.'

'More than fine, from what your father tells me. Not that either of us have any real idea what it is that you're doing. I fear the world is becoming increasingly nonsensical to me. How precisely does this Eudomonia affair make money?'

'Investment. Sponsorships.'

'Oh, well. Maybe you could sponsor your father to finish his damn second novel.'

The waiter brought Alex's drink. She downed half of it in one gulp and said, 'Dom. You've known me my whole life.'

Dom settled back into the cushions. 'I remember the day I met you. Five months old and in the arms of your dear mother, who smiled at me like Julie Christie, then grilled me like David Frost.'

'I'm participating in this research project, you see, about entrepreneurs. They've asked me to interview the people who know me best. To try and get an objective picture of how I became who I am now.' After the calls to Mae and her father, Alex had realized she needed to come up with a smoother explanation for her questions. She'd been practising all the way to the club. 'They're most interested in the struggles. The hurdles I've had to overcome. The self-beliefs I've had to let go.'

'Ugh!' Dom put an olive in his mouth. 'Self-helpease?

And this from the girl who used to be the clammiest of clams? But it's in vogue, of course. Are they paying you?'

'Not exactly. But they think it might help others like me, people who wasted half their life before they were able to release their true potential.'

'You sound like a mortgage advert, Dorothy.'

'*Dom!*' Alex drowned the wobble in her voice with gin. The waiter caught her eye. She nodded for another.

'Sorry. Of course I'll help if I can. Go on.'

'You remember the job offer you got me? With the new office in New York?'

'I do.'

'What exactly did I say, when I turned it down? Did I tell you why?'

Dom smoothed one of his eyebrows with his thumb. 'I believe the essence of it was that you didn't want to let the people at your current company down. You said that they'd taken a chance on you when you were young, provided training and so forth. You said that you felt it would be selfish to leave them in the lurch. I remember that word specifically. Selfish.' He took another olive. 'It was all quite bizarre.'

The waiter handed Alex her second drink. She took a long draught, feeling the alcohol roll the tide of nausea another inch or two away. 'So would you say I was afraid of failure? Or was it more of a people-pleasing thing? Would you say I believed something like: *I will be sad if I don't make others happy*? Or was it more a lack of self-esteem, like: *I must be grateful for whatever I can get*?'

'Dorothy. My dear. What in the name of Christ are you talking about?'

'I just need you to tell me one thing, Dom. Please.' She gulped another mouthful. 'Be as brutal as you can. What would you say has been my main driver, as a person? Historically? How would you sum up the narrative I tell myself about who I am?'

Dom rolled his eyes.

'Dom!'

'Fine.' He picked up his whisky and took a slow sip. He regarded her levelly over the rim of his glass. 'Well, it all depends who you're talking about,' he said. 'Because there have really been three of you so far, haven't there?'

Alex's breath caught in her throat. 'What do you mean?'

'Well, first there was happy young Dorothy, bright as a grasshopper, mouth like a motor, heart on her sleeve. My little chum. Then, shortly after she hit double figures, we got clammed-up Alex, the teenage mutant ninja turtle with a shell that no jokes or bribes could penetrate. My little chum seemed to disappear overnight, like a butterfly popping back into her chrysalis. And if we're being brutally honest, dear, it was quite obvious that her replacement desired to neither see nor hear me. It was probably inevitable, considering the influx of oestrogen, but it did rather bruise my squidgy old heart. And we now appear to be on Ms Moore number three, don't we, my skinny, press-ready media mogulette?' He put his glass down on the table. 'I rejoiced in the first Dorothy. I was sad about the second. But I must admit, although she at least seems to tolerate my presence, I'm most worried of all about the third.'

'Don't, Dom.' Alex stared at her clasped hands. 'I'm trying my best.'

'But what if we don't want your best, my dear? What if we just want *you*?'

'But that's what I'm trying to figure out. Who me is.'

'Figuring's no good, dear. It's quite simple. We are what we do.'

'But that's exactly the problem.'

Alex heard the squeak of springs. One of Dom's large, clammy hands closed around her own. 'Dorothy, what do you think you have done?'

'I hurt someone,' she said, still staring at her lap. 'I hurt someone badly.'

'Your chap?'

She shook her head.

'Are you talking about now, or back then? B.A.?'

'B what?'

'Before Alex?'

Alex looked up. 'Why do you say that?'

Dom gave her hand a little pat. He looked at the wall, where three pencil drawings of vaginas hung in a row. 'I always wondered if there was something more to your volte-face back then. Something less obvious than hormones and performance anxiety at your fancy new school. It was the suddenness of it all.' He looked back at her. 'Did something happen to you?'

Alex wrapped her arms around her chest. 'I can't remem-

ber. I think it might have. He suggested – the Head of
Scholarship at the—'

'OI! YOU!' There was a shout from behind. Alex swung
round to see a skeletal man in a slogan T-shirt – *Love Will
Save the World* – waving an empty martini glass at a waitress.

Dom sighed. 'Look, Dorothy, I'd be wary of suggestion, if
I were you. Of trying to rewrite your childhood. I'm always
on the lookout for a juicy mystery, an unexpected plot twist.
But unfortunately in life the most obvious explanation is
usually the one that fits.'

He crossed his arms across his straining shirt front. 'Of
course, if you really wanted me to, I could enumerate potential *issues*, like the best pseudo-Freud. None of us would
deny, for example, that your father's a melancholic. It has
been truly hard for him over the years, watching the young
guns fire off their debuts, as the gigs slowly dry up. But that's
the nature of the industry, and most of my clients would kill
to have had Tom's one scorching moment in the sun. And it
would be wrong to underestimate him. It takes enormous
guts, exposing yourself like that on the page. Drained him to
the dregs, quite literally, and now it looks like the grand
follow-up might never quite force its way out. But you know,
dear, part of me still thinks, after all this time, that one day
he's going to surprise us all.

'And then your mother . . .' Dom shook his head. 'Well,
your mother's a force of nature. I can imagine that, to a
young girl, she might have seemed – how do I put this? A
touch domineering? Oh, undoubtedly Liz must always be in

control, Liz must always know best. But then again, that's because she generally is, and she generally does.

'And together? Well, I've envied their relationship my whole life. Even when the fuss around Tom was at its height, when he was winning awards left, right and centre, it was your mother's opinion that still mattered to him most. And he has remained her shining knight, whether he's the voice of his generation or a washed-up columnist for a Sunday rag. And you've always been right at the heart of it, my dear, positively swaddled in love. Which is much, much more than most of us can say.' Dom reached again for the olives. 'So whatever you're trying to dig up at the moment, I suggest you'd be much better off doing the opposite. My advice is to simply let it go.'

'Let it go?' Alex blundered to her feet. 'Well, yes, every-one's very eager to give me that particular piece of advice, Dom. But how exactly does that *work*? What exactly am I supposed to bloody *do* to let this damn thing go?'

'Dorothy—'

Alex heard Dom struggle up out of the sofa behind her, but she didn't look back. Ignoring the stares, she thundered across the floorboards and squeezed against the upcoming traffic, down four flights of stairs.

Outside, Soho was sticky and burning with lights. People were pouring out of the Palace Theatre opposite, spilling across the pavement, swilling down interval drinks and using their programmes as fans. Alex forced her way through them and out onto Cambridge Circus. A tuk-tuk laboured past, pop song pumping, cutting up a black cab, which blared its horn. A group of young girls staggered across the junction, giggling, the smell of fried onions mingling with the maple-syrup stench of overheating cars. Two women in burkhas glided past, one of them posting Alex a piercing blue look through the letter-box around her eyes.

Alex ducked her head and strode off up Charing Cross Road, eyes on her feet.

No tears, you selfish, self-pitying freakshow. Don't you dare cry.

15

'Five.'

She had pleaded tiredness.

'Four.'

She had pleaded illness. She had begged Lenni to reschedule. And Lenni had told her, with a core of Nordic ice in his voice, that rescheduling thirty minutes before they were due to arrive was 100 per cent not going to work.

Three was silent, as the floor manager flashed a Brownie salute in the air.

Five in the morning! The *morning*! Once Alex had left Dom the night before, she'd bought a bottle of wine from a mini-supermarket and caught a night bus back to her flat. Shocked to find that she didn't have a single print copy of her father's book on her shelves, she'd downloaded the twentieth-anniversary-edition e-book of Tom R. Moore's *The Switch*. She'd read until two, until the wine was finished and her eyes were so gritty she couldn't keep them open. One and a half hours after that, she'd woken from a night-mare to the unfamiliar ring of her new mobile. In her dream, the half-completed statue of Egan MacCalum had been chasing her through a jungle filled with gripping indigo vines. It took her several disoriented seconds to understand that the call was from the driver that Gemma had so thoughtfully pre-booked, saying that he was outside. Once Alex had phoned Lenni and made her fruitless entreaties, she had barely had time to shower and pull on her dirty jeans before sprinting out the door.

Two: the peace sign.

She felt like her own waxwork. The thick make-up was itchy under the lights, her hair crispy with spray. They'd snipped off the blue thong, without asking, and her wrist felt bare. Beside her the presenter, Corinne, thinner and older than she looked on TV, stopped fiddling with her top button and turned to the autocue.

The floor manager's forefinger sliced towards the camera: one.

'Welcome back!' Corinne chirruped in her Northern Irish twang. 'Now, today's Superwoman is a real personal treat. As you all know, I'm a big fan of self-improvement, and a month ago a friend of mine got me hooked on this new well-being community she'd found online. Well, now *everyone*'s talking about Eudomonia, so I'm delighted to have with me on the sofa this morning Alex Moore, Eudo's *amazing* Founder-CEO.' She turned to Alex with a sisterly smile. 'So, Alex! It's time to confess.'

Alex stared back, rigid. Corinne laughed and pointed downwards, while the cameraman tilted his lens down to zoom in on Alex's feet. 'Come on, now. Where *did* you get those killer heels?'

Alex looked down at the five-inch courts Gemma had

brought to the studio, along with the too-tight digital-pattern body-con dress. 'Um,' she said. 'Um . . .'

Corinne laughed and patted her knee. 'You're right. We probably shouldn't start off with fashion. Because Eudo is about much more than the latest labels, isn't it, Alex? I believe you describe it as a community for those who want to be their best self?'

Alex cleared her throat. She tried to remember the prompts Gemma had typed out for her to read during make-up. *Warm*, that was one. *Feelings-focused*, that was another. *Relatable. Human.*

'Yes.' Alex gave what she hoped was a feelings-focused smile. 'Yes, Corinne, exactly.'

Corinne nodded encouragingly, eyebrows arched.

Alex cleared her throat again. 'Well, Corinne, personally I don't see there's any contradiction between loving a great midi-skirt and wanting to improve your neuroplasticity.' As long as she didn't let her brain intervene, she would get through. She was probably still drunk, which helped. Next was . . . next was . . . 'The media put women in such a box, you see.'

Corinne's head took on a slant of sadness, a slow beat of solidarity.

'We're either damsels or ball-breakers, airheads or blue-stockings. With Eudo, I wanted to break the paradigm.' It was all coming back to her, from somewhere deep in her linguistic muscle-memory. 'I wanted to be something other than what society told me I had to be. To finally let my true potential detonate. I suspected that many others—'

Jesus! Let her true potential detonate? She imagined the Library Board watching her, huddled in front of black-and-white TVs in remote Outside outposts across the world. No doubt rapidly revising their opinion of her semi-innocence.

Corinne looked pained. 'That's definitely something I can relate to,' she said. 'And we know there are many others who feel the same. Because six months on, you're growing fast. Eudo now has several million monthly users, and interest from international investors. So how do you combine being a woman with being a business owner, Alex? Have you struggled to balance your home life with the responsibilities of leadership?'

Alex looked at her fingernails, freshly painted scarlet. Maybe it hadn't been the best idea to ignore all of Mac-Brian's calls. But the thought of having to report her as-yet-total failure to either figure out the meaning of her Storyline, or uncover its surge-enabled root Memory, made her feel even sicker than usual.

'Alex?'

'Sorry?'

Corinne laughed again, more sharply. 'Seems you're still a little dazed by your own success. Now I understand you have a fiancé, Harry Fyfield, a shipping analyst. I've seen a picture, and I must say you're a lucky woman! I'm sure that Harry is a big support?'

He had sent her a text at 6 a.m., checking that she was still coming for dinner. How right he had been, at that lunch in the fancy chapel – more right than he knew. She certainly wasn't the Alex he had met five years ago. How appalled he would be if he knew, if he could comprehend, the full truth about the woman he no longer recognized.

'No-go area?' Corinne smiled brightly. 'Fair enough. But I *am* hoping that you'll give us the skinny on your father.' She leaned forward and picked up a hardback from the coffee table. 'Now, book-loving viewers will know that our current Book Club Pick is *The Screaming Girl*, the debut novel from Adam Hussein. Adam won a place on Novus's Young Novelists to Watch list earlier this month. It's a rare honour, as the list is only released once every ten years. And our viewers may be surprised to learn that you are in fact the daughter of Tom R. Moore, who featured on Novus's first-ever list, back in 1985 – for his widely acclaimed debut novel *The Switch*. Now, unfortunately I couldn't find a copy, and your dad has somewhat dropped out of the limelight. But *The Switch* was a phenomenon in its time, and it was famously written in just five months, straight after you were born. It must have had an impact on you, Alex. Did your father encourage the daughter who inspired his masterpiece to reach for the stars herself?'

Dom's wry voice drifted back through Alex's mind. *It was the suddenness of it all . . . My little chum seemed to disappear overnight . . . clammed-up Alex, the teenage mutant ninja turtle . . .* He had been spot-on, give or take a ninja turtle. Everything he had said backed up Taran's hypothesis.

She looked up. The floor manager was rotating his arm clockwise above his head.

'Okaaaaay . . .' Corinne gave a strained smile. 'So, returning to Eudo itself. Every week, on the Founder's Blog, you discuss your own favourite pieces of content on the site. Why don't you tell us about the most powerful stories you've recently shared?'

'Um, I . . . I don't think I've . . .'

Corinne reached for a clipboard on the coffee table. 'Well, for example, I believe that yesterday you blogged about how Hillary Gibson's low-sugar programme has given you real clarity of mind? And on Sunday I see that you described how Flaural, a company that creates soundscapes from the cycles of blossoming plants, has helped bring a sense of the interconnection of the planet to your urban lifestyle?'

'I did?' Alex gazed hopelessly beyond the camera. Gemma, standing behind the cameraman, holding a coffee and a pastry, was nodding vigorously. Beside her, Lenni was mouthing something. Alex squinted. WARM, he silently bellowed. WARM!

The floor manager's arm had turned into a windmill in a gale.

'And what about the future?' Corinne asked. 'I understand that you've recently been working on a collaboration with a prestigious institute up in the Ork—'

'NO!' Alex bellowed. She looked wildly from Corinne, whose smile had frozen, to Lenni and Gemma, whose pain-aux-raisins was arrested halfway to her mouth. 'I mean—' She tried a laugh, but it came out all wrong. 'I mean, it's just a personal project. Nothing worth sharing at all.' She tried another laugh, which was even worse. She swallowed. 'You have to understand, all I ever wanted to do was help people.' She cleared her throat. 'You see, I . . . Everyone has to

261

understand that they have the power to change. We can all face up to our Storylines – I mean, no, sorry, I mean our narratives, our limiting narratives about ourselves, and we all have the power to break free of them, all by ourselves, even if we can't be Read . . . I mean, um, helped.' She sniffed. 'I mean obviously, a Library – that is, a community – can be a great source of support. But no-one should rely on there being someone there to Read . . . or, no, I mean . . .' She rubbed at her eyes. 'All I'm trying to say, the message I'm trying to send out to the world, is that people simply have to take matters into their own hands, if they want to be – to be their best . . . their best . . . their best . . .'

And then they came, finally – the tears that had been waiting to fall ever since Finn MacEgan had slammed into her, seven days ago, on De Beauvoir Road. Alex stared helplessly into the camera as water streamed silently down her face, snot bubbled out of her nose, and the unctuous mixture dribbled into the rictus of her smile.

The floor manager made a vicious grabbing motion with his hand and balled it into a fist.

'And that's all we have time for,' Corinne said smoothly. 'Now, I don't know about anyone else, but I'm starving. Anjit, what have you been concocting for us today?'

The floor manager made a slashing motion across his throat. Corinne pulled off her microphone and stalked away, leaving Alex stranded on the sofa. 'Christ,' Alex heard her mutter to a researcher as she stepped off the living-room set, 'where do you find these psychopaths?'

*

The row of bay windows overlooking Arundel Gardens was wide open, gasping for breeze. As Alex clacked unsteadily past each cream villa she was granted a blast of expensive noise: the squawk of a learner violin, the drill of builders renovating a basement, the chatter of Czech nannies on a play date. At number 119 she climbed up to the shady portico and pressed the buzzer for the top-floor flat. She pressed it twice more before she heard a crackle, and a breathy pan-European accent came through the grille.

'Sorry, wrong number!'

'No, Chloe, it's me, Alex. Alex Moore.'

'Alex? Wait, I . . . I think there's been a mix-up? Hold on, I'm coming down.'

Chloe opened the door, her slim sienna body robed in a white maxi-dress. 'Alex! Namaste!' She wrapped her arms lightly around Alex in a waft of coconut. 'Oh, Alex, did you think you had an appointment? I've taken today off!'

'No, no, I just hoped you might have time for a quick chat. It's really important, and I couldn't get through on the phone.'

Chloe leaned close. 'That's because I spent last night with Mother Ayahuasca,' she whispered. '*Amazing!* But the thing is, the shamans ask that we spend some time alone afterwards to fully process the journey.'

'Could I come in for a minute?'

Chloe looked at the stairs that rose into the gloom behind her. She turned back. 'The thing is, Alex, between you and me, one of the shamans is actually helping me process it right now.'

'Can I take you out, then? Buy you lunch? Please, Chloe. I wouldn't ask if it wasn't important.'

Chloe half-turned to the stairs, looked back at Alex's face, then sighed. 'Let me get my keys. But I'll have to charge full price, okay?'

Chloe led her round the corner onto Westbourne Grove and into a farm-shop cafe. They sat at a corner table beneath a tower of knobbly vegetables. Chloe ordered the chilled raw cashew soup, then tutted when Alex pushed the menu away.

'You're looking thin, Alex. Is this a new look? Very . . . glamorous. Although you've got a bit . . .' Chloe tapped under her eyes. 'Just a bit of slippage.'

Alex touched her cheek. In her rush to get out of the studio, she had neglected either to change or wash, and her make-up had a clotted, tacky feel where it had mixed with the snot and the tears. Well, fuck it. At least she finally looked how she felt.

'Chloe,' she said, leaning forward, 'I have to ask you about our first meeting, back in February. The evening of the seventeenth. Do you remember what happened?'

'Of course. It was an incredibly powerful session, am I right?'

'Well, yes. I Read . . . I mean, I know that I spent the whole time crying, but the problem is: I can't remember why.'

Chloe nodded and sipped from her elderflower pressé. 'You chose not to vocalize what you were feeling, Alex, and frankly I thought that was a very good decision at the time. You're someone who naturally gets very attached to language, to logic, to labels. But in that session you simply *unleashed* your emotions. It was very pure. Very raw. I'm not going to deny it, you were a tough nut at first. Very defensive, very closed. But once you broke through, well. Kaboom. There was a lifetime of pent-up anger in the room, Alex. A lifetime of fear.'

Kaboom. Alex gripped her teaspoon. 'But *why*? What was I angry *about*? What was I frightened *of*?'

Chloe wrapped a cold hand round Alex's. 'The why doesn't matter, Alex. What matters is how you've used that power since. How you're going to use it today. This hour. *Now.*'

'But . . . but you made me look at all those pictures, do those word-association tests. You must have had some kind of instinct, Chloe, even if I didn't say anything outright. Would you say I was suffering from a fear of failure? Body issues? Low self-esteem?'

Chloe sat back, shaking her head. 'Labels, Alex. Labels and words. This sounds suspiciously like your cognitive dissonance at work, trying to rationalize. Trying to separate you from the emotional immediacy of your experience.'

'So you can't give me a single clue as to what my . . . er, my personal narrative could have been? Or what events in my past it might have grown out of?'

Chloe sighed again and sipped at her soup. 'Well, I did ask if your reaction concerned your family, because emotional blocks so often do. You didn't reply; you were still deep in the sub-vocal stage of your transition at that point.

265

However, I do remember picking up on some body language that suggested I was right.'

'My *family*?' Alex thought, again, of Dom. 'But my parents are rock-solid. I can't think of anything in our family that would have made me . . . *unleash* my . . .' She stopped. She imagined her Storyline, lassoed around Egan MacCalum's wrists, getting slower and denser until it suddenly whoom-phed out in a white-hot nuclear blast. Chloe was doing her drawing-out-with-silence routine, her face beatific. Alex felt the urge to hit her, then noticed the impulse and felt even more sick.

'Why are you raking all this up now, Alex?' Chloe said eventually. 'You know I'm not a fan of traditional psychoanalysis. I don't believe you should fetishize the past. You haven't felt the need to trawl through the whys in our sessions, you've been focused on the future – and look at what's happened. You've freed yourself. You're forging a positive, resourceful path.'

Alex put her head in her hands and stared at the spirals in the grain of the wooden tabletop. 'Chloe,' she said, weakly. 'Do you believe there is more to the world than we realize?'

'Oh, Alex.' A fluting laugh. 'Do you really need to ask me that question?'

Alex looked up. 'What would you say if I told you there was a Library of human consciousness, then? A place where the Stories we create about ourselves are alive?'

Chloe placed her hands over her heart. 'I'd say that was beautiful, Alex. Really beautiful.'

'No, I don't mean like Paulo Coelho. I mean a real place. *Real*-real. A place I have actually gone inside.'

Chloe nodded. 'You have, Alex, you have gone inside. And I'm *so* proud of you.'

'No, a physical location. On the map. With coordinates.'

'And once you have those coordinates, Alex, you never lose them. It will only get—'

That was it then, Alex thought, tuning Chloe out. Another dead end. And if someone like Chloe wouldn't believe her, who would? For the first time since she'd left the TV studio, she reached into her bag and took out her continually vibrating phone.

'I think this is a really important conversation, Alex,' said Chloe.

Alex had twenty-six missed calls, several of them from an unknown landline. She checked her emails and there it was, flagged with another red exclamation mark. Sender: <u>sorcha.macbrian@gcaseu.org</u>. Subject line: *Urgent Development*.

Miss Moore,
  We need to discuss an urgent development. Please call me on 01857 391542 (GCAS EU North Ronaldsay Office) <u>as soon as possible.</u>
  Sorcha MacBrian

'Alex,' Chloe said. 'Alex!'

Alex looked up.

'Don't be scared of it, Alex. Don't retreat from your full power just because you're scared.'

Alex looked back at her screen. Below MacBrian's email was one from Lenni, sent half an hour ago, also flagged as urgent. Subject line: *WE NEED TO TALK.* She opened it and found no message, only a link. She could feel Chloe's eyes on her, disapproving. She didn't care. She clicked on the link.

'The will to win, the desire to succeed, the urge to reach your full potential: these are the keys that will unlock the door to personal excellence,' Chloe said gently. 'That's Confucius, Alex. *Confucius.*'

The YouTube clip took a few seconds to load, and then there was the ad to skip.

'Or,' Chloe said, 'possibly Bruce Lee. Alex? Alex, what are you looking at? What's wrong?'

And there it was: her breakfast TV meltdown. Every ugly, messy, indiscreet second of it. Alex wondered if their Internet was fast enough to stream video, in North Ronaldsay. She grabbed her bag and, without another word to Chloe, stumbled out of the cafe.

There was a man camped against the front of Rotherhithe Tube station, shouting 'CUNT!' every time someone emerged. Alex, in a daze of exhaustion, spent the ten-minute totter to Harry's flat trying to imagine the homeless man's Storylines. Were they chaotic, juddering medleys, or sleek white dynamos? Was his madness an aberration he fought against, or was it simply his version of sense? Had he, six months ago, been happily employed and housed, until his slowly dimming Story, languishing un-Read, finally drove him insane?

She suspected that she knew exactly what Harry's Storylines would look like: steady and smooth. She doubted

that his Story had ever surfaced to be Read. Harry's flat contained the same few pieces of IKEA furniture that he had
bought when he first moved in. Neatly arranged inside them
was a well-cared-for capsule collection of possessions that
was only added to in times of pressing need or deep sentiment, such as the set of cashmere jumpers he'd bought after
the moth infestation of 2011, or the metronome his grandmother had left him in the tearful winter of 2013. His library
consisted of three novels (*The Da Vinci Code*, *The Runaway
Jury* and *Misery*), a dozen sporting autobiographies and an
illustrated collection of poetry that he had received as a
school prize. Alex had never seen him open it. She had also
never seen him wearing an apron, which he was doing, without irony, when he opened the door.

He was, as always, so much more handsome than she
remembered; so sharp-edged and brightly coloured he might
have materialized from a high-definition screen. She saw
him take in, in turn, her dress, her heels, her scrubbed face
and swollen eyes. She still hadn't had a chance to go home
and change. She'd spent the whole afternoon in the office at
a crisis-limitation roundtable. Even so, she and Lenni had
had an argument in front of the whole team when she'd
insisted that she had to go.

For a moment she thought Harry wasn't going to kiss her,
but then he leaned in and brushed his lips against her cheek,
in a fug of garlic and Polo Sport. 'Come and sit down,' he
said. 'Jamie's Fifteen-Minute Thai Curry has so far taken me
an hour.'

She sat on the corner sofa while Harry busied himself

behind the counter of the galley kitchen, his face obscured by the low-hanging extractor hood. Staring out at the Alice-in-Wonderland cityscape of Gherkin and Eye and Shard, Alex belatedly tried to compose an internal Venn diagram. Things she needed to say; things she was allowed to say; things Harry would understand. Instead, her thoughts kept flitting back to MacBrian and the scene that must currently be unfolding on North Ronaldsay, and in the other tech-enabled Library outposts around the world. Surely nothing in that tearful babble could have constituted a security breach? Surely they could see that going on TV hadn't been her choice, that she was under intense pressure, that she was doing her best? Surely they couldn't think that a single one of those 1,003,567 lunch-break time-wasters who had watched the YouTube clip so far would consider her anything other than a joke? She knew that she should call MacBrian and defend herself. She should reassure the Iskeullians that she was, as promised, doing everything she could to engage with that damn Storyline. But the thought of that brisk Celtic accent invading the south London air, of letting them back into her world barely thirty-six hours after she had escaped from theirs, was too much to bear. The next time she spoke to them, she wanted it to be on her terms. She wanted to be armed with something positive, with proof that she was going to make things right. She needed more time.

'So how are you?' Harry said. His tone was determinedly light, his chopping brisk, his gaze riveted to the board.

Alex groaned. 'You saw it, then?'

The knife paused. 'Someone at work sent me an email.'

'Great. If I've reached the inboxes of IMARR, I've officially gone viral.'

'Chip-shop paper. It'll blow over in a couple of days.'

Alex gripped a Union Jack cushion to her chest. Numbly she parroted Lenni's words. 'Not online. This could dominate our search rankings for months. I assume you've seen the memes? Lockie thinks the first few came from the production agency on the ninth floor. Lenni's furious, of course.'

'Well, I suppose you have to give to them, really. The graphics. That Roy Orbison song. Where do you even get footage of a crying sloth?'

'Have you got any whisky?'

'Oh. No. I keep forgetting you drink now. I've got some red in the rack, will that do?' Harry poured a glass and brought it over to her, perching on the arm of the sofa.

'Alex,' he began.

'Harry, I'm so sorry. Last time we met, you were right, I had no idea how—'

'Shhhh.' Harry put his finger on her lips.

She was so startled, she almost bit it.

'This time,' he said, 'I'm going to talk.'

'But I need to apologize,' she said against his finger, then batted it away. She gulped some wine, felt her hangover momentarily revolt, then welcome it in enthusiastically. Oh, for oblivion. For forgetting. Yes, please. 'And I need to ask you some questions. About me. They're going to seem strange, but it's for the—'

'*Alex,*' Harry removed his stripy apron and took both her hands. 'Listen. While you were away, something changed.'

271

Alex swallowed, pulling her hands away. 'It's okay, Harry. I understand. I've become a terrible person.' She felt, once again, the weight of Finn MacEgan as he pressed against her in the archive room, every inch of his stringy flesh hot with grief and hate. 'To be honest, it's probably for the best. You shouldn't tie yourself to someone like—'

'ALEX!' He grabbed her hands again. 'Will you please shut up and listen?'

She hesitated, then nodded. She owed him this, at the very least. 'Sorry.' She took another slug of wine. 'Go ahead.'

Harry cleared his throat. 'That lunch,' he began stiffly, 'last time we met. You were right. I *was* scared. I have to admit that when you told me you were going off on your retreat or research project, or whatever it was, I was cynical. I thought it was a cheap attempt to prove that we still shared the same values. I expected you to spend the whole time sending me photographs of sunsets.' He paused. 'But I need to apologize, Alex, because you did take proper time out, didn't you – not just from me, but from Eudomonia? When I hadn't heard from you by Sunday morning I called Lenni. It was only then that I realized then how hard taking a step back must have been for you. I could tell he was furious that you had gone, that you hadn't called him either, and it made me question whether I had underestimated you. I couldn't stop thinking of you, trapped in the middle of nowhere with all those Neanderthal men, and all because I'd asked you to go.'

On Sunday morning she'd been standing inside an un-imaginably ancient tower, Reading the deepest secrets of a sixty-five-year-old Kosovan. She reached for the wine. 'And then you saw that bloody clip, and all those horrible memes, and realized that I was a total fuck-up after all. I get it, Harry. You don't have to—'

'No!' Harry slid off the arm of the sofa and onto the cushion beside her, angling his knees so they touched hers. 'You don't get it, do you? When I saw that stupid clip, I saw *you*. The Alex that I know and love. A bit confused, admittedly. A bit overwrought. But so authentic. So *human.*'

Human? Human, again? 'You know what, Harry? Being human is seriously overrated.'

Harry took her wine glass, put it on the coffee table and gathered her hands back into his. 'Don't get defensive. You know what I mean. Your true spirit shone through in that interview. Was this Alex Moore a strong woman? Yes. An independent woman? Absolutely. A successful woman. A Superwoman, in many ways. But she was also vulnerable, she was sensitive, she made mistakes, she wasn't a . . . a feminist cyborg. And when that presenter asked you about me, I realized that I *haven't* supported you at all. I've stepped back when I should have pushed forward, and forced you to accept help. No wonder you felt you had to create this invincible persona to cope.'

Alex untangled their fingers. 'You have no idea who I am. You don't know what I'm capable of.'

'No, that's the point. I finally do. I don't want you to give up Eudo any more, Alex. I want to help. I mean, Lenni's obviously good at what he does and you've obviously assembled a clever team, but none of them understands how *you* work. What *you* need.' Harry jumped to his feet. 'I wasn't going to do this until after we'd eaten, but hell, I don't care.'

He laughed, a little wildly, jumped to his feet and gave a bow.

'Ms Moore, I would humbly like to nominate a candidate for the position of Eudomonia's COO.'

'You – *what?*'

'You know, when it comes to data, shipping isn't all that different from self-development. I'm an excellent analyst and an experienced project manager.' Harry spread his arms. 'Think of it, Alex. A *family business*. It's everything you said you wanted at lunch last week, and more.'

'Harry.' Alex ushered him off his knees and back onto the sofa. 'This is . . . I didn't . . .'

'I know! I swore Mae to secrecy—'

'You told Mae all this?'

He grinned. 'I'm not a total idiot. I sounded her out first, and I called your mum as well. Of course, neither of them could really grasp how much sense it would make, in terms of the business. But the moment I walked into that dreary bloody office on Monday, my head buzzing with reasons why you could still be stuck in that Bear Grylls backwater, I knew it felt right. For the first time in my life I was truly ready to throw caution to the wind. I handed in my notice yesterday.'

'I—'

'Wait. Don't say anything yet. There's one more surprise.' Harry rushed back to the kitchen and retrieved an A4 plastic folder from between the pages of his cookery book, then laid it ceremonially on Alex's lap. 'Now the next few week-ends were all booked up, but you said sooner rather than later, so . . .'

She lifted the flap, pulled out a sheaf of leaflets and print-outs and looked at the top page:

<u>ITINERARY</u>
<u>Wednesday 5 August 2015</u>
<u>Dorothy Alexandra Moore</u>

07.00: *Alex Moore (AM) wake-up call*
(Flat 12, 37 Dunnett Street)
07.30: *Mae Tsang (MT) and Liz Moore (LM) arive*
at Dunnett Street from Premier Inn Old Street
(tel: 0871 527 9312)
07.45: *Protein-rich, low-GI breakfast (to be arranged by*
MT & LM)
08.15: *AM hair and make-up with Shelley Hubert of*
The Modern Bride (tel: 07786 546532)

On it went, all the way to *12.00: AM arrives at Shoreditch Town Hall for wedding service.* When Alex looked back up, Harry's face was radiant.

16

Trying to maintain a casual air, Alex accelerated through Waterloo Station concourse. When she reached the south end, she marched through the open doors of the Whistle-Stop, took a sharp left and halted with her back to a display of two-for-one Amstel six-packs.

Seconds later, a small, pale, dark-haired girl wearing lace-up calf-length boots appeared in the doorway. She took one step inside and then stopped, scanning the aisles.

'I knew it,' Alex hissed, stepping away from the lager, making the girl start. 'I bloody knew it. Well, you can tell Captain bloody MacHoras that his people might be a dab hand at online censorship, but they make rubbish real-world spies. And you can tell Director bloody MacBrian that I AM DOING MY BEST. I AM GOING AS FAST AS I CAN.'

'Holy shit!' the girl said. 'You really are a nutter, aren't you?'

Alex found herself staring into the small reflective eye of a vampire. 'Crap,' she said. She swiped at it, but the girl stepped back, her special-edition Twilight iPhone case still trained on Alex's face. 'You can't do that!' Alex hissed. 'This is a . . . a contravention of my human rights!'

'Whatever.' The young Goth lowered her phone and thumbed at the screen. 'Already uploaded, babe. Thanks for the hits.' She flashed Alex the victory sign, revealing a pentagram inked on her wrist, then slouched back towards two other black-clad teens, who were sniggering beside the ticket machines.

Feeling the tears start to prickle, Alex swiped furiously at her eyes and growled, 'Get a grip', surprising a guy in a Rasta hat who was heading for the Amstel.

MacBrian's latest email, which had arrived late the night before, had contained just one line:

Alex. 01857 391542. Call me now.

She hadn't. The last thing she needed was another lecture on how she was drowning the Iskeullians, not to mention screwing up the mental health of the entire human race. Or, indeed, denying the world the possibility of an unending supply of clean energy, with a side order of empathy and creativity to go. She had been serious when she'd told the Goth that she was going as fast as she could. Ten minutes ago, when she'd phoned Lenni to tell him she was about to get on a train to Fring, he had greeted the news with ominous silence.

'Alex,' he had eventually said, his Nordic accent suddenly thick, 'I'm starting to think I have made a mistake. When I came on board with this company, I thought I knew what kind of person you were.'

So she'd told him, improvising, about Harry's surprise

277

wedding plans, insisting that she had to arrange some last-minute details. She had, of course, been careful to omit Harry's other, Eudo-related surprise. Even so, the moment she had heard Lenni's stiff congratulations, she realized that she'd pulled the female card. The family card. The queen of hearts. The one card she'd been determined, ever since becoming a Founder-CEO, to excise from her pack.

But then what the fuck did it matter any more? Her self-respect, the sisterhood, even Eudo? If she didn't find some way to cross herself off the Library's most-wanted list and halt the rot eroding her system, all she'd be CEO of was a mental ward, followed swiftly by a body bag. And at least Harry still loved her. Although, in retrospect, Harry not loving her any more had been one of the few sane developments to occur in the past six months. Now even that anchor had been cut loose.

On board the train, the wi-fi remained maliciously healthy. It enabled her to find, watch and minutely track the progress of her latest YouTube triumph. Comments from concerned Eudomos were pouring in as @EudoGemma tried to pass off Alex's wild-eyed Waterloo outburst as self-satire. Forty minutes of obsessive refreshing later, Alex stepped through the sliding doors of Fring Station, to find her parents' old Astra idling by the kerb.

'Darling! The very-soon-to-be Mrs Fyfield!' Her mother leaned across for a kiss while Alex climbed into the car. 'But look at you. You look terrible. What on earth did they do to you in Shetland?'

It was no good. Alex swung round blindly and clung to

her mother's cardigan, weeping into the soft, thumping dark. After an initial exclamation, her mother lapsed into soothing murmurs and held on tight, stroking her back. Eventually, exhausted, the sobs tailed off into sniffles and hiccups, and Alex reluctantly allowed her mother to lever her upright.

'Come on, my darling, now come on,' her mother tutted, fishing a crumpled tissue from her pocket and dabbing at Alex's face. 'I knew something was wrong the moment I saw you in London, but nothing in the world is worth getting this upset about. There's nothing we can't sort out somehow.'

Studying the lines of Elizabeth Mary Moore's face, Alex wondered how many times over the years her mother had lied to her like this. How many tiny deceits had she performed, as she instinctively tried to protect her daughter from a world that was far stranger and more terrible than the Grimms' Fairy Tales they used to read together every night?

'Now tell me,' her mother said, decisively pocketing the tissue, 'is this about that silly breakfast television interview?'

'*You've* seen that?'

'Caroline Wrigley showed me on her iPad in Waitrose.'

'Great – so now everyone in Fring knows that I'm crazy, too.'

'Don't be silly. You're not crazy, darling. You're tired and you're overworked.'

'But I am crazy, Mum. I'm a total freak. You have no idea—'

No, she didn't. And she wouldn't. And she couldn't. It was Alex's turn to protect her mother from the bogeymen now.

'Darling.' Her mother was watching her closely. 'Is it Harry?'

Alex rubbed vigorously at her face, tried to wrestle herself back under control. 'Harry?'

'Oh, well, we're delighted that you've decided to crack on with the wedding, of course. Only – only after our conversation in London, I *had* rather started to assume you were about to call the whole thing off.'

'No. I – we're fine.' Alex thought miserably of how excited Harry had been last night. How he had countered the questions she had tried to ask about her bad Storyline with a maddening pep talk, clearly believing that she had been deeply scarred by his bluntness the week before. 'Honestly, Mum,' she said bleakly, 'everything's fine. You're right. I'm tired, that's all, and this last trip was the last straw.' She had a stab at her by now well-practised fake smile. 'All I need is some of your food and a good sleep. Really. Please. Can we just go home?'

Her mother stared at her for a moment longer and then, with a tiny fluttering sigh, put the Astra in gear. 'You and your father,' she said, shaking her head, 'blood from a stone.' She embarked on a determinedly cheerful stream of local gossip as they stop-started down the zebra crossings on the High Street.

Murmuring responses on autopilot, Alex stared out at the double row of charity shops and grocers and chemists. The street looked more dilapidated than ever, window after painted-out window gaping like knocked-out teeth. As the Astra passed over the controversial rumble strips at the outskirts of town, the stagesets of Alex's youth juddered by. The crumbling community hall, where she had clapped her hands and stamped her feet through dozens of birthday parties. The primary school with the yellow slide, down which she had forced a screaming Andrew Bullen, splitting his lip. The park where she had dragged their ageing terrier, getting yelled at by the cool kids doing drugs under the monkey bars. But there was no sudden outpouring of emotion, no in-situ lightning bolt. And now the dizziness was starting to rise.

'Mum,' she said, turning away from the window.

' . . . don't seem to realize that they have to be built *somewhere*,' her mother was saying. 'And, really, I think the Poles have been a godsend. My boiler man is very good value, and the woman in the place that used to be Hollingsworth's does an excellent rye.'

'Mum, why did I change my name when I was eleven?'

Her mother glanced sideways. 'Goodness! Where did that come from?'

Alex took a deep breath. 'It's this research project. The Orkney thing. I'm trying to fill in some gaps.'

'Gaps?'

'They're trying to identify the characteristics of high achievers.'

Her mother rolled her eyes. 'Like hard work?'

'Do you, though? Remember why?'

'Well, no, in the sense that you never told me. But then you never told me anything back then, darling. *Plus ça change*. It wasn't hard to guess that it was some sort of adolescent bid for independence, though, with you being about to start at St J's.' She paused. 'Your father was terribly upset, because of Gramma Dot, although he would never have admitted it.'

Alex gazed at a cordoned-off building site that had once been a field. 'That was the beginning of my downward spiral, don't you think? Going to St J's? Wouldn't you say that was the first time in my life I failed, and badly? Enough for me to form a horrible new self-belief inside?'

'Nonsense.' Her mother stared fixedly at the mini-roundabout ahead. 'You did perfectly well. And look at where it's got you now. Anyway, I'm not sure that I approve of all this navel-gazing, darling. People aren't jigsaw puzzles, you know. You can't just click them together, piece by piece.' She hesitated. 'Although—'

'What?'

'Well, I will admit that for years I wondered if we had made the right decision. With St J's. You were so moody that summer before you went that your father and I talked seriously about turning down the scholarship and sending you to Fring. But Dad said that we shouldn't clip your wings before you'd even given it a try, and once you were there' – she swept the wheel round – 'well, you eventually settled down.' She shook her head. 'You know, I'm sure that whole phase started the day you had to miss the Kapurs' camping trip.'

'The camping trip?'

Her mother glanced across. 'Oh, darling, you must remember. That same summer, '95 it must have been, mid-July? Diya and her father had gone out to the car with the

282

bags and you were almost out the door, too, when you dashed back up the stairs. You didn't come back down, so I followed a few minutes later, only to find you throwing up all over the bathroom, poor thing. You were awfully dizzy, you could barely move. I had to tell them to go without you. You spent the whole week in bed, and even when you finally emerged, the funk never seemed to lift.' She chuckled to herself. 'My goodness, what fun we had from then on. The silences! The rows! In retrospect, I wonder if perhaps it was something Diya had said – something that made you scared at the thought of starting St J's. All I knew was that my bright little girl seemed to switch from light to dark in the course of a morning. And from then on, that was that.'

Of course she remembered the aborted camping trip; she had Read the technicolour version only three days before. She had hunched with her eleven-year-old self over the toilet bowl. Lain curled with her in bed. Tasted the hot Ribena that her mother had forced her to drink. Watched her scribble her angst into her diary as soon as she was alone. At the time, inundated with hundreds of Memories, she hadn't given that one a second thought. But now, as she lowered the window and stuck her face into the breeze, the significance of her mother's words hit her with visceral force.

She'd been sick. She'd become dizzy. And, more to the point – stupid fucking idiot – *she'd had a diary.*

Seconds later, 20 Cedar Drive rose over the hedge like some half-forgotten childhood dream. Its mismatched extensions looked diminished and dirty in the morning glare. The lawn was singed from the heatwave. Even the trees seemed somehow to have shrunk and bowed. Gulping down bile and fighting off a rush of light-headedness, Alex slammed the car door and crunched doggedly over the gravel to the front door.

'Before we go in,' her mother said, coming up beside her, key in hand, 'It's probably best not to mention your five min-utes of televisual glory to Dad. He hasn't said anything, of course, but you know what he's like. I suspect he's feeling a little sensitive, considering the things that presenter woman said.'

Alex thought of what Dom had said in the club. 'I think you underestimate Dad, Mum. He's tougher than you real-ize.'

Her mother snorted. 'You both like to think you're tough, darling, but I know better. Those Moore hearts bruise like September plums.'

Alex stared into a withered hanging basket, feeling the tears start to sting yet again. 'Please, Mum,' she mumbled. 'Can we just get out of this sun?'

In the cool dark of the hall her mother turned into the kitchen, already talking about lunch. Alex continued straight up the stairs, shouting that she was going to dump her bag.

Her bedroom had been a guest room for over ten years, but when she opened the door she was still surprised to be greeted by the scent of a freesia reed diffuser, instead of the whiff of Eternity stewed with mouldering tights. She slumped onto the embroidered cream throw that had replaced her old purple duvet cover and wondered helplessly exactly how she expected to have a Proustian epiphany when all traces of her younger self had been so efficiently excised. The posters had long ago been stripped from the walls, the Blu-tack marks covered with paint, the books on her shelves replaced with *Homes & Gardens* back-issues. Her desk, once littered with hair bands, novelty mugs and caseless CDs, held nothing but a box of tissues and a single framed photograph.

Forcing herself to her feet, she went over to the desk and picked up the photograph in a rush of mingled hope and dread. Of course. The familiar faded image had been taken on that fateful afternoon: Saturday, 16 July 2005. There they were, the two of them, standing in the downstairs hall. Her father was cocking one eyebrow, wearing a horrible floral shirt and holding a glass of champagne. Alex was smiling grimly in an unflattering brown dress, gripping his arm like a prison guard. In the background, various family friends could be seen progressing from the lounge to the kitchen; one side of the frame showed an encroaching bulge of purple belly that was unmistakably Dom. Dom, about to break the news of his coup in New York.

But as Alex stared back through ten years and into the face of her twenty-one-year-old self, trying to fathom the feelings encoded into that brittle smile, nothing came up to greet her. No sudden revelation, no moment of emotional engagement, no flash of self-discovery. Just the same old sickening symptoms of an encroaching episode. She would have been about the same age in the photograph, she thought dizzily, as Finn MacEgan was now. Did they allow cameras on Iskeull? Or would they not even risk some blurry analogue shot with a background sliver of Stack finding its way

Outside? Had Finn MacEgan ever posed for an awkward family photo? Had he ever pretended to look happy for the camera and clung onto his father as if he might be about to disappear?

Abruptly she replaced the frame on the desk, face-down. The boy might have attacked her four times in the space of four days, but she owed him more than self-pity disguised as sympathy. She began to search the room, opening drawers and rifling through guest linen, poking about in the wardrobe. Pushing aside the empty hangers, she realized she couldn't think of a single non-clothing-based item that had survived her move to London. She found herself wondering whether the comprehensiveness of her cull had really been due to the cost of square footage in Zone 2. She was the one who had insisted on being so ruthless. Her mother, muttering about grandchildren, had spent most of the sort-out taking things back out of bin bags and squirrelling them away. Could her own desperation to make a clean break from her past have been prompted by her first, failed Reading? Had she been reacting to some subconscious intimation of exactly what it was that had been growing inside her all those miserable years?

She got down on her belly and groped around under the bed. A coffer of heated rollers. A stack of board games. A crate full of foreign editions of *The Switch*. A bag of her mother's old clothes. Then she felt the corner of a large shoebox, and even before she had pulled it out and brushed off the dust to reveal the words *Dorothy's Tresures* scrawled across the lid in marker pen, she knew she had found what she was looking for.

A silk scarf that had belonged to Granny Jean. A thumb-sized good-luck bear. A *Blue Peter* badge, worn to blank plastic. A pair of clip-on enamel earrings that she'd made at Brownies. And then, right at the bottom, a fat book with a squashy pink-and-purple cover.

The *Diary of Dorothy A. Moore* began on 1 January 1995. The first page offered a list of thirty-six resolutions in neat new-stationery handwriting (23: *Stop eating licourish allsorts in bed*). Subsequent entries were sporadic and random, covering everything from reasons she loved Diya, to the lyrics of charting pop songs. There were several big gaps in the chronology, and as Alex turned the pages she began to fear it would turn out to be yet another dead end. Then, about three-quarters of the way through, she stopped breathing.

Sunday 16 July 1995

I want to tell someone. I want to tell someone so much it hurts.

But its a SECRET

MY SECRET

Sick and sick and dizzy and black and lonely and horrible inside.

To think that I was supposed to be camping with Diya today. How can I ever be with Diya again? How can I be with Mum and Pippa and Mrs Mulvony and everyone doing all those normal things like camping and homework and eating and playing, how can I pretend that evrything is normal and that I am OK when I am NOT OK.

I WILL NEVER BE OK AGAIN.

I am going to say I've got a bug so I can stay at home. If I can stay here at least I can keep watch. I can keep control. But how can I stay at home my whole life?

I'm so scared. I wish I was still happy stupid little smiley baby Dorothy but I'm not.

Dorothy is dead.

Its like a lump a big lump inside me and I cant tell anyone and one day its going to birst.

But if it birsts theyll all get hurt. Way way worse than Me.

The day her mother's bright little girl had contracted mysterious germs and switched, just like that, from light to dark. The day that the Story-surging mutation, finding a new Memory fertile with her blossoming fear of St Joseph's, must have planted itself inside. Worse: the day she had *realized*.

Alex blundered up from the carpet and lurched across the corridor, just in time to vomit her train-station granola into the toilet bowl. When the heaves were over, she remained kneeling on the bathroom floor for a few seconds, her head too heavy for her neck, the bones of her knees sharp against the tiles. Swilling her mouth out at the sink, she was shocked to see how bad she looked: not only thin and tired, but positively feverish, her eyes too big and too bright. She could also make out, she was sure, a yellowish tinge to her skin.

'Kansas?' A tap on the door. 'Are you alright?'

'I'm fine, Dad,' she croaked. 'Dodgy takeaway. Sorry. Give me a sec.'

She listened to the floorboards creak as her father walked away, then sat on the side of the bath and gathered her strength. When she felt steady enough to stand, she went back to her bedroom and retrieved the diary from the floor. Every page since the entry on the 16th was blank. She stuffed the diary in her bag, then climbed the stairs to the top floor and pushed open the study door.

Her father looked up from his mess of papers: black coffee in one hand, black Fineliner in the other, framed by the dark wooden beams that met in a peak high overhead. He dropped his pen and gave her a worried beard-crease. 'You okay?'

She bent to kiss his cheek. His skin was warm. He smelled of soap and ink. She found herself having to turn away and feign interest in the Cy Twombly calendar on the wall. 'I'm fine.'

'You don't look fine,' he said gently.

'I'm just tired, Dad,' she said, not meeting his eyes. She leaned against the desk and fiddled with a stack of Post-its. 'How's the book?'

Her father waved a hand over the papers spread across his desk. 'Fine, Kansas. Everything's fine. I'm more interested in how you are. You're not dieting for the wedding, or something dumb like that?'

'No, of course not. It's just a . . . a bug.' She swallowed, started to fold one of the Post-its into a crane. 'The wedding. You don't think it's a bit . . . rushed?'

'Not if it's what you really want. What you both want. Although I have to say I did find a spelling mistake in our laminated itinerary.'

Alex snorted. They locked eyes. She quickly looked away. The things she could not say to him, the knowledge that he knew there were things she was not saying to him, felt like a clamp on her heart.

'Dominic told me that you two met.'

'Mmm.'

'He said you asked him some questions?'

'Yes.'

There was a pause.

'The other—'

'Dominic—'

They both spoke at the same time, both stopped.

Get it together, Alex. Your father isn't your protector any more. You're thirty-one years old and you're not built like him – or anyone else on the planet, as it turns out. *This is your burden. Your Story. Leave his alone.*

'Look, Dad,' she said brightly. 'About the other day – how I was on the phone. And Dom . . . whatever Dom told you. I don't want you to worry. I've been doing a lot of thinking for this research project, that's all. And I wanted to ask you something, about *The Switch*.'

She looked up. Her father – brown eyes riveted on her face – had gone very still.

'I know it annoys you when people try to draw real-life

290

parallels, but was there a reason why you wrote it, when you did? I mean' – she pinched the crane's beak – 'this might sound odd, but did you see something strange in me, when I was born?'

'Strange?'

'Because,' Alex rushed on, 'I was rereading it the other night, and I couldn't stop thinking about Lyman. About how he's born with all this anger inside him, even when he's a tiny baby, and how he manages to hide it away for years, but how eventually, when he becomes a teenager and all that stuff happens with his dad, it starts to come out.'

'Alex. What are you trying to ask me?'

She folded the tail. 'Am I Lyman?'

'Alex.' Her father reached out and squeezed her hand, crane and all. 'Stop.'

'LUNCH!' her mother bellowed from the hall.

'Lunch!' Alex cried, thrusting herself away from the desk and flinging open the door. What the fuck was she doing? she thought, as she thundered down the stairs. Even if he had seen it inside her – her painfully perceptive father – even if he had seen some sort of terrible difference waiting to grow, what good would it do to let him know that she had finally seen it, too? What good would it do to let him know that his lifelong attempts to protect her had failed irrevocably?

In the kitchen, her mother was bending to take a roast chicken out of the oven. Alex was instantly reminded of that other photograph, the one she'd called up on her iPad on the train to Edinburgh, the one from New Year's Eve. It was all too easy, now, to see a direct line from the tortured adoles-cent of the diary to the haunted woman captured by Harry's flash. The woman who had known what was inside her, and who had spent almost twenty years trying to stop it bursting out. But then it had broken free with the help of a brilliant Reader, and neutralized her memories, and for six short months it had succeeded in setting her free, too. Six months of freedom in twenty years. With a God-awful catch.

Alex sat heavily at the kitchen table and stared, fizzing, breathless and nauseous, at the pears and partridges on the PVC cloth. Her mother placed a glass of Prosecco in front of her. There was the shuffle of slippers as her father walked in. Serving dishes slid onto the middle of the table, then chairs scraped as her parents took their places at either end, with Alex in the middle, just as they always had.

'Darling!' Her mother raised her glass. 'To you and Harry! To TRM and LM getting the Waterloo train next Saturday at o-six-hundred hours!'

Alex realized they were waiting for her to lift her glass. She lifted her glass. Her mother clinked and took a sip. Her father silently drained his glass in one and reached for a refill. Alex stared into the bubbles. Oh God, had she avoided drinking all those years because she suspected it would make it easier for her to 'birst'? Slowly she returned the brimming flute to the table.

'Now, darling,' her mother said, brandishing the sharpen-ing steel. 'Louise Parker's cousin volunteered on a dig in Orkney and she said that it's magical. I want to hear every last detail.'

292

17

Sitting alone in the attic on the same old broken wheelie chair, hunched in front of the Mac that had replaced the Gateway, Alex scrolled through images of sports-day races and prize-giving speeches and exam-envelope-opening tableaux. She wasn't in touch with any of her former classmates from St Joseph's. She'd barely spoken to them when she was there. An inveterate loner, a vapid fringe-floater, she'd paired up with other misfits only when projects or PE required.

With one exception: an old friend from Fring Primary. Another scholarship girl who had refused, despite Alex's increasingly sophisticated portfolio of avoidance techniques, to entirely let her go.

It took Alex only a couple of minutes of browsing to find a comment from a name she recognized ('OMG Major memories!!') under a photo of the drama block. Julia Bristow had been the meanest of mean girls, a bulimic redhead with a hot brother and a talent for haughty put-downs, but it seemed that time and boredom dissolved all hierarchies, because Julia now appeared to be friends with everyone who had been in their year. It didn't take Alex long to spot, amongst Julia's connections, a head-shot of a dark-skinned woman smiling out from the ghost of her younger self. Diya Goldsmith, née Kapur.

Alex send a friend request with a short note: *Hi, Diya. Remember me?*

The acceptance came back instantly.

> Alex Moore!! Of course! Wow, hiiii! :)
>> How are you?
> All good! Living in East London now, coding 4 a creative agency. Supercool :) :)
>> That's great
> Thanks!! How things change, right? Julia B is divorced w 3 kids in Fring & you're like St Js official superstar!! They never stop boasting about you in that sodding newsletter! So cool!
>> Thanks, Diya. Hey, you remember the summer before we went to St J's? 1995?

There was a pause, then:

> Yeah sure
>> Do you remember that I was supposed to go camping with you and your parents, but then I couldn't go because I got a bug?
> Oh yeah. I was really disappointed! But that bug was pretty serious, wasn't it?

Another pause.

TBH my mum wondered if it was M.E., but I never
really knew.

So you don't remember me talking to you about
it at all? About what it was?

Er not really, no. I don't think we met up for the whole
rest of that hol.

And I didn't mention it when we got to St J's?

Um well, I'm pretty sure I tried, but TBH you didn't
really want to talk to me at all once we got to St
J's!!

The message window said that Diya was still typing, but
although Alex waited for almost a minute, no more text
appeared. She was just about to log off when another speech
bubble popped up:

Except for that batshit bust-up in the changing rooms.

Alex wheeled back in the chair. Now that she thought
about it, she did vaguely remember a Memory from her bad
Storyline featuring her and Diya shouting at each other in a
square of benches and lockers, wearing nothing but their
grotty underwear. She hadn't paid much attention to it at the
time, dismissing it as a typically melodramatic adolescent
argument; and now, when she tried to dredge it back up, she
felt the dizziness come on so badly that she had to jerk her
mind away. She wheeled forward again to find a fresh message on the screen, longer this time:

Actually I'm really glad you got in touch TBH. I've thought about what you said back then quite a few times over the years. I always wondered what all that was really about, if there was stuff going on at home or something. I always felt guilty that I didn't make more effort to find out, but TBH you kind of freaked me out & I didn't know how to handle it.

Alex grabbed the keyboard:

That's okay. You were great. But can you tell me what you remember about that fight?
Seriously?
I know, I know. It sounds mad. But the thing is I think I've kind of . . . blocked it out. I think that time was really traumatic for me, and I repressed a lot of my memories. That's partly why I got in touch. You know – for closure. I'd really appreciate if you could give me all the detail you can. Help me get inside the emotions I was feeling at the time. I'm trying to make my peace with it all so I can move on.

A long pause. But Diya was typing, apparently. Then:

OK. If it might help you – sure. Well, I know it was end of the autumn term, just before we broke up, cos we were supposed to do the Xmas stall together, but after we had that fight I ended up partnering with

296

Susie K (bitch!) instead :(We were the last to leave one afternoon after P.E. & I was pissed off with you really because you'd been avoiding me ever since we got to St Js & I felt like you'd kind of left me in the lurch. Anyway we were the last to leave the changing rooms & I think I made some sarky comment about you being a loner & you sort of went mental, started kicking the shit out of the lockers. It was totally not like you. Obvs I asked you WTF was going on and that's when you said all that crazy stuff.

What crazy stuff?
Seriously???!!!

Please . . .

OK, well I can still remember every word clear as day because it was like some crazy horror film. You said that you had this secret, that you were afraid that someone was going to die & that you didn't know how to stop it happening.

Alex scooted back so fast that the broken wheel caught and the chair toppled over, depositing her onto the floorboards. Heart leaping, she jumped up, dragged the chair upright and reached for the keyboard:

What secret? Who did I think was going to die?
You tell me!! I asked you about it but then you calmed down & clammed up. It really freaked me out. I was going to tell my mum but then I thought it

297

sounded too mad, so I told myself it must have been a horrible joke. Was it a joke?

I wish. I bloody wish.

After a moment, Diya added:

Look, does this have something to do with that viral from that morning TV interview? :/ Wasn't going to bring it up but Julia B sent everyone a group message. Plus my mum texted me.

Oh.

Hey don't stress about it, Alex. They're just jealous. You're doing something big with your life now. Who cares if you let it all out. Don't let them fence you in :)

I'm sorry if I freaked you out. Then. Or now.

No worries. Every story's got 2 sides, right? Anyway we should def go for a cocktail. I was actually thinking of getting in touch myself. Our agency would be a GREAT fit for Eudo.

Alex fobbed Diya off with some dates, then powered down the computer and climbed back down the stairs. Her mother had returned; she could hear her talking on the phone in the kitchen as she opened her bedroom door. She was just about to go in, when something in her mother's tone made her pause. She tiptoed over to the top of the stairs and crouched beside the bannister.

'. . . feel like whatever I say might be wrong, but I was worried, seriously worried, Barbara, from the moment I saw her get off that train. Mmm. Yes. No, terribly thin, and she didn't eat a scrap of lunch. Yes, well exactly, I don't want her to think I'm not proud. I mean, she's always been bright, in a way *too* bright for her own good. And of course I'm delighted she's finally found her – yes. But that's it. All this pressure, all the articles and interviews, and now that awful – Well, *exactly*, Barbara. What's wrong with normal? We can't all be extraordinary, can we? That's the point. And – well, yes, I know. You have, Barbara. And so have I. And it's not that I don't admire ambition, I mean look at Tom. And – yes, well, that's exactly my point. There *is* a price. And the main thing, Barbara, is that she's running on empty. She's burnt-out inside.'

Alex tiptoed back to her room and shut the door, feeling end-weighted ropes begin to grapple the muscles of her mouth, her ankles, her diaphragm. Moments later, she heard a creak from the stairs that led down from the top floor. The shuffle of footsteps. A knock.

'Kansas?' A pause. 'Kansas, please?'

She crawled under the throw.

She caught the train back to London that evening, despite her mother's protests. Her father, lumbering out of his study at the last moment to say goodbye, had held her so tightly she thought her ribs might break.

At least once she was back in her own small, bare flat, where everything was bright and disposable and shinily non-adhesive to the past, the dizziness receded a bit. Thankfully, too, MacBrian had stopped inundating her with missed calls. Alex knew she should contact MacBrian now and tell her what she had found. But as she stood at the window, watching the Haggerston kids jump on broken bottles beneath the recycling bins, she began to feel that Iskeull had finally become the place that felt like a dream.

It was clear, now, that she'd never be able to uncover the true meaning of that Storyline, or push past the rot to reconnect with its root Memory. She'd never be strong enough to force her Story out of that wall. Never become the energy-wielding superhero Taran thought she could be. All she could do was lie to the people she loved – pretend pretend pretend – while she waited for it to erode her body and her mind. In the meantime, there was only one way she could undo a tiny bit of the damage she was causing to all those un-Read people in the world.

She could keep Eudo afloat.

She took some painkillers, opened her laptop on the sofa and read back through the past week's worth of content on the site. Then she opened her email and found, among the 2,748 messages, a conciliatory note from Lenni.

> Alex – Looks like there could be a backlash in the works. It was rough for the first 3 days, especially after Waterloo-gate, but over the weekend we've seen a load of members leap to your defence. Consensus seems that both inter-view and virals show you as 'refreshingly vulnerable'. Same in the site comments – 'I know how that feels, she's a real woman', etc. Broadsheets have run a couple of op-eds about emotionally open female leadership styles. And – wait for it – Gemma is this close to securing a piece

from Helena Pereira. She has a new range to promote, and her people want to ghost a 'women in the spotlight' solidarity thing. A small part of me thinks you planned this all along. Do I owe you an apology? – L

In the shower the next morning Alex murmured, 'Alex Moore, Founder-CEO, Alex Moore, Founder-CEO' while she washed her hair. She would keep her head down, let Lenni take on Eudo's public engagements, stop drinking, stop going out. She would delete her social profiles, change her phone number, put a block on gcaseu.org emails. And she would work.

She towel-dried her hair, dressed in black jeans and a black T-shirt and dug out an old baseball cap. Forcing down a banana and more Nurofen, she put on her sunglasses, pressed in her earbuds and cued up a 'Friday Focus' playlist, then set off along the canal. She made it to the bottom of New North Road without thinking about Iskeull once.

Finn MacEgan was standing beside the hire bikes.

She was running before she'd had time to think. Instinct drove her towards Old Street Tube, where she knew there would be crowds, cameras, police. Then, halfway down the steps to the underpass, she slipped and felt someone catch the top of her arm, grab the other, drag her upright.

'I'M SORRY!' he bellowed, pressing her against the wall, her shock buying him time for another line. 'I'm not going to hurt you. I promise.'

'You alright, love?' A man in a high-vis vest and paint-splattered boots had paused on the stairs. Finn was bone-white and sweating in a hideous orange jumper, brown trousers and chunky ankle boots. His grey eyes were wide, blue-socketed, pleading. 'Listen,' he panted, dropping his hands. 'Please. Just listen to me.'

Alex took a shuddering breath and straightened her T-shirt. 'I'm fine,' she told the man in high-vis, who raised his eyebrows, shook his head and moved on. She remained where she was, reassured by all the bodies swerving past, and eyed the canvas holdall slung over Finn's shoulder. A documentary she'd once seen about crisis negotiators came to mind. She took off her sunglasses and hooked them onto the front of her T-shirt.

'Finn,' she said slowly. 'I hear what you're saying. I appreciate the apology. And I'm sorry about your father, truly I am. But I didn't mean for what happened to happen, you have to believe that. And I've tried everything, I really have, but there's nothing I can do about it now. Don't you think you should just go back – *there* – and get on with your life?'

'I don't have a life there, any more.' He was shuddering, squinting in the sun. 'But that's not why I'm here. I'm here for you.'

'Seriously, guys, take it somewhere else,' snapped a girl in a topknot and a tiger backpack, jogging down the steps.

'Please,' Finn repeated, flinching as a truck belched past. 'I just want to talk.'

Alex Moore, Founder-CEO, her shower-voice said. Then: *You killed his dad.*

'Okay,' she said. 'One hour. Somewhere public. But if you touch me again, I'll scream.'

She led him into Shoreditch Grind and told him to find

a seat while she went to the counter to get a bottle of water and buy some time. She watched him through the breakfast crowd as the card machine whirred. He looked like an over-grown child, perched on a stool in the window, alternately gazing around the room and looking back at her. Alex was scared, so scared that her fingers fumbled when she tried to key in her PIN. But she couldn't pretend there wasn't a tiny thread of relief spinning through the guilt and the anger and the fear.

He knew about the Library. Whatever he was here for, at least she was with someone who *knew*.

She took her water and pushed her way through the crush. She moved the stool next to his as far back as possible before she climbed on it, still close enough to smell the acrid tang of his sweat. He watched her wrestle with the bottle-top, the tip of his tongue darting between his lips. Alex took a defiant slug and screwed the top back on.

'I need—' Finn began, as a hip-hop song blasted out of the speaker on the wall. He cleared his throat, leaned closer. 'You have to come back,' he repeated in a hoarse shout.

'I beg your pardon?'

He swiped at his hair, his hand shaking. 'I mean, please. For your sake, you have to come back to Iskeull.'

The nest of snakes in her stomach erupted. Faintly she asked, 'Why? What have I done?'

'You – what do you mean, what have you done?'

'Have I—?' She paused, tried to breathe. 'Is someone else dead?'

'No! No. Not that I know of.'

She closed her eyes as the snakes exploded into sherbet, fizzing through her veins. Thank God. Or the Library. Or whatever it was that called the shots in this crazy world. Then she opened her eyes again and narrowed them at him. 'So why on earth would MacBrian send *you* to herd me back in?'

A spark of the old fire flashed in his eyes. 'I don't take orders from Sorcha MacBrian.'

'Then why aren't you still in prison?'

'Taran got me out. Professor MacGill.'

'*Taran* put you up to this?'

A man sat down on the other side of Finn and swiped at his iPad. Finn glanced at the man, then the screen, then turned back and shuffled his stool a couple of inches closer to Alex. 'No, Taran got me transferred to house arrest. His house. He was supposed to keep me locked in, but I got out. He doesn't know I'm here. No-one does.'

Alex crossed her arms, afraid that he would see her heart thumping through the thin cotton of her T-shirt. 'So why the hell would *you* want me to come back?'

'Because you're in danger. You have to realize that they won't leave you alone until you fix this.'

'Oh, Christ. Look, you don't seem to understand. It's not that I don't want to fix it. Why doesn't anyone get that? Do you think it doesn't bother me, discovering that I've killed someone I've never even met? Do you think I don't care that I'm hurting millions of people, just by being alive? Well, I *do*. It's a fucking nightmare. And I wish – I *wish* there was some way I could get my mutant bloody Story to stop whatever it's doing, but I can't, okay? I don't know how to get it under control.'

'But it's *you*! It's part of you. How can you not get it under control?'

'I don't fucking know!' Alex slammed her hand down on the counter. The man with the iPad glared at them, then angled his back to block them out. Alex lowered her voice to a hiss. 'Anyway, isn't this supposed to be *your* department? Isn't this the whole *raison de* bloody *être* of your precious bloody tribe, understanding how this shit works?'

Finn ran his shaking hands through his hair again. 'Sorry. You're right. And no-one understands what's happening. Not really. Not even Taran. They're just fighting among themselves and blaming my father, while the Library gets worse and worse. That's why you have to come back.'

Alex groaned. 'Look, if I thought it would help, I would. But I went down into my Story and' – she swallowed as the bile began to rise – 'it didn't work. The rot was too strong. I was too weak. Even if I did return to Iskeull, I don't see what more I could do.'

'Try again. Go back down there and try.'

'I tried, Finn, alright! I tried! And I've been trying here too, trying and trying, and it hasn't helped at all. In fact, it's made things worse.'

'Then MacBrian will have you killed.'

There was a moment of silence, in which she could hear the shallow wheeze of his breath. Then 'Nonsense,' she said firmly. 'You're just trying to scare me. I know about that Covenant thing.'

'The Covenant was written when nobody believed anything like this could happen. Half of the Readers are on strike, afraid it might happen again, with a different Story. The Stacks are slowing down, the rain is getting worse, crops are failing, we're running out of fish. The Council is in chaos. The Board's threatening to intervene.'

'That still doesn't mean MacBrian's going to murder me, for God's sake!'

'She's already proposed it to the Board.'

'And how would *you* know that?'

'Taran. He made me swear not to tell anyone, but he couldn't help but tell me when he came back from the Council meeting. He says she panicked when she didn't hear from you. He says she's out of her depth.'

'Okay. Fine. Let's say you're right. Why would you come here and warn me?' She forced herself to meet his eyes. 'I killed your father, for God's sake. I'd have thought you'd be the first person to dance on my grave.'

Finn licked his lips. 'I – I got you wrong. You aren't what I thought you were.'

'What, you mean a monster?'

'It was a possibility.'

'Before you met me, maybe! But you came to my office, you drank my coffee, you listened to me talk.' Alex paused. 'You looked into my eyes. Did you see a monster?'

'No! No. Not exactly. But I did see . . . I saw . . .' He was doing it again, then; looking at her the way he had before. She made herself stay open to him, offer herself up. The cafe's industrial pendants danced in his Atlantic irises.

Micro-expressions swept his craggy face like island clouds. 'I didn't understand what I saw,' he said eventually. 'That was the problem. You're like a storm without an eye. You don't make sense.'

'And that, Finn MacEgan,' Alex said, looking away, 'is the most sensible thing you've said so far.'

They sat in silence while, one by one, spots of Finn's sweat rained onto the concrete floor. Eventually Alex unscrewed the bottle and handed it to him. He drained the remaining water in a single draught of great animal gulps. 'You have no reason to trust me,' he said when he had finished. 'But I wasn't the one who attacked you outside your home, or the man who was taken away by the police. And I don't know what I thought I was going to do by coming to your office, but I definitely didn't have a gun. Although—'

'Although what?'

'I don't know what I might have done, when I found you spying in the index. If you hadn't—' He reached into the neck of his orange jumper and pulled out the same blue leather necklace he had been wearing when he had visited her office. Hanging from it, beside the carved pebble and a plastic-topped car key, was the yellow Lego USB stick she had rammed into his throat. 'I could have hurt you then. After you'd seemed to mock me in your office, talking about death and readers and stories, after you'd managed to convince Taran and MacBrian that you were innocent. That's why I kept this. To remind myself how easy it is. To become like her. To give into what's wrong because it feels right.'

Alex knuckled her eyelids. 'So what, you're saying that MacBrian tried to kill me even before I came to Iskeull?'

'Maybe. I don't know. But I do know that Dughlas is lying. Was lying. My father would never have acted like that, compromising the records, sneaking around behind Sorcha MacBrian's back. If he'd wanted to work extra shifts, he'd just have argued it out with her. He wasn't afraid of her. He wasn't afraid of the Council. He wasn't afraid of anyone.' He let off a salvo of full-body hacks that made his stool shake. 'He'd have been horrified,' he gasped, 'if he knew what they were planning to do. The precedent it would set. He made me learn the Covenant by heart when I was five years old. It's another reason why I had to come. He'd have wanted me to stop it. To help you.'

Alex looked round the cafe. There were so many people; so many of them pale and dark-haired. 'Okay,' she said. 'So let's say I trust you. Let's even say I agree with you. Let's say, for argument's sake, that I'm fed up of doing the wrong thing. Of *being* the wrong thing. That for once in my life I want to face up to who I really am, or die trying. If the Board has given the go-ahead for this bloody fatwa, how exactly am I supposed to get back onto Iskeull, and into that tomb place in the middle of the Stacks, without getting shot in the head?'

Silence. She looked back. Finn's stool was empty.

'Hey!'

She looked down. The man with the iPad was kneeling on the floor.

'Hey,' he said again. 'I think your friend needs an ambulance.'

18

They made her wait in a crowded oasis of plastic chairs while they 'performed tests'. The paramedics had assumed that Alex was his girlfriend, and it was easier just to go with it. To jump into the back of the ambulance. To field their questions with vague lies while they strapped an oxygen mask to his dark-lashed, bloodless face. To follow them into the Homerton and watch them wheel his twitching body on a trolley down a strip-lit corridor.

She knew without a doubt that it was bad for him to be there, for tests to be performed. But she hadn't known what else to do. As the minutes and then the hours trickled past, she watched those around her come and go in a swatch-book of skin colours and a babble of languages. Some looked scared and others looked sad, but most simply looked bored. Her phone remained in her bag, and she let others pick through the dog-eared magazines. She sat in silence and let the tide of humanity roll around her – fragile, damaged, bored humanity – and waited to find out what she was going to decide to do.

'Jesus, Alex! Thank God. I've been looking for you everywhere. No-one had any record of you being admitted.' She blinked up. Harry was staring down at her, chestnut hair ruffled, stubbled cheeks flushed. 'What the hell happened? Are you alright?' He crouched down in front of her. 'Alex? What's the matter?'

'Harry,' she said dazedly. 'Why are you here?'

'Why am *I* here? I spent all morning trying to get hold of you, to make a decision about the cake. I phoned your mother, but she said you'd got the train back last night, so I tried your office and they told me you'd had to go to hospital. Why didn't you call me?' He grasped her knees. 'Alex? What on earth's wrong?'

Alex desperately tried to engage her brain. 'Nothing. Nothing's wrong. Well, not with me. It's a . . . a colleague. They fell ill. When they were with me. I thought I should come.'

Harry rocked back on his heels and blew out a heavy *whooo* of air. 'Thank God. Jesus, Alex, I've been frantic. I thought you'd been in an accident.'

'I'm sorry. I didn't think—'

'No.' Harry rose to his full height. 'No, obviously not.' He straightened his T-shirt, ran a hand through his hair. 'Are they alright?'

'Who?'

'Your colleague, Alex. Are they okay?'

'Oh, they're . . . I don't know.'

'What happened?'

'They . . . um, they fainted.'

'And what? Hit their head?'

'Alex Moore?' A short, plump Indian doctor walked up beside Harry, holding a clipboard.

310

'Yes?' Harry said, turning round.

The doctor looked from Alex to Harry and back again. 'Are you—'

'Yes,' Alex said wearily. 'I'm Alex Moore.'

'Okay.' The doctor rubbed her forehead. 'Well, we've done the tests on your boyfriend, and although he's currently in a stable—'

'Boyfriend?' Harry said.

The doctor looked from Alex to Harry and back again. 'I was under the impression—'

'No,' Alex said quickly, not looking at Harry. 'He's not. We're not. We're . . . um, colleagues. Is he alright?'

The doctor rubbed her forehead again. 'Well, as I said, he's now stable, but he's still very weak, and at this point we're still not sure what's causing his symptoms. We'd like to run further tests, but he's proving very resistant. He's rather upset.' She glanced at Harry. 'He's been asking to see you ever since he came round. He should be strong enough to see you now, but it would be very helpful if you could try and persuade him to cooperate.'

Alex stood up. 'Right.' She turned to Harry. 'I should – do that.'

The Air Force blues were trained on her face. 'Who is he?' he said.

'He's, um . . . well. He's one of the students I'm working with on this research project.'

'From Orkney?'

'Yes, he – uh, he came to catch up with my progress.'

'You didn't tell me.'

'It was a – a very last-minute thing.'

'And he fainted? I thought they were all macho outdoor types.'

'Yes, well, he's . . . um, he's not used to the city. The pollution and everything.'

'Okay,' Harry said, after a beat. He gave a strained smile. 'No problem. If it's important for you. For Eudo.' He sat down in the chair Alex had just vacated. 'I'll wait here.'

'Oh, no, really, you don't have to—'

'No problem,' Harry replied calmly. He held up his Black-Berry. 'I'll keep working on the P&L I've been drawing up for Eudo. Take your time.'

Alex stared down at him.

'Miss Moore?' the doctor prompted, gesturing with her clipboard.

'Um,' Alex said. 'I – um – okay.'

She followed the doctor down the corridor, trainers squeaking on the linoleum. She glanced back at Harry, who looked up from his BlackBerry and gave her another tight smile.

'We thought it was drugs, initially,' the doctor said, 'but all the tests have come back clear. It's a strange collection of symptoms, and quite debilitating, but since he woke up he's refused to let us take any more blood. Is there a relative we can call?'

'No,' Alex said quickly. 'No, they're . . . um, estranged.'

'Ah.' The doctor stopped in front of a curtain. 'Are you quite alright yourself? You look quite – run-down.'

'I'm fine.'

The doctor shrugged. 'Okay. Well. If you could do what you can. I'll be back in ten minutes.' She moved the curtain back an inch, and headed back along the corridor.

Finn was hunched over at the end of the bed, stark naked but for the full-torso tattoo and the farmer's trousers he was pulling on. He looked up. Their eyes locked. 'Thank the Library,' he said, straightening up, the trousers suspended halfway up his thighs. 'I thought you'd gone.'

Alex dragged the curtain closed.

'We have to get out of here now,' his voice said from behind the curtain, the shiny fabric imprinted with a vista of indigo-inked muscle that she was never going to shake. 'They can't get any DNA.'

Deciding this wasn't the time to tell him that the police were already puzzling over his – no, someone else's – Iskeullian DNA in one of their labs, Alex edged the curtain back. By now, thank God, his trousers were buttoned, and he was pulling on his shirt. On the hospital bed behind him lay a crumpled gown and the abandoned snake of a saline drip.

'The ferry will take too long,' he croaked, reaching for his boots. 'Have you got enough money for an aeroplane?'

'Yes,' Alex said, surprising herself. She wasn't aware that she'd made a decision, sitting back there in the waiting room, but apparently she had. 'I'll put it on the Eudo credit card. But are you sure you're alright to fly? Can you even walk?'

'Don't worry about me,' he said, fumbling with the laces. He was so pale as to be virtually opalescent, his forehead glistening, the sooty hair matted in clumps. He grabbed his holdall from beside the bed. 'Just get us out of here.'

Alex tweaked the curtain aside. Amongst the bustling nurses and slow-moving patients, their doctor was nowhere to be seen. 'It's just down there,' she said, 'but there's a complication. I need to find a way to—' But he had already pushed past her and was striding unsteadily along the corridor.

'Wait!' Alex hissed, rushing after him, but it was too late. He had almost reached the waiting room, and now Harry, who had been gazing in their direction, had seen them and was rising to his feet.

'Hey,' Harry said, spreading his arms like a bullfighter. 'Hey, mate, steady on.'

'Finn!' Alex yelled, noticing the predatory tension that had stiffened his back. 'It's okay! He's a – he's a friend.'

Finn stopped and turned on his heels, wobbling.

'I tried to explain,' Alex panted, rushing into the space between them. 'Harry – Harry came to see if I was okay. He didn't know you were here. He doesn't know – about—' she petered off, seeing Harry's face.

'Friend?' Harry said.

'Fiancé,' Alex said. 'Finn, this is Harry, my fiancé. Harry, this is Finn MacEgan. He's a—' She swallowed. 'He's . . . um, well, he's part of the . . . the GCAS.'

Harry and Finn were eyeing each other like a lion and a hyena might, across the body of an injured gazelle. Harry had never looked so vital, so broad, so clean. Finn, a blue vein juddering across his temple, looked like a complete wreck.

314

'What don't I know about?' Harry asked, without moving his gaze from Finn.

'We don't have time for this,' Finn said, without moving his gaze from Harry.

'The trip.' Alex touched Harry's wrist. His eyes flickered down to her face. 'I didn't get a chance to tell you. Finn has come to ask me to go back with him. To the island. There are some . . . uh, more interviews they need to do.'

Harry thrust his arm across Alex's back. He swept her away to a wall covered in posters displaying grisly images of organs in various states of decay. 'Alex,' he said. 'We are getting married in five days.'

'I know.' Alex glanced back at Finn, who was riveted by the tech-wielding human circus sprawled across the waiting-room chairs. 'It'll only be the weekend, I *promise*. There are just a few last things I need to help them with, then it'll be over for good.' One way or another, she thought hopelessly, staring at a photographic cross-section of a nicotine-ravaged lung.

'You need,' Harry said slowly, 'to step away from this research project, Alex. I know you've only been trying to do what I asked – to do some thinking about yourself – but it's clearly gone too far. It's obviously upsetting you. Look at all those questions you asked me on Wednesday night. A well-meaning idea has turned into unproductive naval-gazing, and now you need to let this introspection go and focus on the future. *Our* future – together in every way. I feel responsible for pushing you away, and I want to help you, but you have to let me in.' His arm was still across her back, and he gave her a little shake.

'I can't, though,' Alex whispered, looking up at him. 'Not with this. If you're truly willing to support me now, you have to trust me. You're right, I never should have got mixed up in this thing, and I wish I could just let it go. My God how I wish. But now I have to finish what I started. It's out of my control.'

'What about *your destiny is your responsibility*? I've memorized Eudo's core values, you know.'

'I'm sorry, Harry. I have to go.'

He clenched his jaw, but he didn't drop his arm. 'Have you told Lenni that I'm coming on board?'

'Oh. Um. Not yet. He's still a bit sensitive after the virals. I need to pick the right time.'

'You will, though? Before you go?'

'Um, yes, I – yes. Okay.'

'And you'll need to let me know about the cake. Almond polenta or stack of Hertfordshire cheese.'

'Okay, I – um, polenta sounds good.'

'And the flowers. Lily-of-the-valley or amnesia roses.'

'Right. Yes. The second one.'

'And the music. I've found a Guildhall student who could do a classical medley on the violin.'

'Sure.'

'Alright. I'll action those. Wednesday, then.'

'Yes. Wednesday.'

Harry curled his arm round and swept her into his chest. Tilting back her chin with his spare hand, he cupped her jaw and kissed her, passionately and for a very long time. As Alex staggered back, Harry nodded at Finn, who had, like the rest of A&E, turned to watch.

'Have a good trip, mate,' he called, wiping his mouth with the back of his hand. 'And take care. You look pretty weak to me.'

Curled on a leather sofa in a quiet corner of the airport lounge, Alex tried to focus on composing her Eudo out-of-office autoreply. But every few seconds she found herself looking up, searching for Finn. There – he was there, rounding the central buffet station, heading back her way. He did not, she thought, look well. At all. When he reached the sofa he swung his holdall off his shoulder and onto the cushions beside Alex. It landed with an odd crackling noise. Then, before she could say anything, he turned and wobbled back across the lounge. As soon as he had disappeared around the complimentary newspaper stand, Alex leaned over and peered into the holdall.

A base layer of balled-up cape was just about visible beneath a vast mound of foil-covered chocolates, bags of pretzels and crisps, individually wrapped *cantuccini* and can upon mini-can of Coke, Red Bull and Sprite. No shotgun. She sprang back as Finn returned, his arms laden with copies of *Grazia*, *Intelligent Life*, *Wallpaper* and *Men's Health*.

'What are you doing?' she asked.

'Big market for Outside gear,' he said, piling the magazines into the bag.

'Taran told me you flew in supplies.'

'Essentials. A few luxuries, allocated per family on a rotating basis. We exchange some local specialities with the other Chapters. Only Council members have credit cards.'

She thought, giddily, of Tim at Eudo, who regularly dis-coursed upon his village in *Clash of Clans* as if it were real. 'But . . . where do they even get *money*?'

'We export produce we don't need. It goes for a lot, espe-cially the fish and the beef. Each island pays a tithe into a shared account in Luxembourg that the Board reallocates in emergencies. Any extra funds we need, Iain MacHoras's team gets online at Ronaldsay.'

'What do you mean, online?'

'Library people are good with networks. Better than Out-side banks.'

'Wait . . . you mean you're *hackers*?'

'Library Tax, MacHoras calls it.'

'It sounds like stealing to me!'

He gave her a level look. 'It seems like a fair exchange for what we do,' he said and walked off unsteadily.

Alex returned to the text she had been composing.

Think it'll be good for me to stay under the radar for a while, she tapped.

You can stay under the radar, Lenni's reply shot back, *in the office.*

Sorry. I have no choice.

I thought we already talked about priorities.

I know. I promise, once I get back – if I get back – no more trips.

At this point, Alex thought, if only I could get back for good, I'd happily stay in my flat for the rest of my life. The smell of New York and the heat of the desert and the noise of Tokyo can go hang.

We need to capitalize on the backlash, Alex. We need to show you're not afraid.

Just give me a few days, Lenni. A few more days.

Alex looked up. Finn was back, his pockets bulging. He unloaded a fistful of boiled sweets, two dozen sachets of instant coffee and an aerosol of magnolia air freshener into the bag.

'Seriously?'

'Iskeullians like to complain about Outside materialism, but half of them would trade their prize heifer for a stick of chewing gum.'

'And you?'

'Full-time Readers are different.' He sat, suddenly, on the sofa and closed his eyes. Alex watched his eyelashes flutter, his face tight with pain. 'Not,' he said tightly, 'that that's an option any more.'

'They banned you,' Alex said, after a moment.

A tiny twitch of his shoulders. 'I knew the rules.'

'Taran said you loved it. More than anything. Just like your dad.'

He didn't reply.

'I can't imagine what it would be like, doing that full-time. Spending hours upon hours Reading other people in the dark. Knowing that you'll never get to see what they see, go where they go. Isn't it torture?'

After a moment, he said, 'It's everything.'

'But don't you feel trapped?'

Another twitch. 'It's all I've ever known. Anyway, Read enough people and you come to realize that everyone is trapped in some way.' He opened one eye. 'When I came to your office, you said you were trapped.'

'Yes. I suppose I was. Until—'

'Until.' He closed the eye.

Unbidden, Alex saw a face staring out from between rotten shutters, a halo of dusky hair. 'I met Taran's sister,' she said.

He opened both eyes this time. 'Freya?'

'We saw her on the beach below Taran's house. She was steaming drunk. She asked a lot of questions about real – I mean, about life Outside. Taran said she struggles.'

'It's harder, if you're not allowed to Read. And Freya's a special case.'

'Why?'

'She fell in love.'

'And what's so bad about that?'

'With an Outsider.'

'Oh.'

He picked a boiled sweet out of the bag. Unwrapped it. Rewrapped it. 'She was sixteen. She told him she lived with her mother, that her mother was ill, that she couldn't often get away. They met in Kirkwall every time she had leave, two days every three months for years, until someone from Iskeull spotted them together. She was ordered never to see him again.' He paused. 'She disobeyed. She got pregnant. They found her trying to smuggle him onto the island. He was beaten up and warned off. She was banned from the Library, and her Outside leave was permanently revoked. That's when she started to drink.'

'Jesus. What happened to the baby?'

'It miscarried. They always do, if they're got from Outside men.'

'*Fuck.*'

There was a long silence.

'Must've been strange for you,' Finn broke it abruptly. 'Finding out about us.'

'Honestly,' Alex said, admitting the truth only as she said it, 'I think I knew about the Library already. Deep down. I think everyone does. We're all part of it, after all, aren't we? It's part of us.' She sighed. She looked across the lounge at all the faces around them. Young, old, fat, thin, brown, black, yellow, white. Anxious, excited, irritated. Mostly blank, in the pale light of a screen. 'But coming back to London? Being the only person outside those seven islands, walking freely around the world, who has actually seen it? That's hell. Oh, it's lonely, not being able to talk about it with anyone. But that's not the worst part. The worst part is watching everyone plough through their lives without realizing that what's going on in their brains *matters*. That they're making real things out of their thoughts. Real, glowing, living things. And that so many of those thoughts are holding them back. Everywhere I look I see people creating Memories that are like tiny blocks of concrete, dragging them down. People operating from Storylines that are like handcuffs, tying them to a rigid idea of who they are. I want to scream at them all.' She picked at a frayed thread on her jeans. 'I want to scream at myself.'

'It doesn't really change anything, though,' Finn said. 'Knowing about the Library.'

She stared at him. 'It changes *everything*.'

'Not really. As you said, the Library's just . . . people. You don't need to Read Stories to know that's how we work.'

'Just? *Just?*'

He closed his eyes again. 'Except it *has* changed, now. All of it. Because of you.'

'Yeah,' Alex said bitterly. 'Thanks for reminding me. All hail the evil mutant.' She thought of the words scrawled inside the diary. She thought of the words Diya had typed.

I thought it sounded too mad, so I told myself it must have been a horrible joke. Was it a joke?

'Do you think that Taran's right? Do you think it could be this Story-surging thing? Do you really think my Story could have evolved to use consciousness as a . . . a *weapon?*'

Another shoulder-twitch. 'My father knew the Library better than anyone, and he never put much stock in Taran's theories. The scholars on the Board are divided. But then I suppose the only thing we've ever really known about the Library is how much we don't know.'

'So tell me again exactly how you think I'm going to—' She stopped. Finn had put his head in his hands. His shoulder blades, through the fabric of his shirt, were as sharp as wings.

'Are you alright?'

He moved his head, the tiniest shake.

'What does it feel like?'

He didn't reply for several seconds. When he did, he spoke into his hands. 'Like I'm on a fishing line,' he said, 'with a hook in my heart. And every second I'm away, Iskeull is reeling me back in.'

Above his head, the digital display started flashing.

'So the good news is that it's time to go,' Alex said. 'The bad news is you're going to have to get up.'

They just about made it to the departure gate. Finn stood very straight, grim-faced and glitter-eyed, while the security desk made a series of calls to verify his Microstate of Iskeull identity card. But as they queued in the tunnel for the plane, his knees buckled, and Alex had to wriggle her shoulder beneath his arm and wedge him upright against the hoard-ings. *In the future*, declared the HSBC ad behind Finn's drooping head, beside an image of an office water-cooler with a slot for swiping a credit card, *growth has a cost*.

'Muscle relaxant,' Alex said breezily to the flight attendant as she hauled him into the cabin, flashing the expensive last-minute tickets she'd put on the Eudo account. 'He's afraid of flying.'

It wasn't, as it turned out, a total lie. As the Airbus taxied down the runway, Finn opened his eyes, looked out of the window and gripped the armrest so tightly that Alex thought the tendons on his wrist might burst through his tattoo. When they took off, his jaw dropped and she thought for one awful moment that he might yell. But then his features soft-ened for the first time all day and he suddenly looked like a little boy, transformed with awe. It lasted perhaps a minute, before a spasm of pain closed him up again. He glanced at her and muttered something.

'What?' She leaned in.

'Sometimes,' he whispered.

'Sometimes what?'

'I feel trapped, too.'

19

By the time they changed onto a propellor plane at Edinburgh, Finn had become very still. It reminded Alex of how Curstag MacRob had looked, preparing to Read. She guessed that he was drawing on his training, suppressing his feelings, locking down into survival mode. The only part of him that moved during the whole hour-long journey was his left hand, which he kept wrapped around his throat. At first she thought he was struggling to breathe. But as the plane touched down into Kirkwall, his hand jerked and she got a glimpse of the pebble clenched in his palm. A piece of Iske-ull, helping him to hold on.

She was afraid that his appearance – both of their appearances, judging by a glimpse in the airport loos – would create a problem in Arrivals. But when it came to their reclusive neighbours, the Orcadians appeared to have a remarkable blind spot. With no luggage except for Finn's holdall and the ruck-sack Alex had thrown together while a taxi waited outside her flat, they passed through the airport without being asked a single question. Barely ten minutes later they were walking out of the double doors.

Alex had forgotten how much brighter the light was here,

even at 7 p.m. It was cooler, too, with a breeze coming off the bay behind the terminal. It was hard to believe that Iskeull was being lashed by storms only forty miles away. She put on her sunglasses and turned to Finn, who was standing with his face raised to the sun.

'So,' she said, 'what exactly is the plan?'

His eyes slid sideways, then widened. His whole body went stiff. For a moment Alex thought he was having some sort of fit. Then he cuffed the crown of her head and pulled it down into his chest, squashing her nose against his pecs and sending her sunglasses skittering across the tarmac.

'What the—?'

'Quiet,' he hissed. 'Move. Move!'

He hustled her towards a loitering cab, shielding her all the way with his body, then yanked open the back door and bundled her in, smacking her elbow on the frame. He threw himself in after her, chucked the holdall on top of her and slammed the door.

'What the *fuck*?'

But he was staring out of the window, gripping the handle. She peered past his ear. She could see nothing more threatening than a group of Germans in matching T-shirts, a young couple with multiple piercings and a heavyset musician in black with a violin case slung over his shoulder.

The musician was Iain.

He was striding towards the departures gate of the terminal, scrutinizing the tourists as he passed. Then the automatic doors split before his bulk and he disappeared inside.

'Shit,' Alex murmured, slumping back against the seat. 'Shit shit shit shit shit shit—'

'I can't believe they did it.' Finn's voice was bleak. 'I can't believe they voted it through.'

'I can't – they can't – I didn't think it was just – it's like I've gone from *Labyrinth* to fucking *Pulp Fiction* in less than twenty-four hours.'

'How could they? Break the Covenant, and there's no point to any of us.'

'So what's the idea: he rocks up at my flat and guns me down? Drops into the office and sets to with a Kalashnikov?'

'They'd need to have taken a decision like this to the Board. The Yíngzhōuese would never have agreed. Never. And I can't believe it of the Pasca Nui. But if the Menikuki felt threatened enough . . . and they'd bring the Buyaniners . . .'

'Oh my God. Finn? Finn! What happens when Iain gets to London and finds me gone? What about my family? Would he try to get to me through them?'

'No, they'd never—' Finn stopped. 'I don't know. I don't know what they'd do, any more.'

Alex grabbed the door handle. 'We have to follow him.'

Finn closed his hand over hers. 'And what?'

'I don't know. Get to him before he boards? *Reason* with him?'

''Scuse me,' the cabbie said. He was watching Finn in his rear-view mirror as if a scorpion had been thrown through his window. 'Are thoo twa gyaan somewey?'

'Dislodging that Story is your only hope,' Finn said grimly. '*Our* only hope.'

'Fuck!' Alex said. 'FUCK.'

'That's why you came back, isn't it?'

'Yes. I suppose. It's just that now it's so fucking *real*. FUCK.' Alex hugged her chest and rubbed her arms as if she could weld herself together. 'Okay. Okay.' She looked at Finn. 'What the fuck do we do next?'

'We stick to my plan,' Finn said. 'It's all we can do.' He caught the cabbie's eye in the mirror. The cabbie looked away. 'The Reel,' Finn said.

After five minutes of speeding through fields and another five jerking through narrow streets, the car braked sharply in the centre of town. They were outside a white rendered building, opposite a majestic red cathedral. Alex got out and began to search her wallet for cash, but as soon as Finn's door slammed, the cabbie ground into gear and accelerated away.

Alex looked up at the cathedral. With 800 years of weather in its sandstone bones, it looked older than the flatscreen sky. As she gazed at the confident thrust of its walls, she felt a hypocritical urge to go inside and pray. But Finn was already heading in the opposite direction, weaving between half a dozen folding chairs' worth of tourists. She rushed after him and through the white building's open door.

Inside The Reel, Finn's 'plan' revealed itself to be a some-one. Sitting at a table at the back, slumped against the wainscoting with his black head bent over an untouched beer, the plan was doing his best to look invisible. He could almost have passed for a brooding immigrant, until he looked up, and Alex saw a face that was unmistakably a product of Iskeull. On the meaty wrists sticking out of his sloppy green jumper, she spotted a telltale coil of blue tattoo.

Finn slid in beside the man and bumped his shoulder with his own. '*Laochyn dhy*,' he said.

'*Beullych*,' the man muttered back, giving Alex a hard stare. He was stouter than Finn, more grizzled and less pale, but he looked just as ill. His eyes were glazed and his body was racked by a low-level shudder that Alex could feel through the floorboards. He looked back at his pint as Finn talked to him in Iskeullian, then shook his head and made some sort of objection. Finn pressed his point. The two of them began to argue.

Alex rapped on the table. She did it again, louder. They fell silent mid-bout and stared.

'Sorry,' Alex said. 'But I've just seen my own *assassin*. Or wannabe assassin. I'm feeling a tiny bit fucking shaky. So it would be really nice if you could, y'know, tell me the fucking masterplan.'

'This is Lucas,' Finn said. 'He's a friend.'

'Hello, Lucas,' Alex said. 'I'm Alex.'

'He knows who you are.'

'Of course he does. Dorothy Moore the bloody mutant Reader-slayer.'

'He brought me here in his boat. He's been waiting to bring us home.'

'In a *boat*?'

'It's late, but it's light, and the weather's good. If we leave in an hour, the tides will help us to Sanday. We'll sleep there and go on to Iskeull at first light. That part will be difficult, but if anyone can sail it, Lucas can. He's been fishing Iskeull's coast since before he could walk.'

'Define difficult,' Alex said.

Lucas muttered something.

'You should eat,' Finn said. 'Keep your strength up.'

'Define strength,' Alex said, but she walked over to the bar anyway, and bought three sandwiches from a woman who looked at her strangely. She was carrying them back to their table when a man with a violin case walked through the door. She stumbled, and half a prawn mayo slid across the tray and into Lucas's lap.

'Sit down,' Finn hissed.

The man with the violin case went over to the bar. He threw a casual glance their way, then turned his back to them and bent heads with the woman who had served Alex. Another man followed him in, carrying a recorder, then a teenage girl with a guitar. A woman meandered over to a small upright piano and placed sheet music on the stand.

Alex sat down and picked up the other half of the sandwich, but she couldn't bring herself to eat. Finn and Lucas ignored theirs, too, their eyes trained on the newcomers. The man with the violin case moved away from the bar, slung his case on a table and took out a fiddle. The other musicians gathered round, tuning up, swapping jokes with the regulars, swigging beer.

The first piece was a rousing foot-stamper. The second was a catchy, repetitive reel. On the third – a dissonant, melancholy air – the fiddler began to sing.

The lyrics were in the Orcadians' mashed-up Scandi-

Scots-English dialect, so Alex couldn't understand every word, but she caught the general drift. In olden times, a local man had voyaged across the sea to find a mysterious island that would, now and then, materialize out of the mist. The man found the island, but as soon as he set foot on its shores he was abducted by a kingdom of *trowies*, or trolls. The trolls took him deep underground and tied him up with rainbow ropes of magic. His son sailed after him, but he too was captured and bound. Back home, their wife and mother prepared to head out and rescue them – singing as she stitched a sealskin coat, from which she hoped the magic ropes would slip.

From the first note to the last, as he swung his bow and sung his song, the man looked straight at Lucas and Finn.

At the end there was a long, heavy silence. Then a muted smattering of applause. The musicians fiddled with their instruments. Some people turned away and began to speak loudly, while others stood to get a refill at the bar.

'Time to go,' Finn said, hefting his bag.

It was a short walk to where Lucas's boat was moored between two high-tech white vessels in a disproportionately large space. Squatting between the catamarans, it looked like a dugout with an outboard motor stuck on the back, and it stank of fish. Lucas started the motor while Finn untied the rope, then offered his hand to Alex, who clambered in and settled herself on a bench at the front. There was a sheet of canvas lashed across the space behind the bench. Beneath it she found nets, oars, ropes, a lifebuoy, a spare cape and a pile of blankets. She donned the cape and draped a blanket around her shoulders. Then she put the lifebuoy on her knees and let the vibrations and the tiredness sink her scudding thoughts.

The next few hours passed in a blur of sights and sounds. Nests. Gulls. Rocks. Seals. Green fuzz. White paint. A finger of rust-coloured cliff, layered like a wafer. A slice of shale. A hoop of cut-out rock with white water pouring through it. A lighthouse, white with a black cap. The moon, silver on grey.

They growled up to a small jetty just before midnight.

'You can park wherever you like?' Alex asked. The words came out garbled, her face stiff, her lips tart with salt. Cautiously, she stood up to stretch as Lucas did Boy Scouty things with rope.

'Orcadians leave us alone,' Finn said. He was shivering hard, although it wasn't cold.

'Can't we find somewhere to stay? There must be a B&B?'

'They leave us alone if we leave them alone.'

Lucas fetched a blanket, curled up on the bottom of the boat and lay twitching like a dog. Finn sat beside him with his arms around his knees and a blanket round his shoulders, and dipped his chin to his chest. Alex lay back on the bench, squashed her bag into a pillow, tucked her own blanket round her, then tilted the peak of her cap over her eyes.

The water lapped and sploshed. The twilight that passed for darkness this far north crept in through shades of grey.

'Finn,' Alex said. She could hear him breathing, fast and ragged.

'Uh.'

'Do you think it was Iain who attacked me in London, before I came?'

'Perhaps.'

'But I've been thinking. It doesn't really make sense. Why would MacBrian try to kill me *before* she knew that I couldn't unstick my Story? When the Board hadn't even voted on breaking the Covenant?'

'I don't know.' A pause. 'I did think it might have been Dughlas.'

'Dughlas? The one who was helping your dad?'

'So they say.'

'Why? Was he violent?'

'Not so far as I know. But he – Dughlas – got ideas. About people.'

'What do you mean?'

'He was strange. No-one really liked him. His parents died when he was young and the Council tried to help him with extra training, but he was a useless Reader. He preferred Outside novels – romance, historical fiction, thrillers, all that nonsense. He worshipped Freya. He thought my father was a hero. I thought that maybe he thought – maybe he thought he could be a hero, too. Go vigilante. "Take you out".'

A pause. 'You really think it could have been him?'

'He hasn't been seen for two weeks, so—' A sigh. 'I don't know.'

There was a squawk. A scrabble. The plip-plip-plip of falling stones.

'Finn?'

'Uh.'

'Your dad.'

A beat. 'Uh.'

'I saw the statue of him. In town. That morning you caught me in the index room.'

Silence.

'MacBrian said everyone loved him. She said he was a prodigy.'

Silence.

'Finn, what was he like?'

Eventually: 'He was the most successful Reader on record, in terms of volume and change rate, across all seven islands. He was the best.'

'No, I mean what was he *like* like? As a person?'

Silence.

Then: 'I didn't see him very often. He was always working. He was obsessed with work. He was stubborn. He always had to be right.'

Silence.

Then: 'He said I was too impulsive. Too emotional. I wanted to show him. I wanted to be *better* than him. Better than the best.' A humourless *hnh*. 'Too much wanting. He was right. I probably wouldn't have made professional, even if I hadn't been thrown out.'

Silence.

Then, all in a rush: 'But when he wasn't trying to teach you something, when he wasn't thinking about the Board or the paperwork or whoever it was on the Council that was annoying him that month . . . When he was at home on the farm with us, with me and my mother, talking about the

333

people he'd Read that day, the things they'd done, the way they'd changed their lives once they'd dispersed an old Storyline . . . Then he'd made you feel like nothing in the world was impossible. Nothing.'

'I'm so sorry, Finn,' Alex managed eventually. 'I'm so, so sorry.'

Something blew and slapped in the water, far off.

'There's a theory,' Finn said.

'Another bloody theory?' She paused. 'Sorry. Go on.'

'Some scholars think that if you love someone enough, if you spend enough time with them, something happens in the Library. They think that, just once or twice, when you hear about a certain significant experience they went through for the hundredth time, or imagine them going about their life vividly enough, you're able to create a Memory inside your Story that exactly matches theirs. Even if you were never there. Even if your Stories live on islands thousands of miles apart.'

The breeze plucked goosebumps from her arms. 'That's beautiful.'

'It's bullcrap,' Finn said angrily. 'It's bullcrap that people make up to comfort themselves when someone they love dies. They want to think there's something left, even just one tiny Memory, living on in them.'

'But didn't you say that the only thing you knew about the Library was how much you didn't know?' Alex asked gently.

'Yeah, well. I know *that's* bullcrap.'

'Like someone's Story being able to kill someone else is bullcrap?'

334

Silence. The breeze sighed.

'That man,' Finn said, after a moment.

'What man?'

'In the hospital.' A beat. '*Harry*.'

'Yes?'

'Are you really going to marry him?'

Alex frowned into the darkness. 'Well, that kind of depends on whether I get gunned down by Iain MacHoras. Or whether this thing eats me up from the inside. But if I'm still alive on Wednesday, I suppose that, well, yes, that's the plan.'

Silence.

'Why do you ask?'

'He seemed like a *chluidsea*.'

'What does *that* mean?' Silence. 'Okay, fine, I'm pretty sure I can guess. That's bloody rich, coming from you!'

'You really love him, then? Someone like that?'

'What do you mean, *someone like that*? Harry's honourable, he's reliable, he's thoughtful, he's loyal. And he loves me, he really does.'

Finn muttered something under his breath in Iskeullian. Alex, her fingers furiously gripping the hem of the blanket, refused to react. Several minutes passed. A bird shook out its feathers. A rope creaked.

'Finn?'

'Uh.'

'Shut up,' said a new, heavily accented voice.

There was a pause. 'You speak English,' Alex said.

'Of course I speak English,' Lucas said. 'Everyone on

Iskeull speaks English. We also like to sleep.' He said something in Iskeullian. Finn muttered back.

Alex waited until she heard both men's breathing slow and deepen. Then she sat up and unzipped her rucksack. Taking out her phone, she tilted the screen to catch the moonlight and saw that some mast on Sanday was gifting it a single dot of signal.

H, she typed. *I had an idea. Why don't you try out some of those hotels on your list? Go and stay a night in each one with Mum & Dad? On the Eudo card? We want it to be perfect, right? And we can't recommend people stay in places we don't know. So pls. Tomorrow. The 3 of you, a pre-wedding jaunt. 4 nights, 4 different hotels. Bonding with the in-laws. Then I'll see you all on Weds. Please take care of them. And yourself. I DO love you, Harry. I really do xxx*

Alex swiped to power off. The screen flashed once, then died. She tucked the phone back in her bag, rearranged herself on the bench and blinked up at the stars.

20

Alex and Finn sat beneath the canvas with the lifebuoy between them. Their arms were braced along the sides, their hands secured with quick-release knots of rope. When the first coal-coloured clouds descended and the first eddies spun the boat around, Alex watched Lucas from where he sat at the motor. His face was impassive, his body swaying easily with the roll. This was, she told herself, no worse than the Congo River Rapids at Alton Towers.

Two hours in, drenched to the bone, her throat burning with acid and the wind stabbing her ears, she was longing for Iain and his violin case of mercy. The sky screamed. The sea bellowed. Waves as big as whales tossed them up then smashed them down, nail-bombing the deck with spray. The great rabid tongue of the world bucked and belched and tried to vomit them out.

In the next rain-lashed lull, Alex disentangled her stiff fingers from the rope and splashed along the planks in a freezing belly-crawl. She stalled, her ankle caught in a vice-like grip. She looked back. Finn's mouth was open, his jaw working. She donkey-kicked and felt his fingers slip away. She wriggled onwards and managed to poke her head out of the canvas, her hood dropping back, her baseball cap flying up and away.

Punched. Water-boarded. Instantly blind.

'COME ON, THEN!' she shouted, struggling to her knees. 'COME AND GET ME, ISKEULL!' She wedged her foot against the strut of the bench and levered herself upright, then spread her arms full crucifix and felt the wind fling a cannonball. 'YOU WANT REVENGE? YOU WANT ME TO FUCK OFF OUT OF THAT STACK, YOU FUCKING . . . DEWEY . . . DECIMAL—'

She hit the floor. Lucas was sitting on her abdomen, one thick knee planted on either side of her hips. He was swollen, shining, pink as a baby; his eyes salt-crusted slits, his hair glistening eels. He leaned down so that his mouth was close to her ear. 'Not helpful,' he said. He shoved his hands under her armpits and hauled her back under the canvas, then threw the ring at her chest and bellowed, 'HALF AN HOUR.'

She had no idea if it was half an hour or twenty, but eventually the lulls did get longer and the tantrums milder, until the boat settled into a drunken rock. She heard birds. A splash. A clonk. Voices. Finn's voice, saying one of her names.

She staggered up the slope while Finn and Lucas dragged the boat high enough to avoid the tide. It was raining steadily, but she was so cold she didn't feel cold any more. The thing out there was pretending to be the sea again: flirtily brooding, Turner-esque. The men unfolded the canvas to its full size and used it to cover the deck of the boat, tying it round with side-ropes. Then they tramped over to where

Alex sat on the waterlogged white grit, numb-arsed, numb-everythinged, sodden rucksack heavy on her back. They looked different, she saw; exhausted and half-drowned, but somehow more solid, cleaner, as if some primal tension had lifted from their flesh. Finn had also, somehow, held onto his stupid holdall full of airport-lounge freebies, which was banging against his hip with every step. He stopped and looked down at Alex. She looked back. She contemplated standing up. She considered her knees, her trainers. She scuffed her toes through the silt. Thrust her fingers into it. Filled her lungs. Stood.

They climbed the bank of the cove onto a rise of mossy scrub, where the landscape offered itself to them in that brazen Iskeullian way: miles of moorland, gentle hills, the blind eye of a loch, a coronet of standing stones. Not far off, she could see fences, and low handfuls of houses and barns. It wasn't until Finn and Lucas crouched down that she noticed the hump in the grass, the blunt mouth of piled rubble, which they now began to pull apart.

'Don't worry,' Finn said, looking over as if he knew that her thoughts had immediately turned to that other, pretend-tomb in the centre of the Stacks. Even his voice sounded wider here, as if it had opened to fill the space. 'This one's man-made. And much younger. Bronze Age. Nothing in here but . . . *gnuhhh* . . . this.'

It was a bike, an old red-and-black Honda that it took all their combined strength to drag out and upright. Finn removed the thong from around his neck and slotted the plastic-topped key in the ignition.

'That doesn't look like a horse,' Alex said.

Finn brushed wet soil off the seat with his cape. 'First thing my father did when he got his credit card was to ship this in. Caused a big storm in the Council. He was supposed to have got rid of it, but everyone knew he hadn't. He'd sneak it out, now and then.'

'He put this on *expenses?*'

The corners of his mouth lifted, ever so slightly. He threw his bag to Lucas, straddled the bike and revved it to a throaty growl. 'Wait here,' he yelled.

Lucas settled behind Finn, bag on lap, and they roared off. Alex could see them for a long time, bouncing over heath, looping round fields, dipping into basins, then reappearing as a distant, incongruous glint. She sat on the excavated rubble and unzipped her rucksack. Her spare clothes were soaked and the new phone was a mess of warped plastic. Thinking of the last message she had sent, she reached up and put her hand on the ancient hump of grass.

'Please,' she murmured. 'I know we've got our issues. But call Iain MacHoras back? Please? Reel him in, as hard as you can.' She left her hand resting there and took the rain as due penance. She found that she felt oddly calm. Post-traumatic shock? Adrenaline comedown? The onset of hypothermia? Probably all three.

When he returned, spraying mud, Finn must have thought the same, because he gave her a worried look. 'Can you stand?'

She could, as it turned out, but he had to help lift her

onto the bike. She dug her fingers into the front of his jumper, laid her cheek on his wet back and closed her eyes.

When they slowed to a putter, she opened them again, but found that she had no strength to lift her head. She caught sideways glimpses of fence and hedge, and saw straggly sheep or goats with their bums to the wind. When the bike stopped she forced herself upright, pushing against Finn, and saw that they were parked outside a big stone barn on the edge of a field. He helped her off and they performed a reverse version of their shuffle through the boarding tunnel at Heathrow, her arm over his shoulder this time. They moved through the double doors and down an aisle between roof-high stacks of hay bales to the back, where there was some cast-iron farm machinery and several large stone bins. Finn kicked aside a pile of leather harness and sat Alex down on a bale. He opened one of the bins and retrieved a towel, a pile of dry clothes, a blanket and a basket. He took the cloth off the top of the basket to show her a flask of water, a piece of cheese and a loaf of dark bread.

'Eat,' he said. 'Sleep. It'll be warmer if you dig yourself into the hay. As soon as my mother leaves, I'll bring you in.'

'She doesn't know? Where you've been?' Alex pressed the towel to her face. It had a comforting herbal smell, like thyme.

'No.' He rose from the crouch. 'You're not weak at all, you know,' he said abruptly. 'You're strong.'

She was too cold to laugh or cry. 'I'm not strong enough to go down there again. I'm not ready.'

'My father used to say that no-one's ever ready for any-thing,' he said. 'You just have to get on and do it.'

Alex gave a bleak huff-laugh. 'Your dad would've liked my mum.'

They both almost smiled, a split second. Then Finn turned and walked back down the aisle, leaving a trail of muddy boot prints in his wake.

The light was failing by the time he came to fetch her. They walked silently, heads bowed, through the driving rain, past field after field of soggy animals and slimy crops. Eventually they came to a stable yard, scattering chickens and passing two yellow horses with bottle-brush manes that snorted at them over half-doors as they crossed. At the end was a long, low farmhouse, old but immaculately kept. Finn lifted the latch and ducked his head to avoid the lintel – carved, Alex noticed, with knots and swirls and figures-of-eight – as they stepped into a fug of sweet-smelling warmth. He took off his boots while Alex gazed round the kitchen. At one end there was a cast-iron range and a long stone table stacked with pottery cups and plates. At the other there was a black peat-burner, framed with shelves crowded with books. In front of the burner were two of those high-backed wicker chairs.

'Shoes,' Finn said. 'Please.' She toed off her still-sodden trainers. 'Follow me.' He led her up a narrow flight of stairs and into a small room almost wholly taken up by a steaming tin bath. 'My mother's with Freya,' he said, already retreating back through the doorway. 'She won't be back until late. I'll be downstairs.'

Lowering herself into the water was throbbing, itching agony. More than once Alex had to grip the sides, to stop herself from jumping out. Once she was in, though, she stayed until the water was tepid, delaying the moment when she would have to go downstairs, while her thoughts sloshed and bobbed. She silently begged Harry to have been swayed by her text. She tried to imagine her parents ensconced in the safe anonymity of some boutique hotel. Her father would be laid out on the bed with a book and a vodka. Her mother would be tutting over the price of the artisan popcorn in the minibar. She found she was still too tired, too shocked, too numb to cry.

Her own clothes were still damp, so she used the ones Finn had left for her in the barn: sludge-coloured drawstring trousers, a chunky mustard jumper and a pair of hand-knitted red socks. When she walked back into the kitchen Finn was sitting in one of the chairs in front of the peat-burner, ripping bites from an apple while a mottled cat with tufted ears watched him from a windowsill.

'Tea,' he said, glancing over and nodding his head towards the table on the other side of the room. 'Bannocks, if you want. We should start. My mother wants you back in the barn by the time she gets home.'

'You told her, then?'

'She has a way,' Finn said, 'of getting at the truth.'

'Is she angry?'

'She doesn't want to know about it,' he said, in a tone that discouraged further questions.

Alex walked over to the table and poured tea from a blue ceramic pot into a matching mug. Sipping the hot herbal brew, she wandered over to the shelves behind Finn. Expecting to find unintelligible leather-bound tomes, she was surprised to see a full set of Penguin Classics, plus modern novels by everyone from William Gibson to John Grisham. She spotted choice collections of recent pop science along-side psychology books ranging from Freud to Malcolm Gladwell. There were magazines, too, dozens of back-issues of *Wired* and *New Scientist*, bookended by random objects: a kitsch plastic robot, a pristine pair of Nikes, a twisted iPod.

She took down a hardback copy of *Maus* and leafed through the pages. 'Are these your dad's?'

He grunted assent. 'There's a whole barnful out there. My mother was always pretending she was going to sell them.' He considered the *Maus*, as if seeing it for the first time. 'I suppose she might, now.'

'Finn, I really am—'

'It's alright.' He took the book from her and slotted it carefully back into place. 'You don't have to. I know. And we have to get on with your training. Innate autoReading skills obviously aren't going to be enough to tackle whatever's going on with your Story. We have one night to get you as near to professional as we can. But, first, sit down and tell me everything you know about what's happened. From the beginning, in your own words.'

She tried to touch the recollections as lightly as possible to avoid an episode. Once she started, however, it all began to spill out in a furious, rambling rush. The events of

344

17 February. The attack and attempted attack, six months later. Her arrival on Iskeull. Her first interview with Taran and MacBrian.

'That was the night I went for my wander on the peninsula,' Alex said, pausing to drink more tea, in an attempt to soothe her lurching stomach. 'Obviously, after our little altercation and my detour into the Library, the GCAS cover was blown. I was totally freaking out, so MacBrian took me into one of the Stacks and gave me a demo with a woman called Curstag MacRob. Then she took me into I-537 and showed me my Story.' She swallowed, feeling the horror rush back. 'I knew it was mine as soon as I saw it.'

Finn nodded. 'No-one can mistake their own Story.'

'Deep down, I'd known there was something wrong with me for months.' She described the episodes. The slipperiness of her thoughts. The months spent on a hollow, manic high. The dizzy, exhilarating feeling of having been cut free from everything she had been before. Then she related, as accurately as she could, what she had been told about the night Egan MacCalum had died.

When she'd finished, Finn continued to sit in silence, staring at the fire.

'Is that what you heard?' Alex asked.

'It's the same as what Taran told me.'

'But you think Dughlas was lying?'

Finn grunted. 'Everyone thinks I'm trying to defend him, but my father would never have lied like that. And he was just as good a Reader as he'd ever been. Reading gave him energy. It was the political bullcrap that made him tired.' He leaned forward and stabbed at the fire with a poker. 'Anyway, Dughlas was the last person he would have asked to help him, even if he had gone mad and decided to take on secret shifts. He barely even knew Dughlas was alive.'

'So you think MacBrian is in on it? That she was trying to set your dad up?'

'She's always been ambitious. Pushy. Cold. A bad Reader but a clever politician, clawing her way up.' Finn gave the fire a final rattle, then propped the poker back on the hearth. 'Anyway. Go on. Taran said they showed you your Reading record?'

So she told him about the abortive first Reading. About Dom's job offer. About the miserable summer before St J's. And about Taran's hypothesis.

'And I'm afraid that he's right, you know,' she added. 'About Story-surging. About that mutated Memory. I didn't want to believe it, but I found evidence, at home.' She took the pink-and-purple diary out of her rucksack and rifled through the pages. 'I described it taking root in me, when I was eleven years old. And even back then, I knew what it was capable of. That's the worst thing.' She handed it to him, open on the final entry. 'Look. I *knew*.'

He read it several times, then looked up. 'I can't believe it,' he said.

'Well, I tried pretty damn hard not to believe it, either. I wish it wasn't true. But there it is, in black and white. Everything my mother told me corroborates it. And everything I heard from Mae, Chloe, Dom. It seems that I really have spent my whole life trying to keep this power where it belongs

– inside me, wrapped up inside a big fat Storyline, nice and safe, only screwing up *my* life. Until your dad got his hands on it. And now my Story's trying to stop me from getting control of it again. It's rotting my Memories. It's rotting *me*. I saw it. I *tasted* it.' And then she told him, as best she could, with the hopelessly inadequate words she had at her disposal, what had happened when she'd gone through that dark chamber at the centre of the Stacks. When she'd walked all the way down the tunnel to her Story, and tried to Read her Storyline.

The next thing she knew, Finn's face was slowly solidifying into existence inches away from hers.

'Dorothy?' he was saying. 'Dorothy? Alex?'

'Ngg,' she said. She licked her lips, stirred, located her hands, tried to push herself up from where she lay curled on the floor.

'Careful.' Finn kneeled behind her and scooped her into a sitting position, propping her against him.

'Are you alright?'

She shook her head.

'That was it, wasn't it?' he asked. 'That was an episode?'

She nodded. She licked her lips again and rolled her eyes wildly until Finn, finally getting it, reached over to the other side of her chair and passed her the mug of cold tea.

'Mild,' she mumbled, after she'd slurped some down. 'That was mild compared to the episode I had down there, when I tried to Read my Storyline. I got close to that mutated root Memory, I know I did, and my Story didn't like it one bit.'

She sank back against him and let the heat from the fire

soak through her body as it tried to stitch itself back into something resembling a whole.

'I did try, Finn,' she said quietly. 'I did. But this mutation is too powerful. It's so powerful, so dangerous, that none of the other Stories in that Stack can bear to even be near it, for goodness' sake. It's preventing millions of people from being Read. It's devastating this place with storms. It's forcing your leaders to override their deepest values and agree to murder, just so it can be stopped. You say I'm strong, but how can you expect me to overcome something like that?'

'Because it's *your* Story,' Finn murmured. 'You've asked all these people what they think of you, but none of that matters if you can't hear what your own Story is trying to say. You need to start trusting your instincts, Alex. There has to be a missing piece. There has to be something we don't know.'

'Like the time?' said a voice from the doorway.

Finn sprang to his feet, depositing Alex in an ungainly sprawl onto the floor. The cat trotted over and rubbed itself against the mud-splattered leather boots of the woman standing framed in the doorway.

Alex hauled herself up with as much dignity as she could. The woman was short and solid with a thick black plait, badger-streaked with white, pinned round her head. But the eyes were his: chips of bright, shifting flint-grey.

'I'm sorry,' Alex said. 'I'm really sorry about what happened to your husband.'

Cait MacMorgan gave her a steady appraisal from head to toe. 'I wondered where that jumper had gone,' she said.

'I know it doesn't help,' Alex said, 'but I didn't mean to do it.'

'So they say,' she said. 'And no. It doesn't.'

Finn spoke again, rapidly, and Cait replied without looking away from Alex. Her tone was calm but, from the look of Finn's clenched jaw and stiffening posture, it couched a robust bollocking. Finn started to reply, gesturing, but Cait spoke over him until he fell quiet.

'Are you going to give me up?' Alex said when she could bear it no longer. 'To them? To her?'

Cait turned to look at her. 'Of course not,' she said. 'If it is true that Sorcha MacBrian has somehow gained permission to order your death, I am appalled. Every right-minded Reader across the world will be appalled.'

'I'm going to try again,' Alex burst out. 'To fix it. I'm not sure what good it will do, but I really will try.'

Cait bent to pull off her boots. 'As my late husband would say, do, or do not. There is no try.'

Alex blinked. 'I think that was Yoda,' she said.

'I know it was Yoda,' Cait said witheringly. 'Egan insisted on watching that ridiculous film every time we went to Kirkwall. Now, is one of you going to get me a drink?'

21

Her parents' skulls exploded like watermelons. A sniper bored a hole in Harry's temple. Lenni was stunned by a rifle butt, then bundled into a revving van. As she rode through the cold morning rain, Alex cursed all the movies and games that had given her imagination such a spectacular collection of snuff scenes.

Iain could be in London by now. Or Fring. Or Twickenham, dear God. Of course he might simply leave, once he realized she'd disappeared. He might already be getting shaky, losing focus. Perhaps he was making mistakes, like the ones he – or Dughlas, or whoever her previous would-be hitman had been – had made outside L'Antiga Capella. Then again, he might already have kidnapped Bo. She'd told MacBrian and that doctor so much about her loved ones, both friends and family. If the health of the Library and the civic order of Iskeull were at stake, wouldn't it be a no-brainer for them to use all the leverage they had, to bring her to heel?

Alex had snatched a couple of hours' sleep in Cait MacMorgan's spare room, after a gruelling all-night Reading training session with Finn. But the sleep simply appeared to have given her system just enough time to reboot out of shock-induced safety mode and into fully functioning what-the-fuck-am-I-doing alert. Cait's stoic presence had somehow kept her calm as she forced down 3 a.m. eggs and tea. But now as she glanced at Finn, paler and bonier than ever in the moonlight, she could only think of how young he looked – a thought that segued into a panicked internal plea about how young *she* was. Too young to save the world. Too young to die.

Her plodding farm horse snorted and threw up its head. Finn turned to look at her. Alex took a breath to tell him that it was all a mistake. That she didn't give a shit about humankind any more. That all the mind-calming techniques on the planet weren't going to help her in that lonely chamber, and that she'd take her chances with the killer thing inside her and a succession of half-crippled assassins back home. But then Finn put his finger on his lips and pointed, and Alex saw the hulking shape of GCAS EU HQ solidifying out of the mist. They had reached the outskirts of the town.

They tied the horses in an open-fronted shelter, then continued on foot into the streets. As they wended their way along the cobbles Alex saw, from beneath the curve of her hood, a trickle of people in grey Reading uniforms emerging out of doorways, some of them still chewing on breakfast bannocks. They clumped into groups as they walked, exchanging subdued greetings, but the drum of the rain kept their heads down and their conversations to a minimum. None of them wasted a glance on the antisocial pair skirting the edges of the buildings and slipping off, wherever possible, to follow a parallel path up the town through emptier alleyways.

After half an hour or so Alex caught a glimpse of the public arena, at the end of the street they were crossing. At its centre stood the statue of Egan MacCalum, in profile. Even from this distance, she could see that the sculptor had been hard at work. Last week, MacCalum's arms had dissolved into formless stone below the elbow. Now the one facing them was complete, its hand spread like a star in the direction of the Director's gaze, as if the long, elegant fingers were being pulled by some invisible force towards the peninsula beyond the roofs. Feeling her stomach plummet and the dizziness rise, Alex turned away to look at Finn. But Finn's hood was fixed ahead, and something about the set of his shoulders warned her not to comment.

Eventually they reached the north end of the town. As they emerged out onto the avenue, the rain-spiked wind attacked with ferocious force. Alex's hood flew back, and for one terrible moment she found her face exposed, before Finn helped her wrestle the wax-cloth back over her head. Thankfully, the others walking out around them were too busy battling their own way through the gale to notice. But Alex had already snatched a glimpse of the picket lines snaking away on either side of the bell tower in front of the causeway, and she suddenly found that her legs wouldn't work. Finn had warned her about the protests, of course. He had told her about the islanders who felt that Reading was now too risky, and that all activity in the Library should cease. Mixed in with them, he said, were a number of MacBrian's political opponents, who were calling for a vote of no confidence in her leadership – as well as a good dose of generic troublemakers who were just happy for a chance to shout. However, knowing to expect them didn't make the sight of the makeshift shelters, with their banners and fires and angry Iskeullians with underlit scowls, any less terrifying. Then, as Alex stood paralysed, the first great boom of the shift-change bell rang out. She let out a strangled moan.

Finn's hand closed around her wrist. 'Alex,' he said, his voice loud in her ear, 'remember. You're strong.' She took a deep breath, returned her gaze to Cait's spare boots and forced them to uproot themselves, one step at a time. Still holding her wrist, Finn steered her forward, right into the stream of commuters. The bell struck again. Alex heard the snap and flap of canvas, the shuffle and thump of boots, the mercifully unintelligible rumble of a chant. Then the bell rang out a third time and Finn tightened his grip.

They were right at the front of the bell tower now, shoulder-to-shoulder with the islanders still willing to Read. Alex heard the murmur of voices as Readers exchanged words with guards, the rustle of papers as they took shift-chits from pockets and bags. Then the bell boomed a fourth time and Finn's grip was gone, leaving her wrist weightless and cold. He had been careful to explain what she should expect to happen at every stage of their journey, up until the point at which they had no idea what was going to happen – which was around about now.

A female voice, somewhere just in front of Alex, asked a question in Iskeullian.

She's talking to someone else. Come on, Finn. Come on.

The woman repeated the question, louder. Alex stared at her toes.

Finn. What the fuck are you doing? Hurry the fucking fuck up.

The woman spoke again, sharply, and touched Alex's shoulder. Alex was about to throw herself, sobbing, on her mercy, when she heard him shout.

Several voices started up at once, loudly. There was a yell, then a cheer; another cheer, a tumble of cries. Alex was jostled sideways, bumped between bodies. She risked a glance in the direction of the noise. Finn was over on the far side of the bell tower. Hood thrown back, he was bellowing protestations of his father's innocence and accusations against MacBrian, while a big male guard tried to drag him away. The other guards were instinctively flocking towards them, including some of those patrolling the picket lines. As Alex watched, the strikers furthest from Finn broke rank. At their head, she thought she recognized the bullish green shoulders of Lucas and the deep burr of his voice leading a chorus of outraged shouts.

The woman who had stopped Alex had turned to watch. Alex slipped past her into the bell tower before she could change her mind. *Don't run,* she told herself as she walked through the passageway, staring at the hoop of grey waves ahead. *I'm just a regular islander on my way to work. At 4 a.m. To Read a bunch of sleeping Europeans. Nice and easy.* As her mother always said: *More haste, darling, less speed.*

Alex didn't dare look back as she strode across the causeway, but from the sound of the racket behind her, Finn's distraction had worked better than they could have hoped. Feeling the path shudder beneath her boots, she glanced up, then jumped sideways just in time to avoid being mown down by a massive yellow horse. On top of the horse she saw MacBrian, her chin jutting grimly as she galloped back along the causeway with a dozen guards in her wake.

The sight of MacBrian gave Alex a burst of resolve. She clenched her fists and marched on, briskly now. How dare that haughty bitch have made her feel so guilty? MacBrian had switched from protector of the species to murderer in a matter of days, without any sort of genetic excuse. The Iskeullians might have to nurse human consciousness in order to keep their island afloat, but it was becoming increasingly clear that they were no more noble than anyone Outside.

Safely on the peninsula, she crossed over the road to the rotunda and climbed the steps. Every moment, she expected to hear a shout or feel a hand on her arm. But everyone else was heading the other way, running out of the index or emerging from doors along the length of the archives to watch the drama unfolding at the other end of the causeway. Alex reached the top of the steps and passed through the double doors. And now there was nothing but the glow of lamplight, the squeak of her soles on the flagstones, the susurration of the rain on the domed glass. The voices around her were barely audible, the atmosphere subdued, and Alex realized just how skeleton the Library's spooked staff had become. It took her three minutes to cross the index, and a heart-stopping moment of dithering deadlock

355

with a pair of grey-booted feet before she could pass through the arch. Then she was out, on the other side of the rotunda, back in the rain.

She glanced up, now, from under her hood. More than half of the flares had been extinguished, turning the Library into a broken jumble of peaks and lumps. A few riderless horses grazed beside the remaining fires, and barely a couple of hundred mounted ones were emerging from the stables behind the archives and spreading out across the sandy paths. Bad for humankind, good for her right now. Thanks to the slope of the land, it was easy to make out the black hump at the centre of the Stacks. That hump was her target – the tomb that hid the tunnel that would, in turn, take her deep beneath the Library. After tracing the route that would take her there most quickly – a winding diagonal line – Alex focused on the dark bullseye and set off.

She had rounded two Stacks – left wall, right wall, left wall, right wall – when she felt the thunder of approaching hooves. She crouched beside the wall of the nearest unlit Stack and watched two riders gallop past, turn round another one ahead and disappear. She straightened up and returned to the path, only to run straight back as she felt another rumble, but the hoofbeats receded and no-one appeared. She continued in the same stop-start routine for what was probably only a few minutes but felt like hours. Finally all fell silent. She imagined the couple-of-hundred islanders installed in their assigned Stacks, both part-time farmers and full-time pros, shrugging off their wet capes and limbering up for a six-hour Reading shift. A couple of hundred people determined to keep Reading, despite what she'd done. Stubborn. Brave. Afraid.

From then on, the only surprises she had to contend with were the horses. Irritable in the rain despite their waxed rugs, they looked up from their piles of hay to snort or stamp as she jogged past. She was growing cold now, cold and tired. But the grim determination she had found on the causeway still held – and the improbable success of her journey so far made the whole crazy mission feel not just lucky, but somehow preordained. Chloe would say that was because Alex's will was aligned with the universe. But then Chloe was probably, at that moment, tied to one of her shabby chic chairs with Iain poking forks in her eyes.

When Alex finally reached the central tomb, it was dark and deserted, indistinguishable on the outside from the Bronze Age hillock that Finn had used to store his father's bike. She knelt in front of the carved stones set around its grassy entrance, then hesitated.

What the fuck was she doing? Why was she here? Wouldn't it be better just to keep walking until she came out the other side of the Stacks, then throw herself off the peninsula's northern cliff? It would be a better way to go, surely, than getting gunned down by a guard or slowly putrefying from the inside out. A heroic gesture of self-sacrifice. She imagined it: the long, stomach-twisting dive; the single, swift moment of rock-smash oblivion. Her broken body would reach an honest, useful end inside the bellies of gannets and whales. But then suicide wasn't heroic, was it? It was the ultimate cop-out. And as she gazed into the tomb, Alex realized something startling. Despite all that had happened, despite all that was probably about to happen, she still appeared to have a delusional amount of hope.

She wriggled her way through the passageway into the central space, barely five foot high. A slanting beam of grainy moonlight perfectly framed the mouth of the tunnel cut into the floor. She turned and sat on the edge of the hole, her legs dangling into the darkness, and tried once again to take stock, to reason, to doubt. But she found that she was bored of thinking, bored of imagining, bored even of being afraid. She threw off her cape and bum-shuffled over the lip until her heels found the rope ladder. Then she climbed the wobbling rungs to the bottom and jumped the last couple of feet down to the rough earth.

It was like jumping into a dream that she dreamed every night, but forgot during waking hours: the springy, sloping floor; the fibrous walls; the blackness that swallowed her in a single gulp. The hours stretched and bulged, and for a while she lost all sense of time as she walked.

When her legs became so tired that she was forced to slump to the ground with her back against the wall, she wondered whether it really had taken her so long, before. She couldn't shake the feeling that her Story was shrinking back from her, with every step she advanced. She nibbled some of the dried beef that Cait had wrapped up for her, then fell into an exhausted doze. When she woke, she felt thick-headed and bleary, but she hauled herself to her feet and set off again. She wondered what time it was, on the surface. She wondered what had happened to Finn. For all she knew, MacBrian had already discovered that she was inside the tunnel – not that it really mattered. MacBrian had said it herself the first time Alex had gone down: the path to every Story was unique, and only you could find yours.

Alex had forgotten why or where she was walking, by the time she found the door – or, rather, by the time the door allowed itself to be found. It didn't shift so much as a millimetre when she pushed at the inscribed letters of her name. Nor did it budge when she rested her forehead on it, as before. She tried shoving and caressing; she tried sweet-talking and swearing. It ignored every strategy. Eventually she sat down, rested her back against it and closed her eyes.

She was half-asleep by the time it swung open. She scrambled to her feet and stepped down onto the walkway, still dangerously woozy, but scared it would close again before she could get through. As the door swung shut, the calm rolled through her, sigh by sweet sigh. Fifty feet above, in the cinder-coloured space over the platform, her Storylines were still dancing, swarming in and out of their rainbow fugues. But she noticed at once that they were even dimmer than before, and much slower too. The temperature in the chamber had also increased by at least fifteen degrees, and the billows of calm around her now felt feverishly hot rather than pleasantly warm. Alex took off Cait's jumper and boots and walked barefoot across the walkway. Despite the rot that she knew lay behind the muted loops, the craving instantly took hold.

She wanted to Read them all. She wanted, so badly, to taste again every significant Memory of her past. She wanted to decode every single one of the Storylines that, spun together, would tell her the whole no-holds-barred, beauty-and-beast tale of Dorothy Alexandra Moore. But she knew it would be pointless. They would tell her nothing, bleached and barren as they were. And this time, she knew, she needed to direct all her strength onto just the one.

It took less than a minute for it to appear: her nemesis, that great murky slug backlit by a scum of flickering Memories. It too, she realized, had changed. It was visibly longer and fatter than it had been six days ago. Bloated clusters of Memories now bulged out from its current like half-digested mice. At first, she thought it had entirely frozen, but then it suddenly spasmed, as if it was trying to throw up, and juddered around an inch before stalling once more. Sucking in calm, Alex gazed up at where it coughed and swelled. She called to it. She offered it love and acceptance, if only it would let her in, let her cradle and guide the power at its heart. As she settled into the Reading posture and raised her arms, she was sure she could feel it calling back, simultaneously pushing her away and begging her to keep reaching out. And, when she closed her eyes and lifted her wrists, it immediately locked on.

As soon as the first Memory exploded, she realized how much worse the bad Storyline had become. It was so dense and noxious that Reading it was like feasting on her own fetid corpse. Her body instinctively tried to pull away, although her brain knew that once she was in the grip of the Storyline, she had to see it through. However violently her system heaved, however deep the pain and the disgust became, she simply had to stand and bear it. And so she stood and bore it as Memory after Memory exploded into her, calling up the same putrid jumble of false starts, failed ideas and unfulfilled dreams that she had tasted a week ago.

She was eleven, scribbling furiously in her pink-and-purple diary, propped up on pillows with a backpack full of camping gear discarded on her bedroom floor. She was in the kitchen, telling her mother she had decided to change her name, but stubbornly refusing to say why. She was traipsing alone through the crowded corridors of St J's. She was arguing with Diya in the changing rooms, shouting that someone was going to die. She was sitting in the attic night after night, pounding away at the computer while her homework languished untouched in her bag. She was twenty-one, sitting in front of a plate of salmon amongst her parents' pissed friends, listening to Dom announce that he'd found her an incredible opportunity in New York. She was alone in her room later that night, slumped on the floor, reading her diary entry from ten years' before. She was in her parents' frosty garden ten years after that, on New Year's Day, hearing Harry propose. She was in Mark's office six months ago, staring at his nose hairs while he offered her the promotion. She was in Chloe's flat, gripping the edge of the vintage sofa, shaking with silent tears. And in amongst those Memories were hundreds of others, good and bad, and new ones, too – Memories that had been created since she left Iskeull. The disastrous TV interview. The viral videos. The discovery of her diary. The exchange with Diya. Even several moments from the past two days with Finn. But it was impossible to string them together with one clear clasp of meaning, because every one of them remained as emotionless as computer code. Even Memories that had touched her deeply, as lived experiences only hours before, had been bled dry.

She could sense the thing getting nearer now, as the Storyline came close to completing its circuit; felt her distant body buck as it tried to break its hold. This time, rather than waiting to be tossed into oblivion, she reached out to it, tried to get purchase. But it was like trying to grab at air. Before she knew it, the void had split open and gulped her in.

She woke with a retch, half-digested beef jerky streaming out of her mouth. Groaning, sobbing, she rolled onto her side, then retched some more while her vision sparked and her stomach cramped. But as soon as the calm had plugged the worst of the pain, Alex got back to her feet and glared up at the lurching snake. It had instantly re-formed above her head, as if it knew exactly why she was there.

'Listen,' she whispered, 'you mutant piece of shit. You're MINE. I bred you. I own you. And I'm going to try again and again and a-fucking-gain, until you let me into that root Memory. I'm going to take back my Story and reclaim my past. And I'm going to force you to unleash your crazy fucking surging power only how and when I say.'

She adopted the posture. She closed her eyes. She breathed her way back into calm. She raised her arms and felt the burning loop lock on. And then the whole revolting rollercoaster slid round again. She re-Read every Memory; came close to the root; fought the void; and once again tumbled in and lost consciousness. When she dragged herself back to standing, she forced herself to draw on the intensive training top-up Finn had given her in the farmhouse kitchen the previous night. She thought of his hand, firm on her belly. She heard his voice, lilting in her ear for hours. She straightened her spine. She breathed in more calm. She looked back up at her bad Storyline. She Read.

Alex held on through twelve sickening bouts until – as she neared the end of the circuit and felt the thing approaching yet again – she couldn't take it any more. Finn was wrong. She wasn't strong. She was a weak pathetic failure, and she was never going to be able to wrestle this thing back under her control. This time, when the void cracked open, she didn't try to resist it. She didn't struggle. She opened her eyes and jumped right in.

22

You're like a storm without an eye, said Finn.

She's running on empty, said her mother. *She's burnt out inside.*

Their voices chased each other through Alex's head as she lay curled against the Stack, draped in her cape. What light there was, filtering through the pounding rain, suggested that it was mid-morning. She had no idea how she'd managed to stumble back through the maze from the tomb. She'd tucked herself behind an unlit tower on the perimeter of the Library before she'd collapsed and had been drifting in and out of a doze for a while. In the space between her cape and the ground she could see a flickering barcode of legs, as islanders passed in and out of the arch at the back of the index. She wondered whether they would hate her more or less, now, if they knew what she had found.

A prodigy, really, said MacBrian.

When you were with him, said Finn, *he made you feel like nothing in the world was impossible. Nothing.*

The shift bell rang out, just once. Ten a.m., then. She must have been inside her Story for either six or thirty hours. She really should get up. She was ambivalent about her chances of making it to their agreed meeting place, even if Finn had somehow managed to avoid getting locked up. Anyway, at this point she wasn't entirely sure what would be worse: getting caught, or having to tell Finn what she knew. Horses were beginning to thunder in and out of the Library, shaking the ground beneath her. Perhaps one of them would trample her. She wasn't sure she had the energy left to care. But then the changeover finished and the peninsula quietened down again and she found that she was doing it: pulling the cape onto her shoulders, drawing the hood over her head, gripping onto the lichened wall of the Stack. Standing up.

It was all too smooth. Too easy. Too unlikely, when she was such a shambling mess. But she was too tired to question her luck as she retraced her steps through the index, down the steps, across the road and onto the causeway. Mingling with the others crossing over to the main island, Alex moved doggedly through the cross-current of voices, noticing their subdued tone against the hiss and smack of the waves. She wondered how many Storylines the Readers had managed to disperse, despite their increasingly stubborn Stories. She wondered how many hours the scholars had wasted, studying their misguided theories.

There has to be a missing piece, said Finn.

As she approached the end of the causeway, she heard the chanting and stamping start up and risked a glimpse ahead. There seemed to be more picketers than before, packed behind a double rank of guards. The atmosphere was electric. A few of the younger Readers around her threw back angry shouts, but most of them seemed too exhausted to make trouble. The guards were too busy checking the chits of incoming workers to bother examining those returning from the peninsula. Alex passed through the bell tower without challenge and joined the tired Readers heading home along the western side of the avenue.

As soon as she was clear of the picket lines, she hung back and let the others draw ahead. Every few minutes a handful of people peeled off down towards the town. An hour or so later she was the only one left on the wide street, save for the occasional horse clattering past. Far from restoring her energy, the rest she'd managed to snatch seemed to have given her system time to register the full impact of what she'd just been through. As the last traces of calm seeped away, she found herself slowing to a shuffle. What had taken ten minutes to ride six days ago now took at least two hours to walk.

By the time she saw Taran's house crouching high on the cliff above, she was drenched. Planting one squelching boot on the churned-up turf, she began to trudge up the spine of scaly black mud that led to the house. Sixty-three steps later, with every inch of her flesh stinging and booming, Alex found herself standing outside the professor's front door. This time, when she glanced at the smeared windows, only her distorted reflection stared back. The front door was flaky with old indigo paint, the knocker a rusty twist of metal shaped into a figure-of-eight. Alex took hold of it and banged.

A loud silence. Then, what felt like an age later, heavy footsteps.

It would be MacBrian, of course. MacBrian with a dozen

of Iain's toughest tough-guys in tow. Finn would be back in prison. Taran would be disgraced. They probably wouldn't even pause to hear what she had to say, before they blew her apart.

The door creaked open a few inches. A collection of large, pale features floated in the darkness for a moment. Then the gap widened to reveal Taran's face. He peered beyond Alex, looked back over his shoulder, then jumped down onto the driveway. 'Alex!' he stammered as the door blew shut behind him. 'I can't believe you're—'

'Is Finn here?' she croaked, stepping back into a pothole ankle-deep with freezing water.

'We'd given up hope,' Taran gabbled. 'We couldn't imagine you'd managed to—'

She raised her voice as loud as she could. 'Finn?'

'No, no.' Taran lurched forward, shaking his big hands. 'No, Alex, you mustn't—'

'Finn?' She was about to fall. '*Finn?*'

Then the door banged open and she saw a flash of orange jumper and Finn was there, ducking under Taran's arm. He stared at Alex open-mouthed, then gave a strangled laugh and crushed her against his warm, thyme-scented chest. She held herself rigid until he moved her out by her shoulders and subjected her to the drill-bit gaze.

'You did it, didn't you?' he murmured. 'You found it, whatever it is? I can tell from your face. I *knew* you would, I knew it. Alex. Alex? What did you find?'

'Not here,' Taran blundered between them. 'Not now. We must get inside. I'm sorry, Alex, but we were sure that you

367

were lost . . . and Iain's men have already been here, asking about Finn.' He reached an arm around her shoulders and hustled her through the door into a dim entrance hall.

'What happened?' Finn said, rushing after them, kicking the door shut with his heel. 'What was the Storyline? What was the root Memory? Can you control the surge?'

'Finn,' Taran said, 'wait.' He threw Alex's sopping cape onto the floor, then steered her through a doorway into a large living room lit by a blazing fire.

As he manoeuvred her onto a sagging leather sofa, Alex looked dizzily around. Piles of books climbed the walls on all sides, teetering up to the peeling plaster of the ceiling. Other than the sofa, the only furniture was a low table, scattered with papers, empty plates and mouldy food. The only decoration was an ornate filigree silver box, incongruously elegant, displayed on the mantelpiece above the fire.

'You've had a huge overdose of radiation,' Taran said, kneeling before a battered bucket of peat in front of the hearth. Rummaging inside, he withdrew an unlabelled bottle and held it up to the flames, revealing a few inches of tawny liquid inside. 'Here.' He carried the bottle over and pulled out the cork. 'Drink as much as you can.'

The handmade bottle was so heavy she could barely lift it. Alex necked a mouthful of raw heat, then lowered it, coughing, blinking at Taran through watering eyes. He gestured for her to drink again, then turned to Finn, who was hovering behind his shoulder. 'It was a ridiculous idea. Unforgivable. She'd already tried her best. How could you expect her to be able to control Story-surging, when *we* still don't fully understand how it works?'

'It's not,' Alex gasped, 'Story-surging.'

Both men turned to stare at her. She put the bottle on the floor. 'The thing inside my Story – it's not a mutation,' she croaked. 'It's not a power. Or a weapon. It's a hole.'

'A what?' Finn said.

'It's a hole.'

Finn looked at Taran, who opened his mouth, but no words came out. Finn flung himself onto the sofa beside Alex. 'Alex? What do you mean?'

She'd been trying to work out what to say during the long journey back up through the tomb, through the Library and to the house. But now that she was sitting inches from his face, all her carefully constructed sentences shattered into monosyllables. 'It was the void.'

'The void?'

'It's been there from the start, from the night of the seventeenth, waiting for me in my episodes. I thought it was just fear, the edge of panic, the start of unconsciousness. But it wasn't unconsciousness. It was *anti*-consciousness.'

'I don't understand.'

'I kept trying, like we agreed. I Read that Storyline again and again. And every time I Read it, I could feel the thing – what we thought was this mutated root Memory – at its core. And every time I got close, it would tumble me down into the void. I tried my best to fight it, so that I could stay conscious, so I could grab the root Memory and get it under my control. But in the end, after I had Read the Storyline maybe eleven, twelve times, I was so knackered I couldn't fight any more. I gave in, Finn. I finally let go, just like everyone's been telling me to. For the first time since the night of the seventeenth, I didn't resist the void. I opened my eyes and jumped right in. And that's when I saw it, in the split second before the Storyline fell apart. That's when I saw the hole.'

Taran was frowning down at her, shaking his head. 'Breaking a Reading before the Storyline is finished does bad things to the system. Very bad. No wonder you're in such a state.' He looked at Finn. 'She needs drugs. Do you think you could get away unnoticed, reach Cait?'

'No.' Alex grabbed Finn's arm. 'Listen. You have to believe me. I'm telling you, I know what I saw.'

'Alex,' Finn said, glancing at Taran, 'what you're telling us doesn't make sense. Stories are made of pure consciousness. They don't have *holes*.'

'Well, mine does. I saw it. It was the size of a Memory, but it wasn't silver, or shimmery-black like the calm. It wasn't any colour at all, not light, not dark. It was nothing, total nothingness, and it was sort of . . . *tattered* round the edge.' She gave Finn's arm a shake. 'You said that no-one could mistake their own Story and, believe me, I knew exactly what this was. It isn't some magic mutant power. It's the opposite. It's a *wound*.'

Taran grunted, as if he had been punched. Finn appeared to have stopped breathing.

'Finn.' Alex squeezed his elbow as if she could tourniquet the pain of her words. 'I'm so sorry that I have to tell you this. After everything I've done to you so far. But there's no doubt in my mind what happened. Your father ripped out my root Memory.'

Finn's face turned white, then red.

'Alex,' Taran said. 'This is madness. I don't understand what you're trying to do.'

Alex looked up at him. 'I wish I could think of some other explanation. But you all keep telling me how talented Egan was. The best Reader for generations. This fearless prodigy. A man who didn't care what others thought. A man who thought anything was possible.'

She looked back at Finn, who still hadn't moved. 'It all adds up now. It all makes sense. Your father refusing to stop Reading, concealing it from the Council. The changes in his mood. He was trying something new, wasn't he? *Experimenting*. You told me how passionate he was about the impact that being well-Read could have on people's lives. So what if he found a way to actually *remove* a root Memory? That would shatter even the most stubborn Storyline, wouldn't it? Force its owner to change? And wouldn't it give Readers so much more control than they have right now, when people can simply feint, or re-form their Storylines a few days later? Wouldn't it mean that you guys – all of you, around the world – would finally be able to keep the Library working the way it should?'

She was getting through to Taran. She knew she was. He was agitated, rubbing furiously at the back of his neck, refusing to meet her eye. She turned back to Finn, desperate now for him to react, even if it was to punch her in the face.

'Don't you see?' she pleaded. 'Your dad managed it, Finn. He did what no other Reader had ever managed to do – what no other Reader had ever even *thought* to do. And it worked, in a way. It forced me to change, so quickly and thoroughly that it felt like a miracle. Because it was a miracle. It had nothing to do with me. He ripped out the eye of my storm.'

Finn was still as stiff as a corpse. Taran was pacing, looking anguished. Alex slumped back against the sofa and stared at the cracks cross-hatched across the ceiling. She was so very tired.

'It backfired, though, didn't it?' she ploughed on, determined to get it all out while she still could. 'My Storyline didn't just fall apart, once the root Memory had gone. I understand it now, you see. Poor thing. It's like it remembers that something should be there, like it's still trying to hold onto the pattern. But without that first, crucial Memory, it doesn't make sense. Nor do any of my other Storylines. That Memory must have been a part of all of them. Without it, *I* don't make sense.'

One of the cracks looked like a long, thin finger, reaching out from the corner, preparing to rip the ceiling apart.

'Sure, once it was gone, I could finally get free of whatever crap was holding me back,' she murmured. 'But that crap made me who I was. Now I'm *too* free. Free-floating. Free-falling. Constantly trying to stitch myself together from other people's ideas and words. Improvising myself, moment to moment, which sounds kind of Zen, but isn't really Zen at all. It's absolutely bloody exhausting.'

The sofa creaked. Alex looked over to see that Finn had stood up. One of his hands was buried in his hair. The other was clenching and unclenching by his side. 'You have no idea what you're talking about,' he said.

'I *know*!' Alex let out a hysterical laugh. Finn's face darkened from Eudo scarlet to Iskeull indigo. 'I'm so sorry, Finn. I'm so, so sorry. But you're the one who wanted me to go back down there. You're the one who told me I need to start trusting my instincts. And my instincts are in absolutely no doubt about what I saw. An ex-Memory. A *grave*. And, God, I wish I hadn't seen it, because now I finally understand how utterly fucked I really am. And I wish – I really do wish – that it wasn't your father who had done it. But who the hell else could it have been?'

CRACK. A shard of glass ripped across Alex's cheek. A spray of whisky hit her face. Finn made a sound as if he was going to be sick. His complexion switched back from purple to bone-white. A single rivulet of amber liquid rolled from his hairline into his eye. Then he crumpled to the floor to reveal Taran, holding a broken bottle, watching him fall.

23

They remained like that for several seconds – Alex on the sofa, Taran in front of her with the bottle, Finn on the floor between them. It was as though, if no-one moved, they might be able to pretend that it wasn't happening. Then Alex tried to launch herself out of the sofa in a desperate leap for the door. But her ankles wouldn't take her weight. The back of her knees buckled, and she flumped back onto the broken springs. She turned and grabbed the back of the sofa. Hooked one foot over the top. Tried to climb over. Felt her elbows buckle. Crashed back down.

'Stop,' Taran said, still looking at Finn. 'You don't have the strength. And there's nowhere to go.'

He was right. Already, from her one pathetic fumble, her ears were ringing and her vision was perforated with flashing lights. Alex hauled herself back to sitting, her heart making strange arrhythmic leaps. Her cheek was stinging and she could feel liquid rolling down her skin, although she wasn't sure whether it was alcohol or blood. Beneath her, his hair shining purple in the firelight and his prone body giving off an overpowering stench of acrid malt, Finn still hadn't moved.

ABC, her mother's voice said. *That's the first thing you need to remember in an emergency, darling. Airway, breathing, circulation. ABC.*

They looked up at the same time. 'Taran,' Alex said. She had been going for calm and rational, but her voice came out too high and she had to fight down a wave of panic that threatened to black her out. 'What are you doing?'

Taran sighed. 'I am trying to do what's best for us all.'

'Did MacBrian put you up to this?'

He snorted. 'Sorcha? Sorcha's nothing but an overblown secretary. I told you, Alex, you and I, we're pioneers.'

'I don't want to be a pioneer,' Alex croaked. 'I want to be alive.'

'But you have been, haven't you?' Taran swept his hand through the air, taking the half-bottle with it, in a glinting arc. 'Truly alive, for the first time in twenty years? Oh, it didn't quite work, as you said. There are issues to iron out. But while it did – *ppppfffff*.' He gave his hiccupy-gasp laugh. 'It's been a testament to what we might achieve.'

He looked back down at Finn, who was leaking blood from a clotted nest of hair just above his ear. Grasping the opportunity, Alex tried to propel herself forward again. But her legs ignored her, her arms crumpled like paper and she collapsed back onto the cushions with a cry. Taran didn't even bother to look up. She closed her eyes and tried to summon some calm, but her chest was a birdcage: brittle, fluttering, leaking breath.

'Please,' she whispered. 'Finn needs help. Let me get him out of here.'

'What a waste.' Taran shook his head. 'Not a patch on his father, of course, but still. What a waste.' He levered the heel of his boot beneath Finn's shoulders and rolled the boy to one side – thump-thump-thump – his head bouncing on the flagstones as he turned.

'Taran—' Alex pleaded.

Taran looked up at her. 'I'm sorry, Alex. I really am. This has all been as difficult for me as it has for you. I didn't think for a moment that you'd come within a thousand miles of this place again, once they let you go. But what's done is done. And your sacrifice will allow me to keep working. It will buy me time. This may not have turned out quite the way I hoped, but then this isn't about us. It's about the Library. It's about what's right.' He stepped forward, readjusting his grip on the half-bottle's base.

Alex's bowels tried to empty their non-existent contents while her stomach heaved the whisky back out of her mouth. She swiped at the sticky mess with her sleeve. '*Please.*'

'Be brave, my pioneer,' he said, bending over her. 'We'll get it over quickly now, you and me.'

With a final, mammoth effort, Alex jerked her knee up and into Taran's balls. He grunted and reeled back, but now she found that she didn't even have the strength left to slither past him onto the floor. Turning back, pink-faced, Taran grabbed her wrists. He transferred them both into one big hand and dragged her back up.

'Such an old Storyline,' he said, leaning close to her face, his voice tight with pain. 'Girls and their fathers. Perhaps the oldest Storyline of all. But then the oldest ones are always the most powerful, aren't they?' He touched the jagged glass to her throat. 'Now close your eyes.'

A shout. A jerk. A rumble. A rush of air. An almighty crash. Alex's face smashed into the sofa, her mouth full of flaking hide and dust. A hell-beast was crouching over her, its musky bulk pinning her down, its hot pant in her ear. No. No. She had been here before. She wriggled, screamed, choked. Beyond her head, more shouts, bangs, a grunt, another crash. Beyond her feet, a terrible, low, animal wail.

Then the weight lifted just enough to allow her to flip onto her back and she found herself staring up into the face of Iain MacHoras. He grazed her neck with a rough-padded thumb, then looked up beyond her head. Alex craned her head back to follow his gaze and saw, upside-down, Taran crouched on the ground. He was swarming with black-clad guards, with his bound hands wrenched high above his back and thick strings of blood spinning from his mouth.

Iain barked something in Iskeullian and the men dragged Taran to his feet. Another familiar voice shouted an instruction from the other end of the room. Iain twisted off the sofa in one sideways leap and Alex saw, from over her toes, MacBrian, standing in the doorway. She was restraining the source of the horrible wail: a tall, barefoot woman in a stained white nightdress with a wild storm-cloud of hair.

Iain directed one of the guards to help MacBrian, then knelt beside Finn.

ABC.

Alex tried to speak. She couldn't speak.

ABC.

Shit!

ABC ABC shit shit shit. She couldn't sit up and suddenly, shit, oh God, oh shit, she couldn't see.

ABC ABC ABC ABC ABXYZXHGYUTOPSHJEIYX

A grenade of panic exploded in Alex's chest.

Bang.

Lamplight, dim. Weight on her legs: a blanket. A silhouette in the doorway, facing out. Still in her clothes, stiff with mud and sweat. The sheets beneath her smelling of unwashed skin and alcohol. Splintered shutters, bolted shut, peeling with paint. And, glinting in the shadows all around her, hundreds of pale, sculptural, shining things, bristling with blades and spikes and tubes and curves.

Tech components? Lab equipment? Medical – oh God – medical instruments?

But then her eyes adjusted and she realized what she was looking at: a flock of model aircraft. They were all shapes and sizes, perched on every available shelf, table, crate and chair. Chunky 747s, elegant gliders, giant Space Shuttles, spindly wooden biplanes. A plastic Action Man helicopter. A metal replica of Concorde. A Lego Starship *Enterprise*. In the corners, shadowy stacks of magazines. On top of a chest of drawers, between a khaki fighter plane and a white-and-orange EasyJet, a brown glass bottle and a silver-backed hairbrush.

'Dorothy Moore?'

She tried to scream. She rolled her eyes to the side of the bed and saw Freya MacGill sitting on a wicker chair, arms crossed over her chest.

'They're fetching the doctor,' said Freya. Her voice was slurred, her eyes yellow-tinged. She had covered the white nightdress with a knitted jumper, but Alex could feel her shivering where her bare knees pushed against the bed.

Am I going to die? Alex tried to say.

'I'm sorry,' Freya said thickly. 'I knew something was wrong, but—' She shook her head. 'Please, don't blame him. It's me.' She put a hand to her forehead. 'I'm sorry,' she said again. 'I'm not right. I think, when Taran let me have a drink, he – when Finn arrived – I think he put something in the—'

Is Finn dead? Alex pleaded with her eyes. Finn. Is Finn okay? But Freya had turned to look at her collection of planes.

'Egan used to bring them for me,' she said, vaguely. 'He'd order them to be sent to Kirkwall and every time he went on leave, he'd bring one back. It made my brother angry, but Egan understood. He liked those sort of things, too. Outside things. Things that would help you remember that there's a world out there where people can just – go, wherever, whenever they want.' She shook her head again. 'I know Taran gets carried away with things, but I never thought he'd actually hurt someone. And not Egan, surely, never Egan . . .

Mum? I need you, Mum. I need you. Dad?

Freya turned back to Alex. 'I promise, Taran never confided in me, about what they were trying to do with the Stories. About what they did to you. You have to believe me, I would never have let him—' She paused, squeezed her elbows. 'He used to tell me everything, before. He was always shut away in his room with his books, but I didn't mind. I was just happy to be with him. He was always so excited about one idea or another, tripping over himself, spilling over with thoughts. Our father didn't understand. Our father used to call him a *chneònachat*. A – a – what's the English? A misfit. A geek.'

Girls and their fathers.

'Egan didn't understand him, either.' She sniffed, tossing back the heavy mass of her hair. 'Not really. He was fascinated by Taran, loved to listen to him talk, but he never took him seriously. He once told me he thought that Taran was mad, brilliant but mad. But then I suppose, if what they're saying is true, Taran must have finally convinced Egan to test out one of his theories. To take him seriously.'

Girls and their fathers?

'I wish he had told me. Maybe I could have helped in some way, reminded him that Stories aren't . . . He sometimes seems to forget that they're people, not things. But then when I – after I . . . Tom,' Freya leaned forward, her eyes suddenly lit by the same bright fervour as her twin. 'Tom. Tom Rendall. That was his name. No-one wants me to say it, but I won't forget him, I won't be ashamed. His name was TOM.' Then she shrank back into herself, shivering again. 'After Tom, Taran didn't talk to me like he used to. He didn't understand why I'd done what I'd done. I think being around me made him sad. And angry. He was so angry, all the time.'

What the hell had Taran meant by that? What was the Memory he had stolen from her? What was the meaning of her wounded Storyline?

'Do you understand what it means to love someone, Dorothy Moore? To love them in a way that has nothing to do with books and ideas? To love them in a way that would make you do something stupid, something quite mad . . .'

But when Alex tried to think, tried to understand, her head became as heavy as stone and her chest sparkled like stars; and the void, oh, the void, the bottomless void—

Light. Bright morning light, spangled across whitewashed stone. A linen shift, her body naked, dry, clean. Cool sheets. A red-and-yellow patterned woollen blanket. A circle of warped, bubbled glass, and against it the interminable drum and hiss of the rain.

She turned her head and felt the tiny spines of feathers prick through the pillow. Bedside table. Wardrobe. Stand with blue bowl and ewer. Shelves crowded with books and homespun knick-knacks, battered desk, green-cushioned stool, sheepskin rug. She felt sore and drowsy, as if she had been sleeping for a very long time.

Her toes moved when she asked them to: flexed, pointed, flexed. She drew her arms out from under the covers and twisted her wrists, watching the pale hairs catch the light. She saw her palms glow red in the sun; turned them over and examined the minute crosshatching and fanned bones. Her nails were pink, and she imagined someone scrubbing away whatever must have been under them. She touched her cheek. There was a dressing on it, cottony padding and tape.

She felt the ghost of Taran's breath on her skin, saw the glint of brown glass.

She kicked the blanket aside and sat up. On the bedside table there was a glass of water and a small cardboard packet: Health Essentials Paracetamol Caplets 500mg. She lifted the glass and took some of the cold, sweet water into her mouth. Swilled it around, held it until it had soaked into her gums. Swallowed. Drank the rest. Cleared her throat.

'Alex,' she said. It worked. 'Alex,' she said, louder. 'I'm okay. I'm here.'

Wait. Was that . . . ? She was sure, suddenly, that she had heard the sound of children whispering, a giggle. But when she listened now, all she could hear was the rush of her own blood, mingling with the sound of the rain.

The rug was soft under her toes. When she tipped her weight forward over her ankles, they held. Stiffly, joints popping, she straightened her knees. Yup. She could stand. She bent her left knee, shuffled her foot forward, let her weight sink down, did the same thing with the right. Yup. She could walk, too. She made a circuit of the room, working out the kinks.

Then she sat back on the bed and covered her face in her hands.

She cried and cried and cried and cried until she couldn't cry any more. Then she sat in a daze, trying to piece it all together, until she heard a knock. She didn't speak, but the door opened anyway.

'Miss Moore? I was told—'

'Are my family safe?'

MacBrian stopped with her hand on the latch. 'Your family?'

Alex stood up. 'If Iain MacHoras has hurt so much as a hair on their heads—'

'*Iain?*'

'I saw him at the airport. Sent to blow my brains out. By you.'

MacBrian came in and pushed the door closed. Under the greying crop, her brow was gathered into a whorl. 'I sent Iain to bring you back here, for your own safety.'

'And was the gun for my own safety, too?'

'*Gun?* Iain doesn't carry a gun. There are no guns on Iskeull. The only person who has a gun – *had* a gun – was Dughlas MacFionn. And he bought that in Kirkwall using Taran's credit card.' She took a step forward. 'Listen, before we get into—'

'No.' Alex reached her in three wild strides. 'You listen to me. Has. Anyone. Touched. My. Parents? Harry? Lenni? Mae?' Her voice broke. 'Bo?'

'Your family are fine, Miss Moore. Absolutely fine. By the time Iain landed in Edinburgh, you and Finn had already—'

'Finn!' CRACK. *Thump-thump-thump.* 'Finn. Finn – is he—?'

'Finn's fine. He's got a nasty cut, but the doctors say there's no lasting damage done. Physically, that is. His state of mind is – well, you can imagine.'

Thank the Library. God? Whatever. Alex felt the beginnings of relief sink through her like a shot of gin. 'So if Iain didn't have a gun, what was in the violin case?'

MacBrian frowned. 'The—?'

'At the airport. Iain was carrying a violin case.'

'Well . . .' MacBrian paused. 'I imagine it would have been a violin.'

'A violin.'

'A fiddle. For the homesickness. One of the only ways to delay its progress is to play native music while you're Outside.'

It sounded ridiculous. She had no reason to trust her. She had no reason to trust any of them. But as Alex glared at MacBrian, and MacBrian looked steadily back, the hormonal shot of gin became a double. Alex took a wobbly step back. 'And you're honestly giving me your word that you didn't order me to be killed?'

'Of course not! Why on earth—?' MacBrian stopped and pinched her temples. By the time she'd dropped her hand, the cold-blooded tyrant that Alex had been constructing in her mind over the past few days had become a tired middle-aged manager, squinting in the morning light. 'I'm not a monster, Miss Moore,' MacBrian said wearily. 'I'm just a woman. An ordinary woman, I admit; an unglamorous and un-legendary woman. Neither the best Reader of her generation nor even of her class. But a reasonably skilled, intelligent, hard-working woman, nonetheless. One who is trying her best to do the right thing under very difficult circumstances. Why on earth would you think that I would kill anyone?'

Alex felt the heat rise through her cheeks. 'Finn,' she said. 'He told me that you'd panicked. He said you'd asked the Board to suspend the Covenant, so that I – so that the problem of my Story could be solved.'

384

A shade of hurt crossed MacBrian's face, then was briskly dismissed. 'Well, he's certainly right that things are in a mess. It would have helped if his beloved father had done a little more of his actual job, practised a little more actual leadership in between the secret Reading sessions and the unethical experiments. But, still, to believe I could commit *murder*—'

'Finn told me,' Alex said slowly, 'that he heard it from Taran.'

'Ah. I see.' MacBrian pinched her temples again. 'Another piece of the puzzle we shall have to fit in. I am beginning to suspect that Taran has secretly been trying to undermine my authority for months.'

'But why? I still don't understand what's happening. What happened. With me, and Taran, and Finn's dad.'

'Nor do we. Not everything. We're still unclear on how the responsibility for this falls out between the two of them. We've been trying to piece it together from what Dughlas has told us, and Taran . . .' She sighed. 'Well, Taran is refusing to cooperate until we provide a guarantee that he will be allowed to keep working on what he calls his *project*, which is of course out of the question. Finn is on his way to the guardhouse now to try and get him to talk.'

'Hang on.' Alex's head was spinning. 'Dughlas?'

'Yes. Dughlas is back. It appears that he was the one who attacked you in London last week, at Taran's behest. And he was the one who followed you to the restaurant, too. He was arrested there and detained for several days, and he very nearly ended up irrevocably damaging his Story. He only just made it back to Kirkwall last Wednesday, at which point he threw himself on our mercy and confessed. That's why I was trying to get hold of you with such urgency. We were concerned that Taran might have sent someone else to finish the job. When you didn't reply, I sent Iain to escort you back here. But by that time, Finn had taken the matter into his own hands. You'd been spotted together in Kirkwall by the time Iain landed in Edinburgh. So I called Iain on the mobile telephone and he flew straight back.'

'Wait – what? You've known all this for days? You knew I was here?'

'We've been watching you ever since you left The Reel. We couldn't follow you on the boat, of course, and we knew that part of the journey might be dangerous. But Lucas Mac-Tomas is an excellent sailor, so we took a calculated risk to let you proceed. We assumed that Finn would take you back to his mother's, so we picked up the trail again there. We've been following you ever since.'

Alex thought back to the surprising success of Finn's riot at the causeway, her suspiciously smooth journey to the tomb, the oblivious index, the deserted avenue. Not so lucky, then. Not so fated. Not such a brilliant pair of spies after all. 'You *let* me go down there again?'

'Frankly, we were delighted. We couldn't understand how Finn had persuaded you to give it another try.' MacBrian spread her hands. 'I knew you didn't trust me, Miss Moore. By that point we had Dughlas's testimony, but we still didn't know exactly what Taran and Egan had done. We couldn't simply accept the word of a deeply troubled young man against a professor and the most admired Director in recent history, without further proof. We had no idea what you and Finn were up to, but by then we were hoping that whatever you had planned might, well, help flush out the truth.'

Alex pondered this for a moment. 'So you knew we were in Taran's house?'

MacBrian nodded. 'I followed Finn there with a team of Iain's men and made a cursory search, for appearances' sake. Then we waited nearby until you arrived – closely trailed by Iain, who made sure that nobody interfered with your progress. We broke in through the back while you were at the front door.'

'You were there when Taran attacked Finn, then?'

'We were just outside the room.'

'And you didn't think,' Alex said, slowly, '*that* was a good time to intervene?'

MacBrian hesitated. 'We thought Taran might . . . divulge all. Once you and he were alone. Once he had nothing to lose.'

'What, like some bloody James Bond villain? And what if I *hadn't* made it out of the tomb, what with the addiction and the radiation and all?' Alex paused. 'Oooh. Oh, but that would've still been a win, wouldn't it? You might not have got the full truth about Taran, but at least my Story would have been out of the way.'

'It was not an ideal situation by any means. Personally, I was not comfortable about it at all. But being the Director – serving the majority – involves making complex decisions. Sometimes at the expense of my own feelings. I should imagine you have discovered the same in your own career.'

Alex stared at her for a moment, then walked back to the bed and slumped down on the edge. 'So did I kill him or not? Egan?'

MacBrian followed her over. To Alex's surprise, she sat beside her on the bed. 'It's complicated.'

'What's *that* supposed to mean?'

'As I said, we're still trying to assemble all the facts.' MacBrian paused. 'The one thing we *can* now say is that you are, without doubt, not the slightest bit to blame.'

Alex picked up the fringe of the blanket and rolled it between her fingers. 'Whatever it was they did to me,' she said, twisting the wool until it was as thin and sharp as wire, 'am I more fucked than you thought I was before, or less?'

'We don't know,' MacBrian said. 'Not yet. We have scholars working on some theories. However, until Taran decides to tell us exactly what happened, they're no more than that.'

Alex dropped the blanket. She let out a long, shuddering breath. 'I think,' she said, 'that I would really quite like a bath.'

'Of course.' MacBrian stood up, straightening her tunic. 'I've washed your clothes. And you should eat. Also the doctor will want to see you. I'll have everything prepared.'

'Where are we, anyway?'

'In town. In my house. I hope my children didn't disturb you. I did ask them to keep their voices down, but trying to keep them under control makes dealing with the Council seem easy.'

'You've got kids?' Alex realized that she had imagined MacBrian as a confirmed spinster, working all hours from her soulless office amongst boxes she hadn't had time to unpack.

'Three girls,' MacBrian said, with the first smile Alex had seen from her. It transformed her face. 'And a husband who can cook. There are hot scones downstairs.' She reached for the doorknob, then paused and turned. 'Miss Moore. Before I go—'

The rest of her sentence was obliterated by the single deep boom of the bell. As they waited for the shockwaves to spread and dissolve, something stirred in the back of Alex's mind. Bells. Bells?

'As I was saying,' MacBrian said.

What was the significance of bells?

'I wanted to assure you, when I first came in: whatever it turns out that those men have done, however they've done it, I – we – the Council, the Board, the entire worldwide Readership – will do everything in our power to heal your Story and get you home.'

What had she forgotten? What was she supposed to *do*?

'Of course I can't promise that we can undo all the harm that has been done. I wish we could. But I do promise that we will try.'

'What day is it?' Alex asked.

'Wednesday,' MacBrian said, opening the door. 'Ten in the morning on Wednesday. You've been asleep for almost twenty-four hours.' She stepped out. 'Dr MacDiarmid will be along soon.'

Wednesday 5 August, 10.00 hours. No torture. No terror. No sobbing hostages or gory scenes. Instead her father, cranky

389

with worry, perched on the sofa in her abandoned living-room-diner, silently polishing his uncomfortable shoes. Her mother, unboxing a hat in the bedroom, keeping up a bright stream of conversation and plying them all with tea. Mae, leaning against the tiny kitchen counter, trying to keep Bo quiet with pirated YouTube cartoons while she fired off text after email after call. And, across London in his own neat flat, Harry. Dear, good Harry. Standing in his new dove-grey suit from Charles Tyrwhitt with his handsome jaw clenched, trying to ignore the whispers of his stiffly immaculate parents while he ironed his lilac pocket square.

24

It might have been a bit of belly-button fluff, except for the fact that it was floating in the centre of a clear plastic cylinder. A cylinder that had once, according to the label, held twenty Ryman's Assorted Ballpens.

'One of Iain's men found it in his living room,' MacBrian said. She was hovering in front of the table, as if Alex's root Memory might suddenly do something she needed to triage. 'It was in a silver box on the mantelpiece. Unlocked.'

Alex watched the scrap of fossilized consciousness spin in the pale, watery light streaming down from the dome. Had Taran and Egan spent their evenings sitting side-by-side on the broken-down sofa, clinking tumblers of whisky, watching her Memory glitter through the latticework? Had it given them a thrill, having their smoking gun on such blatant display?

More importantly, what crucial piece of her past was spun into that silver crumb?

'We didn't even know it was possible.' MacBrian, looking queasy, pulled out a chair and sat down. 'A real live Memory, outside its Story. Outside the Library. I never could quite bring myself to believe in Story-surging, but Editing? Dear Library. *Editing*. And Taran's always been a little . . . unpredictable, but the irreproachable Egan? Two elected Council members, in cahoots to commandeer the Library? How exactly I'm going to break this to the Board, I have no . . .'

There was a knock and the secretary popped her head round the door. Alex thought: Finn? He was still with Taran at the guardhouse, had been for more than two hours. But then Iain entered MacBrian's office, with an unfamiliar figure in tow.

'Miss Moore,' MacBrian said, 'this is Dughlas MacFionn.'

The boy who had attacked Alex on De Beauvoir Road and got himself arrested outside L'Antiga Capella was just that, a boy. He was sixteen at most, tall but still gangling, his features yet to settle into definite form behind a pointillist varnish of acne. Two hairy slices of flesh showed between the bottom of his brown trousers and the top of his boots, and his coarse mulch-coloured jumper stretched tight across his shoulders. No Reader's uniform now, no shotgun. Yet Alex could still feel his weight on top of her, smell his unwashed teenage flesh, hear the huff of his breath. She was disproportionately glad, suddenly, that she had had a long bath and was wearing her own clothes. She drew back her shoulders, shook out her freshly washed fringe and glared.

See? Boy? Outsider. Outsider who refuses to die.

Indestructible bitch of an Outsider, who left her devoted fiancé stranded at the registry table, a little over two hours ago.

Where, Alex wondered, would Harry be now? Already in the car back to St Albans, listening to Elaine enumerate the ways in which 'that girl' had never been good enough for him anyway? Or waiting in a side room at Shoreditch Town

Hall, still hoping for her to call from Heathrow with gushing apologies?

Iain grunted something and prodded Dughlas between his shoulder blades. The boy lurched forward and crashed into the seat opposite Alex and MacBrian.

'English,' Iain said, sitting beside him.

The top of Dughlas's head, dandruff-flecked black, dipped.

'Dughlas,' MacBrian said. 'You already know Dorothy Moore.'

A flash of grey eyes. A mutter, cracked in the middle. Iain growled a few words and Dughlas raised his head, shades of pink washing across his pimples like an LED light display. Looking somewhere beyond Alex's left ear, he seemed about to speak when his gaze caught on the Ryman's pot. He froze, his mouth half-open. His expression flipped from surly defensiveness to the fascinated horror of a child encountering a particularly graphic piece of roadkill. He turned to Iain, rumbling something in subterranean Iskeullian.

'This, Dughlas,' MacBrian said, 'is what your so-called friends did to Dorothy Moore.'

Dughlas rumbled again.

'English,' Iain said.

Dughlas's Adam's apple ballcocked up and down his neck. 'I never knew about *that*,' he said. 'I didn't. I never knew that was even *possible*.'

'Yes, well, there it is.' MacBrian poured water into a tumbler and pushed it across the table. Dughlas drained it in one. 'Now try and concentrate, Dughlas. I want you to tell

Miss Moore your version of events.' She opened her notebook. 'Start right at the beginning, with when you met Freya.'

Dughlas wrenched his gaze from the Memory to Alex's face, veered onto her breasts, then settled for a point somewhere on her chin. He mumbled something.

'Louder,' Iain said.

'I found her,' Dughlas mumbled a little louder. 'In the market, one day. It was cold.' He paused. The pink dialled up to crimson. 'She wasn't wearing enough clothes. People were staring. Whispering. People were always whispering about her.' He looked up, suddenly fierce. 'She's too good for them all.'

'Go on, Dughlas,' MacBrian said.

Dughlas returned his gaze to Alex's chin. 'I was the only one Freya would let help her. Other people tried, but she shouted and pushed them away. She liked me, though. She took my arm. I gave her my cloak and walked her back to her house. The house where she lived with her brother, Professor MacGill.' He swallowed. 'The Professor wasn't there, but he found out. Later that day he pulled me out of the archives and told me not to interfere. He was angry. But when I'd left her, Freya had asked if I would come and see her again. So I wrote a letter to her explaining why I couldn't and put it under the door when the Professor was at work. And then Freya sent me a letter back. And then I wrote back some more.'

'And this happened early last year?'

'March. The twentieth of March was the day we met.'

Watching Dughlas's neck flare, Alex found it all too easy to imagine: the excruciatingly shy teenage bookworm, a mediocre Reader who knew that he was considered a charity case, a joke. How strong he would have felt, how special, coming across the beautiful woman with the tragic past. A woman who had spent her life amongst whispers and stares. A woman who seemed to have eyes only for him.

As for Freya, perhaps Dughlas had reminded her of Tom, her long-lost young lover. Or perhaps her booze-cunning had simply recognized someone who would worship rather than judge her. Someone who would help her romanticize the shitty mess she had become.

Harry, she suddenly thought. *Forgive me. Forgive me what you're going through.*

'But Taran – Professor MacGill – found out about the letters?' MacBrian prompted.

Dughlas shifted in the chair. 'At first he was furious, said he'd get me banned. But two days after that he summoned me again and said he'd talked to Freya and he understood now that we were friends. He said that Director MacCalum was going to try out a new Reading technique that could help Freya and other people like her, people with particularly resistant root Memories. A secret technique.' He glanced up with a flash of defiance. 'They needed my help. Director MacCalum needed time in the Stacks, time that he wasn't going to be hassled about. So Professor MacGill asked if I was willing to give up my shift.'

'And you were to keep this secret? Keep the rota unchanged?'

Back to Alex's chin. 'Professor MacGill said you'd try to stop us, if you found out. He said' – the slightest hint of relish crept into his voice – 'you'd never understand what we were trying to do. He said you didn't have the imagination.'

With an invisibly fast reflex, Iain smacked Dughlas round the back of the head. Dughlas yelped.

'But you didn't talk to Director MacCalum himself?' MacBrian asked. 'About the arrangement?'

Rubbing the back of his neck resentfully, Dughlas shook his head. 'Professor MacGill said the Director wanted to keep as much distance between me and him as possible, so no-one would suspect. He was grateful, though. The Professor told me he was, and I could see it, too. He pretended not to notice me when he was passing through the archives, but it was there in his eyes. Professor MacGill said that the Director was going to make me his official assistant, once they'd proved their idea worked and got approval from the Board.'

'But we questioned you in February, after Director Mac-Calum's accident. You didn't say then that Professor MacGill had been involved in arranging the shifts, did you, Dughlas?'

'He said it was for the best,' Dughlas said miserably. 'He said that they had been really close to refining the technique, when the Director died, and if the Council found out that Professor MacGill was involved, they'd force him to stop. Then the Director's sacrifice would have been for nothing.'

MacBrian turned to Alex. 'Of course we re-questioned Dughlas last Wednesday, on his return to Iskeull. That's when we found out all the extra details about Taran's involvement.' She swivelled back to Dughlas. 'And you told us then that you did talk to Director MacCalum in person after all, didn't you, Dughlas? Just once, the evening he died?'

Dughlas nodded. 'He came to the house.'

'Professor MacGill's house.'

'Yes.' A note of pride, now. 'The Professor let me spend my shifts there with Freya. She loved having me in her room, showing me her planes. He had told me not to answer the door to anyone, but when I saw it was Director MacCalum, I knew it would be alright. But then when I did open it, the Director seemed very upset. He asked me where Professor MacGill was, and I told him that I didn't exactly know. I said I'd assumed he was in the archives, but that maybe if he wasn't there, he might be trying out stuff in our Stack. The Director got this funny look on his face and asked me to remind him *which* Stack was our Stack. I didn't understand why he would ask that, but he was getting really angry by then, so I just told him. I-537.'

'What happened after that?'

'Nothing. I stayed with Freya until fourth bell, then went home. I only found out what had happened to the Director the next morning.'

'When Professor MacGill visited you?'

Dughlas visibly cringed. 'He was so angry with me for talking to the Director. I thought he was going to—' He realized what he was about to say, and stopped. 'After a while he calmed down a bit and told me there might be a way to make up for it, if I kept my mouth shut. He told me that if I did exactly what he said, we might be able to hide what really happened in the Stack that morning.'

'And what,' Alex said coldly, 'was that?'

Dughlas's Adam apple started careering up and down again. Unexpectedly, Alex saw two bright rims of moisture collect on his downcast lashes. 'I killed him,' he whispered.

Alex looked wildly round at MacBrian. '*He* killed Egan MacCalum?'

'Wait.' MacBrian held up a hand. 'Go on, Dughlas.'

'Professor MacGill said he'd taken the shift that night.' His voice was barely decipherable now, gravel mixed with glue. 'He said he thought that Director MacCalum had been working too hard, what with his official duties on top of the experiments. So he'd decided to give him a break. He said that he was Reading a really stubborn Storyline, one that was fighting their new technique, when Director MacCalum came in and disturbed him. He'd jerked out of the Reading and somehow the root Memory had let out this blast of energy and hit the Director, right in the chest.'

Dughlas stopped snuffling then and looked fiercely at Alex. For a moment she saw how he could have done it; how he could have invented a Storyline where he became some sort of jihadi warrior – defending against the evil Outsider – and set out to gun her down.

'And Taran told you to keep all this yourself?' MacBrian asked.

'He warned me that you'd come and see me, to ask questions about that night. He told me what to tell you. He even made me rehearse it. Then he told me to stay quiet, to take time off work, not to come to the house. He said he needed time to work out what to do.'

'Until two weeks ago. When we found the right Dorothy Moore.'

'He said it was the only way I could make up for what I'd done. He said I had to destroy her evil Story.'

'So you came to London and tried to kill me,' Alex said. 'Twice. But you screwed up, didn't you, Dughlas? Got your arse whipped by a couple of city kids. Lurked outside a res- taurant' – oh, Harry, forgive me – 'in broad daylight. Let the homesickness drive you nuts.'

Dughlas glared at her, twisting his hands, no doubt im- agining her neck.

'After he was arrested, the police drove him to a local station,' MacBrian said. 'By that time he was ranting about all kinds of strange things they took to be delusions, thank- fully. And despite the accusations of this' – she checked her notebook – 'jewellery designer? there was no real evidence of a crime. They transferred him to a drug rehabilitation unit in' – she glanced down again – 'Uxbridge? By this time he was in a very bad way, but the unit wasn't particularly secure. Dughlas managed to escape and, using Taran's credit card, found his way back to Kirkwall, where we were tipped off.'

'Tipped off?'

MacBrian looked at Iain. 'We get the odd problem with islanders on leave: people trying to travel too far, youngsters testing their strength. For such purposes we maintain a number of . . . contacts around Orkney and Scotland. Noth- ing official. No governments. Just hand-picked individuals, contacted anonymously and compensated handsomely. Associates.'

'Oh.' Alex raised her eyebrows. 'Associates.'

'Anyway,' MacBrian continued briskly, 'Iain's team picked Dughlas up in Kirkwall, at which point he begged them to take him back to the island in exchange for everything he knew.'

'I couldn't help it,' Dughlas muttered, his skin flaming. 'The homesickness – it's *torture*. It feels like you're being ripped apart inside.'

'You know what, Dughlas?' Alex said. 'I know *exactly* how that feels.'

Dughlas looked back at the Memory. Panic crossed his face. 'He never told me they'd hurt you,' he stammered. 'He never said anything about – that. He said it was all your fault. That there was something wrong with your Story. That it was built wrong. That it was . . . That you were—'

'*Sa il-onaidh*,' Iain said succinctly. Dughlas shut up.

'Take him out, Iain, please,' MacBrian said wearily. 'And find out what's happened to Finn.'

Iain stood and Douglas lurched back to his feet without having to be asked. He shot a final horrified glance at Alex's Memory, then followed Iain out.

'So,' MacBrian said.

They both looked, again, at the Memory.

'Can I touch it?' Alex asked.

'I don't see there's much harm. Iain carried it here, after all.'

Alex leaned across the table and picked up the Ryman's

pot, then almost dropped it. The thin polyethylene tube felt as heavy as lead. She rearranged her grip, then almost dropped it again, as the Memory began to dart around inside like a deranged insect.

It *recognizes* me, she thought, holding it up to the light. She felt a sudden, unlocatable jab of pain, somewhere between a gunshot and grief. What *are* you? she begged. What terrible secret do you hide? 'So I was just a lab rat, then?' she asked out loud. 'A test subject for this Editing thing?' She thought of the statue, so beautiful, so lofty, reaching out towards the Library. 'Your glorious Director ripped out part of my soul because he thought it would – how did you put it – *serve the majority?*'

'No,' said Finn.

25

Finn looked ten years older and exhausted. There was a bandage turbaned round his head and a purple bulge above one of his eyes. Alex wanted to jump forward and hug him, like he'd hugged her when she'd arrived back from the tomb. But he didn't look like he'd want anyone to touch him for a while.

'Can I . . . ?'

'Careful. It's heavy.'

He received the Ryman's pot as carefully and reverentially as if it were a newborn. As soon as it transferred hands, the Memory stopped rocketing and hung tranquilly in the centre of the cylinder again. Iain returned, closing the door behind him. After a while MacBrian said, as gently as Alex had ever heard her say anything, 'Finn?'

'He seemed pleased to see me,' Finn said. 'He actually seemed pleased to see me. He said that he wanted me to try to understand. I think he believes he's done the right thing, even now. I think he's *proud*.'

After a few more moments he handed the pot back to Alex and went and sat in Dughlas's vacant chair. He threw his head back and watched the rain slide down the dome.

'Dughlas doesn't know the full story,' he said. 'My father did discover how to Edit, that part's right. But he didn't hurt you, Alex. He never touched your Story. Taran was the one who took your Memory out.'

'Taran?' MacBrian pinched her temples. 'Dear Library, *Taran*? How?'

Alex put the pot back on the table. The Memory stabilized.

'It began early last March,' Finn said, his voice distant, his face Reading-still. 'The day my father told the Council he'd decided to stop Reading after all. Taran found himself summoned here, to this room, shortly after second bell. My father was pacing around, still in his damp Reading clothes, obviously upset. He told Taran to shut the door and swore him to secrecy, then explained that he had just beaten his personal Reading best. Four hundred Stories in six hours, without a single feint. He said he felt like he'd reached a new level of connection with the Library. What he called a pure state of flow.' Finn paused. 'Towards the end of the session my father had come across a Storyline with a particularly tough root Memory. He did what he always did, what any good Reader would do. He waited, breathed through it, gave it space – and after a while he felt it yield. The meaning of the Storyline gushed out, as usual. But just before it broke apart, he felt something *detach*. And then, while the other Memories rushed back into the Story, he saw that one of them was still there. On his fingertip.'

The slap and plish of old rain, sliding over the glass.

'I don't understand,' MacBrian said slowly. 'He must have

done something different. Something unusual. Something new.'

'My father said not. He told Taran that he'd asked himself the same question, over and over. Yet he was certain he hadn't done anything different from the last thousand Reads, or the thousand before that.'

MacBrian spread her palms. 'So you're telling us this Memory simply Edited *itself*?'

'Apparently my father thought it had happened simply because he Read so much. You all know the numbers. He'd Read millions of Stories over the years. He'd taken multiple shifts when he was young, more than anyone else on record. He told Taran that he believed he'd reached some kind of – and these were his exact words – tipping point. He reached a whole new level of integration with the Library, which allowed that Memory to simply – let go.'

'Sweet Library!' MacBrian murmured. 'So much for Taran's elaborate calculations and models. When all you have to do is keep Reading. Read *enough*.'

'What did he do with it?' Alex asked. 'The Memory?'

'The Story was still in its dock in the wall, still open, still re-gathering its Memories, in preparation for its return to the Library. So my father simply climbed up the wall and dropped the detached Memory back in. The Story simply closed over and vanished, as normal, into the energy behind the wall.'

MacBrian leaned forward. 'But why didn't he tell the Council, Finn? The Board? Your father may have been frustrated with the politics at times, but I can't believe he would have hidden a discovery of that magnitude.'

'Taran couldn't believe it, either. He told my father he should be thrilled.'

Finn looked round at them then, and the grief that cracked through his mask made Alex long to reach across the table and take his hand. 'Of course my father loved being loved,' he said. 'He loved being a star. But the real reason he loved Reading was because it allowed him to become part of something bigger than himself.' He looked at MacBrian. 'I know you think he was selfish. Vain. But I saw what it really meant to him, whenever he talked about Reading, to my mother and me. He told Taran that when that Memory came away in his hand, it felt *wrong*. He said it felt dangerous, being able to force someone like that. Taking away their choice. He said it felt like he'd stepped outside the Library, rather than gone deeper in. He said it felt *cold*.'

Finn stood and walked over to the empty spaces on the wall where his father's pictures had once hung, faced the empty shelves that had once groaned with his father's Outside trinkets and books. The rain had started again, whispering insistently on the glass. 'He said he never wanted to feel it again, and he didn't think that anyone else should, either.'

'Let me guess,' MacBrian said. 'Taran disagreed.'

'Taran thought he was a coward. Taran said that the Library had shown him the path to the future and it would be irresponsible of him not to take it.'

MacBrian made a grim sound in the back of her throat. 'And did Taran tell you how your father responded to that?'

'He said he was going to stop Reading altogether, from that night on. He told Taran he wasn't to speak a word about what had happened, and that he never wanted to discuss it again. Taran told me his exact words. *Just because something is possible, that doesn't mean it's right.*'

In its plastic tube, the Memory danced.

'Taran said,' Finn went on, after a moment, 'that I wasn't to feel ashamed of my father. He said that people who were successful in the present were always afraid of change. He said that sometimes' – a beat – 'for new growth to come through' – a beat – 'the dead heather has to burn.'

'*Finn.*' Unable to resist any longer, Alex crossed the room and placed her hands on Finn's shoulder blades. He twitched, like a horse with a fly, but he didn't turn round.

'He kept saying,' he said, 'that the thing people never understand is that free will isn't free will if you don't have self-control.'

'I bet he did,' Alex said. 'It's like he told Dughlas. This whole shit-show is about Freya, essentially?'

Finn turned. 'Freya?'

'Well, it's obvious, isn't it? The guy's your classic geek, a kid who lived his life through sci-fi books while his hot mate aced sports day and got all the girls. And then the only person he ever really loved, who ever really loved him, fell for the wrong guy. She let one stubborn Storyline destroy the rest of her life, and probably quite a big chunk of his, too. And so he went back to his books with even more fervour, desperate to believe that if he just found the right theory, he could bring the whole world under his control.'

She threw up her hands. 'Jesus! I mean, Taran's been waiting his whole life for something like this to come along. Imagine how frustrated he must have been when this "breakthrough" passed him by, for all his cleverness. Instead it went to his perfect friend, simply because he *got on and did it*. And imagine how angry he must have been when Egan *rejected* the treasure that had fallen into his lap.'

Finn was staring at her. She shrugged. 'Two thousand three hundred quid's worth of therapy. It had to come in useful sometime.'

'And did he tell you what really happened that night, Finn?' MacBrian asked. 'On the seventeenth?'

Finn turned, scrubbed at his hair, nodded. 'By the seventeenth Taran had been trying to Edit for almost a year, secretly taking Dughlas's shifts under my father's name.'

He leaned against the shelves and Alex realized that this room must be familiar to him, more familiar than it was to MacBrian. 'At first he didn't expect to get anywhere. He was never a great Reader, and he hadn't worked a full shift for years. But he said that the very first time he Read a root Memory in I-537, he felt the change straight away. It was very small, he said, the faintest tug. He said that a busy Reader in full flow wouldn't notice a thing, but of course he knew what he was looking for. He said that the first Edit must have taken extraordinary talent, but that now, it seemed, my father had created a pathway anyone could find – if only they knew it was there.

'Over the months, as he tried to sink deeper into that tug, it became stronger, then stronger again. By the beginning of February he was able to keep Storylines suspended for several seconds while their root Memories struggled to detach.'

He looked at Alex. 'That's what he was doing with your Storyline, when my father appeared. He was sure the root Memory was finally about to come free. My father shouted at him to stop, but Taran was Reading too deeply to hear, so my father grabbed him and shoved him the ground. Apparently Taran took your Memory with him. It didn't just slide out, like the first one had with my father. This one *ripped*. And as it tore away, the wound let out a burst of Library energy that hit my father right in the chest.'

Meanwhile, Alex thought, back in Haggerston – I woke up, puked and proceeded to become the sort of person I'd always dreamed I might be.

'He says he's sorry my father had to die,' Finn said. 'Or rather, *be sacrificed*. But he still thinks he was right, to do what he did. And he's been trying to do it again, all this time. He's been taking advantage of the strikes, working in the deserted Stacks. He thinks that if he can only prove it can be done without ripping, he can take it to the Board. He's sure, if they believed it could be done safely, they would approve Editing as a standard Reading practice. He plans to write manuals, so the other Chapters can learn it. He thinks he's about to usher in some sort of new age for the Library. He even has a name for it. *Assisted intelligence*. He seems to think that if only the Board could be made to understand the potential, they'd let him *carry on*.'

MacBrian pinched her temples. Iain, arms crossed, shifted in his chair.

'Would they?' Finn asked.

'No,' said MacBrian, without hesitation. 'No. Not if I have anything to do with it.' She cleared her throat. 'It seems that I owe you an apology, Finn. I underestimated your father. I admit, I was envious of him. Everything always came so easily to Egan, ever since we were children, and I let my personal feelings blind my judgement. But I promise you, as long as I am Director, I will do my very best to ensure that his integrity is upheld. All the rules of the Board, all the principles of democracy, demand that I make the truth of this public. That I open it up to debate. But quite honestly, I am going to think long and hard before I do so. And I also promise you this. Taran MacGill will never set foot inside the Library, ever again.'

Alex said, as firmly as she could, 'And what if he's the only one who can fix me?'

They all looked at her.

'I'm just asking,' she said. 'Seeing as he's the one who ripped it out it in the first place.' She looked at Finn. 'Do you think he can?'

'I don't know,' Finn said. 'I don't think *he* knows.'

Alex walked back to the table and picked up the Ryman's pot. Her Memory went batshit. The void ached. 'So what is it?' She asked. 'What's my Memory about?'

'That,' Finn replied, 'he wouldn't say. He said he'll only tell you.'

*

A guard and two horses were waiting at the bottom of the index steps, being steadily pickled by the rain. Iain cupped his hands beside the nearest horse's stirrup and nodded at Alex to put her foot in it. Alex walked towards him, then stopped.

'Thanks,' she said. 'For coming to get me. Outside.'

Iain said nothing.

'I hope it didn't hurt too much.'

Raindrops bounced off his back.

'Okay. Well,' Alex slotted her trainer onto his interlaced fingers, 'I wanted to say thanks. And sorry I thought you were, you know. A killer. And thanks.'

They cantered down the road along the front of the peninsula, Iain keeping her horse in line with a rope. As Alex jolted past the archives' seemingly endless wall, she imagined the billions of cards tucked into cubbyholes on the other side. Centuries of human hope and fear and hubris and frailty, laid bare in Ryman's cheapest paper and ink. She thought of the text that Taran believed all the strongest Storylines in the Library were collectively building towards, and wondered what it might boil down to. All you need is love? Trust no-one? Forty-two?

She started to laugh. By the time they reached a tightly packed jumble of grey buildings perched at the end the cliff, the laugh had a distinctly hysterical note. By the time they stopped outside a dark entryway, it had morphed into something not unlike a sob. Thankfully, there appeared to be something caught in Iain's horse's foot. The good ten minutes it took him to dig it out gave Alex just about enough time to downgrade the sob to hiccups.

At some invisible signal, two guards came to take their horses. Alex followed Iain through the entryway and into a tiled lobby that smelled of leather and wax. Two more guards, stationed behind a desk, nodded at Iain. They passed through a door into a bewildering warren of whitewashed corridors, stairs and more corridors. There were none of the spikes or bars or echoing screams Alex had been expecting; overall the guardhouse seemed more utilitarian public-sector office than Castle Black. Eventually they reached a door with a young male guard stationed outside. He saluted Iain, gawped at Alex, then caught himself and stared back at the wall.

Iain unlocked the door, then paused. Alex became suddenly, ludicrously aware of the wet saddle-patch straddling her crotch, the crusty yellow streak of indeterminate equine origin ingrained in her jumper, her rain-frizzed hair, her puffy eyes. No. She wasn't ready. She wasn't ready at all.

'They're right, you know,' Iain said. 'You *are* extraordinary.' Then he opened the door, put a hand on her back and prodded her in.

The room was square and windowless. There was a low, unmade bed set along one wall, and a small table and chair pushed against the other. Taran was sitting at the table, hunched over a sprawl of papers. As they walked in, he looked up and smiled his crooked kid-about-to-show-off-his-science-project smile. 'We're nearly there, Alex,' he said.

There was a dressing over his nose. One side of his bottom lip was swollen. His left canine had been snapped in half.

411

'Nearly where?' Alex said.

'Guidelines,' Taran said, gesturing at his paperwork with a Ryman's Assorted Ballpen. 'Rules. A suggested method for training. Ways to track the effects of Editing on early test subjects, using the GCAS cover story and social media surveillance. Nice neat processes to make Sorcha MacBrian and her small-minded international counterparts feel safe.'

Realizing that her hands were shaking, Alex shoved them into her damp back pockets. 'Small-minded,' she said, 'because they don't think people should be given a physiological lobotomy – just because they struggle to cope with the basic un-copeableness of life?'

Still writing, Taran gave one of his hiccupy-gasp laughs. 'Come on, Alex. These have been the best six months of your life. You said so yourself many times.'

'Maybe they have been. But they haven't been *mine*.'

'You said you felt free.'

'Maybe I did. At first. But none of it was real, was it?'

'No more or less real than any Story.'

'Except it isn't a Story.' Alex took a step forward, itching to wrench the pen out of his fingers. 'You've made me into a . . . a bloody *compilation*. With a gaping hole at its heart.'

Taran put down the pen. 'Maybe that gaping hole is the door to your cage.'

'At least the cage was *my* cage,' Alex spluttered. 'I had no choice about the hole.'

'So you would rather return to being the miserable trapped animal you were before the seventeenth of February?'

'Yes. No. I don't know. I don't know what it really felt like, to be her. But that doesn't matter. I can't stay like this, even if I wanted to. It's hurting me. It's hurting everyone. Don't you care that Iskeull is drowning? Don't you care that millions of people are suffering from un-Read Stories, because of what you've done?'

'Of course.' Taran nodded sadly. 'Don't imagine that these things bring me any pleasure. Of course I wish that breakthroughs could happen without something having to break. But this one failure with your Story has been more valuable to the Library than a billion routine Readings. You know, Alex, you made an inspired comment, back at that first interview. You said that entrepreneurs must be willing to fail.'

'Oh God.' Alex gripped her forehead. 'I meant, like, getting the colour of a Buy Now button wrong. I didn't mean they should go around *killing people*.'

'No. But Egan died, in the end, because he was not brave enough to embrace progress. The Library killed him, Alex. You and I were only its instruments.'

'Oh, right! So was Dughlas MacFionn's shotgun an instrument of the Library, too? And was the Library mystically channelling itself through that broken bottle you held at my throat?'

Taran sighed. 'That was a mess, I admit. I panicked when I heard you had been found. I should never have sent Dughlas to London. It turned out to be much more valuable to meet you in person, even if I had to persuade everyone we were investigating a case of Story-surging, to make sure no-one suspected the truth. I mean – Story-surging! Imagine! Editing is a hundred, a thousand times more exciting. But

413

the farce served its purpose. What you told us about your experience of the past six months helped me understand so much more about what the procedure had done.'

'Procedure?'

'Once I had heard your sorry tale, of course, it was clear that there was no way you were going to be able to piece together the truth about your Storyline and identify your missing root Memory from the outside. I was nervous about you visiting your Story, of course, but there was nothing I could do about that. And, as I suspected, the experience was far too overwhelming for you to identify the tear.

But I didn't count on the depth of Finn's need to prove himself to his father, even once he was dead. Nor, I admit, did I foresee your willingness to come back to Iskeull. And so I panicked again when I heard you tell Finn what you had found. I needed more time. I needed to show them that Editing didn't have to be done that way. That it could be done right.'

He shrugged. 'Perhaps I could have handled things better. I'm only human, after all. Unfortunately. But I'm sure that once the Board understands the potential we have here, I mean really understands it, they'll forgive a misstep or two.'

'Look,' Alex said, feeling her dread start to harden into rage. 'I didn't come here to listen to your fucked-up manifesto for some Reader-controlled dystopia. I don't really give a toss about poor wounded Freya, and poor misunderstood Taran, and why you think it's okay to rip a stranger's consciousness apart and kill your best friend. I just want you to

414

tell me two things, Professor MacGill. One: how I can repair my Story.'

'Ever the woman of action!' Taran chuckled. 'Oh, Alex, I really do hope we can continue to work together. Well, to begin with, there's a decent chance your Story might repair itself without that Memory. The Storyline with the tear might eventually give up the ghost, so to speak, and disperse. The others would probably find a way to adapt, rearrange, maybe swap in new root Memories. Stories can be incredibly adaptable, when they want to be. In that scenario, you'd continue as you are now, liberated from your past. But the rot would stop, and your Story would eventually unstick. The other Stories would no longer sense that it was dangerous to surface in that Stack, and they would flood back into the wall to be Read. And *that* should convince even Sorcha MacBrian that we have an unmissable opportunity here.'

'And what if none of that happened? What if it never recovered and just kept rotting, and both of us withered and died?'

Taran tutted. 'Come on, Alex! Dear me! Where's your famous positive attitude?'

'So there's nothing I can do? Except wait and see?'

'Far from it.' He gestured to his papers. 'I've worked through all the possible scenarios, and frankly it would be fascinating to test any one of them out. Of course I suspect that, as ever, the simplest solution is the most likely to succeed.'

'And what would that involve?'

'Physically transferring the separated Memory back into your Story.'

'Okay. And how would that work, if none of the Readers can open it?'

'You'd have to take it down there yourself. Through the tunnel in the centre of the Stacks.'

No. Please, no. Not there. Not again.

Alex took a deep breath.

You're extraordinary, said Iain. *You're strong*, said Finn.

'How sure are you that would work?'

'Fifty–fifty, I'd say. It's perfectly possible your Story will simply reject the Memory. Who knows what being outside the Library has done to it? On the other hand, of course, it might simply reintegrate, just like the first time Egan Edited.'

'And if that happened, I'd be okay? Healthy? Back to how I was before you got your hands on my Storyline?'

'Maybe. Maybe not. Even if the root Memory *did* reintegrate, I suspect that your Story would then have to suppress all the Memories you've created since that night. Thanks to the tear, they're probably riddled with scar tissue, imperfectly formed. To get your Storylines back to normal, those recent Memories would have to be left out.' Taran had picked up his pen and was sketching deformed-looking squiggly lumps.

'So – what? I'd forget everything that's happened, since the seventeenth?'

'Mmm.' He started to add random splatters all over the page. 'Then again, your Story might have some kind of complex immune reaction, and die.'

Alex looked from his face to the sketch, all out of words.

'Now,' Taran continued, adding a final splatter, before replacing his pen with a satisfied air. 'I think I can guess the

416

second thing you want to know. You want to know what that cage door looks like, before you try to slam it shut, don't you, Alex? You want to know the contents of that poor little root Memory?'

Alex crossed her arms. 'Are you going to tell me?'

'If you're really sure that's what you want. I'll give you a clue. It dates from the sixteenth of July 1995.'

Alex closed her eyes. *I want to tell someone. I want to tell someone so much it hurts.*

'What was it?' she asked hollowly. 'What was so life-changing about that bug I caught?'

'That's just it,' Taran said. 'There was no bug. You were only sick because of what you saw. You were late for a camping trip, weren't you, Alex? You should have left half an hour before. But you took longer than expected to pack your bags, and then you ran up to your father's study to say a final good-bye. That's why, when you opened the door, you saw an empty bottle of vodka roll out. That's why, when you walked in, you were just in time to find your father standing on a chair, with one end of a tie secured to the beams and the other knotted around his neck.'

26

Egan MacCalum's Honda roared, jerked, roared, lurched, then settled into a juddering thrum. Alex laced her fingers, wrapped in Egan's wife's gloves, against Egan's son's hard stomach. She leaned the unscratched side of her face against his back and felt her heart bump faster than the motorcycle against his spine. Then, as they sped through the rain, she dropped what Taran had told her into the iridescent dark behind her eyes and watched her fuzzy past slowly sharpen into vivid polychrome.

Sunday, 16 July 1995. The day she should have been on her way to a Lake District campsite, 300 miles away from Fring. The day she had vomited, to her mother's consternation and concern, all over the bathroom. The day she had spent curled in bed, angsting into her diary. The day, it now seemed, that her childhood had died – a milestone that had nothing at all to do with the prospect of a fancy secondary school.

Then, the age of the miserable shadow. The abandoned friendships, the academic backsliding, the withdrawal, the rows. Without full access to her Memories, Alex couldn't begin to imagine the unspeakable, unspoken emotions she had been feeling. The ones that her mother and Diya, Dom and her teachers had so badly mistaken for fish-out-of-water nerves and teenage hormones.

So why hadn't she spoken up? Why hadn't she run straight out of her father's study that morning and into her mother's arms?

Had she wanted to pretend it never happened? Had she been trying to limit the damage, to quarantine that poisonous Memory in some far corner of her Story? Vain hope. From the evidence of her uniformly nonsensical Storylines, that Memory had become part of every single adult belief she'd created about herself. Without it, none of them – life-affirming or self-destructive – worked.

But there was another possibility, one that sprung back up higher every time she tried to push it down. Her father could have asked her not to tell. Explained that he'd been playing a game, acting out a plot point; insisted that she'd misunderstood what she'd seen. Begged for it to be their special secret. Entreated her to think of Mum – how she wouldn't get the joke, because she never did. Emphasized how much it would hurt her, if she got the wrong end of the stick. Or the tie.

Your father might not buy me flowers, her mother had said in that seemingly random Memory in her bad Storyline. *In fact he often neglects to say a single word from breakfast until dinnertime. But I know he would never purposefully do anything to hurt me, and that's everything, Alex. Everything.*

Not so random, then, after all.

A freezing, briny breaker of grief and anger and sorrow smashed over Alex's head. Finn must have felt it, because she felt his abs tense and his shoulders shift. She relaced her fingers, already numb despite the gloves, and pressed closer into his back – squeezing the sobs out of her ribs, holding her skeleton together with his own.

Could he really have been so fucking selfish? So fucking weak? That mild, wry, self-effacing man who had always defended his awkward little Kansas from the conformist tyranny of the world?

Another unbearable thought: his loyalty fuelled by guilt, bestowed as part of the trade. *You watched my back, Kansas, I'll watch yours.*

Feeling her throat clench in a paroxysm of horror, Alex scythed the idea down in a single furious swipe. Her father had been her champion from the moment she was born. She couldn't let this one awful incident rewrite everything about their relationship. It was hard, though, so hard, trying to understand what fit where, what caused what, what was connected and what wasn't. She longed to know, to feel, and not just figure out the truth. Yet with that crucial Memory missing and all the others disconnected from her emotions, her only bullshit detector was her brain. And she knew from long experience that trying to detect bullshit with a bullshit-generating organ was a sure-fire way to drown.

It all came down to the same question Finn had asked her back in the archives. *Why?* Back then, she'd been trying to make sense of her own cast-change from heroine to murderer, not of her father's from comic bit-part to tragic wannabe suicide. But the same problem with motivation applied. *Why?* What would have driven him to do such a thing? Which

Storyline could he have knotted, over the years, into such an irresistible noose?

And why *then*? What was so special about 16 July? About 1995?

And then, as the bike tipped sideways in a turn so low that Alex felt clods of mud hit the back of her hood, she suddenly made the link with the exact same date ten years later. The date of the garden party.

The second crisis in her Story hadn't been prompted by Dom's offer of a job in New York. Or at least, not entirely. The crucial link she had been missing was the one fact she hadn't thought to question: the reason her mother had thrown that party in the first place.

16 July 2005 had marked the release of Novus's third Young Novelists to Watch list. Novus's editors had decided to make a fuss: profiles of the original 1985 authors in a special *Guardian* supplement, newly issued editions of the books that had made their names, a glamorous press-packed supper in Bloomsbury. Her father had unequivocally declined both the interviews and the supper. Nevertheless, Liz, who remained both fiercely proud of *The Switch* and fiercely dismissive of the suggestion that her husband was a one-hit wonder, had insisted on organizing a surprise party for him at home.

With a surge of sickness, Alex recalled how fervently she had tried to persuade her mother that it was a bad idea. The Memory remained bleached of all emotion, but how full of dread she must have been, knowing that the day marked not one, but two anniversaries. How keenly her father must have known it, too. How hard he must have worked to show her that he was fine, posing for the camera in his jaunty shirt with his glass of champagne and his sardonic smile.

Because a decade before, that very same day would have marked the release of the *second* Novus list. The first follow-on from the now-infamous inaugural line-up. The absence of any relevant Memories suggested that Alex's happy eleven-year-old self, consumed with pop songs and liquorice allsorts, had been oblivious to the inevitable anticipation and gossip. But Tom R. Moore would not have been oblivious at all.

Ten years on from his moment of glory, her father would no longer have been able to pretend that his much-debated follow-up was magically going to materialize. In the morning's *TLS*, the critics must have picked over his early promise and mourned, or even mocked, its demise. Alex imagined her father's frustration at proving Gramps right, that Midwestern bully who made pointed jokes about arty fags over Thanksgiving dinner. She imagined her father's shame at failing his wife, who had always staunchly insisted that the sequel would find its own way out. She even imagined him feeling that he'd become a man whom his adoring daughter, born into the sunburst of his fame, would no longer recognize.

The chronology of her neuroses finally made twisted sense. On 16 July 1985, Tom R. Moore had sprinted to the balmy peak of his career with his very first book. Twenty years later, on 16 July 2005, he had mocked its stone-cold corpse with poached salmon and cheap fizz. But on 16 July 1995 – a time when the taunts of squandered potential and unfulfilled hope still stung – Tom himself must have privately, despairingly condemned his career as terminal.

Or perhaps it was all too easy, Alex thought, shivering in the wind. So much neat pop psychology. Surely her mother had been right about people not being jigsaw puzzles. Alex was only just beginning to comprehend how complex and contradictory Storylines were. She knew that her father would have thousands of Memories she wasn't aware of and couldn't begin to understand. He may not even have had a coherent why. An instantaneous bundle of overwhelming instincts, a handy bottle of booze and a dash of wonky brain chemistry may well have been enough.

What she *was* increasingly clear on was the nature of her own dominant Storyline. She'd nurtured a fear of failure to protect herself from the horror of what she had seen in her father. But in a way that she was beginning to see as characteristic of Storylines, it had only led her to replicate that horror every day since, in many mundane little epilogues. Throughout her teenage years, in a thousand small ways, she'd forced her head to stay below the parapet in case she exposed herself, in the way her father had so dangerously done. Squashed her natural talents. Refused to let her work become too good. And she was the one who had been her father's protector, not the other way round; clinging to his side, scurrying home from school as soon as she could.

So the Storyline that began with that hideous root Memory in July 1995 must have been chafing like hell ten years later, when Dom offered her a chance to blow it apart. At that point she had been brave enough to surface her Story and offer up the crippling Storyline to be Read – but not quite brave enough to let Greum MacTormod help her prise it apart. And so she returned to the same old pattern through-out her twenties, continually trying and failing to throw off the shackles of her self-imposed mediocrity. Sticking to the same undemanding job. Still not able to face a single glass of alcohol. Still not able to face the sight of a single copy of her father's famous novel on her shelves.

After yet another decade of the same old loop, Mark's offer of a promotion must have felt like a crossroads. Like Dom's job offer, it was a chance to finally reject all those years of aborted ambitions and change the game. So, provoked by Chloe's blunt therapeutic mash-up, Alex had summoned the courage to surface her Story a second time. And then Taran MacGill had, as he'd boasted, torn her free. Free from her twenty-year-old certainty that if you flew too close to the sun, you'd eventually crash and burn.

Fear of failure. They'd been right all along, except for the underlying why. It was so obvious, so pedestrian, so pathetic. But then, as Taran had pointed out, the oldest Storylines were the most powerful of all.

She was starting to become overwhelmed by dizziness, to sense the void where her Memory had once been opening up. She didn't have long now, she knew, whatever Taran had said about natural reintegration. The rot, some biological instinct informed her, had burrowed mitochondria-deep.

Jerk. Splash. Splutter. Dragging her thoughts back to the present, she realized that the bike was slowing, turning, stop-ping. The engine cut out. Alex lifted her head.

They were parked on top of a cliff, surrounded by wheeling birds. All around them, scales of sandstone broke through the furzy turf, cradling pools of rainwater. Below them, the sea spewed and sucked over a dice-roll of rocks. Behind them, perhaps a mile inland, she could see the outskirts of some sort of fishing hamlet, a doll's-house cluster of low houses fringed with dark squares of cultivated earth.

Finn kicked down the stand while Alex wrenched her fingers apart and inched her leg over the seat. He threw back his hood, pulled off his woolly hat and fiddled with the bandage, which had slipped down from his forehead over his eye. Alex felt a belated pang of guilt.

'Are you okay?' she said. 'I should have thought . . . I was in a mess when I came back from Taran. I shouldn't have asked . . .'

'Cape,' he said, spreading his own over the seat.

'It's still raining.'

He held out his hand. 'Take it off.'

She unbuckled it and passed it to him. He tossed it on top of his own, then readjusted the holdall, strapped across his chest, and took her hand. 'This way.'

Alex's brief to Finn had been to transport her somewhere a very long way from the peninsula, somewhere she could forget the Library, Taran and her father. And they *were* a long way from the peninsula, if the journey was anything to go by – right down at the southern tip of Iskeull. And it *was* a very nice cliff, what with the rocks and the birds and the sea. She shouldn't feel ungrateful, Alex thought, as she clambered after Finn through the pools, cold water splashing through the eyelets of her trainers. Only a landlocked Outsider would think that if you'd seen one rainy cliff, you'd seen them all. The rain was slackening. There was a flat slab not too far ahead that she could sit on. She could only hope that the view would be enough to sweep her mind temporarily clean.

Then Finn jerked her to a stop and she saw, inches from her feet, the ground drop away into a steep teardrop-shaped gully.

'Come on,' he said, lowering himself in backwards before she could say: I'm too ill, I'm too tired, I'm too weak.

Alex had climbed once, strapped into a harness, on a St J's activity holiday in Normandy. Thanks to her screwed-up Memories, she had no sense of how it had felt, but she was pretty sure it had felt nothing remotely like this: primal terror, toddlerish helplessness, wild self-pity. Her toes found holes then flipped straight out, her fingers scrabbled on wet rubble, her hips banged, her knees buckled and scraped. After a timeless stretch of mayhem, she suddenly found herself anchored on a miraculously safe perch, at which point her body refused, for long panicked seconds, to give it up. Then Finn tugged at her ankle and she found herself fumbling down again. The dressing on her cheek slid off. Her jumper snagged and tore. Her trainers were too clumpy, their treads non-existent. How was it that there were Reading boots all over the fucking place until you actually needed a pair?

When Finn finally gripped her waist and lifted her down onto a narrow platform, she looked straight back up and was amazed to see how sheer the precipice had been, how far

above the steely jewel of sky. Down in the gully it was shel-
tered and warmer than on the surface, with only a few drops
of rain making it past the overhangs to spit in her eyes. Panting, flushed with triumph, Alex twisted in Finn's hands to
face him.

'See?' he said. 'I told you you were strong.' Then he
stepped aside so that she could see the pool.

Her grasp on coastal geography had always been weak, so
she found it impossible to fathom how the sea could wriggle
up and under to erode a perfectly still, glassy basin in the
middle of the cliff. She was about to ask Finn when she
realized that he was dragging his orange jumper, bundled up
with his shirt, over his head.

'What are you doing?'

She might have forgotten the most significant event of her
life, but she remembered every inch of his naked torso:
youthfully lean but deep-scored with muscle, the ridges and
furrows distorting the twisting blue leylines of his tattoo.

'Swimming,' Finn said, dragging the bike-key-USB-
pebble-necklace over his head. He pulled off his boots, then
unbuttoned his trousers and yanked them down in one
smooth move. 'Hurry up,' he said, with a hint of a smile, 'it's
cold.' Then he turned and executed a perfect swan-dive into
the middle of the pool.

Seconds later his head popped up, arcing back in a spray
of water as he let out a roar. His bandage, sopping, was hanging over one ear. He barked something in Iskeullian, which
Alex interpreted as 'It's really, really, *really* cold' and then
began to scull, vigorously. 'I am going to get out,' he said, the

427

words forced between lips the same colour as his tattoo, 'in thirty seconds. Get in.'

Alex hesitated, her skin already shrinking, then thought: Fuck it. I'll probably be dead tomorrow, after all. She fumbled with her laces, tugged off her trainers and jeans, wriggled out of her jumper and T-shirt. Determinedly not turning her back on Finn, she unclipped her greying bra and pulled down her cherry-print multipack pants. Then, before she had a chance to think, she took two not-quite-running steps and leapt.

Cold. Cold. Heart-attack cold. Her scalp contracted to the size of a pin. Bubbles streamed through her aching teeth as she surged back up, imagining slimy creatures and gripping weeds. She broke the surface with a gasp. 'FUCK FUCK FUCK.'

A proper, joyful grin split Finn's juddering face. 'Keep. Move. Ing,' he ordered, in staccato bursts. Alex sliced her arms and legs through the water, trying to kick the cold down. She gulped a mouthful of brine, felt it shrivel her gums. The scratch on her cheek was stinging. Her eyes were stinging. Her belly was turning inside out.

He was laughing. The bulge over his eye had split open, streaking one side of his face with watery blood. The bandage was slipping further, barely clinging onto a thick white pad that was now exposed at the back of his head.

'Get out,' Alex shrieked, laughing now, too. 'Get the fuck out!'

Striking out for the ledge, she discovered, mercifully, that the pool sloped upwards around the sides. By virtue of flailing her feet in all directions, she just about managed to get purchase on the submerged rock. Hauling her elbows onto the platform, she found herself shooting up, as Finn boosted her from behind. By the time she had got to her feet he was already behind her on the outcrop, cradling his holdall, rummaging inside. The towel he tossed her had the thyme smell that she associated with Cait's house. She caught it, then punched it into his solar plexus, still laughing, still coughing. 'You fucking idiot,' she gasped, her teeth chattering. 'You'll give me pneumonia.'

He was holding both of her elbows. He raised an eyebrow. 'You jumped,' he said.

They looked at each other for a moment. Then Alex stepped back and pulled the towel around her chest. 'Idiot,' she muttered again. She turned her back, scrubbed herself dry, dressed clumsily.

'Here.' She turned. Finn was back in his clothes. He'd wiped the blood from his face and improvised a replacement bandage with a strip cut from his towel. He looked both ridiculous, like a boy playing doctors, and beautiful, his bones algae-green in the light of the cave. He held out a flask. 'Drink.'

Alex took the flask and swigged, relishing the whisky's burn. The spectre of Taran made a brief appearance, standing in front of her with his broken bottle. It was swiftly followed by an image of her father, draining vodka before climbing onto his chair. Alex blinked them both away and drank, defiantly, again.

'You first,' Finn said, shoving the towels and flask back in the holdall. 'Quickly. The climb will make you warm.'

Going up was, against all her expectations, easier than climbing down. High on some epic adrenaline rush, her brain still on hold, she pushed and pulled from crag to crag with strong, instinctive grace. Seconds after she had flopped over the edge, Finn came up behind her, swinging effortlessly sideways onto his feet. The rain was back in earnest, the sky a bleary veneer of pearl, the evening sun beginning its long, slow journey towards its short northern rest.

'Thank you.' Still panting, Alex turned to Finn. 'Thank you. It was perfect.'

Finn nodded, then reached out and lightly placed his palm in the space between her shoulder and her neck. 'You're getting cold,' he said. 'We should go.'

Back at the bike, they shook out their capes and buckled them on. Finn settled himself on the seat with the bag in his lap and started the engine, while Alex clambered on behind. She wrapped her arms around him, amazed that he could still be radiating so much heat. The bike roared, jerked, roared, lurched forward and settled back into a juddering thrum.

Cait's barn seemed far smaller than it had been when they'd come to pick up the Honda a handful of hours before. Finn drove straight in, leaning out of the seat to open one of the doors, then puttering the bike through and down to the end of the aisle. The door banged shut in the wind behind them. The silence, when he finally turned the key, was loud.

Alex dismounted, threw off her cape and leaned against

the hay bales, breathing in the sweet dust. When she opened her eyes, Finn was standing by the bike, watching her from beneath his ridiculous towel-bandage. 'Your cheek,' he said. He took off his cape and lifted the satchel over his head, then rummaged inside and held out his mangled towel.

Alex accepted the towel, then held it to one side and let it drop to the floor. She took hold of his outstretched wrist, turned it over and pressed her thumb into the Story symbol inked there. Then she rolled up his sleeve and slowly, millimetre by millimetre, traced her fingers along the blue rope that coiled up his outstretched arm. When she reached his neck, she buried her hand in his thick, wet hair.

Finn grabbed her arms and flipped her round, face-first into the bales. He tugged impatiently at the back of her jeans. As soon as she'd popped the button and dragged down her pants, he pushed straight up into her from behind. Alex reached round to grip the hard, round swell of his arse. He groped under her jumper and crammed one of her breasts into his hand. Then she braced against the hay and groaned while he thrust, breathing fast, his mouth in her hair.

When it was over, Alex did up her jeans and collapsed weak-legged onto the nearest bale. Finn stood looking down at her, flushed beneath the towel bandage, his hair mussed into peaks and his jumper rucked up to show a flash of blue-mapped skin. He grinned. Then he dropped onto the bale behind her and scooped her backwards, so that she was leaning against his chest. As his long, delicate Reader's fingers reached round to stroke her collarbone, she thought, briefly, of Harry. But Harry seemed to have become a character in a book she had once read, long ago.

'Are you frightened?' Finn asked, from behind her.

'Mostly tired,' she said, 'thinking about that bloody tunnel. But yes. Also fucking terrified.'

'Stories are tough. They'll do anything to survive.'

'Well, we'll see, won't we? Or rather, I will.'

'The other one reintegrated. The one my father Edited. Taran said that my father slipped the Memory back in, and the Story simply closed.'

'Here's hoping.' Alex shrugged, her shoulder blades raking his chest. 'Honestly, I just want it over with now.'

'Really?'

'Fuck. God. I don't know.' She traced a figure-of-eight on his knee. 'But then we know what's going to happen, don't we?' she said, falsely bright. 'What's going to happen is that my Story will accept my Memory back in, happy as Larry. Then it'll repress that little bastard, and my Storylines will heal without it, in lovely new patterns. The secret of the Library will be safe, as I won't remember any of it. I will remain in blissful ignorance as to what my father tried to do. And we can all get on with our lives, just as they were two weeks ago. Happy endings all round. Well, except for your dad. And you. And your mum. And Taran. And poor bloody Sorcha.'

But at least, in that case, she would never know what it felt like to know what she knew now. From the inside.

'Did Taran say—?'

'No. NO. It's simply one option. Probably the least likely

of all.' She twisted to look at Finn with a poor attempt at an insouciant smile. 'But, hey, when it comes to Iskeull, I specialize in the impossible, right?'

He looked back at her, steadily. Seeing what she was. Seeing what she was not.

'Or,' Alex said, 'or I might die, then and there, while my Story shrivels up around me, deep under the earth, all alone.'

After a moment, Finn toppled her forward. 'Come home,' he said. 'Have some tea. My mother says you're welcome to stay, if you don't want to go back to town tonight.'

At least, Alex thought as she let him help her up, at least if she did shrivel up and die in the dark all alone, she'd have signed off her Story with some pretty kick-ass Memories.

∞

'Alex?'

Alex looked up groggily from a blank sheet of paper to find them all staring at her.

'Sorry,' she said. 'Sorry, Mark. I didn't quite catch that.'

'The CoreCo contract, Alex. Timeline for a release.'

'Of course.' She bent over the paper and made some meaningless squiggles with her pen. 'Sorry. Got it. All good.'

Mark bestowed upon her a smile of great fatherly patience, then offered it around the boardroom. 'No problem, Alex, no problem,' he said. 'The last thing we want is for you to push yourself. Take your time. So: on to agenda point fifteen. Matt?'

Matt tapped a key on his notebook and pulled up a Power-Point deck on the big screen. 'Thanks, Mark. So, if we take a look at the data for last quarter—'

Alex found herself zoning out again as Matt droned on. Her squiggles morphed into figures-of-eight, each one connecting to the next in a baroque pattern that snaked down the page. She hadn't slept well – she hadn't slept well since the accident – and she felt painfully tired. She was hot, too, and the pink blouse Harry had bought her as a back-to-work present was pulling uncomfortably across her breasts. She pressed

434

her phone to check the time and saw with relief that there were only nine and a half more minutes left until lunch.

She dragged her attention back to the chart on the screen and tried to concentrate. Mark had been very generous, agreeing to let her step straight back into her old job. There was a consensus that the best thing was for her to resume normal service, as quickly as possible. She would need to keep going for check-ups, according to Dr Dasgupta at the Homerton's Regional Neurological Rehabilitation Unit. She must eat well, sleep well and take care not to get too tired. The best medicine of all right now, apparently, was routine. Dr Dasgupta, whose diagnoses and advice had up to this point consisted of a series of elaborate and jargon-couched variations on 'I don't know', had seemed relieved finally to be able to offer something concrete. Yes. Routine. Familiar, comfortable, soothing routine. That was the answer. The doctor had repeated it, nodding, to Harry and Alex's parents, several times.

Matt's notebook, which looked like something investigative journalists took into war zones, had a flashing USB sticking out of the side. Alex brought her hand to her collarbone and touched the blue leather necklace that lay under her blouse. She had found it amongst the belongings they'd returned to her in hospital, presumably having bought it in some tourist shop in Orkney. It was awful; the dual pendants, a carved pebble and a crumpled Lego memory stick, were obviously intended to be some kind of lame arty metaphor. But for some reason she found herself sleeping in it and showering in it and tucking it under her top, every day.

435

She dragged her gaze back to the screen, on which there was now a long list of bullets. She nodded thoughtfully, in case anyone was watching her, which was likely. It was all they'd done, these past few days. She could only hope the novelty value would wear off soon.

TOP BRIT TECH-HOPE LOSES MARBLES IN FREAK TRAGEDY, had screamed the *Daily Mail*. *The Guardian* opted for the more sober 'London Entrepreneur Contracts Amnesia in Island Accident'. *Flair* had run a special report on 'Women Under Pressure', illustrated with a giant hazard sign; *Wired* a wry op-ed called 'Eudomonia: On the Rocks?' They had all wanted interviews, the very idea of which made Alex want to throw up. She had spent hours staring at the press cuttings that Harry had got off some girl called Gemma, amazed that the confident woman smiling back at her from the glossy headshots, with her good hair, expert knowledge of 'omnichannel well-being communities' and witty pull-quotes, was her. Less surprised to recognize the hapless mess melting down on YouTube. Twice.

Gemma had been very helpful, actually, in deflecting the journalists and trying to persuade them to run positive pieces on Lenni instead. Lenni Kauppinen – whom she vaguely remembered as a friend of a friend from uni – had apparently been her business partner at Eudomonia. He was now its majority stakeholder and CEO. They'd needed a string of meetings to disentangle her from the company, and Lenni had been very understanding. He had even insisted that she hold on to some of her shares. But the truth was that, despite all the meetings, Alex still hadn't been able to figure out exactly what Eudomonia was, what it did. She found the whole thing utterly bewildering.

A sudden rock-fall in a broch, they'd said, but she'd had to google it even to know what a broch was. A sort of mysterious ancient stone tower, apparently, native to northern Scotland and popular with tourists. She'd supposedly been in Orkney to finish off a research project with some academic institute, but when Harry spoke to GCAS, they said that they'd completed the project on her first trip and hadn't seen her since. It was a mystery as to how she'd ended up in North Ronaldsay, let alone gadding about in brochs.

Alex did have a few memories: hauling herself out of a tunnel; jolting along in the arms of a pale young man with thick black hair; being airlifted in a rickety plane through a piercing blue sky over a still, luminous sea. But the order of events was confusing, and nobody seemed to be able to locate her rescuers. The locals on North Ronaldsay claimed to know nothing, to have seen nothing and had no idea who had called the emergency services in Kirkwall.

When she'd asked Harry why he thought she'd gone back to Orkney, something in his manner had put her off probing too far. She got the distinct impression that he thought she'd been having an affair. The idea of it, like the idea of the interviews, made her feel sick. It was hard enough to accept that her accident had effectively left him high and dry at the altar, although he had been so forgiving, so strong, so wonderfully *Harry* about it all. It wasn't her fault, he had said gently, as they sat snuggled on the sofa in his flat, cradling cups of tea, after her parents had finally gone. She hadn't been herself for a long time. He had tried to warn her that she was overreaching, that she was in danger of burning out. It had been scary to watch, he said – although, yes, impressive in a way. There had been a moment or two when he had even thought of encouraging her, of helping her out at Eudo. But now he had accepted an offer from a new shipping firm, with a super-fast route to the Board. It was time for him to support her properly, find them a lovely new place they could hunker down in together. Be her rock. It was so good to have her back, he had said, clinking mugs. There had even been, she thought, the trace of tears in his eyes.

Someone knocked into the back of Alex's chair and she realized the rest of the team were on their feet, wending their way out, glancing at her and muttering. As she rushed to stand, Mark paused to put a hand on her shoulder, his fingers splayed across the front of her blouse. 'No pressure, Alex,' he said, squeezing. 'Steady as she goes.' Squeezing again.

Out on the Farringdon Road, the early September afternoon was chilly and overcast, whispering of winter before autumn had officially begun. They said there'd been a heatwave that had broken a month ago, around the time she returned. But that was hidden in Alex's mental blind spot, and she found it hard to believe as she pushed her way through the whey-faced lunchtime crowd, every other neck wrapped in a scarf. She found it all hard to believe – the six months of life that had slid right out of her brain. There were still times when it threatened to overwhelm her. It was as if she'd been given a glimpse of the struts and paint pots behind the stageset of reality, and now she found it hard just to get on with the play, knowing that at any moment it might all come crashing down. Everyone had told her it was a perfectly normal reaction. That it would pass.

Everyone except her father. He had listened properly, offered no specious reassurances and only mentioned it days later, as they stood on Fring platform. They were waiting for her train back to London, after a fortnight convalescing at home.

'Hold onto that feeling, Kansas,' he had murmured, as Liz retrieved a block of foil-wrapped sandwiches from her hand-bag and Harry hefted Alex's wheelie bag onto the train. 'That space, between you and everyone else. It feels like a curse, but it can be a gift.' He had pulled her close, kissed her hard on the forehead. 'Don't worry,' he had said, fiercely, into her hair. 'You learn to live with it. It can make you a better person even. A stronger person. You'll be fine.'

Mae was already sitting in the restaurant when Alex arrived, flanked by a buggy and a high chair. She was surrounded by a litter of plastic containers holding half-chewed bits of food, scrunched-up baby wipes and anthropomorphic toys. When she saw Alex approaching, she stopped spooning purple yoghurt in the general direction of Bo's face and waved.

'Al,' she said, sliding out of the booth for a hug. 'It's so good to see you. We're all sorted. Go get some grub.'

Alex kissed the top of Bo's head, then fought her way through the scrum to the chiller cabinets lining one side of the room. Browsing the bento boxes with their neon slices of fish and translucent tangles of wakame, she realized she

439

wasn't hungry after all; in fact she felt ever so slightly nauseous. Snatching a box at random, she joined the back of a
long queue and began pulling faces at Bo.

'Revenge of the geeks!'

Alex swung round. The comment had come from one of
two thirty-something women who were queuing in front of
her, both dressed all in black, their heads bent over a single
iPad. The phrase snagged the corner of her consciousness, as
if it should have some particular significance, although she
couldn't imagine what that might be. Some relic of her lost
six months, she thought, as one of the servers beckoned her
forward and she slotted her card in the machine. She remembered how, in the press cuttings and blogs, she'd banged on
about all the time she'd spent on the family computer, when
she was a teen. How she'd made herself sound like a geek, a
gamer, a tech-savvy maverick, when really she'd only ever
been filling time. Staying close to him. Standing guard.

She carried her tray over to the booth and settled herself
on the other side of Bo, who was trying to fit an Octonaut
into his yoghurt pot.

'How are you?'

'How are you?'

They spoke at the same time. Mae raised an eyebrow. 'You
know how I am, Al. Every day the same. An endless round
of suburban maternal joy. The important thing is: how the
hell are *you*?'

'Oh, I'm okay.' Alex unpicked the tape from the plastic lid,
then focused on smearing wasabi that she didn't want onto
sushi she didn't want, and carefully arranging thumbnail-

sized slivers of ginger she didn't want on top. 'I'm good. I'm fine.'

Mae stuffed two pieces of sashimi into her mouth at once, closing her eyes and moaning with pleasure. 'Oh my God. London food.' She used Bo's fork to trowel in some salad, then waggled it at Alex's chest. 'Your tits look massive in that blouse.'

'I know.' Alex plucked at it, readjusting. 'Mark noticed, too.'

'Ah.' Mae snorted. 'No change there, then. Honestly, Al. What *is* it like, being back there?'

'Oh, you know, a bit weird. But it's bound to be, isn't it? The whole situation's weird.'

'And you're seriously feeling okay, health-wise? No black-outs? No headaches?'

'No. I'm getting fat, and I've got a serious dose of overdue PMT, but other than that, I'm fine.' Alex snapped her chop-sticks in two and pincered a California roll. 'Seriously, Mae, I'm bored of talking about myself. It's all anyone wants to do.' She leaned across and growled at Bo, pretended to nibble his cheek, made him laugh. 'Tell me about you. Tell me about suburban maternal joy. Tell me the latest on the Octonauts.'

But Mae just gave her a silent, sceptical look, so Alex turned back to her food, ploughing through two salmon nigiri and an avocado maki before a surge of queasiness forced her to put her chopsticks down.

'Have you seen Chloe?' Mae asked. She was chewing slowly now, studying Alex's face.

'Chloe? Oh. The therapist. No.'

'You were mad about her. Before.' Mae hesitated. 'Have you thought whether she might . . . help bridge the gap?'

Alex's first session with Chloe was one of her last vivid memories. All it had done, she seemed to remember, was rake up that old stuff about her dad, which she couldn't do anything about, and make her feel worse. She shook her head. 'It's the last thing I need at the moment, if I'm honest. More talk. I just want to get on with things now.'

'Fair enough.' Mae put her small hand on top of Alex's. 'But it's weird thinking of you, back there. At Minos. When I know how much you hated it. When you'd only just broken free.'

'Yes. Well.' Alex slid her hand away. 'That was SuperAlex. We never met.'

Mae sighed. 'And I'm not saying you should. If I'm being honest, Al, SuperAlex could be a bit of a dick. But she did have a few things going for her. She was open about her feelings. She was, I have to admit, pretty damn brave. She was a bit self-obsessed, sure, a bit shallow, but she also knew how extraordinary she really was.'

Alex fiddled with her tiny plastic bottle of soy sauce. Something about that word stung. 'Sorry that I'm such a disappointment,' she mumbled.

'No!' Mae gripped her hand. 'No. Al! Please! That's not what I mean. My whole point is that you've still got that in you, deep down. I'm so glad you're back – you-you, I mean: non-dick Alex. But I hope you're not letting people make you feel like you've become some kind of invalid now.'

Bo started making indecipherable complaints, which

quickly dissolved into angry tears. Mae tried suggesting a fresh nappy, a book and a banana, before rummaging in her bag, pulling out a muffin, ripping off the cellophane and shoving it on the high chair's tray.

'Harry said he could see it coming,' Alex said, as Mae settled back down, Bo now intently stuffing gummy wodges of high-fructose corn syrup and gluten into his mouth. 'Accident or no accident. He said it was clear I was heading for some sort of burnout. A meltdown.'

'I bet he did,' Mae muttered, then said, 'And sure, he's probably right. You went about your whole grand reinvention in a seriously full-on way. But that doesn't take away from what you accomplished in those six months, Al. You should be really proud of everything you achieved.'

Alex unscrewed the soy and balanced a dab of sauce on her fingertip.

Mae sighed again. 'How *is* Harry?'

'He thinks we should finally move in together.'

'Okaaay. And you?'

Alex touched her tongue to her finger and tasted the salt. It had been a long time, she thought, since she'd seen the sea. Too long. She should plan a trip. 'I don't know. I don't know how I feel. Not yet, I don't think. I feel like I need to get myself a bit more sorted first.'

'And what about the wedding?'

'Oh, he's been really wonderful about it all. He says we can talk about it when I'm back in the . . . um, the flow of things. Plan it all out properly, book a slot in St Albans cathedral, do it right this time. But only once I'm back to full strength.'

Mae raised both eyebrows, then tugged a baby wipe from the packet near her elbow and began to attack Bo's face.

'Is something wrong?' Alex said.

'God, I'm such a cow. But Harry—' Mae scrunched up the wipe and threw it on the table. 'Look, I'm so relieved you're okay, Al, of course I am, but I also don't want to see you lose all the ground you gained before the accident. You may have been a bit of a dick for a while back then, but you also seemed so energized, so *alive*. I can't bear to see you slide back from one extreme to the other. I know I sound like a bitch, but it's only because I love you. Because I believe you can be so much better than okay.'

Quietly Alex said, 'I know. I want to be better than okay, too.'

Mae leaned forward. 'So did you look at that thing I emailed you?'

'Oh. Yeah. Thanks. Nice thought, but it's a bit out of my league.' Alex took her phone out of her pocket and checked the time. 'Sorry. I should get going. You know what Mark's like.'

Mae folded her arms. 'Out of your league? You could do that job with your eyes closed. Copywriting, new media, flexible hours – it sounds tailor-made. And Singapore! Imagine! Wouldn't it be the perfect time to get a proper fresh start, seeing as you're having to start again anyway?'

Alex began to slide out of the booth. 'It's very sweet of you, but I'm just not sure it's what I want to do. I have no idea

444

what I really want to do; I never have, you know that. So it would be an awfully big risk to go halfway across the world for something I'm not even convinced I want, and which I'd probably fail at anyway. And I'm really not sure that Harry would be up for Singapore.'

'I'm not talking about Harry, Al. I'm talking about *you*.'

'Well, I'm not ready. It's too soon to be thinking so big, Mae. But I do appreciate the thought, honestly I do.' Alex stood up. 'Sorry. Duty calls.'

Mae got up and began to sweep detritus into her holdall, while Alex lifted Bo out of the high chair, enforced a squirmy cuddle, then buckled him into the buggy.

'Have a great afternoon,' Mae said, leaning in for a goodbye hug. 'And I'm sorry if I was, you know, too full-on. As usual. Too me.'

'No,' Alex said, gripping Mae's shoulders with sudden fervour, her throat thickening. 'I love it. You being you. Don't ever stop. Promise me.'

'Only if *you* promise *me* not to settle? To aim for better than okay?'

'Okay. Sure.'

They disentangled. Mae pushed the buggy forward a foot, then suddenly stopped and turned.

'You know, Al,' she said quietly, 'it's the story of your life. I don't think you're afraid of failure, not really. I think you're terrified of success.'

Alex sat back on the edge of the booth as Mae pushed her way out of the doors. For several minutes she simply sat there

445

in a daze, her thoughts shattering and colliding while the packed restaurant receded into impressionist shapes.

When she finally stood, a wave of nausea rose with her. She only just had time to push her way to the loo, lock the door and hunch over the toilet bowl before she threw up a stream of undigested fish and rice. As she washed her mouth out at the sink, the unfamiliar mirror confirmed how much her face had filled out over the past month. She had a rash of spots on her cheeks, too, and an uncharacteristic pink flush. As she stared, fragments of images began to dance over her reflection.

A broken stiletto heel, a pair of grey eyes, a giant stone tower, a red index card. The smell of industrial bleach faded into an echo-scent of salt and peat and wild thyme.

She left the toilet, light-headed, tingling with oxygen, as if she had just taken her first real breath in a very long time. Through the glass frontage of the restaurant, above the heads of people on stools bolting their food and swiping their phones, she saw that the sky had turned a stormy mineral grey.

The splash of hooves. The thrum of an old bike, swerving low. The thud of mud on her hood.

She walked shakily towards the double doors and, sure enough, as soon as she pushed out onto Cowcross Street, a few drops of rain began to spit. She reached for the sensible mini-umbrella in her tote, then stopped, lifting her face to the damp air.

A constellation of sparks. A spark in her hand, shooting upwards. A lifetime of moments wheeling around it, wheeling around her, as she fell to the bone-white floor.

She stumbled through the jostling pedestrians.

A maze of stone giants. A toy aeroplane. A great glass dome.

Somewhere deep within her abdomen, something started to ache. It wasn't a bad ache; more of a yearning. A tug. A pull. The nearest way Alex could think of to describe it was as if something inside her – some tiny, deep-rooted, slowly growing thing – was *homesick*.

Her pace increased to a jog.

A vodka bottle, rolling on floorboards. A memory stick, hidden in her fist. A pool, cradled in the middle of a cliff.

At the corner where Cowcross Street became Turnmill Street, she flung her Minos lanyard into a recycling bin.

A novel. A pearl.

She paused to lean on a rack of hire bikes.

A rainbow. A noose.

She fished in her tote and swapped her sensible kitten heels for the water-stained trainers she had been wearing when she had been rescued.

Darkness. Total darkness. Endless darkness.

A pair of strong, blue-mapped arms, lifting her out.

He had been waiting there inside the tomb, beside the mouth of the tunnel, for days. Everyone else had eventually given up, but he had stayed behind. He had seen her stumbling towards him, barely alive. He had reached down into that darkness and pulled her back into the light. And as he handed her over to Iain in that rickety plane, he had said something, soft and lilting in her ear, but she hadn't been able to make it out.

What had he said? And what would she say to him? Where on earth would they start?

On Clerkenwell Road a man outside Sainsbury's looked up from his phone with a jerk, as a sodden woman in filthy trainers sprinted past.

Look, she wasn't expecting happy-ever-afters. This wasn't a bloody fairy tale. But what if two strangers from opposite worlds, brought together by a dead man, divided by genes and personality types and tastes in knitwear, could in fact forge some kind of relationship that wasn't a total disaster?

I'm coming, Finn, Alex thought, upping her pace until she felt like her heart might burst out of her chest. I'm coming back.

Acknowledgements

Thanks, first, to two wonderful women: my agent, Cathryn Summerhayes, and my editor, Bella Pagan, both of whom saw the potential in a mad book and had the talent and tact to help me make it work. Thanks also to the wider teams at Curtis Brown and Pan Macmillan – I feel truly lucky to have such skilled and passionate people on my side. And thanks, too, to Antony Topping, without whose initial encouragement this journey might never have begun.

Alex Moore would never have been born without Richard Skinner and my beloved cabal from the Faber Academy writing course. Richard, Julia, Judith, Laura, Georgina, Jonathan, Wendy and of course my first reader, Matt Blakstad – you are all indispensable and irreplaceable. A big nod, too, to my other first reader and friend, Annie McKie. Her magical room in the forest was where Alex first found her true voice. Woody, come!

And I am of course indebted to all those who helped me get a feel for the extraordinary place that is Orkney, especially Stewart Bain and the team at Orkney Library, Tom Rendall and Fran Flett Hollinrake.

Finally, I am forever grateful to my friends and family for their patience, humour, love and support. You know who you are. And you are everything.

Permissions Acknowledgements